SARAH MARIE PAGE

ILLUSION
OF
STARS

SHADOW FORGE
PUBLISHING

Jacket art: Franziska Stern

This is a work of fiction. Names, characters, places, and incidents either are the product of the author's imagination or are used fictitiously, and any resemblance to actual persons, living or dead, business establishments, events, or locales is entirely coincidental.

www.shadowforgepublishing.com

www.sarahpagestories.com

ISBN: 979-8-9899831-1-7 (print)

ISBN: 979-8-9899831-0-0 (ebook)

To the people who see in us
what we can't see in ourselves

and

To Sarah Eliason.
for believing in this story first.

This book contains content that may be upsetting to some readers.

For a list of **trigger warnings**, please flip to the last page. For information on what to expect for **sexual content**, please flip to the second to last page.

Take care of yourself.

The Hjertalend Countries

Volgaard

Boreal Sea

Karlsborn Castle

Hjern

Saeby

St Kilda

Esbern

Pebble Beach

Cobble Cove

The Sanok Isles

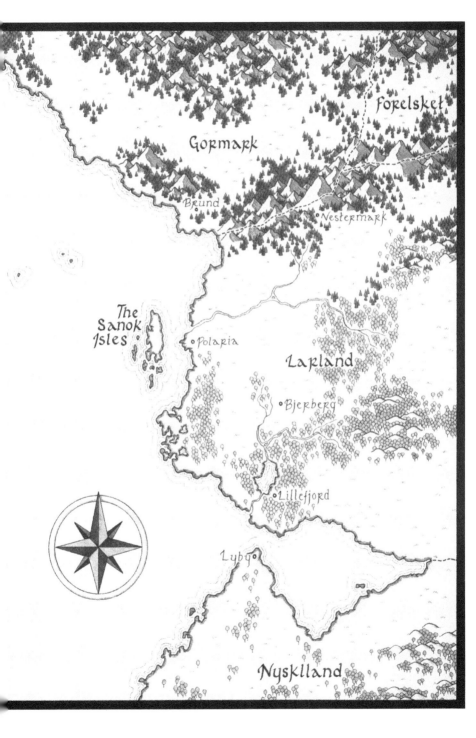

"And Vega found him?"

Chapter One

I'VE LET KATRINA TALK ME INTO a lot of bad decisions. Cutting bangs. Buying a sweater in the illustrious, never-popular goose-turd green. Drinking an entire bottle of holiday wine. The wine itself wasn't bad; but after I was well and drunk, she goaded me into flirting with a cute stable hand. The night ended with me running my hands over his abdominals and telling him the hard ridges felt like a ten-pound wheel of cheese.

So, yes. Lots of bad decisions come from Katrina.

This, however, might have been the worst.

Katrina dropped from the second-story window and into the thatch of rhubarb and wild thyme. I edged down the trellis after her, my heart pounding, the cotton lace of my nightgown sticky against my legs.

It might have been easier to leave Karlsborn Castle through the front door, but if Frue Andersen saw, she'd know we were going to be late for work. Katrina said she could slip into her position in laundry as late as she wanted, *if* she wasn't caught traipsing the grounds. My day started after Katrina's, but I still needed to be back before Queen Margarethe woke.

"Stop being a wimp and jump," Katrina said. "It's not that far."

I gripped the trellis, the wood groaning under my boots. Beneath me, the garden seemed to spin and twist, a tangle of copper, green, and bleached oyster shells the gardeners used for fertilizer. "I'm going back up."

Katrina raked a hand through her hair, dark brown and cropped short at the collarbone. Her lips pursed into a slash. "Isabel Annis Moller, do not go up that trellis."

"I'll head out the main door and meet you outside the kitchen." I clawed at a handful of half-dead leaves.

"You're already halfway down."

"I don't want to break an ankle."

"You're the next royal physician. You can fix a broken ankle."

"First," I said, taking a moment to decide whether I wanted to go up or down. Down. I'd go down. "Just because I can fix a broken ankle doesn't mean I want one. Second, Jens-Kjeld's not making that decision until the fall."

Condensation sparkled along Karlsborn Castle's chalky white exterior, making the granite glitter like cut glass. Birds chittered and morning bells pealed, bright and songful. The air held the shimmery taste of marigolds and fresh-tilled mud.

Katrina snorted. "Okay, but you're not *not* the next royal physician."

"Shush." I jammed the toe of my boot into the latticework. The paper-thin wood bent and warped under my weight. "I'm trying to concentrate."

Katrina pinched the bridge of her nose and stared at the sky. "This is painful. Like, actually painful. Just jump."

Fine.

My boots hit the ground with a *thump* and my knees buckled, my palms squelching through the mud.

"Morning, Isy," called a pink-cheeked Carl. He stood by the hedges, thick and dewy mist muting his form like a knit sweater. He gave a little wave of his garden sheers. "Glad to see you got down."

"Shit." I wiped my muddy hands through the grass. "We've been spotted."

Katrina hooked her arm through mine and tugged me up. "Relax. He won't rat on us. He likes you."

"Does not."

She picked a speck of dirt off her dressing robe. "Hmm."

"He doesn't!"

And just like that, her neutral expression gave way to the tempest that was Katrina, all untamed hair and feral grins and a dimple that tugged at the corner of her cheek. "Say what you will, but I've noticed he turns a very suspicious shade of pink every time you pass." She elbowed my ribs and dropped her voice to match his. "Good morning, Isy."

I shoved my hands into my pockets and hurried around the kitchens, starting for the path that led to the best place to see the ships—the bluffs. "Now who's the slow poke?"

Katrina jogged to catch up. "Oh, Isy." Her voice was still low like Carl's. "I love your beautiful brown eyes. They are the exact color of a mouse's butt."

I flicked her nose and dangled the one subject she couldn't resist. "King Christian's getting worse. Last night he threw his wine bottle at my head and stripped."

"Naked?"

"Stark."

She gave a sly glance. "Why didn't you tell me?"

Because I wasn't supposed to? Because she was terrible at keeping secrets and now half the staff at Karlsborn Castle would know? I shrugged, plucked a stem of a pink-lipped poppy, and pearled it away in my pocket.

"We're taking bets in laundry, you know," Katrina said. "About how long the king's going to last. I say until the end of the year, Elin says not even that."

"The king won't die."

She clucked her tongue and ran another hand through her hair. "That's not what Elin says."

"Is Elin his physician?"

"I bet three gyllis he'd get worse."

"That's a bet you'll probably win."

"It's not too late to get in on it." She snatched a handful of wispy buds off a bush and offered them to me. "Tiny daisies?"

"That's chickweed."

"I know." A wicked grin cracked across her face, bringing out that dimple in the hollow of her cheek. "Bet with me."

"I don't need the headache."

The grin deepened. "I hear winning is the best cure for headaches."

"*Peppermint* is the best cure for headaches."

The manicured path ended with three rocks set in a line. I pulled my dressing robe tighter and stepped over the barrier. Plants scratched my ankles, and my hair—the same dark brown as Katrina's but longer—hung in clumps. My bangs plastered my forehead, no doubt making me look more like a cliff troll than an eighteen-year-old girl who was going to be late for work.

Behind us, something snapped.

"The two of you aren't heading off into trouble, are you?"

I whirled and met a familiar pair of brown eyes. My breath hitched.

The speaker smirked. "And you thought you'd go without me, tsk, tsk."

"Hans!" Katrina shouted. A few smaller birds scattered from the grasses. She bunched the skirt of her nightgown and tromped through the underbrush. "What are you doing here?"

He extended his hands, which were cradling a gray pigeon. A ruff of turquoise and plum feathers sheened its neck. "Training." He squinted at the castle. His soft brown curls usually stood out in an unruly mess, but today, they clung to his cheeks and forehead.

I tugged the belt on my robe tighter, suddenly aware of the way my nightgown clung to my body.

The three of us had grown up together, had skinned our knees scrambling over boulders, splashed through the Colt in nothing but our underthings, had even shared a sickbed the year the pox swept through Hjern, but things had changed. He'd grown up and I'd, well…

Katrina, on the other hand, hardly seemed to notice the way her dressing robe hung off her shoulder. She'd stopped a few feet away and cocked her head, her lips parting. "Aren't you supposed to take your pigeons farther from the castle?"

"This is fine." With a smooth motion, Hans tossed the messenger pigeon in the air. The bird unfurled its wings and the silver band around its ankle flashed once before it disappeared into the haze. "Now tell me. Where are you two going and why didn't you invite me?"

"We're spying," Katrina said. "On the ships."

"The two of you make terrible spies. I heard Isy grumbling from a mile away."

I placed my hands on my hips. "I wasn't grumbling, and we didn't invite you because we only decided to go this morning."

"In that case," Hans said, "I need to train a pigeon to fly between our rooms."

"Frue Andersen wouldn't let you."

"Frue Andersen doesn't need to know."

Katrina bunched her nightgown and started up the bluff. "I think it's an excellent idea. Then Hans can write letters about how pink Carl turns every time Isy's name is mentioned."

Hans gave a musing grin, the type that quirked the left side of his lip a little higher than the right. "He does turn a rather suspicious shade of pink…"

Katrina threw her hands in the air, scattering another bird. "That's what I've been saying."

"I hate this conversation," I grumbled, tugging the belt of my robe one last time and falling into step behind them.

"Though you and Carl aren't a good match," Katrina continued. "You need someone who smells yummy. Like smoke. Or wool. Or rosemary or juniper or amber…"

"What do I smell like?" Hans asked. The question was meant to sound casual and teasing, but his gaze caught mine, warm and careful. It lingered. He swallowed.

Please don't, I wanted to say.

Katrina gave him a sly glance and tromped several feet ahead. "Pigeon."

The spell broke.

I ducked my head to hide the fire rising in my cheeks. "Come on. I need to be back before the queen wakes." The old woman complained about almost everything, but making her wait to get her bandages changed wouldn't get me any closer to becoming the next royal physician.

The path inclined to a near-vertical slant, with boulders arranged into steps. Clusters of heath-spotted orchids grew between splits in the rocks, and then we were over the hill, standing on top of the bluffs.

On a clear day, a salty sea breeze might have ruffled our hair or blew through the grass and made the dogwoods quiver. But on a day like today, mist hung over the ocean like a sheet of paper, gray and flat.

But even with the mist, we should have been able to see the ships.

The three of us stood there, scrub grass tickling our ankles, the dull roar of the ocean below. A drizzle freckled our hair and our lashes.

Katrina's mouth tugged into a frown. "You can't see much."

My breath fluttered. "You can't see...anything."

But that was impossible.

Katrina and I saw ships from our bedroom window, had snubbed our palms against the glass and watched at least a dozen black blots cut through the star-speckled sea. Even last night, they were too close to the coast to pull away, or, if they had, we should've been able to see them teetering on the edge of the horizon.

Ships didn't just disappear.

They couldn't...could they?

Hans furrowed his brow and stepped forward, sending pieces of gravel skidding over the edge. Below him, the waves continued to churn like a cauldron, spraying foam and froth against the rocks. "I thought you said there were ships?"

"There were," I replied.

"Then…"

"I don't know."

"Maybe they already pulled into port?"

"They weren't that close."

Or maybe they were? I blinked again and squinted through the rolling fog. Maybe they were closer to shore than we thought. If they'd veered to port, we wouldn't see them from the bluffs.

Katrina nudged my ribs. "Do you want to do the screaming thing?"

I shoved my hands in my pockets. "I don't want to do the screaming thing. Let's get back. I can't be late for the queen."

"Come on. You like it." She turned toward the sea and lifted her arms like a bird. "Ayeeeeee!" The wind caught her voice, ripped it backwards.

Eeeeeeya.

Hans let out a whoop that caused a few seagulls to scatter.

"I kissed Oskar!" Katrina shouted over the ocean.

RaksO dessik I, said the backwards echo.

"I spilled tea on Stefan's sweater!" shouted Hans.

Retaews s'nafetS no aet dellips I.

"Frue Anderson's a bitch!" Katrina.

Hctib a s'nosrednA eurF.

"Pigeons are friends!" Hans.

"Pigeons are *food*!"

Katrina turned toward me, her eyes bright, mist clinging to her cheeks, her hair. "Come on, Isy. Scream."

"Scream! Scream!" they both chanted.

I spread my arms like Katrina. "Hello!" I shouted.

Olleh.

A beat, a pause, and then we were all screaming and shouting, the actual words getting jumbled with the gibberish ones. It always reminded me of a child catching a cat's tail, the wind grabbing the secrets, pulling them back.

"I think Katrina makes terrible tea!"

"Hans loves my tea!"

"Sometimes I steal Isy's wildflower perfume!"

"And I always steal it back!"

Behind us, something snapped, and I whirled to see Carl, eyes fixed on the ground and fiddling with his garden sheers. "Um... Isabel... Frue Andersen's looking for you. Something about...uh, the queen's feet?"

Katrina squinted at him. "The crone's awake already?"

Awake...already?

The words hung in the air, suspended like petals tossed atop a puddle, spinning and spinning...

The fluttery air slammed back into my stomach.

Shit.

I bunched the skirt of my nightgown and broke into a sprint down the path.

Shit, shit, shit.

My robe had slipped open during the trip back, and the ties flapped against my leg.

"I'll sneak down to see you a little later," Katrina shouted.

Retal elttil, said the echo.

It took me a moment to realize she and Hans hadn't followed.

I remember looking over my shoulder and seeing the two of them set in shades of green and gray—Katrina windswept and wild, her dressing robe slouching off one shoulder, and Hans, his jacket sleeves rolled to his elbows, an empty pigeon cage at his hip.

And smiling.

They were smiling…

I can't get that image out of my brain. It's preserved there, hanging in the gallery of my memory like a painting that's fallen out of style. And no matter how many times I try to take it down or cover it up or walk away, I always come back to it—that day on the bluffs, trapped under the silver sky…

This is supposed to be my confession. The Red King himself deigned to tell me that. He visited my cell with his entourage of dukes and earls, mistresses, and princes. He tossed these papers with a flick of the wrist and commanded me to write.

A confession.

I suppose this is a confession, though not the type he wanted. And while it brings me great satisfaction knowing the Red King is not getting what he wanted, my hands still shake.

The stories I grew up with had happy endings. The river trolls are slain, the nokken is banished, the mapmaker's daughter finds her way home. Although this is the start of a story studded with monsters, madness, and magic, all that awaits at the end of these pages is death.

I will die tomorrow.

Why is that so hard to write? I chose this, sealed this fate upon my head when I let that grate go. And though I know I don't have to be the hero, don't have to walk to my death lewd and tonguing my teeth, I should have made my peace.

But I'm afraid.

I'm afraid to see the sunrise. I'm afraid to hear the clock. I'm afraid of footfalls, the rattle of keys. I'm afraid Signey wasn't able to—

I'm sorry. I'm getting ahead of myself. I still have many pages, a full inkwell, and one last evening.

So, I write.

Chapter Two

"YOU'RE NOT JENS-KJELD," Queen Margarethe said. She tried to pull herself higher but ended up slumping halfway against the pillows, mauve silk and feather-fluff boxing her shoulders and salt-white hair. She stuck out a whiskered chin and pursed her lips, drawing the wrinkles around her mouth taut. "*Jens-Kjeld.*"

I peeled back the duster, the duvet, the knitted throw embroidered with geese and tiny peonies, and found her feet nestled between the sheets. The bandages wrapped around her heels were crusted yellow with puss and black with blood.

"No," I said, uncorking a bottle of vinegar and cradling her heel in my palm. "I'm not."

Queen Margarethe waved her hand. "I don't like being waited on by some silly assistant."

"Apprentice," I corrected.

"I don't care who you are. Fetch Jens-Kjeld." She made a point of peering around me and into the hall. "Jens-Kjeld?" Her voice cracked. "Jens-Kjeld?"

I scrubbed away the puss and blood, taking care not to tickle her toes.

The ships must have been closer than we'd thought, or they'd been faster. Or maybe the mist made it hard to see.

Nothing else made sense.

Queen Margarethe lifted her heel out of my hand and rolled to her side, shoving the quilted duvet off her lap. "Where's Jens-Kjeld?"

I grabbed her heel and pulled her back.

We'd had this conversation yesterday, and the day before that. In truth, we'll probably have it again tomorrow, the next day, and every day until the royal physician returned with a cure for the king's madness.

But I didn't say that. Instead, I forced a smile and said, a little too cheerily, "Your feet are looking better." A lie, but the old woman loved to be puffed.

Queen Margarethe sank into the knot of pillows, a glass doll in a padded box. "Of course, they're looking better, you twit. Jens-Kjeld's been taking care of them." Still, I caught the shadow of a smile tugging at her wrinkled lip.

I smoothed calendula honey over the bedsores and fumbled behind me for the bandages.

Someone—probably the queen's maid—had thrown open the windows. Ocean air, still thick with fog, rinsed away most of the queen's sour smell and the rose perfume she tried to cover it with. But up close, with her withered heel sitting in the palm of my hand, I smelled the way death clung to her bedsheets.

She was fading. Fast.

A dying queen, a mad king, a drunkard prince who went to Gormark and hadn't been seen in eighteen months.

"Tell Jens-Kjeld to come next time," Queen Margarethe said, patting the pillow beside her. "Tell him I deserve the best. Tell him it's not enough that he sends his assistant."

Not enough.

Those words curled like an eel in the pit of my stomach, but I forced another smile and shoved the vinegar bottle into my bag. "He's in Nysklland, remember?"

"Nysklland? Oh my. What's he doing there?"

"Searching for a way to help your husband."

We'd talked about this. She knew this. Still, Queen Margarethe looked at me like I'd sprouted fangs and grown horns. "Why couldn't he have one of his assistants do *that*?"

Because it's for the king? Because medical texts are dense? Because the bookish royal physician would rather spend his time in the library than dealing with you? But I didn't say any of that. Instead, I slipped a fresh pair of lacy socks onto her feet—inside out, so her fictitious trolls wouldn't get them. "I'll pass your message along."

Then I left.

I hurried through the lacquered halls, past glittering marble busts and vases of buttercups, my head down, hands tangled in my skirts. The windows had been propped open and a thin drizzle flecked the sills and thick cobalt rugs, fogging the glass.

The fact of the matter was, I *was* searching for a cure to King Christian's madness. Jens-Kjeld preferred Stefan as his successor, but finding a cure would tip the odds in my favor. So, a few months back, I'd struck up a correspondence with Gormark's royal librarian. We'd made an arrangement—I'd send him oatmeal salve for his wife's eczema and he'd send me books. If I finished my rounds quickly, I could spend a few hours reading the newest one, a white leather volume with crabbed text and a grassy smell.

The bells pealed, marking a new hour. I gritted my teeth and walked faster.

I hadn't had much time for research lately. Two days ago,

every guard came down with a violent case of the stomach flu, and the week before, Costall Bridge collapsed, killing seven people and injuring half a dozen others. It hadn't always been like this. When I started at Karlsborn Castle, things had been slower, plenty of time to read and learn, but lately, there seemed to be one disaster after another.

From around the corner, there was a snicker, a snort. Then— "I heard they kill boars and use their tusks as cups."

Katrina.

She stood next to a lowered chandelier, her arms wrapped around swaths of organza curtains. She beamed at the lamplighter. "What do you think?"

The lamplighter snuffed the candles and hoisted the chandelier to the ceiling. "I heard they don't even bother with cups. I heard they drink straight from the animals." He winked. "Like brutes."

I tried to duck around them, but Katrina was faster, nearly dropping the curtains. "Isy!" Her cheeks were flushed a rosy pink and several wisps of hair had fallen out of her lopsided bun. "The ships? Henrik says they're from Volgaard. Everyone's scrambling, and I mean *everyone*. The minister of trade wasn't even out of bed! Kitchen's supposed to serve them, but no one knows what they like. We're taking bets. Animals or cups. What do you think?"

Ships from Volgaard? That was strange. Volgaard was a recluse of a country, curled tight like a fist and just as hostile. I thumbed the buckle on my medicine bag. "Do we know why they're here?"

"That's the mystery of it," Katrina said. "No one knows."

"I'll buy you in." The lamplighter—Henrik—dug in his pocket and flicked a silver gyllie in the air. "Do they drink straight from animals or use cups?"

Katrina snickered. "Definitely from anim—"

"Isabel?" Frue Andersen stood at the end of the hallway, black dress stark against the pale blue tapestries and pearly damask walls.

Katrina pulled the organza off the floor and the lamplighter shoved his hands in his pockets and walked in the opposite direction.

"Ships have ported," Frue Andersen said, "from Volgaard." She paused, letting the words sink in. The tip of Katrina's lopsided bun peeked around the corner. "King Christian insists on greeting them himself. Is there something you can give him so…"

So he doesn't have another breakdown? So he doesn't have a repeat of yesterday, when he came to breakfast believing he was a bear, believing the world was on fire, believing *he* was on fire, scratching his skin, calling it fur, making it bleed. Stefan had to give him søven, had to press the warm cloth to his nose and hold it there until he slumped forward and fell, snoring, into his bowl of porridge.

Why wasn't Stefan helping now? He'd been tasked with the King; I'd been tasked with the queen. Two apprentice physicians, two ailing monarchs.

I licked my lips, still salty from this morning on the bluffs. "Valerian. And lavender." A cure for nerves, not for madness.

Still, the tension eased from her shoulders and the lines on her forehead smoothed. "The king's meeting them in the Rose Room."

I nodded, curt, adjusting the strap on my pack.

"And Isabel? Be discrete. We don't want the Volds to know he's slipping."

THE DOOR TO THE ROSE ROOM was ajar, the smell of ink and leather oozing into the hallway, musky and rich, mixed with the crisp of rain.

My fingers brushed the handle, and I readied myself for the vase of buttercups to be thrown at my head or for screaming or scratching or the snarls of a man who teetered on insane. I could do this. I'd managed worse before.

The guard stationed outside cocked a bushy brow. "You sure you want to go in there?"

"Yeah. Why?" This shouldn't be hard. Find the king, administer the valerian and—

"Unacceptable. Irresponsible. *Lazy*." The whispered words came from inside the room.

I paused, the metal scrolling cool against my palm.

The guard's mustache twitched. "Because of *them*."

From inside, there was a pause. Then—"Understood," said a second speaker.

"It was weak and reckless," whispered the first.

"I know."

"Embarrassing."

I cracked the door.

Inside stood a Vold about my age, wheat-colored hair and a thick traveling cloak wrapped around his shoulders, as if he'd just stepped off the boat. His hands were clapped behind his back, high cheekbones and a harsh mouth. Handsome in a stormy sort of way.

"A stain on House Rythja's name," said the first speaker. His back was to me, though he seemed older than the other one. "A stain on *my* name."

The handsome Vold kept his face forward, his expression fixed.

The first leaned forward. "Nothing to say?"

The handsome Vold's lips pulled back from his teeth. His eyes went feral. "What do you want me to say? I'm weak? I'm worthless? *I'm sorry?*"

My hand hovered on the handle. My heartbeat thrummed through my fingertips. *Ba-dum, ba-dum.*

A scrape. "You're valuable for one reason," the first speaker hissed. "Don't make me regret my decision."

The door flew open and the first speaker stormed out. Hard. Angry. Rainwater clung to his hair, misted his beard, the droplets glittering like knives. A fur had been wrapped around his shoulders, curly and tan. A sheep, or maybe some sort of goat. Beneath it, a red cape swirled.

Our eyes met, his gray as steel. The corner of his mouth tugged into a sneer.

The guard glanced between the door and the man. Door. Man. Door. "Watch the other one," he said, then hurried after the man.

I took a shaky breath.

Okay. Volds. But I could do this. King. Valerian. Be discrete.

I shouldered my way into the Rose Room.

The handsome Vold had balled his hands into fists. His chest heaved and a lock of hair slipped over his forehead. Beneath it, his eyes burned.

"You...okay?" I asked.

"Fine."

Okay. Ignoring him, and back to the king. I glanced around. Dark credenza. Lambswool settee.

So King Christian wasn't in the Rose Room.

The Vold scrubbed a hand over his face. "Actually, could I get a drink?"

I backed toward the door. So where was the king? Had he been here and left? Or was he in transit? *Don't let the Volds find out he's slipping.* Those were my instructions, but if the older one ran into King Christian in the hallway, who knows what would happen. Well, I knew. Bad things. The worst things. So, should I leave to look for him or should I stay here? What if I couldn't find him? What if he was off terrorizing someone or ruining something or—

"Make sure it's strong," the Vold continued. "Vodka? Or do you have absinthe?"

Or maybe the king was hurting *himself.* Last week, we'd found him trying to climb out a second-story window, and now the Vold was watching me, his eyes gray as cinders, gray as smoke. Light gilded his hair, and I needed to find the king, but a drink, the Vold wanted a drink and—

"Do you know how to use a cup?" The words dropped out of my mouth. Worse, they seemed to float between us, suspended on some invisible thread. Save for the rain pattering on the windowsill and the billow of curtains, the room became very, very still.

The Vold blinked once, blinked again. "Do I know how to use a…cup?"

Heat rose in my cheeks. "I, um, heard some of you don't."

His eyes narrowed. "My horse, maybe. But what would I use?"

I didn't answer. I needed to find the king. Speaking of—

"You, uh," I bounced from one foot to the other, "haven't seen King Christian, have you?"

He turned to the map, stretched and pinned and hanging in a dark wood frame. "No, I haven't seen your king."

"Great. Well, goodbye."

I guess I was committing to scurrying around the castle. But what if King Christian walked in the moment I walked out? Isn't that how these things worked? As soon as you went to look for someone, the person magically appeared in the place you just left? So, if King Christian was on his way here, maybe it was better to wait. Lest he terrorize this stormy, sort of scary-handsome Vold.

Said scary-handsome Vold was now wandering around the Rose Room. He picked up a magnifying glass. Looked at the inkwell. Inspected the map.

Was this allowed? Were they allowed to wander?

The Vold leaned closer to the map. His fingers skimmed the empty arch of a country simply marked *"VOLGAARD."* No other detail beyond that. Stark white and barren compared to its neighbors, Larland, Gormark, and the Sanok Isles.

"There should be a city here." He tapped the left corner of his empty country. "A mountain range here." He traced down the middle. "A river."

For a moment, I could see it, too—the black ink whorls of cities and forest-land, the jagged cut of a snow-capped mountain range, the narrow curl of a river, carved in pen and ink. A country almost as full as its neighbors, but not quite. A country that left just enough space for wild things and wild people.

"It's a shame your cartographers left it blank."

I glanced at the door. "Well, maybe your king shouldn't have sent back our ambassador's head on a spike."

The whorls on the map disappeared with a *pop*. His lips flattened. "That."

"And slaughtered every merchant who set foot on your shores."

"Slaughtered them, did we?"

Another glance at the door. Okay. Yes. Be patient. I let out a shaky breath and turned back to the Vold. He quirked a brow as if he found the idea of murdering our merchants amusing.

"You sent back their bloody hearts," I said. "Floated them across the sea in cedar boxes."

Wild, wild, wild, that blank country seemed to say. *Wild things, wild people.*

He shrugged. "Hearts tend to do that."

"Do what?"

"Find their way home."

A long pause. Long enough for the lamplighter's words to dance round my brain.

Like brutes.

Brutes, indeed.

What sort of people would carve up bodies and return them piece by piece? What sort of people would send back the head of our ambassador on a spike, eyes stitched shut, a rotted heart and a bloody letter shoved in his mouth: *We do not care that you no longer fly under Larland's flag. We have no interest in relations. Regards.*

And so Volgaard was left blank, a statement as much as a question. We do not know you. We have never known you. You are not our friend, our partner, our ally.

"Perhaps we haven't been so kind to our young neighbor," the handsome Vold murmured. "But this is as much for you as it is for us." He took two steps, closing the distance between us, and reached toward my face…

My heart roared in my ears, and all my nervous energy returned.

He plucked something from my hair, the back of his fingers brushing my temple. "You had a leaf."

Like brutes.

21

The door swung open, and the king shuffled in, his shirt half-tucked, boots unlaced, silver-white hair falling out of his ribbon. Pink rimmed his lips and a sore puckered at the corner of his mouth, almost a shaving nick, but the king's barber did not miss.

King Christian's eyes slid over me, and he smiled wide, a little mad. "He comes, he comes. Red hair, red teeth." He took a wobbly step in my direction, then another.

The cherub-cheeked minister of trade hooked an arm around the king's shoulders and shepherded him toward the settee.

"Ingrid," the minister said, but I didn't bother correcting him. "Be a dear and bring us something to drink."

The handsome Vold caught my eye, a smirk tugging at the corner of his mouth. "In cups, preferably."

Chapter Three

I SHOULDERED MY WAY into the Rose Room, a tray of fluted glasses in my hands. I'd swirled valerian root into a dessert wine—a dark vintage dug out of the back of the pantry—to mask the bitter taste.

Once the king drank it, the herb would soothe the shiver in his spine and the jitter in his hands. It wouldn't ease the madness nipping at the back of his brain, but it would make him seem more relaxed.

We don't want the Volds to know he's slipping. We didn't want anyone to know. A mad king, a dying queen, a country still in the soft of its infancy, barely older than I. We were teetering on the edge of a succession crisis, dancing dangerously close to the cliff.

Inside, the king had wedged himself between the settee cushions and goose-down pillows, his fingers laced around a bouncing knee, pink-rimmed lips pursed as if he were sucking a lemon. His entourage stood behind him—the minister of trade, once a trusted advisor, now a babysitter, and two stewards, immaculate in their polished boots and wing-tipped jackets.

The Volds had sprawled across the room, out of place against the warm wood and faded florals. There were three—the two I'd seen arguing earlier, stiff and apart, and a woman with sharp features and the same blonde hair. A family, then. A father and his children? An uncle with a niece and nephew? Kohl rimmed the woman's eyes, and she fingered a knife, flipping it back and forth so the gems in the hilt cast a spray of red shadows over the room's coffered ceiling.

"Finally." She dropped the knife into her lap and reached for a glass.

I plucked King Christian's off the tray and let her take another—a trick I'd gotten from Stefan. We'd both gotten good at administering medicines, at slights of hand. Grape seeds slipped into a jar of pickled herring, charcoal creamed into crab.

Rain pattered on the recess of the window, beads pilling on the glass. The sky outside gloomed a shallow and smudgy gray.

I handed King Christian his wine, then waited for him to take a sip. He needed to drink most of it to get the benefit. Afterward, I'd need to watch him to make sure the herb took effect.

The king's throat bobbed. He raised the fluted glass to his lips, then pulled it back. "He licks me with his frog tongue, ties it round my neck. He tells me to drink, but I do not want to drink. I do not."

A stewards snorted, and the minister scowled. Rain continued to patter.

"King Christian," the oldest Vold said. "We were hoping to speak with you in private."

In private? That was a weird request. Even before he was mad, the king was always accompanied by half a dozen others—stewards and spectators, servants and seneschals. Lately, the number of people allowed near him had shrunk, but he was never left alone.

The minister rubbed the whiskers on his lip. "Due respect," he said, "I don't think—"

"Alone. Yes, alone." The king stood, then paced around the room on wobbly legs, his shirt hanging out of the back of his pants like a duck tail. "The dark devil comes to me alone."

The fluted glass of wine sat on the table, deep red and untouched. It would help, but he needed to drink it first.

King Christian licked his lips. "Everyone can leave."

The stewards exchanged a glance and shuffled toward the door. The minister clapped his hands, face beseeching. *Do something,* he seemed to say.

My gut lurched. "I…erm, I believe a toast is customary."

All eyes slid to me.

Please. Just drink. It will help you.

Tick, tick, tick went the mantle clock. Its scrolled, silver hand made its way around the pearly face. *Tick, tick, tick.* Rain billowed the curtains, soft wisps of cotton and champagne.

"An excellent idea," the minister said. "A toast to new allies." Had he caught on to what I was trying to do, or did he see this as an excuse to delay leaving?

The king lunged forward, reaching for the glass in the oldest Vold's hand.

"Actually, Your Highness, I think you have one right…" I plucked the king's cup off the table and gave it to him. His fingers were bony and cold, limp as chicken flesh. "Here."

He took it. Thankfully.

The king raised the wine to his lips, where it hovered for a second, the bow of glass catching the light, pulling his upper lip wide like a frog's. His mouth parted and—

He stuck out his tongue and lapped it like a dog.

The handsome Vold gave me a look that said he was seriously questioning whether *we* knew how to use cups.

My cheeks burned. So much for discretion.

Dribbles of red streaked down the king's chin, staining the white of his cravat. "More," he said. "The rest of you can leave."

No one moved.

The oldest Vold clapped his hands. "You heard him. You're dismissed. Now go."

The minister touched my elbow. "Watch him."

I'd try.

The minister and the two stewards filtered out of the room, but we were staff, what else could we do? Even the minister didn't have the power to disobey a direct order from the king.

I opened the credenza and found a dusty bottle in the back. The king said he wanted more wine and it was customary to keep at least one serving girl in even the most private meetings. There were still a few from Larland's rule who had their tongues cut out, a way to ensure the glasses stayed full and the secrets never spilled. I wasn't a serving girl, but I'd try to stay in the shadows, try to blend with the scrolled sconces and the white walls the same way the stewards—

The oldest Vold plucked the bottle from my hands. "We will serve your king. Now run along."

He waited, hulking and wolfish, at least a head taller than the average man. His face was hard and battle-lined.

"Run along," he repeated, and there was a bite behind those words, a warning.

The minister, two stewards, and the guard nearly toppled through the door when I opened it.

"He drank valerian root," I said. "That should relax him." Though it wouldn't be enough to keep him from spouting nonsense about the dark devil or to stop him from lapping his drink like a dog.

"Is there anything else you could give him?" the minister asked. "Anything stronger?"

One of the stewards flicked a gloved hand. "I don't see why it matters. We don't have a relationship with Volgaard."

True. But Volgaard didn't seem like the type of country you wanted to trifle with. Even if the Volds weren't terrifying, they could take the news to our neighbors. At some point, they'd all ruled us—Larland, Gormark, even cold and rugged Forelsket. We'd been traded, given like rubies in dowries, won and lost in smoky gambling rooms. The Hyllestad Treaty protected our sovereignty, but if the Sanok Isles collapsed into crisis, they might take it as a sign that we were not smart enough, not shrewd enough, to rule ourselves. Did they want us back?

The minister waited for the answer to his question. His cherubic cheeks flushed red, a rash from the liver disease I'd been treating. *Was* there anything else I could give the king?

My hand crept to my hip where I'd stashed a clear vial. Søven. A wet rag held against the mouth would make him slump forward, his eyes lidding heavily. If I used that, the Volds would definitely know he was slipping, but what would be better? The king doing something ridiculous or using søven to knock him out?

Or maybe everything would be okay, maybe the valerian would be enough.

I pressed my ear to the wood and tried to untangle the sounds, the vowels, but everything blurred together like I was listening underwater. Was the king scratching? Growling? Pawing at the furniture?

No. They seemed to be talking. Or rather, the *Volds* seemed to be talking.

If I strained, I could catch snips of the conversation, voices vibrating the wood in a honeyed thrum. "… protection… resources… peaceful transition…"

It must be the oldest one, his tone teasing out the sharp consonants of each word, making them hard like metal.

"… before we start a war…"

My heart kicked. Before they start a…*what?*

I caught one of the steward's eyes. His brow furrowed, jaw falling slack as if he was trying to puzzle through the same thing.

"Do you think they mean…?" I whispered.

The steward shook his head. "I don't know."

"Shhh," the minister of trade hissed.

"… enemy… allies…"

From inside, something *thunked*. Then a shatter. Another scuffle, another *thunk*. A muffled, "Your Highness?"

What was the king doing? It might be fine. It should be fine? Or was he hurting himself? Hurting the Volds?

Scuffle, scuffle, *thunk*, *thunk*… *crash!*

I grabbed the søven and barged into the Rose Room.

Curtains billowed. Papers rustled.

King Christian had climbed atop the settee, his silver hair out of the ribbon, cascading wildly down his back. One of the oil lamps had been knocked over, and his wineglass lay broken at his feet, the pieces glittering.

I uncorked the søven bottle, wetting the corner of my rag. "The king's feeling unwell," I explained, bunching my woolen skirts and climbing onto the settee. "He's having a reaction to something I gave him earlier. He's not normally like this."

I needed to keep a firm grip. I'd seen the way the king fought Stefan when he tried to sedate him, thrashing and tearing like a fish caught in a net. He may be mad, but his years as a commander in Larland's army had drilled combat into his muscles in a way that could not be unlearned.

I grabbed the king's shirt by the ruffles and stuffed the søven-soaked rag into his face.

He tensed, then twisted, shoving my shoulders with the flats of his hands. Any minute now, he'd slump forward, unconscious. Breathe. He just needed to breathe. A few deep breaths.

"It's okay, Your Highness," I murmured, trying to mimic the milky tone Stefan used. "You can relax. Take a deep breath." The settee groaned under our weight.

King Christian's hands roved my torso, my arms, his nails raking the back of my neck. His fingers tangled through the fabric of my dress, tugging at the ribbing of my sweater. His grip seemed to loosen.

This was it. A few deep breaths and he'd be on the ground. I pressed the rag harder. "Breathe. It's okay."

It was as if someone sent a surge through the room. King Christian shoved me and scrambled up the side of the settee, perching there like a giant bird. "You're working with him," he shouted. "You're working with the dark devil." He hugged his knees and rocked. "The dark devil puts me to sleep, but I do not want to sleep. I do not."

I glanced at the bottle of søven, still open on the credenza, only the shape was too big, too fat, the liquid inside missing the pale champagne shimmer.

I sniffed the corner of my rag and my stomach crumpled. The queen's foot vinegar.

The king scrambled off the settee and into the space between the back of the chair and the bookshelves. "I do not want to drink, I do not." His lips sheened with vinegar. He tore off his jacket and tossed it to the ground. "The only way I am safe is to become the bear." He pulled his breeches over his boots, exposing his penis.

One of the stewards pushed past me. "Give it to me," he murmured, lunging for the open bottle of vinegar on the table.

"Wait." I pulled the real søven bottle out, taller, more slender. "Use this." How had I switched the two?

The steward took the rag and søven bottle and crept toward the king, his footsteps soft against the floral rug. "Your Highness," he said, his cadence calm like waves. "I know a way to get rid of the dark devil. Come closer. I'll tell you."

King Christian's arm slacked, his fingers loosening around his waistband. He shuffled forward one step, then another.

The steward lunged forward, shoving the rag against the king's nose. King Christian flailed, raking his fingers along the steward's coat, tearing the fabric, popping buttons.

The steward's elbow clipped a bird on the bookshelves. It shattered into a spray of glass. The king stumbled back, knocking into another bookshelf with an *oof*, just as—

The king groaned, then slumped against the steward, who lowered him to the floor.

Everyone stared, mouths agape. The handsome Vold swirled his drink and took a pointed sip.

The room was so quiet, the only sounds were the rustle of pages and the lull of the ocean.

The minister clapped his hands. "Well," he said. "That was exciting. Now if you'll follow me, I think a better place to talk would be the *Orchid* Room." He led the Volds down the hall. "I can relay your message to the king when he's feeling well again…"

I grabbed the king's coat off the ground and draped it over his waist. "Thanks for that."

The steward picked the vinegar bottle off the floor and took a sniff. His expression pinched. "Is this…?"

I snatched it back. "The søven should wear off in a few hours. He'll need to be dressed and moved. Discretely. Make sure he has a warm bath when he wakes. He'll probably soil himself."

The steward gathered the king's clothes and his boots, then eased his pants around his belly. Broken glass littered the floor like confetti and three half-drunk wineglasses shimmered, red like rubies, red like blood.

We don't need the Volds to know he's slipping.

We couldn't have told them any louder.

Chapter Four

I PUSHED ASIDE A STACK of blot papers, a bowl filled with garden thyme and pulled the book off the shelf, a slim white volume that smelled like grass. The lettering in the title might have been silver, or it might have been gold, but all that had been rubbed away by years of hands, years of tracing thumbs, and now all that was left was the soft indent of the words *Index Catalogue* embossed in leather.

I flipped to the section on *M*. M for madness, M for mind, M for maybe, because maybe if I'd given King Christian søven instead of vinegar, I could have stopped him from stripping. That was the worst part. The stripping. We could try to explain the nonsense about the dark devil, the way he'd lapped up his wine like a dog, but that?

And the steward knew it was my fault. He would tell, of course he would. If Jens-Kjeld found out…

I shook my head.

When Jens-Kjeld found out, his eyes would darken. He'd *tsk* his tongue, shake his head, and say the next royal physician couldn't make such a mistake.

I followed the words, tight text that seemed to crab across the page.

Outside, the rain still pattered, fogging up the apothecary windows, beading along the glass. Beyond it, a ribbon of green flecked with white and the whistles of goose girls herding their flocks.

The door creaked.

"I did your job," I said, slipping the book into a drawer and dropping to the cabinet below the long worktable. "You can thank me later. Also, we need more valerian." I rummaged through the empty gray-green bottles.

Sometimes I forgot it was a competition between Stefan and me, that Jens-Kjeld would choose just one of us to be his successor and the other would be sent home. Stefan, with his wide forehead and easy smile. Stefan, who knew exactly what to say to make a bad day better. Stefan, who was more like a brother than my real ones.

And I wanted to be the next royal physician, I did. I wanted it so bad my heart clenched and my ribs ached, but there was a reason Stefan was taking care of the king and I, the queen. There was a reason he could get away with disappearing for hours at a time, and I had to be there the moment the queen woke. Stefan, who was so kind-hearted, so easy to love. And me?

The queen's words from this morning slipped into my mind the way wind slips through eves.

Tell him it's not enough.

Would she have said that to Stefan?

I swallowed the lump forming in my throat and found the crackle glass vase stashed near the back of the cabinet. "I guess I should tell you the king is about the same as yesterday," I continued. "Any word from Jens-Kjeld?"

ILLUSION OF STARS

I glanced up. But it wasn't Stefan.

It was Hans.

He leaned against the wood doorframe, hands in his pockets, his faded sea foam staff jacket rolled to his elbows, dark curls matted from the rain.

"You're not with your pigeons," I said. A stupid thing to say. Of course he wasn't with his pigeons. He was here.

With me.

A smile tugged at his lips. "Katrina sent me."

I placed the poppy from this morning's walk in the vase, grabbed a pitcher from the windowsill, and eased the belly to let out a thin stream of water. "You can tell her the Volds use cups."

He shrugged. "I know."

"You know?"

"That's why she sent me, but that's not why I came."

"Why did you come?"

He paused, fiddling with the button on his jacket. Then—

"You found a poppy." He reached for it or maybe it was my hand he was reaching for. His fingers folded over mine, his pulse quick.

My heart knocked against my ribs, and I noticed the two buttons still open at my throat. I tugged my hand away and retreated to the window.

Hans took a step back and shoved his fists into his pockets. "Gustav has a fishing boat. We could take it out to Catchfly Cove. Go swimming?"

I opened my mouth to say the queen needed her feet cleaned and bandaged every morning, that most of the guards were still sick with the stomach flu, that one of the royal singers had a nose condition and needed spearmint steams twice daily.

"Katrina, too," Hans added. "If you want her to come. I mean, she definitely doesn't *have* to come, but—"

"Hans, I—"

"You know what?" He opened and shut his fingers, wiped a hand on his pants, turned and studied a shelf full of pinkish shells and pearlescent powders. "Maybe we should invite her. We don't want her to feel left out, and—"

"I can't." When Hans didn't reply, I added, "I tried to give the king vinegar instead of søven. I have to double down. Work harder." Find a cure for his madness.

Hans fiddled with a bottle of poppy seeds. His jaw tensed, then relaxed, tensed, then relaxed, then—

"Do you really think you'll be happy spending the rest of your life taking care of the queen's feet?"

"What kind of question is that?"

"You don't have to prove yourself."

I grabbed a ball of twine and a bunch of rosemary cuttings. "I'm not trying to prove myself."

"You're telling me your fixation on being royal physician has *nothing* to do with sticking it to your louse of a father?"

"Absolutely nothing."

"Uh huh."

"Really."

"But your father—"

I looped the twine so tight, the stems snapped. The air filled with a bright, lemony scent. "My father doesn't matter."

And he didn't. Of course, he didn't. My father, the best physician in Hjern, who taught me to use wormwood for an upset stomach, white willow for pain, who promised I could help run his practice when I was just a little older, the two of us, always just the two of us.

35

After he left, Hans had found me crying behind the chicken coop, red-faced and raw, barely thirteen-years-old, knees pulled to my chest.

"He abandoned us," I'd said, resting my cheek against the splintered wood. "He abandoned us because we weren't enough."

"You are enough," Hans had replied, running his fingers through my hair. The gesture might have been sweet, except he'd been thirteen and awkward, too. "You'll always be enough. And I will never leave you."

So far, he'd kept that promise.

The day I turned sixteen, Mama gave me her fringed shawl, a rind of cheese, and five gyllis for the coach. "Find work and write home." Her sun-spotted hand slipped down the side of my face. "Be safe."

When Hans found out, he begged and *begged* his father to let him follow, then chased after the coach, running barefoot down the lane and waving like a madman until the driver stopped.

"Someone has to keep you out of trouble," he'd said when he climbed aboard, as if I was the one in our friendship trio who needed that sort of help.

Although I never admitted it, I was glad he came. His presence was a balm that soothed the angry sting of leaving home. Back then, he smelled like sea and wind, and that smell clung to his clothes and his curls and made the entire ride less miserable.

I wanted to tell Hans, *See?* My father has nothing to do with it. See? This isn't about making him regret his decision to leave. It didn't tear my world in two. My vision didn't line red and I'm not trying to hurt him, I'm not. I'm not trying to show him I can be better than him—the best physician in our little town—by becoming the best physician in the whole damn country.

There was a knock at the apothecary door.

I pulled it open and took the pail of milk delivered by a rain-drenched dairy maid. "Are you happy sorting letters and cleaning pigeon poop?"

Hans crossed his arms and shouldered the wall. His dark hair and jacket set him off against the sun-bleached paint. "Royal postmaster is not what I want from life."

"And what do you want?" The question was a mistake. I realized as soon as I asked.

His blue eyes found mine, and there was something so cautious in them. He opened his mouth then closed it, bit the inside of his lip. "A fishing boat," he said after a moment. "I want a fishing boat."

I glanced down at the milk, cloudy with rain, and caught my own eyes, the wide shape of them, a freckled black-brown, just like my father's. Just like his babies. Water pilled along the pail, slipped down the side.

Tell him it's not enough—

Hans's face fell and he took a seat at the long table. "Just…tell me about this vinegar-søven mix up."

I kept my gaze on my hands. I'd simmer the milk with tansy and twinflowers to make a slurry for the sick guards.

"Isy," Hans said, a note of exasperation in his voice. "You can talk to me. I'm basically assistant secret keeper."

He was. As assistant postmaster, he saw most correspondence others preferred to keep quiet—trysts between lovers, treaties, alliances, backroom business deals perfumed with patchouli and pipe smoke. Sometimes I wondered what secrets Hans kept locked between his lips.

A strand of hair slipped out of my braid, curling at the corner of my vision. I swiped it away. "It's nothing. Just—I have to work harder."

Hans snorted. "There are at least a dozen solutions that aren't 'work harder.'"

"Like, write Jens-Kjeld and ask him to forgive me? Because I'm pretty sure that would get me fired."

"That's one option. Or you could bribe the steward to keep quiet."

"People do that?"

He shrugged and shoved his hands into his pockets. "Everyone wants something." For a moment, his expression was so bare, every hope, every dream, every want written in his features.

Something hard lodged in the back of my throat and I wanted to be somewhere else—*anywhere* else, not here, not now, not with him.

I tore myself away, placed a fresh log in the hearth, struck the strike once, twice. A fire roared and I felt Hans's steady gaze, felt the way he watched me with that cautious hope.

I wanted to tear it out.

Rain drummed the roof, slipped down the windows and that soft *patter, patter* was the only thing that broke the silence.

I turned to Hans, the yellow-tongued fire warming my back. As much as I wanted him to go, to leave, he had a point about the steward. Everyone wanted something.

But if I tried to bribe the steward, he could ask for anything and I'd be at his mercy. Was that better than Jens-Kjeld finding out? Better than the whole of Karlsborn Castle learning I'd let the king pull down his pants in front of the Volds?

Maybe.

And if I could buy the steward's silence, maybe I wasn't as doomed as I thought.

Chapter Five

I LEANED AGAINST ONE of the arching windows, the crisp cold of the glass cutting through the wool of my sweater, my bag heavy with the herbs and medicines people always wanted me to make. *Vanity potions*, Jens-Kjeld called them. Peppermint chews to sweeten breath, linseed oil to make hair shine, jars of glittery mica that a person could swipe on their cheeks or collarbones. I just needed to convince the steward to pick one or two or ten and promise to stay quiet.

Moonlight ran up and down the hall, casting off coffered ceilings, twinkling through chandeliers, dancing across picture frames and plush settees hand painted with pale green poppies. Outside, the sea shimmered like a pot of ink.

The steward would probably want my tooth whitening powder or cedarwood cologne. Still, I'd lay everything out on the credenza. If he was like everyone else in Karlsborn Castle, then he'd have a hard time choosing.

The door to the bedroom swung open and the steward wandered out. He shucked his jacket and gloves, tugged lose his cravat.

"Hey," I said, pushing myself off the windowpane.

"Hey." He didn't look up. What was his name? Henrik? Anders? He pulled the satin ribbon out of his hair and shook his head, letting the golden locks tumble free.

"Can I—?"

Before I finished, the king's door opened again and the second steward trotted out, his beard trimmed short, eyes bright as sugar cubes. "I thought you were going to wait for me."

Shit. I needed to get the first steward alone.

I sidled next to Henrik-Anders. "Can I borrow you?"

He eyed me sidelong. "About this morning?"

"Erm. Maybe?"

A shrug. "Don't worry about it. Everyone makes mistakes."

The second steward snorted. "Yeah, I mean, who *hasn't* tried to suffocate the king with vinegar?"

Double shit. They'd talked. Well, good thing I'd brought extra. I gripped the strap of my leather bag and hurried after them.

"We're friends, right? Henrik? Anders?"

"Pehr."

"I knew that."

"Did you?"

"I make cosmetics. Maybe you might want something? Because, you know, we're friends." The portraits of women in fluffy-dresses glared down at us, red-lipped and cold. I skipped a few steps.

"You're trying to buy our silence?" Pehr asked.

The other—*Loren, maybe?*—snorted. "Why would we keep that to ourselves? That's fantastic gossip. Assistant physician smothers ki—"

I crossed my arms. "Okay. I wouldn't say 'smothered.'"

"Mmm, you definitely smothered."

We were coming to the edge of the hallway. Soon, we'd round the corner, push through the doors that marked the end of the king's suites, and the odds of running into a third person would increase exponentially. I had enough to buy the silence of two people, but did I have enough to buy the silence of three?

I hooked an arm around their shoulders and pulled them to a stop. "Gentlemen. I think we can reach some sort of agreement."

I pushed aside a vase of buttercups and the statuette of a swan and laid out my cosmetics—a bottle of ointment to brighten eye circles, salt scrub to buff fingernails, breath chews wrapped in the silver-speckled paper I'd bought from the Merchant's Market last spring.

"Stefan brings us this sort of stuff all the time," said maybe-Loren, sniffing a stick of underarm cream.

I caught a whiff of the aroma—blood orange and clary sage, sunny and sweet. One of my favorites.

Pehr picked up a tin of tooth whitening charcoal and flicked it open with his thumb. "He said he'll provide it to all staff at no cost when he becomes the royal physician."

A lump lodged at the back of my throat. Is that what everyone thought? It was only a matter of time before Jens-Kjeld chose Stefan? "You must want something." The words came out smaller than I wanted.

Pehr put the tin back on the credenza. "Not really. At least…not cosmetics."

Maybe I could trade something else. "I—I make bouquets? From the flowers I pick on the bluffs. I could make one if you…want one for your girlfriend?" There. Something Stefan didn't do.

41

Pehr shoved his hands in his pockets and took a step back. "Eh."

Eh? That was it? That was all he had to say?

Loren rubbed his beard. "What about the boat?"

"The boat," Pehr repeated. "Huh. Maybe."

I raked a hand through my hair. No, no, no. How was I supposed to get a boat?

"Gustav said any of us could borrow his fishing boat to impress a girl," Loren clarified. "Girl. Swimming. Catchfly Cove. Bound to lead to kissing." He puckered his lips for emphasis. Then to Pehr, "You could have her cover for Elin."

Pehr rubbed his jaw. "I *could* have her cover for Elin."

Okay, this was worse than them asking me to buy a boat. I had to take care of the queen's feet, help the sick guards, find a cure for the king's madness. I couldn't take a day off *to do someone else's work*. I wrapped both arms around their shoulders and tucked them close like a mother duckling tucking in her chicks. "Friends."

Pehr opened his mouth. "We aren't—"

"I think we can come to an agreement."

I dug in the bag's bottom and pulled out a canvas purse. One week of salary—my last resort. "Twenty gyllis."

"I still want you to cover for her."

My smile slipped. "With that money, you could hire a scrape."

He hefted the purse in his hands, then tossed it back. "I think I'd rather have you do it."

Was this about Stefan? Some sort of ploy to get him named as the royal physician? Did they want to see me fail? Pehr propped his elbow against the credenza, golden hair falling around his shoulders like an angel, like a god. They were going to tell everyone, or I'd be at their mercy. Still, he was only asking for a day…

"Where does Elin work?"

"Laundry."

Laundry wasn't bad. Katrina worked in laundry. If she helped, it would go twice as fast. Maybe I could beat them at their own game.

"Just one day?" I clarified.

A golden brow arched. "You willing to trade more?"

"And you promise to forget about the vinegar?"

He smiled, sharp like marran grass. "Like it never happened."

"Then you have a deal."

"YOU PICKED THE WRONG DAY to cover for Elin," Katrina said. She squatted on a wash stool and scrubbed a curtain panel against a wood board. Cream brocade swirled in sudsy liquid, and soap bubbles fizzed around reddened knuckles. "Or maybe she picked the right day to skip."

The other laundresses were folding and pressing and stirring, some up to their ankles in water, their cotton smocks hitched to their knees. Three giant pots bubbled over a fire, pumping out thick braids of steam and the scorched-milk scent of washing ash and lye.

I toed a second curtain panel. "What do I need to do?"

"It's not hard. You're just changing bedsheets." Katrina wiped a strand of sweaty hair off her forehead. "But there are a lot of them, and it'll keep you past dinner."

"Shit."

"Exactly. You'll want to start in the east wing, do the lords and noblemen there. Then the bedrooms in the South Hall, the bedrooms downstairs, the bedrooms looking out over the courtyards, the bedrooms in the Blue Tower and oh—uh, the Volds. They're in the North Wing, looking out on the beach."

My heart kicked. "I thought the Volds set up camp *on* the beach."

Katrina dunked her curtain panel into the washbasin a few more times, churning a white froth. "The important ones are here. Queen Margarethe insisted."

"She can't even get out of bed."

"She insisted *from* her bed."

"You're coming with me, right?"

"Can't. It's curtain week." Katrina hefted the curtain panel out of the wash bucket and carried it, dripping, to the line. The steam had fogged the windows, beads of water trickling down them. "If you're worried about the Volds, you shouldn't have agreed to cover for Elin."

"Pehr and Loren didn't tell me that."

"Just don't make eye contact with them."

"With Pehr and Loren?"

She snorted. "With the *Volds*. I hear it melts your eyeballs."

I remembered the handsome Vold, the way he'd caught my eye when the king had lapped his drink like a dog. At least that rumor was false.

I pushed aside the curtain panel. "Wait. *Is* everyone worried about the Volds?"

From behind us, someone coughed.

We both glanced to see Sofie, her pale hands clasped in front of her, hair falling in a thick braid down her back. "Excuse me," she said. "Where's the washing ash?"

The tips of Katrina's cheeks turned strawberry pink, and she ducked her head. "It's, uh…in the cabinet."

"You know," I said when Sofie was out of earshot, "you could ask her to go dancing."

Katrina shook her head, her eyes fixed on her hands. "She wouldn't say yes."

"You never know." Truthfully, I liked Sofie better than Oskar.

"Well…" Katrina chewed her bottom lip. She stole another glance at Sofie, who was now perched on a stool and riffling through a cabinet, moving aside waxed packages of soaps and linens, threads and dyes. A few strands of hair had slipped loose from her braid.

"Well?"

Katrina's eyes snapped back to her work. "Never mind."

"Tell me."

"I saw her flirting with a stable hand."

"So?"

"A *male* stable hand."

"She might like everyone. A lot of people like everyone. I mean, you. You like everyone."

Katrina dunked the entire curtain panel under the water. "The bedsheets and the basket are in the closet at the end of the hall. If you take the biggest basket, you can minimize the number of trips. You're welcome."

I FOUND THE BASKETS WHERE KATRINA said they would be, took the biggest one, a round wicker hamper, and loaded it with throws and sheets. When it was full, I ventured back into the hallway, tugging the laundry door closed with my boot.

Hans shoved a letter and writing stick into his pocket and scrambled from the floor. "Isy." He fell into step beside me.

My traitorous heart kicked, but I shoved it down and hurried past him with clipped steps. "Can't talk today. Covering for Elin."

Hans trotted after me. "She has you changing sheets?"

"Something like that." I shouldered my way into the first bedroom.

Peonies and blue crabs patterned the walls and a vase of sweet peas sat on the inlaid table, their feather-pink petals curling inward, browning at the edges. A salty breeze riffled the curtains like a pair of lazy hands.

I stripped off the duster, the duvet, lemon organza, the sheets, turned the fringed pillowcases inside out. Hans lingered in the doorway, a ghost twisting the paper in his hands.

"Want help?" he asked.

Yes. I shoved the pillow into the case. "No."

"You sure? I thought—"

I gave him a hard look—the type of look that said, *Please don't get into trouble for me.* "Go train your pigeons or sort letters or whatever you're supposed to be doing."

Dappled sun highlighted the arches in his cheekbones, softened his jaw, played through his hair. "I'm supposed to be cleaning the dovecote today."

"The inside or the outside?"

He grimaced and ran two fingers along the door handle. "Both." His gaze softened. "But I'd help you first."

The words snagged something inside my heart, a loose thread on a sweater. I swallowed, folded the duster in half. "Both, huh? Better get to it."

He opened his mouth, closed it. His charcoal-dusted thumb traced the fold of the paper, blackening the edge. "Actually, can we talk? I want to read you something."

I wadded the dirty sheets and tossed them into the basket. "Can't."

"Tonight?" His eyes caught mine and there was that same cautious expression in them.

"This is supposed to take all day."

He rubbed his palm. "You know, you probably shouldn't be doing this alone."

"Why?"

"The Volds. They're dangerous."

My mind flashed back to that moment in the hallway, when the oldest Vold stormed out. The snarl. The sneer. I shook my head. "I'll be fine."

"Isy…"

"I'm staff. They probably won't even notice I'm there. It's not worth the trouble." *Go. Please.*

He shoved the paper into his pocket and caught the other end of the sheets, pulling them taut across the bed. "I don't care about trouble. You're worth the trouble."

The words were another snag, another tug on that loose thread in the back of my heart. And I knew, *knew* if he kept tugging…

Hans leaned over the mattress and reached for one of the pillow shams, a decorative one embroidered with buttery blackberries.

I snatched it away. "Go help Katrina. It's curtain week."

"I'll find you later?" Again, that hopeful note. "I don't mind staying up."

If he kept tugging…

If he kept tugging…

I'd unravel.

"Maybe." I shooed him away. "Now go."

He nodded, leaving me alone with my mottled heart and mountain of laundry.

I SPENT THE REST OF THE DAY stripping bedsheets in rooms that smelled like dust and rose petals, rooms with cold fireplaces and plush armchairs and with beds draped with heavy canopies. Sometimes the nobles were there, reading books or changing clothes or playing with puppies and a string. Their eyes would slide right past me as if I was nothing—no more than a shadow or a piece of wallpaper or a beam of light banding the floor.

Why wouldn't they? I was staff.

The sun peeled across the sky, casting white spears, then soft yellows, then fiery orange and tender violet, before it slipped off the horizon all together.

Lamps were lit, chandeliers hoisted. Women donned their fluffy gowns and powdered their noses. The hallways filled with the sour bite of pickled herring and the sweet scent of macerated berries.

Room after room, sheet after sheet. More rooms, more sheets, more trips to laundry, where the air steamed with lye. I stripped and swept, tucked and folded, the South Hall, the Blue Tower, the bedrooms downstairs, all of it done until I had one more set of rooms, one more set of beds. The rooms in the North Wing, the rooms overlooking the silver-black sea.

The rooms Queen Margarethe had given to the Volds.

Moonlight pooled on the polished floors, winked off the wrought gold sconces. Spiders spun webs in deadened corners.

I swallowed a shiver.

Three more rooms. Three more rooms, and I'd fulfilled my end of this cursed bargain. Three more rooms, and I wouldn't have to worry about the stewards or the søven mix up or anything else, just taking care of the queen and the guards and finding a cure for the king's madness.

Three more rooms.

I adjusted my grip on the basket of linens, pushed opened the first door...

And walked straight into a forest.

Chapter Six

HAZY MOONLIGHT FILTERED between tall pine trees and the air—musty and sweet—cooled to a chill. Overhead, a bird's wings clapped, causing a few pine needles to twirl through the air and land atop the crisp linen.

I set the basket down and touched the trunk of a tree, my fingertips catching on feathery bark and hardened sap. Trees. They didn't grow in the Sanokes. I'd only ever seen pictures in books. How…?

I turned back, half expecting to find myself marooned in the forest, but the hall was still there, a yawning doorway to another world—a world with tile floors and damask wallpaper, separate and apart from this strange land unfurling in front of me.

"Augh!" a voice behind me said. "What are you doing?"

I whirled.

There was the stormy-handsome Vold from King Christian's study, his shirt untucked, hair tussled, his mouth pulled into a frown.

"What are *you* doing?" I asked, snatching the basket off the ground.

All at once, the trees began to fold, shriveling and shrinking until they disappeared into pale whips of smoke he waved away with the back of his hand. And just like that, we stood in an ordinary bedroom, complete with a floral rug and a tufted settee. Moonlight poured in through windows as the ocean waves lapped below.

"Do people knock in the Sanok Isles?" He stalked toward the settee. "Because in Volgaard, people knock."

My heart thundered. I pressed a hand to my waist to steady myself. "Why are you in a forest?"

He shot me a glare. "That's none of your business. Why are you here?"

I could keep pressing about the forest, but—*The Volds. They're dangerous.*

"I came to change your sheets."

His jaw tensed. "Fine. Do it quickly."

I carried the basket to the side of the bed and prepared to strip away the blankets, but his bed hadn't been slept in. The blue duvet was still turned down, the sheets crisp, the warming pan nestled beneath the mattress.

I ran my fingers along the embroidered fringe and turned. "You didn't—"

The settee was empty, and the room was still. The only reminder he'd ever set foot in the place was his traveling cloak and a handful of pine needles scattered across the floor.

SOMETHING POKED MY RIBS. I groaned and rolled over, throwing the pillow over my head and smothering some of the gray light that filtered through the window. A freezing hand snagged the blankets and a finger jammed into the soft spot right above my—

I sat up and glared. "Stop trying to tickle me. It won't work."

Katrina merely smiled—a gesture that brought out her dimple—and held out a handful of stolen candies. "I want to hear more about the Volds."

"I already told you," I said, throwing the pillow over my head, "I don't know how he got the forest in his bedroom."

"Tell me again what he did with the map."

"*Leavemealone.*"

Katrina pinched my cheek. "Wake up, sleepy." Then, in a saucy whisper, "Let's go to the beach."

I slapped her hand. "Go away. Take your contraband candies with you." I hiked the quilt around my chin to make sure she got the message.

Katrina scrambled to the foot of my bed. The quilt tangled around my legs lifted ever so slowly. Then an ice-cold hand pinched my big toe, followed by another poke to the arch of my foot.

I kicked her. Hard.

"Ouch!" she said, clamping her hand around my ankle.

I kicked again. "I'm not sneaking out with you today. I have work."

From the other side of the room, blankets rustled and someone grunted. I squinted through my lashes and caught a pebble-black pair of eyes.

"You're being awfully loud." Gretchen propped herself up onto her elbow, the corners of her mouth twitching into the lazy half-smile of a cat who'd just caught a mouse.

Katrina scrambled off her perch, wide-eyed and hunch-backed, nightgown clinging to her legs like a surrender flag.

"Sorry," she whispered. The sheets rustled as she slid into her own bed.

I twisted from one side to the other, boxed my pillow, flipped again. I shoved my arm under my head. There was a lump in my mattress, a ball as hard as a goose egg that punched against my shoulder blade. I tried to tamp it down, tried to let the sweet tug of sleep take me back…

A bird chirped. From somewhere, someone snored.

I cracked one eye open. There was Katrina, the slope of her shoulders, her back to me, her body still. Katrina lived for the morning hours—the trips to the bluffs, the beach, the time she could spend walking along a world washed of footprints, smoothed from sleep. And I knew better than to let myself be sucked into her schemes, I did, but her shoulders sagged and she lay so, so still.

"Fine," I said, peeling off the blankets. "As long as we're back before the queen wakes up." *Well* before the queen woke up.

Katrina scrambled up, raked a hand through her hair, and pulled on her boots, skipping her stockings.

I tugged the goose-turd green sweater over my head. "And as long as you help me catch a starfish."

GRAY FOAM BLEW ACROSS THE BEACH, tumbling over seaweed. Sand nipped at our ankles and water sprayed against basalt bluffs, a low and gentle roar. The air was salty and briny and cold.

"Do you think it's magic?" Katrina asked. She'd walked out to the water's edge, her silhouette ribboning pink and copper in the sand.

I picked up a broken shell and tossed it into the waves. If I let her, she'd talk about this ad nauseam. To some extent, she already had. "Dunno."

"It would explain it," she continued, dark hair whipping around her face in loose snaps. "But why come here? Why now?" She pursed her lips and squinted toward the horizon.

"Maybe they want to apologize for cutting out all those merchants' hearts."

"Then why send so many men? Have you seen the beach they're camped at?"

I shrugged and tossed another stone into the sea. "Maybe they're just passing through on the way to something better."

"What's better than the Sanokes?"

Lots of things. Everything. We were a windswept country, an island with no trees, no wealth, a place as bleak and barren as the bottom of the sea. We were a stop-off for whalers and wanderers, a pinprick on the map of the world. We were a country of nobodies.

I flicked wet sand with the toe of my boot and said, "Tide pools are over here."

Katrina tucked an errant strand of hair behind her ear. Her brow furrowed in the look that said she was worried about something. "What are we going to do about it?"

"Do about what?"

"The magic."

"What is there to do about it? We're staff. Now come on. Starfish."

She broke away from her spot on the sand and jogged to catch up. "I thought we were going to do the screaming thing."

"We're at the beach. We can't do the screaming thing."

"Come on. You love the screaming thing."

"You just like secrets." That was the rule with the screaming thing. You could scream anything you wanted, so long as it was a secret. Big secrets, small secrets, silly secrets. It just had to be a secret.

She grinned and tweaked my nose. "Why do you need to catch a starfish?"

I shrugged and shoved my hands under my arms. "Potential madness cure."

"I wish my boss let me out to catch starfish."

Well, Jens-Kjeld didn't exactly *ask* me to catch a starfish. Last night, I'd come back from laundry and searched the white reference book for anything that might help. I had to wade through a lot of irrelevant information—how to knead plaster to pull inflammation, what herbs were the best at blood stopping, how to cauterize a wound with willow bark—until I came across a handwritten study about how starfish spines had been used to treat fixation.

Worth a shot.

We scrambled down the beach, to the tide pools, the rocks pocked and sharp, fuzzed with sea moss. Fish darted in and out of our shadows and purple crabs scurried. Wind pricked my eyes, plastered my bangs against my forehead. I tried tucking a strand behind my ear, but it whipped free.

"What's that?" Katrina asked.

She'd stopped on a rock a few feet ahead of me, her mouth pressed into a line.

I followed her gaze until I saw it too—a black and scarlet smear stretching across the tide pools, reddening the rocks.

"It's…"

But she was already running toward it, racing over the beach.

I followed. The wind pounded my skin, my feet pounded the earth, my heart pounded my mouth as we scrambled toward the smear.

Katrina reached it first. And when she saw it, she let out a whimper and dropped to her knees, sending a splash of red droplets. Red. The wrong color. It pushed and pulled, swirled in eddies around the thing.

Not a thing… A body.

A bloated hand splayed across the rock, fingers so swollen, they'd turned a veiny white. Sandflies leapt like fleas through a crop of matted hair and pink-tinged foam clung to its clothes.

"Wh-what do we do?" Katrina asked.

"That's…that's a staff jacket," I said. "We flip them over, figure out who it is."

Katrina stumbled back, her foot catching a rock. "Isy, I—"

I grabbed her arm and pulled her down. "Grab the ankles. Ready? One, two—"

Water sloshed like sudsy soap, stirring up bits of sand and stringy blood to reveal a face.

The world tipped and for a moment—a fleeting moment— I could not think and I could not breathe and I could not feel.

A handful of silver fish scattered, darting into the shadows.

"Is that—" Katrina's voice cracked.

Tears pricked my eyes. "Get help," I said, but the words were wrong, a gargle. I dropped to my knees. *"Get help!"*

The warmth of Katrina's presence disappeared as she tore up the beach.

I clawed at the jacket, then at the blood-soaked cravat, my fingernails slipping over the knot tied too tight, too tight. I threw the fabric into the tide and pumped his chest. Water spurted from his lips.

I pumped his chest again, and again, and again. Be alive. He had to be alive. Any minute now, he'd sputter and sit up and tell me what the hell he was doing down here.

Pump, pump. Wait.

Pump, pump. Wait.

The sun beat against my arms, my neck. Gulls screeched. The waves pushed and pulled my skirt into a bloody swirl.

Pump, pump. Wait.

Pump, pump. Wait.

The world seemed to stop, seemed to spin, and the only sounds were my breath and the crash of the sea against sand.

Pump, pump. Wait.

Pump, pump—

Then shouting. Splashing. A dog barked. Hands. Wrapped around my waist. Hauling me out.

"Let me go," I shouted, the rhythm of pounding, of pumping still caught in my bones. "I can save him, I can—"

"It's too late," the guard said, pulling me back. "It's too late. Shh. I'm sorry. He's gone."

And then I was on the sand, and the guards were smoothing their hands over my hair, running them down my shoulders, checking for injuries. Someone gave me a blanket like I was the one who was hurt, but I wasn't hurt. I was shivering and I was sobbing, and I wanted to wake up from this dream, this dream, because this had to be a dream.

But I already knew the truth.

The ugly truth.

Hans—the boy who held me crying behind the chicken coop, the boy who chased after our coach, who loved oceans, trained pigeons, who promised he'd never leave—

He was dead.

Chapter Seven

I DIDN'T

Chapter Seven

~~It wasn't~~

Chapter Seven

HOW DO YOU PUT PAIN on a page? How do you say goodbye?

Chapter Eight

THE SOFT GLOW OF CANDLES blinked up the cliff side like a handful of glitter caught in the wind. I shielded my flame and made my way across the dark and dewy lawn, the air catching the ruffles on my dress.

With each step, my heart wanted to crack, wanted to skitter, wanted to snap. Tonight, we'd burn his body, burn our messages, and his soul would climb the smoke to the stars.

The paper in my pocket was supposed to be my final goodbye, supposed to be the words to send him off.

The paper in my pocket, the last thing I'd ever say.

It was blank.

Katrina had known exactly what to write. She'd dried her eyes and scribbled three shaky lines of text. A memory. A message. A goodbye. Three things, that's all it took.

And I should be able to write something, I should. But every time I tried, a lump formed in the back of my throat and my heart clenched like a fist, so I shut it out, shut it down, and pretended that Hans was cleaning the dovecote or on the bluffs, not in the chapel, nuns sponging his gray arms. Not in the chapel, the funeral shroud being stitched around his body.

Wax pilled along my candle shaft, pattered into the catch with slow, slick beats. The lights ahead continued to blink up the hillside.

A memory. Red water swirling around a bloated hand.

A message. You shouldn't have died.

A goodbye—

A goodbye—

A goodbye—

And maybe I was jealous of Katrina because it had been so easy for her. Katrina, who flitted from person to person in the after-hours of that morning, who fell that night into a dark and dreamless sleep. Katrina, who still smiled, still laughed, still stole a handful of candies from the kitchen like everything was normal, like our world hadn't just burst.

She fell into step beside me, looping her arm through mine. "Did you write it?"

I swallowed and kept my eyes fixed on the line of flames peppering the dusky dark. "Yes." A single word meant to end the conversation.

"Here," she unhooked her arm and reached into her pocket, "I can tear mine. I wrote extra, anyway. That's better than sending—"

Nothing. That's what she was going to say. Tearing her goodbye would be better than sending nothing.

My fingers tightened around the candlestick. Beads of wax slipped down the white column and pattered against the catch.

"Isy, he'd want—"

"I wrote something." I quickened my pace, the wind

threatening to snuff out my candle. Waves cracked. Seabirds huddled in scoops of rock.

Katrina jogged a few steps, shielding her flame. "Fine. What did you write?"

I opened my mouth, then closed it.

"Liar. That paper is sitting in your pocket, blank. You didn't write anything. You don't believe—"

I made a point of not glancing in her direction and climbed onward, hoping that would be the end of it.

"He'll look for your message," she called. "He'll look for yours before he looks for mine or anyone else's. And you're sending him to the stars with…with nothing."

I ignored her, wrapped that numbness around my mottled heart and let it squeeze.

"He'll think you didn't care."

A few in the procession slowed. A laundress stopped and tilted her head in our direction, waiting.

I continued, each step heavier than the last, muscles burning from the climb, skirt too heavy, sky too heavy, mouth too heavy. Climbing up and out, out of a world that seemed to close in.

"He loved you."

Blue grass shuttered. A bird arced across the moon.

"Hans was in love with you, and you won't even say goodbye. He came here for *you*. He left home for *you*, and you won't even—"

I bit my bottom lip so hard it throbbed. Tears pricked the corners of my eyes. I knew he loved me, knew he cared, and I hated it—hated his love, the way he looked at me. Because if I wasn't good enough for my father—my lying, cheating father—then how on earth was I supposed to be good enough for Hans?

I pushed on and up, on and up, beads of sweat rolling down my shoulders. The crash of the ocean grew louder.

Katrina dropped to the back of the procession while I pulled to the front. The distance might have only been a few hundred paces, but it felt infinite.

The path opened into a meadow far above the tar-black sea. Without the shield of the hill, droplets of mist fell, coating our lashes, blinking silver against the pyre. I lingered at the periphery, unable to tear my eyes away from the linen-wrapped body resting atop it. Someone placed a bouquet of blue wildflowers by his ear. Another, a handful of currants on his chest. The flowers and berries to remind him of the land he came from.

The royal postmaster gestured at the fat clouds hanging overhead. "We'll have to be quick," he said, the words gruff. "The pyre might not light if the rain picks up." He kept his chin tucked to his chest, but he couldn't hide the way the amber light reflected off his cheeks. I'd heard the royal postmaster say that, of all the apprentices he'd had, Hans was the most like a son.

And perhaps to Hans, the royal postmaster was something of a father.

The royal postmaster's throat bobbed. "Hans was a good boy," he said. "Always on time, never complained. Good head on his shoulders. We'll miss him."

He dug in his pocket and pulled out a piece of paper, which he dipped into the candle's shining flame. "That you find your way home."

An old blessing from a time before we belonged to Larland or Gormark or…anyone.

The edge of the paper blistered, turning orange and black before folding in on itself. With the flick of his wrist, he tossed it on the pyre.

Elin went next. She lit her goodbye and set it on Hans's chest, among the berries. "That you find your way home."

One by one, members of the procession stepped forward, lit their messages, and gave their goodbyes. The words, the wishes formed the steps that carried his spirit to the stars, and those words—*that you find your way home*—said over and over again.

Katrina tore her message in half and said the blessing twice, damp hair hanging loose around her face, black dress clinging to her skin. She didn't bother to look at me as she tossed her goodbye into the flames.

By the time I burned my letter, the yellow fire roared so bright and hot a column of dense smoke chugged toward the rain-streaked sky.

"I'm sorry," I said as the edges of my paper blackened and shriveled. Whether for the fact he was gone or for the empty paper, I wasn't sure. In truth, I could have written a thousand pages, and they would never be enough.

With the flick of my wrist, I tossed the paper on the pyre and watched it burn.

Chapter Nine

I WOKE IN A COLD SWEAT—mouth dry, quilt tangled around my legs, the fizzy images of the dream still popping and bursting behind my eyelids. Red water, pink foam, vacant eyes. The press of his chest beneath my palm.

Pump, pump. Wait.

Pump, pump. Wait.

Pump, pump—

I leaned over the edge of the bed and vomited.

Moonlit fog spilled through the open window, spinning beams of white across the floor and obscuring the shapes of a dozen sleeping girls. Loose hair spilled over pillows, sheets tangled around legs, chests rising and falling. Someone snored.

I rested my cheek against the bedpost. Breathe. It was a dream. Not real.

But my heart still thumped in the back of my throat, and the images still popped, bulging and bright. Brown curls. Swollen skin. A sand fly's wings quivering in the breeze and—

I slipped out of bed, the floorboards cool and smooth and

real. This was real. Here was real, the rumple of sheets, the winter wool so neatly folded. Real.

The roar of waves seemed to grow louder, or maybe it was the ringing in my ears. Too hot. This room was too hot and the ceiling too low and—

Pop, burst. Water lapped over my hands. *Pop, burst.* Seagulls screeched.

I pulled the door open and stumbled into the corridor. Mice vanished and spiders skittered. The air here still too hot, too thick.

My knuckles knocked the edge of the banister. I grabbed it, nails biting into the wood, and jammed my shoulder against the wall to stop the shaking.

Shaking.

I didn't realize I was shaking.

Water. I needed water. A glass. A drink. Something.

THE FOG HAD RINSED AWAY most of the kitchen's food smells, yeast and clams, the sour funk of cheese, leaving nothing but air so thick, the droplets seemed to gather at the tip of my nose.

In a few hours, the cooks would be up, husking crabs, chopping mushrooms, and creaming spinach, but for now, everything was quiet, everything was still.

I stepped over the boxes of old vegetables—cabbages and leeks, a crate of apples with mold dappling the peel—and found a silver drinking bucket in the corner by the hearth.

My reflection stared back at me, rippled and clear.

I ladled some water into a cup, took one sip, then another.

Morning dew had crept in through the windows, beading along the latches, rolling down in pear-shaped streaks.

I let the ladle clatter back into the bucket, pressed my forehead against a pane of glass and let the coolness seep into my bones, let breath after breath fill my lungs. Okay. I was okay. Tomorrow, I'd wake and tend to the queen, boil linen for bandages, and scavenge for wild garlic along the bluffs. I'd push myself on and up, on and up because I couldn't stop.

There was a rustle from the other side of the kitchen.

I paused, squinting through the rolling fog. Another shift, another rustle, and someone was sitting at the long table, the one where the staff ate their meals. Was it one of the stable hands?

I took a step closer, then another, lithe as the tabby that lived in the pantry.

No.

It was the king's cherub-cheeked minister of trade, wearing a floor-length nightshirt and a cotton cap, snoring softly. A plate of crumbs rested on the table in front of him, and a glass of something sat near his wrist. Honey wine, probably—everyone knew that was his favorite.

My foot knocked a bucket of oyster shells and the minister startled. His eyes fluttered open. "Ingrid," he slurred. "I, uh…dinnya hear you come in."

"Sorry. Didn't mean to wake you." I ducked my head. "I'll grab a maid. She can help you with…whatever."

I didn't want anyone to see me like this.

That thought, followed by something deeper: I didn't want to be alone.

The minister tried to rest his cheek on his fist, but ended up punching his cap halfway off his head. "You were friends with the, uh…pigeon boy? Whawas his name? Henrik? Hurr— Hurr— Hurrrman?"

71

"Hans."

"Sorry 'bout…the inquest. It wasn't what I wanted, but you know. He was just assistant postmaster. Inquests? They're…they ruh…" He gave a vague wave of his hand. "S'pensive."

I pressed the heels of my hands against my eyes. The inquest. I wanted to be angry about that, I did. I wanted to rage and cry and shout. But… I understood. That was the worst part about it. The cold, hard weight of understanding. Hans was just the assistant postmaster, a nobody. Inquests *were* expensive, and why would you spend the time and energy trying to figure out what happened to a nobody when the queen was dying and the king was streaking naked and the Volds were doing who knows what on the beach? But I wasn't sure I could tell the minister that without crying, so I pushed aside that gnarled thing and turned toward the set of stairs. "It's fine. It happens."

It happens.

As if people are casually murdered.

It happens.

Because if you're small, nobody cares. If you're staff, nobody cares. I was small, and I was hurting, and this wasn't about me— it wasn't—but I was alone, so alone, and I just wanted someone to see me.

See me.

Morning mist billowed from open windows, the world beyond mirrored in shades of pearl and pewter, the hedges bending like waves in a choppy sea.

The minister nodded, solemn, at his glass of wine. "It's been a rough night for me, too."

I glanced down at my hands, clenched so hard they shook. My nails cut half-moon indents into my palms, and this was a mistake. I couldn't be here. I turned toward the bottom step. "Goodnight."

He continued staring into his wine. "Can I ask'yew something? You're uh…a smart girl."

"The alcohol's making your cheeks worse."

"Not that. Well…" the back of his hand grazed his cheek, "that?"

"Absolutely."

He knocked the glass back and finished the contents with a hiccupy burp.

"Goodnight," I said again.

"Wait. *Waaaaait.*" He wiped his mouth with his sleeve. "If someone powerful asks'yew to do something important. But the thing you don't…you can't…you…?" The minister frowned. "*Aren't* sure if you can give it to them. But the powerful person promises to protect you and says it's the only way. Do you say yes?"

"Huh?"

"If someone powerful asks for something important—"

"I heard that. It's just—was that an actual question?"

The minister reached for the wine bottle but overshot the distance, bumping the green neck. Pale liquid glugged across the wood, shimmering like rainwater. He frowned and tried to grab it, but knocked the cup over. "If someone powerful asks'yew for something important—"

"I heard you. I'd decline."

I'd decline.

The obvious answer, but no, that wasn't right. If someone powerful wanted something important… "I'd be clever," I amended. "Give them all of it or a piece, mince words, play tricks, ask for something in return."

Everyone wants something. Hans's words.

What do you want?

I shook my head and pressed away the memory of him, the feelings that lurked—too big, too raw. "*Can* you ask for something in return?"

The minister let out a burbled "*I dunno,*" and traced a heart through the liquid. "If we ask too much, they cou'just take it."

"All the reason to be clever."

"I suppose so."

A hum and pause, broken only by the chime of the clocktower marking two in the morning.

The minister downed the rest of his bottle, and I left him alone in the dark.

Chapter Ten

I RUBBED MY EYE WITH the heel of my hand and blinked, the fuzzed script coming in and out of focus. The letters balled so tight, they looked like raspberry vines creeping across the page.

… boring a hole in the cranium to relieve pain associated with subungual hematoma…

A fly *tinked* against a bottle of vinegar. Honey hardened in a mixing bowl. Wind creaked through the joists of the apothecary like old bones.

… should occur between the frontal and occipital tissue using a circular trephine to expose the dura mater…

Dura mater?

I placed my hands on my forehead, letting my fingers slide up my scalp.

This didn't make sense. It stopped making sense an hour ago when I got to the part about concussive trauma and even then, the concept was hazy. It had started out simple enough—a story about an ancient king who fell off his horse, underwent a severe personality change, and ordered his husband beheaded. But instead of discussing what had actually cured the king, the author launched into a long and speculative argument about what *might* have helped. All procedures involved cutting or scraping and then…something, something, something.

I took another swig of coffee, black and bitter, and flipped several pages to read it again.

This author recommends attempting these procedures on the deceased before the living. The mind is a delicate organ, easily—

"Hey, Isy."

I jumped, knocking a wooden spoon off the table with a clatter. "Shit." I dropped to my knees. "I didn't hear you come in."

Stefan stood in the doorway, shoulders slouched. Dark circles rimmed his eyes, and his hair, too long, curled over his ears, more like a thief in the night than the other apprentice physician. He'd skipped two buttons on his shirt, and his cravat, a dusky red, hung at an awkward angle. "Nice to see you, too."

Morning sun had burned the fog off the bluffs and streamed in through the windows, lighting blue-green tonic waters and the stems of marsh thistle propagating in the sill. The wood stove smoldered, pumping the heady scent of imported oak and hickory into the air.

I pushed myself up and slapped the dust off my skirts. "What happened to your cravat? You look like a—"

The reference book still lay flat on my worktable, open to the stippled drawing of a skull and a flat-edged knife. If Stefan found out I spent my free time searching for a cure, he'd start looking, too.

It was petty, it was. It shouldn't matter who found the cure. But if Stefan found it first…

He dropped his shoulder bag and unloaded a leather box, a flask, and the seedy fennel bread he took for breakfast. "I look like a what?"

I angled myself between Stefan and the book. "A mess. You look like a mess." I eyed the flask, silver and stamped with twin suns. "Drinking already?"

Stefan's lips pulled into a line, and he shucked the paper off his bread. "It's nothing. Jens-Kjeld had me on an errand."

An errand.

Jens-Kjeld didn't say anything about that. But... Jens-Kjeld hadn't said much. His last letter to me had been brief—

Keep working. Don't let the queen boss you around. Be back in two weeks.

Still. An errand.

Why hadn't Jens-Kjeld asked me?

"That's for you," Stefan said, a little too cheery. He dropped a box into my lap. "They were cleaning out his space this morning, and I thought...well." He propped himself on an elbow and his expression softened, his wide green eyes settling on me. "He'd want you to have it."

I glanced at the box, brown leather embossed with *HH*.

HH. Hans Halstrup.

Acid pricked in the back of my throat, and I wanted to throw it across the room.

"Go on," Stefan said.

I gritted my teeth and flicked the lid.

Letters. Two years' worth. Letters tied up with a red string, letters from friends, letters from home, letters so folded and creased, they must have been read a thousand times. That was Hans, though—always reading, always writing.

I opened one and found the wobbly hand of his sister. *The chicks are growing. They're not so cute anymore.* Another from his neighbor. *I was surprised about what you said about Sonderjem. Are there really that many seabirds?*

Lopsided conversations, fragmented like the metallic shells that scatter on the beach.

I tucked the papers back into the box and my knuckles grazed the supple skinned journal, dark leather tied with a waxy cord. I flipped through the pages, the sprawl of his words, thin and loose like water, his musings, his heart.

And Isy thinks—

I snapped the journal shut.

Stefan rubbed the scruff on his jaw. "Katrina told me about the funeral. Your letter. I can cover for you if you need a few days."

"I'm fine." I set a mixing bowl on top of the book, picked up a bundle of lavender, and knocked the buds off with the blunt of the knife. I should try to get him to leave again so I could put the book back. But...

"What was the errand Jens-Kjeld sent you on?"

"You could go home," Stefan continued. "Spend time with your mother."

"Answer my question."

He sighed and pulled out a stool. "I can't say, Isy. He asked me not to."

A secret errand?

I kept my eyes fixed on the bundle of lavender, the velvet

buds, bruising blue around the calyx, blurring in and out of focus like rain on a window.

I shouldn't cry. It was petty. This wasn't worth crying over. Don't cry, don't cry.

Stefan's shoulders softened and he smiled, something that didn't quite touch the corners of his eyes. "What can I do to help?" The words were so gentle, the way he spoke to a spooked horse or a scared child. "Do you need me to steep bran? Is that a yes? Hmm? I think that's a yes." He tweaked my chin.

But I was tired—so absurdly tired—and maybe Stefan *was* better. Maybe it didn't matter that he was always taking off or leaving dirty bowls in the bin or forgetting to press the bandages. That was the worst part about it because I'd tried, I'd given this job everything.

He set a kettle on the wood-burning stove and measured out a handful of grain. "You know," he said, "I bet your mother would love to see you again. And your Aunt Louise? They're probably getting ready for—"

I wheeled on him. "What are you trying to do?"

"Shit, Isy. Put the knife down."

I glanced at the blade I'd been using to chop lavender, still clenched in my fist.

It clattered to the table.

Stefan raked a hand through his hair. "I know you miss Hans, but there are better ways to cope than pulling a knife *on your friend*. Katrina was right. The letters were a mistake." He gathered up the journal.

"Don't." My voice cracked. Pathetic. "I'm fine. Really. Give it back. *Please.*"

He reached for the letters. "You need to settle down. Grieve. Maybe in a few months—"

I snatched the journal out of his hands and cradled it like a dragon. "I'm fine."

Something white and hot snapped between us.

Stefan blinked, then dove forward, hooking his arm around mine, trying to wrestle the journal back.

"You're unwell," he said, latching hold of it. "I actually think these will make it worse. I'll give them back when you've settled down."

"I *am* settled." The response stuck in my throat, and I tried to wrench the journal free. Stefan's fingers dug into the soft skin right above my hip, harder, harder. Tears pricked my eyes.

"Stefan!" I rasped. "Stef—Stop. You're hurting me."

He continued to press his hand, his other clawing at the journal and—

Someone's elbow caught the box of letters. It tumbled to the floor, scattering papers and powdered inks, scraps of ribbon cut from the spool. A wax stamp hit the table leg with a soft *thunk*.

"Shit," I said, dropping to my knees. My hip throbbed from where Stefan had been holding it.

Stefan began gathering, too.

Letters on card paper, perfumed, pressed flowers, bits of twine. I shoved them into the box.

"Isy." Stefan offered me a thick paper with cream and silver-gray stripes. "You need to read this."

"It's just…" I shook my head. "Put it back." *Pathetic.*

"It's not about you. Here." He extended a paper clutched between two fingers.

I took it. The edges were brittle and curled from the spray of the sea, the writing sprawled and elegant, blooming across the page like a garland of flowers. It smelled of peonies and pipe smoke, of lemons and dried ink.

Dated almost a week ago—

If you didn't want to be gutted, you shouldn't have let the wolf into the henhouse. Perhaps I wasn't clear. The answer is no.

P.S. If Volgaard truly intends to attack Larland, we are more defensible from our own shores.

Signed with a red rose, petals flayed to fit around a stylized W.

Stefan's lips twitched. "If you didn't want to be gutted…"

"That's Larland's royal seal."

"I think I saw another." Stefan picked through the scatter of letters.

He found two more from the pile on the floor, the same cream- and silver-striped paper, the same elegant hand.

This one dated before the other—

We have received your plea for aid. Unfortunately, there are many who are still bitter about Sanokes' independence. I empathize with your situation, truly, but given the situation in my court, I fear rushing to your rescue would be unwise.

Signed again with the flayed red rose.

The kettle let out a low whistle, a blister of steam fogging the window.

"What does this even mean?" I asked, holding out the letter.

Stefan took the kettle off the heat and poured it into the bran bowl. "Think about it, Isy. The Vold ships? Their camp? They're not whalers. They're not merchants."

"Twenty ships isn't enough to take Larland."

"Twenty ships is enough to take us."

If you didn't want to be gutted—

"But why would Hans—a *nobody* from the Sanok Isles—be corresponding with the king of Larland?"

But... That wasn't right.

I'm basically the assistant secret keeper.

"You think the Volds killed him because of these?" I asked.

"I think someone killed him," Stefan replied. "Volgaard makes the most sense. You know what they did to our ambassador, our merchants." He shuffled around the papers. "Wasn't there another letter?"

There was. The same blooming handwriting, the same strokes, long against the gray and cream.

We've heard rumors that Volgaard is in possession of a new weapon, something more terrible and deadly than anything we've seen before. Perhaps you are correct. Given Larland's proximity to the Sanok Isles, it may be wise to help our young friend. I'll make you a deal: find the weapon, deliver it to us, and we will send a thousand ships to your aid.

Dated the day before Hans died. The red rose at the bottom smudged like a blot of blood.

Heat flared through my body, and I read the letter again, slower this time. *Find the weapon. Deliver it to us. Ships to your aid.*

"Hans didn't tell you about these?" Stefan asked.

"He..." The words I wanted to say stuffed into my throat, one after the other. He didn't. But... Maybe he'd tried? Maybe I didn't listen? Maybe I'd pushed him away?

I dredged the day before he died out of my memory, turned

over the details like a shell. Hans standing in the doorway of one of the castle bedrooms while I changed the sheets. Sunlight gilded his curls, a letter in his hand. The paper… The paper…

It was cream, wasn't it? It had to be cream, and I hadn't thought too much about it but now it tumbled from my mind and it was cream, cream, it had to be cream.

You probably shouldn't be doing this alone.

The Volds. They're dangerous.

Why else would he be trying to show me something dated the day before he died? Was his death my fault?

Then I was searching through the letters, tearing them open with blind ferocity.

Gormark's debt to the Sanokes has been repaid. We will not offer support.

And—

Council voted no. Prince-Regent of Forelsket sends his regrets.

And—

Although Nysklland harbors only the best intentions toward our littlest neighbor, sending the men you request would leave us vulnerable. This is Larland's battle. If they have given you a negative answer, I suggest you ask again.

I shoved the papers at Stefan.

He flipped through them, the corners of his mouth tugging into a frown. "No surprise about Forelsket. The others? I would've thought they'd send something. They're supposed to be our allies." He traced the crinkled edge of Nysklland's correspondence. "Ask Larland again. I suppose that's what they did."

Hans was assistant postmaster. The Volds must have found out that he'd been acting as an intermediary between someone at Karlsborn Castle and the foreign nations and killed him for it. Used his murder to send a message of their own: do not cross us. After all, no one would notice a dead assistant postmaster—no one except the people he'd been working with. There was no other reason to kill him, Hans, so easy, so kind. Nothing else made sense. And the Volds?

Gray eyes. Sneer. The scatter of ruby shadows across the ceiling as a dagger twisted and twisted and twisted.

I couldn't breathe.

Stefan gathered the letters in a neat stack and placed them on the table. "I'll ask around, see if anyone's heard anything. Maybe we can figure out who Hans was—wait! Where are you going?"

My chest pounded. My pulse raced.

I needed to think, needed to breathe.

I needed space.

I HIKED UP TO THE SPOT where we'd tried to see the ships. Wind snatched my hair, tangled the grasses, caused tears to pick the corners of my eyes, and it hurt to breathe, hurt to be. And he should have told me. He should have tried harder, shouldn't have stood in the doorway and fingered that letter with so much reserve. Hans, who'd chased the coach barefoot down the lane. Hans, who wouldn't stop until he found a job at Karlsborn Castle. Hans, who always fought for what he wanted.

But no, that wasn't right.

What do you want?

A fishing boat.

Out at sea, the bob of boats cut through the water, lazed and steady, but below, the ocean, wild and breaking, sucked like a mouth, a spray of cauldron and froth and storm.

I screamed at the wind.

The wind screamed back.

I screamed again and again. It tore at my throat, bleeding and raw.

The wind snickered and howled, fluttered the letters in my fist.

Weapon. Delivery. Ships.

Weapon. Delivery. Ships.

Weapon. Delivery—

I wanted to rip them up, to tear them with my teeth, to hurl them, scattering, to the sea. I wanted to bury them deep in the damp earth, to stuff them into a bottle, to let sand and time dissolve them until they were nothing but pulp and powder.

I wanted to find a candle.

It wasn't for the letters.

Instead of doing any of that, I swiped the tears from my cheeks.

I wasn't sure why Hans got involved, but I knew he wasn't acting alone. And after last night, I had a pretty good idea who was helping him.

Chapter Eleven

THE BELLS PEALED ELEVEN as I shouldered my way into the minister of trade's apartments. My hair was snarled from the wind, cheeks sticky from tears. Sunlight streamed through tall windows, lighting the peonies on the walls.

"Ah, Ingrid," the minister said, nearly colliding with me. "You can leave the cheek cream on the credenza."

I shouldn't be here, I should go back and mix my medicines, do my work. I shouldn't, I shouldn't but—

I waved the letters. "What are these?"

Liver spots dotted his cheeks like the freckles on apples, and his gray hair had been combed in careful wisps over his head. His eyes flicked to my hands. "I don't know." He tried to step around me.

I blocked him. "Don't play coy."

He reached for the door.

I slammed it shut. "'What would you do if someone powerful asked you for something important?' Sound familiar? What about 'We have received your plea for aid. Unfortunately, there are many who are still bitter about the Sanokes independence.'"

The minister's eyes darted between me and the door. A pair of goose-gray spectacles perched on the tip of his nose, making him appear owlish. "I've never heard that before in my life."

He had to be lying. I shoved the letters at him. "This is why you didn't do an inquest. You were trying to protect yourself."

He opened the first letter and skimmed the contents. His face softened, his shoulders slacked. "Where did you find these?" He flipped to the second, then the third.

"You admit you wrote them?"

Behind the spectacles, his eyes widened. "Of course not. I've never seen these before."

Wind wisped the curtains, a flutter of gossamer and lace, and the scent of white lilies hit me, pungent and sickly, like funeral, like death.

I wrapped my arms around my middle and doubled over. No, no, no. It had to be him. No one else had been meeting with the Volds, no one else would have written the letters. And Hans—

The door creaked and Gretchen poked her head inside, her dark hair shoved under a ruffled cap. "Sorry, minister, but Lothgar—"

The minister pushed the letters back at me. "Tell them I'll be right there."

Her face paled. "But you—but he's—"

The older Vold from King Christian's study shouldered his way into the room, a wolf, a mountain, hulking with scars and furs. He wore leather armor, supple and stained with seawater. His beard hung in a single braid. He smelled of smoke.

The stormy-handsome Vold ducked in behind him, the one about my age, who'd stuffed an entire forest into his bedroom. His eyes met mine, cool and brooding.

"Have you considered our offer?" the older Vold asked.

"Lothgar," the minister replied. "I have."

The older Vold's—Lothgar—eyes flicked to me. "Who's this?"

Blood rushed to my ears, and I glanced at the letters clutched in my hands.

Had Lothgar ordered Hans's death? Had he done it himself? Had he followed Hans to the tide pools and dragged his knife, carefully, across my friend's throat?

I shoved the letters in my cardigan pocket, but Lothgar's eyes remained fixed and I couldn't shake the feeling that he knew, that he'd seen. What if he sent someone after me? I could probably outrun Lothgar, but could I outrun the handsome Vold?

With his lean body he'd be faster, but I knew Karlsborn Castle. If I could get a head start, I could get away. Hunker down. Lay low. I'd have to be careful traipsing the castle, but I could chop my hair, dye it. Katrina always said I'd make a good redhead.

I edged toward the door.

"That's Ingrid. The physician apprentice," the minister said curt. "Ignore her."

Good. Cover.

I slid my feet over the floral rug. No sudden movements. Stay slow. Stay invisible.

The minister pulled three crystal tumblers from the credenza, then poured a knuckle's worth of amber liquid into each. "We accept Volgaard's generous offer." He offered the Volds the glasses. "One condition."

Lothgar's brow quirked. "A condition?"

"When you send your scouting group, we'll supply a guide."

"A guide," Lothgar repeated.

88

"We don't need a guide," the handsome Vold said. "My men have training. They—"

"Did I ask for your opinion?" Lothgar said.

"No, but—"

"If I wanted strategy, I would have made Signey my Second."

The handsome Vold's mouth snapped shut. His eyes darkened, storms of gray. He looked past Lothgar, at the door.

A breeze caught the curtains, pulling in the faint scents of lemon, wood wax, and salt from the ocean.

"We don't need a guide," Lothgar continued. "Erik's men have training."

I edged around the settee and a rather imposing bust of the minister's late Pomeranian.

"But wouldn't it be fitting?" the minister asked. "If we're going to be allies?"

Lothgar frowned. "I don't think that's something allies do."

I reached the door, the handle cool to the touch. My heart thudded through my fingertips. Breathe. Just breathe. Once I was in the hall, I could run.

I pulled it open.

It creaked.

The minister's head snapped in my direction. His cheeks had deepened from apple red to merlot. "Stay."

He knocked back the contents of his tumbler and poured himself another. The ginger gloss of the credenza reflected his scowl. "A guide would be a symbol, a show to Larland and the rest of the world that we're united."

Lothgar rolled his beard braid between his thumb and forefinger. "I assume you have someone in mind?"

The minister downed the contents of his second glass, poured and drank a third, a fourth. "We'll send Ingrid."

The handsome Vold blanched. "I'm sorry, but saddling me with *her* makes zero sense."

With…her?

I blinked at the handsome Vold.

He blinked at me.

The weight of it came crashing down. I pressed a hand to my forehead, unsteady, ill. *Ingrid.* A thousand times the minister had said that name and I didn't correct him, but I couldn't, I couldn't. The Volds killed Hans, and now they'd seen me with the letters.

"Exactly," I said. The word came out a choke and I ducked toward the door. "I'm probably not the best person to—"

"All my men have training," the handsome Vold added. "*I* have training. And the Sanokes don't seem overly—"

"—job," I continued. "Now—"

"You'll have to excuse Erik," Lothgar cut in, just as the minister said, "Stay."

The room fell silent.

The lull of waves drifted in from the open window. A seagull screeched.

"My son forgets his purpose," Lothgar said. "It's not diplomacy. Or," his lips pursed, "*strategy.* Tell me more about this physician apprentice."

The clock ticked—*one, two, three*—and the chandelier threw rainbows around the room, the light dancing along the ears of the Pomeranian bust and the ruffled petals of the peony wallpaper, tinging everything in peach, mint, and baby blue.

The handsome Vold—Erik—fixed me with a simmering stare. A lock of wheat-colored hair fell over his brow.

I'm not going. I tried to signal with my eyes. *This guide shall not be me.*

A muscle in his jaw twitched. *I will melt you with my gaze.*

Maybe Katrina was right about the gaze-melting. Add that to my growing list of reasons to run.

I dropped my hand to the door handle. If I opened it slowly…

The corner of his mouth lifted.

I tossed him a side-eye. *You didn't win. I'm choosing to leave.*

His brows pinched. A question. He plucked a sweet pea petal and pressed it to his nose.

That's right. Act all innocent. Now if you'll excuse me—

I pressed the handle. *Please don't squeak. Please don't squeak. Please don't—*

A rip of paper tore through the room.

My attention snapped to Lothgar and the minister.

"Erik and his men leave in two days," Lothgar said, handing the paper to the minister. A book lay open on the table, its pages flayed. "Your *guide* will meet them here at dawn."

Chapter Twelve

AS SOON AS THE VOLDS were gone, I whirled on the minister, his cravat tugged loose, jacket open, his cheeks even redder from the alcohol. He rested an elbow on the credenza, the heavy oval mirror reflecting his sun-spotted neck. The tumbler, now full again, dangled from his fingertips. What was this? His fifth? His sixth?

"I can't be their guide," I hissed.

His pupils dilated, dark as beetle skin, and his breath burned. He raised his hands in mock surrender. "You told me to be clever. I was clever."

"Send someone else. A guard. A stable hand."

It wasn't possible, I knew that. Most of the guards were still recovering from the stomach flu, and the stable hands were short staffed. "Send Stefan."

At that moment, a shriek tore through the halls, and the king burst into the room. His shirt was untucked, his hair in clumps. He dropped to his knees and clambered forward, rucking up the rug. "The dark demon! He's here!"

Stefan rushed into the room after him. "Your Majesty," he said, hooking both arms around the king's waist and hauling him up and out, up and out. "There you are."

Fat tears rolled down the king's cheeks. Like a cat being carried to the bath, he grabbed the credenza leg, the settee arm, the rug.

"Carry on," Stefan huffed. "Just ignore us."

The door clicked, and once again, we were alone.

A bond of camaraderie flared between the minister and me, a soap bubble, shiny and warm. The minister cleared his throat. "Stefan. He's, erm, better. With the king."

The bubble popped.

Because the king might have just barged into the minister's rooms, but at least Stefan had taken care of it. The last time I'd managed the king, a steward had been the one to put him down.

My head went dizzy, drunk, like I was drowning. I pressed a hand to the windowpane, cool and smooth and real. "He knows."

"Who?"

"Lothgar. Probably Erik, too. They saw me with the letters and—"

"I'll send you with a separate letter. One of protection." The minister paused, swigged from his drink, then nodded as if his word should be enough to protect me from the people who'd killed Hans.

"They'll kill me," I said. "Dump my body somewhere. I'll never be seen again."

"They don't want war with *us*."

"They brutalized a book!"

A knock rasped at the door, and Stefan popped his head inside, his hair ruffled, cravat askew. "Ugh. Sorry. I thought I had him, but he whacked me with a pillow and got away. You okay, Isy?"

"I'm fine." Because I *was* fine. The minister couldn't force me into this.

"Really?" Stefan asked. "You look like you're going to be sick."

The minister hiccuped and fumbled with the tumbler again, his knuckles now flushed pink. "The Hyllestad Treaty. It keeps us from allying with Volgaard. See?" He tapped his forehead. "Clever."

"I don't follow," Stefan said.

"I told him last night to be clever," I explained. "Now he's trying to send me to be a guide for the Volds." My stomach curled just saying it.

The minister squinted at the ceiling. "The Volds want to use the Sanokes as a military outpost to launch an attack on Larland, the same way Gormark did during the Grain Wars."

"Oh," Stefan said. "That makes sense."

The Grain Wars started when Larland poisoned Gormark's grain supply to drive up the price of their own. The creative price maneuvering worked...until bags of dried silver spire were discovered in an abandoned barn. The poisoners were caught two days later.

When Gormark came for Larland, they came for vengeance, they came for blood. They came with an offer the Sanokes couldn't refuse—our independence for our help.

So, we smuggled Gormarkian soldiers onto our islands, hiding them on beaches and bluffs, stashing them in cellars, tucking them in taverns that teetered on the edge of salt-spewed cliffs, and when the winter-dark wind howled angry off the fjords, Gormark launched the full weight of their army at Larland.

And they launched it from the Sanokes.

Our independence became a footnote in the Hyllestad Treaty, a promise fulfilled with a whisper and two strokes of a pen, one of many concessions a weakened Larland had no choice but to accept.

Twenty years later, and Larland's strength had warmed like the sun, but the terms of the treaty still stood—the Sanok Isles were an independent nation, and no person party to it could interfere with our sovereignty.

Most of the larger nations had signed on, using the treaty as an opportunity to forge trade and foster alliances. Larland was a powerhouse, and everyone wanted a piece.

As a result, the Sanokes' independence was protected from most of the larger nations.

Most.

What would you do if someone powerful wanted something important?

He hadn't been talking about Volgaard's weapon, he'd been talking about an alliance.

An alliance that would pit us firmly against Larland.

"As a condition of our independence, we had to promise we would never assist another foreign nation in raising arms against Larland," the minister of trade explained. "If we do, Larland has the legal right to repatriate us. But Lothgar said he was ready to take the islands by force if we declined, and he brought the manpower to do it. So, we face an impossible choice: ally with Volgaard and violate the treaty, or risk their hostile takeover." His brow furrowed, and he tilted his glass to the glittering chandelier. "Is that dust?"

If you didn't want to be slaughtered…

I pressed my thumb against the sweet pea petal Erik had

picked. "So we're pretending to ally with Volgaard to keep them from attacking while we search for the weapon Larland wants?"

The minister nodded. "Exactly. Lothgar wants to send his son, Erik, to scout the island. Erik is also his second-in-command. High up. Lots of power. Sending a guide is a way to get close to him."

"Because you think Erik's bringing this kingdom-shattering weapon on a scouting trip?" I didn't bother to hide my skepticism.

The minister waved his hand. "I think sending a guide to…befriend their second highest officer is the fastest way to get that information. And who knows? Maybe he *will* bring the weapon on the scouting trip. It could be something they have to plant."

Fine. That made sense. "Don't we have a royal ambassador?"

"Lars is seventy-five years old. He'd never make the journey."

Fair. "Actual spies? We have those?"

The minister winced. "Never got around to it."

Bummer. Back to the ambassador. "Didn't Lars have an underling? That weird boy. What happened to him?"

"He quit."

"Let's get him back!"

"Two years ago. Plus, I'd rather send you. You're a woman."

"What does that have to do with anything?"

The furrow in the minister's brow deepened, and he squinted at the chandelier. "I'll have to call a maid to clean that."

I gritted my teeth. "Why does it matter that I'm a woman?"

"The general has a *son*. You can use your womanly wiles to…" he waved his hand, "I don't know. Woo him. Get information. He seemed to like you. Couldn't take his eyes off you."

Because he was trying to terrify me.

Still, sending a guide wasn't a terrible idea. I almost had to applaud the minister for his creative thinking.

Almost.

The truth was, even if I had the minister's protection, they might still try to kill me. It would be better to stay here, to work, to hide.

"We need two pieces of information," the minister continued. "What the weapon is, and where they're hiding it. Once you find those things, you can come back. I'll send updates to Esbern and St. Kilda. See if you can steer them through one of those two towns." He plucked Lothgar's map off the credenza and extended the paper to me.

A cloud passed before the sun, plunging the room into shadow. The first drops of rain flecked the window.

The paper quivered between the minister's fingers, a fire, a flame.

I wiped my hands on my skirts. "Jens-Kjeld comes back in two weeks."

"I'll cover for you," Stefan said. "We'll tell him you went to get supplies at the Merchant's Market."

My hands burned.

I'd be going undercover with the people who'd killed Hans, with people who might want to kill me.

The rain picked up, plinking the roof, washing the windows. The candles in the chandelier flickered.

I pursed my lips and said the only thing I could, "No."

Chapter Thirteen

MY BRAID SWUNG behind me. My heels clicked on the tile floor.

Stefan jogged to catch up. "Why'd you say no?"

"Because I like living."

Ancient suits of polished armor stood solemn beside faded maritime maps framed in driftwood. Our smudgy shapes glinted through the glass, Stefan's green and cherry-red and mine, blue and brown.

"If you wooed him, he'd protect you. Don't you want his strong hands all over your—"

"His hands are *not* going anywhere on me."

"You say that now, but I bet they'd feel really nice."

For some reason, I had the feeling he was right about that. It was an odd thought, especially considering Erik had just tried to scare me with those angry, angry eyes. Gray, the color of smoke or stone or wild storms.

The thought of them wavered, shifted. Expressive. Brown. I turned, half expecting to find Hans.

Instead, I found Stefan.

Something pricked at the back of my throat. I bit my lip and glanced at the ceiling. Stupid, stupid. Hans wouldn't be in this part of the castle, anyway. He would have been outside in the dovecote, and I couldn't do this. Not here. I couldn't cry in front of Stefan.

I pushed those brown eyes aside and dredged up images of scary Erik.

It worked.

More than likely, he would use those hands to kill me the same way they killed Hans. I needed to get back to the apothecary and hunker down until this blew over. I'd heard of people dying their hair with beetroot juice. I was stuck with the bangs until they grew out, but if I chopped the rest of it above my shoulders, I think I could pass for someone else.

We reached a set of reception rooms that branched off the main hall. Their doors were thrown open, showing slivers of golden sunlight and massive hearths, cold, save for the fjord lilies and mountain saxifrage bundled into vases. One pair of doors, then another, then a sofa set in the hall and—

Katrina. She stood beside a carved oak chest, pulling slipcovers off cushions and throwing them into a wicker hamper.

Her eyes flicked up. Strands fell loose from her bun, unwashed, and her knuckles blistered red. Lye soap. It happened if she spent too many days in the washroom. She usually came to see me before it got bad. I'd smother her hands in beeswax salve, wrap them in gauze, and she'd spend the rest of the afternoon pretending to be helpless.

She always came to see me.

Always.

Her reddened hands twitched.

That thing pricked my throat. I shoved it down.

"I'll be leaving," Stefan said. He tweaked my nose. "Just…think about it."

And he was gone.

I grabbed one of the sofa cushions and shimmied the pillow out. "Want to come see me for those? I'll make the salve. Chamomile or lavender?"

"Go away."

"About the funeral…"

She rolled her eyes and moved the basket to the next sofa. "Don't give me that."

"Give you what?"

"Some bullshit excuse."

"I know you're still angry, but—"

"I'm not angry."

"Yes, you are. It's fine, it's—"

She yanked the cushion from the settee and unfastened the buttons with deft fingers. "I'm not the one who ignored him. *For years*. He was ready to give you *everything*—"

My chest tightened. "Stop."

"And all you had to do—*literally, all you had to do*—was accept it."

"I don't want to fight."

"Then what do you want?" She shoved me.

My body tensed. I stumbled back.

"You ignored him. You broke him. You. Pushed. Him. Away." She shoved me again and again and again.

I fell onto the naked settee. Goose down prickled through the linen, stung my palms, and I should be surprised that Katrina shoved me, I should, but her anger could be a blizzard, and she was wrong—I couldn't accept Hans's love because it was a mistake. *I* was a mistake. But everywhere I looked, I saw him—the kitchens, the hallways—and Katrina's hands, her red, red hands. Why didn't she come to me, why didn't—

It occurred to me.

She was jealous.

My heart raced. I wanted to laugh. "You liked him. You liked Hans, and that's why you're doing this. That's why you're taking it out on me. Well, you know what? I don't care. Go ahead. Hit me." I tipped my chin toward her and barred my teeth. "Hit. Me."

Katrina stepped back, shaking her head. She was only eighteen, but in that moment, she could have been eighty. Her mouth was drawn, shadows rimmed her eyes, and they were dark. Not the dark of anger, but the hollow dark of resignation.

"No, Isy. It just makes me sad. He deserved more than that." Her shoulders slumped. "He deserved more than you."

THAT NIGHT, GIRLS FLICKERED in and out of the dorm room, going dancing or drinking, their skirts whirls of cream and fleecy blues.

I pulled the blanket around my shoulders and waited for someone to come, to laugh and talk to me, to make everything okay, but the girls were chatting and singing, and I was a bird weathering the waves.

The shock of the letters had worn off. So had the shock of Katrina shoving me, the bright and bitter rage replaced with... something else.

He deserved more than that.

More than you.
You could have been there.
Been more.
Been better.
If you'd listened, maybe he wouldn't have died.
You pushed him away.
You shut him out.
You're a disaster.
Who would ever want you?
Not your father.
Not your mother.
Hans would have left you, too.
You failed him.
You fail everyone.
You—

"What if you made him matter?"

The words shook me from my thoughts, a tumble of silk and satin, and it was Sofie from laundry and her words weren't directed at me. They were for Elin, who sat on the edge of another bed, dabbing her eyes with a handkerchief.

I pushed myself a little higher.

"I mean," Sofie continued, "obviously, it would make Pehr jealous but, yeah. What if you *made* him matter?"

"I don't know…" Elin sniffled. "Seems petty."

But—

Make him matter.

A strike of light. A flare in the dark.

I couldn't give Hans my heart, but maybe I could give his death meaning. And someday, when this story was told, the chroniclers would tell of him—how his death was the seed, the spark, the kindling that lit the fire and saved the Sanokes. Hans would be the hero who fought against the Volds, who sacrificed his life to send those messages, the reason for our victory. Ballads would be sung, poems written, monuments erected in his name. Above the ocean, cannons would crack, and swans would fly, and he would go down in history.

I glanced up, caught my reflection in the window. My hair hung limp around my face, and circles rimmed my eyes. The thing that whispered *you could have been better* clenched tight.

Make his death matter.

Maybe that would be enough.

RAIN POUNDED HEAVY AGAINST THE ROOF as I pushed the door to the minister's sitting room open.

A fire roared in the hearth, flames licking up the walls. It stretched the shadows of the minister and a dark-haired girl, delicate hands and eyes the warming blue of lilacs after rain.

"… give him what he wants," the minister said. "Come on strong, but not too strong. Men like—"

They glanced up.

"Ingrid," the minister said. "What are you doing?"

I held up Larland's letter. "The Volds. Send me."

Thunder boomed and firelight caught the metallic threads, making them burn.

Chapter Fourteen

THE NEXT DAYS FELL AWAY like rain, first a pattering, then a pour. The sores on the queen's feet putrefied, creating a black and rancid smell that made her maids gag and run to the door. The harbormaster developed a fever so hot he soaked through three sets of sheets. Then, someone jostled the assistant harbormaster off a loading plank, causing him to break his leg. Without the harbormaster and the assistant harbormaster, a grain ship from Gormark was torched, sending everything up in a yellow-orange blaze.

Eleven workmen came in with burn injuries, and Stefan and I had been woken in the middle of the night to treat them.

"Try to get the Volds to like you," Stefan said, dabbing salt water over a workman's blistered arm. "People tell things to people they like, and you can be a bit, erm, prickly."

"I'm not prickly."

"And practice lying. You're a terrible liar."

I brandished my rag like a sword. "I'm a great liar."

Stefan took a step back. "Whoa, Isy. Not when you say it like that."

The workman grunted in affirmation.

The bells chimed six.

"That's my signal. Handle the rest for me?"

"Of course, but, Isy…" Stefan paused and ran a thumb over his jaw. "I wasn't going to say this, but I've been asking around. You should know the general—Lothgar? His daughter was seen leaving the tide pools the night Hans died."

"She…*what?*"

He held up his hands. "I'm not saying she killed him but… Be careful. Especially around her."

He scooped up my bag and offered it to me.

Be careful.

I'd try.

MIST DRENCHED THE IRON CLIFFS, coated my lips and lashes, glossed the sand so it reflected ribbons of rain-streaked clouds and chicken pens, tents, and the watery silhouettes of Vold soldiers. They lounged on stools and overturned crates, playing cards or eating mouthfuls of runny gruel.

"Ey there," someone called.

Another clicked his tongue. "What brings you down from the castle?"

"Why don't you come sit with us?" A third patted his thigh, a smile creeping over his wine-dark lips. "We could have some fun, you and me."

I pulled my cardigan tighter, walked faster.

Horses snorted, tossed their manes and pawed the earth. A rib-thin dog yanked at its tether and snapped its jaws. The air stank of hot iron and brine.

"Do you have a friend?" called a rat-faced man. He swigged from a green bottle, licked his teeth. "A sister?"

I blinked.

There was another *me* sitting on his lap. A low-cut nightgown hung off one shoulder and her dark brown hair rumpled as if she'd just climbed out of bed. I blinked again. The other me grinned, shimmied her shoulders, then disappeared in a puff of smoke.

His companion nudged him in the ribs. "Why settle for that when you can have—"

The other me returned, prettier this time, better, her skin tone evened, the blemishes smoothed. Instead of being mussed, her hair fell down her back in a shine. The nightgown clung to her belly, her breasts tighter, more sensual, almost sheer, no hide of scars crisscrossing her stomach. The other me bit her bottom lip.

My face grew hot. I turned away, pulled my jacket tighter, and hurried down the beach, away from the men, away from the other me—the better me. Find Erik. That's all I needed to do. Find Erik and don't die. I glanced at Lothgar's rain-speckled map.

"You're not Vold."

The voice caught me by surprise, yanked me back.

The speaker, a woman, stood over a soup pot smoking over an open fire. She paused, the ladle midair and fixed her almond eyes on me. A few strands of blonde hair poked out from under a headscarf. "You're not dadig, either."

I tilted my head. "No," I said, unsure her meaning. "I'm not."

Water beaded along the waxy canvas of her tent, pilled along steel stakes, drummed the sand. She dipped her ladle again and edged the lip of her bowl closer. "It's skause," she said, "with spinach and sour milk. I'll make you some. Show Askel and Holger they don't bother you. Sit."

But I didn't sit. Instead, I stood, the rain misting my hair, patting my cheeks, rising up from the sand in a grayish cloud.

"Do you know Erik?" I asked. I had no family name, no way to identify him apart from, "He's, um, tall?"

She scooped the skause into a wooden bowl. "Lothgar's son?" Her lips drew into a slash. "I know him."

"Is he here?"

"He is."

My hand tightened around the map. "Where?"

A stick in her fire popped and white smoke puffed toward the sky.

"There's a rocky outcropping not far from the ships."

I fisted my skirts and walked faster. The eyes of the rat-faced man and his companion followed me, their snickers carrying over the low lap of waves, and I knew, *knew*, if I turned, I'd see the other me—the better me—sitting on their laps.

My jaw tightened.

"You have an interesting future," the woman called.

I stopped, my back to her. Waves licked the shore like tongues, and a pair of gulls streaked.

I didn't want to turn, didn't want to see the better me, the me without the thread-thin scar under her chin, the burns along her stomach. The me with kinder eyes, softer hands, who looked so at home, so in love with herself.

But—

You have an interesting future.

My belly ached.

"If you let me," the woman continued, "I can read it for you."

I turned.

The better me sat on the companion's lap, her bare legs tossed carelessly, her teeth barred and white. Still there, still perfect.

The woman glanced over her shoulder. "Whatever they're showing you doesn't matter. Come."

I followed her into a tent filled with firewood and fox furs, wild celery buds picked from the bluffs and left in heaps on the floor. A loom sat in the corner, wefted in bands of brown and gray.

"Sit," she said, gesturing to the collection of sheepskin rugs.

I did, tugged my cardigan closed and sank to the ground. Mud matted the sheepskin, flaked off under the press of my thumb.

What would it be like to be that better me? To be stronger, smarter, more beautiful? Still, I had an interesting future, and maybe, *maybe* this woman would tell me I'd do something great, *be* something great.

The woman struck a stone, lit a lamp hanging from the rafter post, and placed a black-brown leaf on her tongue.

She took my hand, pressing her thumb into the soft and fleshy skin of my palm. Her nail pricked a half moon indent.

Rain pattered on the tent, shadows slipping down the waxy sides. From outside, thin laughs and bleats and clucks, but all that seemed blurred, seemed bowed compared to here, compared to her.

Tendrils of tar black smoke snaked from the lamp.

"I see…" she said, her voice husky. Her eyes had gone glossy and white, the irises vanished, pupils blown wide.

My heart quickened.

"I see…" she started again. "A threshold… A mighty

threshold. It will be…difficult to pass. And you…" She swallow-ed. Her lips, bruised and red, parted, revealing that black-brown leaf and sharp incisors.

You will be the royal physician?

"You will hold the door."

My heart plummeted. "That's not an exciting future."

She spit the leaf back into the jar and took a sip of wine from a flask. "I never said it was exciting, just interesting."

Even still. "Can you look again?" I extended my palm. "Look for something else?"

Something better.

Her tongue flicked over her bottom lip, catching one of the ruby drops. "I can only see snips and snaps, key moments that define a person."

And that was supposed to be my key moment? Holding the door?

My face must have fallen, because she placed two fingers on the back of my hand. "You are, of course, free to change it. You could choose not to hold the door."

"What about Hans? Do I make him matter?"

She kept a steady gaze. "In a way."

Something in my stomach fluttered. "And can you tell if I become the royal physician?"

"I didn't see." The color in her eyes returned, her irises now blue as a summer sky. A quizzical expression crossed her face, as if she was trying to puzzle through something herself. "But I don't think you're meant to be the royal physician."

I pulled back the flap on the tent, headed out into the rain. The better me still sat on the man's lap. She blew a kiss as I passed.

In a way.

I don't think you're meant—

One goal, but not the other.

I thumbed the buckle on my bag and followed the bluffs.

Becoming the royal physician was what I wanted. Before Hans died, it had been the *only* thing I'd wanted. And it wasn't about my father—it wasn't. I'd spent years training, studying, devouring every medical text I could get my hands on.

Maybe it didn't have to happen the way she said. Maybe she saw *a* future, not *the* future. Maybe there was still space to claw my way into both things, maybe—

I don't think you're meant—

I'd do it, anyway. Climb faster, claw harder. *Work* harder.

The camp thinned here, fewer people, fewer tents. They spotted the beach like straggle grass. Rain drummed the sand. Ahead, the silhouettes of two dozen men moved about the shore, lifting bags and leading horses. The sky unfurled, long and gray.

"Watch it," gruffed a man leading a stallion. Long hair framed his face, dark eyes and cheeks tattooed with knots.

"I'm looking for Erik," I said.

"He's not here." But the man's eyes gave him away, flicking down a stretch of sand.

The waves had quieted, froth lapping the shores, and there was Erik, hefting a saddlebag off the ground and placing it on a horse's back, stormy as ever.

"You're late," he said as I approached. Rain had soaked through his white shirt, open at the throat, and his wheat-blond hair pressed wet against his forehead. His fingers tied deft knots in the pack. "We said before sunrise."

"I'm sorry I—"

"Where's your horse? Your tent?"

My hand went to the strap of my bag. A horse? A tent? I hadn't brought any of that. Just clothes, medicines, Hans's box of letters, and søven. The clear vial was wrapped securely in a wool stocking and a bit of baker's twine. Just in case I needed to knock someone out.

Erik moved to the set of buckles by the horse's belly. "Lucky for you, we don't need a guide."

A pair of seabirds arced down the basalt cliffs and muted sounds trickled up from the main camp, the bleat of animals, the ring of voices. Fires puffed against the sand.

"You can go home." He clicked his tongue, a hollow sound out of the side of his cheek, and started toward the waves. The horse followed, no reins, no halter, its gray coat blending with the dappled beach.

"If you stop by the supply tent on your way back, you can pick up payment for your troubles," he called. "I think we have gyllis. Otherwise, we'll give you gold. Sorry you came all the way down."

I hurried after him. "You haven't even asked my name."

"It's Ingrid."

"Isabel."

"Well, *Isabel*. The supply tent has a green flag out front. Tell them I sent you." Erik's horse veered off course. He clicked his tongue, calling it back.

Maybe I should have asked the minister if I could take a horse, but the thought honestly hadn't occurred to me. Most of my travel had been done by walking—climbing sweeping planes and scrambling up rugged trails. I'd taken the coach just once on the journey to Karlsborn Castle from Hjern. I'd never ridden a horse.

I squared my shoulders, trying to look resolute. I probably just looked damp. "I'm not leaving."

"Have you ever camped?" Erik asked. "Started a fire? Foraged for food?"

"I've camped." A lie.

Erik eyed me, wary. "You didn't bring food, you didn't bring shelter. You're unprepared and under supplied. Judging by your choice of clothing, I seriously doubt you have any outdoor experience."

I glanced at my outfit: my sturdiest boots, a sage cardigan, and the lambswool skirt I wore out on the bluffs. "What's wrong with my clothes?"

"You'll slow us down."

Change of tactics. "Maybe I'm not the most experienced guide, but that doesn't matter. I'm a…a symbol."

"Oh, just what we need." Erik stopped next to a yellow pack pony and fiddled with the buckles on its harness. "A *symbol*."

"Do you know what it's like to travel around the Sanokes? You don't. But I'll tell you. It's hilly. It's steep. Most of the good roads are flooded two-thirds of the year, and they're packed with mud the other. Taking this many men is far, *far* more likely to slow you down."

The pack pony's bags hit the sand with a *thud*. "There's your horse," he said. "Or did you plan on walking?"

"I thought you didn't want to take me."

He gritted his teeth. "I don't."

In that moment, it all snapped into place. Erik could buy me off, could make fun of my clothes, try to convince me to leave, but he didn't have the power to actually get rid of me—Lothgar must have ordered that.

I stroked the pony's nose. "I suppose you have a tent for me, too?"

A lopsided bag landed at my feet.

"Blankets? I'd hate to be cold."

He gave me a look so smoldering, I thought he might actually kill me.

Stefan's words picked that exact moment to make their grand re-entrance.

I bet his hands would feel nice.

I tackled the thought and shoved it deep, *deep* into the recesses of my brain. I had to maintain a neutral expression. I could not show that he was scary. I could not show that I was thinking about his hands.

His forceful, urgent hands slipping down my body. His knuckles skimming my waist as he held me there, and maybe murdered me.

I wanted to throw up.

Erik's gaze snapped to a woman riding up the beach, sand spraying beneath her horse's hooves, tail streaming behind it like a pendant flag.

He scrubbed a hand over his face. "Perfect." Then louder, "Signey. Right on time."

The woman—Signey—pulled up on the reins, her face more oval than Erik's, but the resemblance was there—their lips, their cheeks, their stormy-gray eyes, the way their hair—his, spun gold and hers, near silver—curled damp around their ears. They wore the same pinched expression.

Signey.

His sister.

The general's daughter.

I'm not saying she killed him, but...

All thoughts of Erik's scary hands vanished and I was standing at the tidepools, red water lapping at my ankles, and I was flicking a blank letter onto the funeral pyre, and I was holding Hans's body to my chest, screaming.

Pump, pump. Wait.

Pump, pump. Wait.

I was falling, flying. I couldn't breathe.

She didn't look at me, didn't so much as turn her head. Instead, she kept her attention on Erik, who was lifting my pony's packs out of the sand.

"You're trying to leave without me," she snapped.

"Believe me," Erik replied, "I wouldn't *dream* of leaving without you."

Rain soaked the furs on her shoulders, ran rivulets down her cheeks. Her horse, massive and black, panted billows. She opened her mouth, then closed it. Her eyes went murderous. "You know why he sent me."

Erik shot her a heated glare.

"You aren't getting another honor bead," she continued.

"I don't need another honor bead." He crouched and began switching the items from my pony's pack with another, rolling a blanket tighter, abandoning a crate of foodstuff. His eyes flicked to Signey. The corner of his lip pulled into a smirk. "I already have two."

Her hands balled to fists.

"Hey, Sig," called a lanky man. He wore a knitted cap shoved over shoulder-length hair, and his jacket collar was popped against the drizzle. "Come to see us off?"

Signey's head snapped in the man's direction. A muscle in

her jaw twitched. She whirled back to Erik. "Don't tell me you're taking *him*."

Erik shrugged, then shoved the blanket to the bottom of the pack. "He's one of my men."

Her finger went straight to her temple. "He swapped my reading candle with a firework and singed off my left eyebrow."

"He's the best swordsman in Volgaard."

"His skause made us all sick."

"I trust him."

"He put hair on a seagull!"

The lanky man crossed the beach. "Something the matter, Sig?"

She seethed. "Signey to you."

At that moment, a seagull flitted down from the cliffs and landed on the sand.

Signey looked at the seagull.

The seagull looked at Signey. Its wingtips quivered in an invisible breeze.

Signey glared at Erik. "Oh yeah, keep that up. That's the only thing you're good at." She stormed away.

Erik's shoulders shook with silent laughter, and the seagull fell away, a slip of smoke on a summer breeze.

"It was the eyes," the lanky man said. "Seagulls don't have them that blue."

Erik shoved a sheet of canvas into the bag. "What are they really? Black?"

"Dunno. To be honest, seagulls kind of creep me out." The lanky man flashed a full smile. "You must be the guide. I'm Kaspar. I would say a pleasure to meet you but, uh—" A glance at Erik. "Well, what do you want me to say?"

Erik pursed his lips. "She didn't bring a horse. Or a tent. Or anything useful." He yanked the leather cording, buckled the flap. Strands of hair clung to his cheeks, his forehead, the water glittering like glass. His white shirt stuck to his chest. He extended the pack to me and his gaze found mine, angry, a little defiant. "Only because you'll slow us down," he murmured.

I snatched the pack. Why did he have to be attractive?

Another man peeled away from the larger group, this one with his hair shaved on the sides, the top curly and long. The haircut stressed his full lips and delicate brows. "What did you do to Signey?"

Erik and Kaspar both shrugged and suddenly, the fulmars roosting on the side of the cliff became the most interesting thing.

"Okay, don't tell me," the delicate man said. "But you should know she just punched Bengt and kicked my bag."

"She *what*?" Kaspar asked.

"I'll handle it," Erik said, storming off. "Signey shouldn't be coming with us, either."

"I'm Björn," the delicate man said. "Call me Bo. And that pony is probably not the best choice."

"She didn't bring a horse," Kaspar explained. "Erik's putting her on that pony."

"Oh." Bo gave a nervous laugh and ran a hand through his hair. "Well, good luck. I hear Buttercup's a bitch."

Buttercup whinnied and dipped her chin.

I reached up to stroke her hairy nose. "A bitch? You're not a bitch."

Chapter Fifteen

BUTTERCUP WAS, INDEED, A BITCH.

She liked to wander, didn't want to listen, would stop and chew mouthfuls of knapweed and carrot blooms, and ignore me when I tried to pull her away.

Some of the men—the thirty or so Erik had brought—joked that they should tether me to their saddles or have me ride double, and once, as Buttercup lipped a cluster of lady's bedstraw, I caught Erik watching me from the corner of his eye.

My hands balled and he smirked.

The gall.

Still, it was easier to be angry, easier to find and fan that spark because if I looked at the Volds for too long, I wanted to wrap my arms around myself and cry.

After all, no one—*no one*—would care if they killed me. Not my lying, cheating father, not my shell of a mother, not Katrina, who hadn't talked to me since Hans's funeral.

And Hans.

People say grief is numbness, but it isn't. It feels like your skin is being opened up and you're being flayed alive. People also say grief is cold, but then why was I burning? Why was every single cell of my body on fire?

If I was going to woo information out of Erik, I couldn't be sad or scared—no one falls for the sad, scared girl. I needed to be like one of the maids, confident and charming, a bright smile with spirit and verve.

I could do this.

I. Could. Do. This.

I turned to him. My heart pounded. "So," I said, infusing my voice with a false sense of cheery, "tell me about Volgaard."

Erik squinted at the ridge line. The corners of his eyes crinkled. "It's cold." His horse, the dappled gray, continued trotting. Its tail flicked behind him, swishing flies and long grasses.

Buttercup veered left to chew on a cluster of common bent, and Signey passed, her shoulders straight as a hunter's, fur vest blowing around her shoulders, pale eyes fixed forward.

A shiver crept down my spine.

I looped my hands around Buttercup's reins and yanked.

Buttercup nickered and moved to a clump of dandelions.

I yanked again.

Another knicker. She tossed her head and went straight back to the dandelions, finishing the yellow buds with two smacks of her lips.

I pressed a palm to my head. I needed to catch up to Erik so I could flirt. Apparently, the reins were for decoration because Buttercup ignored them. But she did like food.

I dug in the bag for a chunk of cheese, shucked off the wax cloth wrapping, and leaned close to her hairy ear. "Buttercup. Psst. Hey. I have a treat for you."

Her ears pricked.

Careful not to lose my balance, I stretched forward and offered the round of cheese…

"Don't feed her that."

I jumped.

Erik and his horse stood a few feet away. He clicked his tongue, a hollow sound out of the side of his cheek and—

Oop. Okay. We were moving. I grabbed the reins. "So. Continuing where we left off, was your father always the general?" That sounded weirdly interrogation-esque.

"Always."

Buttercup veered off course. Erik clicked his tongue again, calling her back.

Flirt. I needed to flirt. Not interrogate him. But the last time I'd flirted with someone, it ended with my hands on his abs and that comment about cheese. No hands on abs. Hands to myself. Better yet, hand on the reins. I looped them tighter and batted my lashes. "You must have grown up with a weapon in your hand."

He shot me a suspicious glance. "I actually didn't."

"So your father taught you hand-to-hand combat?"

"Not that, either."

But *could* I touch him if he was on a horse? I'd probably fall off my horse. Still, a little pat on the arm might go a long way. Did people pat each other on the arm when they were flirting? Was that a thing? Or was that something grandmas did?

The image of Queen Margarethe flashed in my mind—stern faced, pink nightgown buttoned all the way to her chin.

Nope. Do something else. I flashed Gretchen's man-melting smile. "So, children in Volgaard don't learn to fight until they're older?"

"Plenty learn."

"But you…didn't?" Don't interrogate him. Smile. Okay. And then what? Hair flip?

I hair flipped. "You're the general's son. His second."

The suspicion deepened. "I didn't learn, okay?"

I batted my lashes again. My heart pounded. "Why not?"

"Because."

"Because you didn't want to learn or…?"

With one quick motion, Erik spurred the horse, racing down the hillside, sending a colony of graylag geese scattering.

Signey cracked her reins and followed, her white-blonde braid streaming like a whip, and maybe I should have been disappointed that my initial attempts at flirting had failed. Instead, I felt…

Like a blade had just been lifted from my throat.

I placed my palms against Buttercup's hairy neck. Stiff ocean winds flattened fields and blew sharp over the ridgeline, too gusty, too cold for spring. Sweeping planes unraveled like yarn on a sweater, sheer and ancient.

Behind me there was a cough. "Are you okay?"

I turned and found Bo, dark-haired and delicate. Wind ruffled his hair away from his forehead, gusted against his coat. His eyes had reddened, giving his face a watery look. He brought his horse in line with mine.

"Why wouldn't I be?"

"That was just an odd exchange. With Erik. Did you get pollen in your eye?"

"In my…eye?"

"The rapid blinking. The hair flipping?"

"Oh. Um. Yes. I did. But now it's gone."

The men continued to ride through the meadow. The grasses continued to sway. Bo's horse walked alongside mine. Maybe I didn't need to get the information from Erik. Maybe I could get it from someone else.

I turned to Bo. "Can you tell me about Volgaard?"

"About home?" His brow furrowed. "Sure. It's less green than this, but there are trees. Entire forests, even. It rains, but not nearly as often. Kaspar could show you. He uses reykr."

"Reykr?"

"The illusions. He could show you what Volgaard looks like with his illusions."

Oh. That's what they called them. But I didn't care what Volgaard looked like; I cared about the weapon. I needed to take the conversation in that direction. "Did you grow up in the general's house, too?"

Bo blinked. "Too? As in—"

"Like Signey. Erik."

"Oh. Um, Erik didn't grow up in Lothgar's house."

I squinted down the ravine where he'd trotted, a gray blot against the sweeping hills. Interesting. I'd heard of high-ranking children being placed with other families as tributaries, a way to forge friendships with foreign countries. Gormark was fond of the concept, sending us two flighty princesses each summer. Still, the children chosen for such a task were never the important ones, never the heirs, which didn't make sense because—

"Erik is the second-in-command," I said.

Bo pulled his scarf tighter around his neck and swiped the corners of his eyes. "He's better at reykr than Signey. Better at reykr than everyone. Amazing, considering he's only twenty."

Twenty.

Two years older than me.

A few sheep grazed, their hair so long and curly their bells disappeared into their rust-tipped coats. A wagtail fluttered over a stone wall.

"Right. So he's better than you."

"Well, no. I don't use reykr. I'm from House Kaldr-Flodi. We use skygge."

"Skygge?"

"Like reykr, it's a form of projection. Only instead of projecting your mind, you're projecting yourself."

He must have read my confused expression because he held up his gloved hand, the supple leather tailored to the fit of his fingers. "Think of it like this. My hand is my soul. The glove is my body. The glove fits my hand, my hand fits the glove. Most people can't take off their gloves. But when I use skygge, I can slip out of it like—" He pinched the tip of his finger and tugged his hand free. "Make sense?"

Is this how they'd found out about the letters from Larland? Why they'd killed Hans? Did that mean Stefan and the minister could have someone watching them? Did I need to warn them?

"You can just leave your body?" I asked. "Any time you want?"

"Sort of. Bodies don't like to be left empty. They die pretty quickly. It takes someone who can send your body some of their spirit, just enough to keep it alive while you're gone. Someone who can also use skygge. An anchor."

"And when you're a ghost, you walk around like normal?"

Bo shifted in his saddle. His eyes cut to Erik. "I could show you, but I'd need Erik's help. He's my anchor."

Great. Of course, the second-in-command, the best person

at illusion magic, could also leave his body and spy. I glanced at the line of men—strong hands, thick shoulders, scars. "Can the others use skygge?"

"It's a common gift in Volgaard. But here? Just Erik and me." He rubbed his nose, then added, "Being able to use more than one type of magic is rare. It's passed through bloodlines, usually from the father, though sometimes the mother. The others only use reykr. So," he gestured at the men, "they're all from House Rythja. They use reykr. I'm from House Kaldr-Flodi. I use skygge. Erik can use both."

"Are there other types of magic? Besides reykr and skygge?"

"A few."

Buttercup stopped to lip a cluster of white-headed yarrow.

"What about…" I yanked on her reins. Once. Twice. "Seeing the future?"

Bo glanced over his shoulder. "Oh? You met a sooth?"

I thought back to the woman, the blackish leaf on the tip of her tongue, the way she'd said, *I don't think you're meant to become the royal physician.*

One goal, but not the other.

I slid off Buttercup's saddle and grabbed the reins. "I don't know. Maybe."

We reached the bottom of the valley, where the hay-like grass had flattened. A stream cut through the middle like a knife. Water burbled, clear and cold, and a few bugs scudded the surface, leaving a trail of ripples.

Erik settled himself on top of a rock and divided the food from the packs, buckwheat cakes and thick sheep's cheese that smelled like butter and burnt nuts. "We'll water the horses and eat," he said. "Then continue moving."

The men let their horses go to stream, then settled themselves on rocks, arms thrown over legs, stretched toward the sun.

I sat next to Kaspar, who tore straight into his cheese hunk with the ferocity of a fox. He snapped it between his teeth, the grayish crumbs falling into the folds of his shirt. He finished the hunk and reached for another, peeling at the wax cloth, and—

Hans.

The thought snuck up, two hands and a ghost, and I shouldn't think about him now, but there he was—brown hair, smile—and something in the way Kaspar peeled at the wax cloth reminded me of him, and it was *stupid, stupid, stupid*, but that's how Hans peeled the wax cloth, and now all the things I'd been holding threatened to spill.

I bit my lip and glanced at the sky. Pale blue. Watercolor blue. The thinnest threading of clouds. I couldn't cry in front of them. I needed to focus on the task at hand.

My vision wavered. I gritted my teeth. Balled my hands so hard nails pricked my palm and shoved down everything else, the pain, the hurt, the ugly things that wanted to claw their way out of my chest.

Focus. On. The. Task. At hand.

No one likes a sad, scared girl.

I swiped my eyes and turned to Kaspar. "Bo said you could show me Volgaard." Then I plastered a smile on my face. Plastered it so wide and tight, it hurt. "Want to try?"

Chapter Sixteen

TREES. WHITE WAVES against black sand. Winter. Not a dusting of snow, but the full force of it. Mosaics of fractured ice. Waterfalls. Sunsets. A hive of bees built high in the branches of a broken oak. A scraped knee. A dark and churning sea. Lightning. Not a single flash, but full forks that split the sky and fell into butterflies, raindrops, anger. Secrets balled like fists. And fish…thousands of them, silver bodies glinting under a fat, full moon.

I paused, the pen hovering above the page and shaded a spike of lightning, the same flashing forks I'd seen in Kaspar's illusion. Below the lightning, a sketch of bees, and the words, *Reykr, Skygge, Sooth*.

I'd burn this when I was done, kill the chance of being caught, but writing had always helped me puzzle things together, and here, alone in my tent, there was no risk. I turned the lamp brighter, the wick hissing.

E—Potential tributary? Two types of magic. Best at reykr.

Wind snapped the canvas fabric. Shadows skittered across the walls.

S—

I hooked my stockinged feet and underlined the letter twice. I hadn't learned much about Signey. She'd stayed away from the men, had taken her dinner and sat alone on a rocky outcropping.

W—

The weapon. I hadn't learned anything about that, either, not where it was or what it did. *Potential ideas to find W?*

A droplet of water landed on my journal, running down the page. I swiped it away and sketched one of the silver-bodied fish Kaspar had shown me.

Being friendly seemed to work with Bo. The rest of the men didn't care, but maybe I could win them the same way I'd won the stewards. Everyone wanted something.

Two more droplets drummed the page.

I squinted up at the blot blooming across the tent canvas, water whiskering like a rose. I pushed myself onto my knees and swiped it with my thumb. Was it raining? It couldn't be raining because there was only one blot, one black blossom. Unless Erik had somehow given me a defective tent.

I wouldn't put it past him.

Then water, cold as ice, dumped over my head, soaking my hair, my papers, my bedroll. The oil lamp fizzled out.

And laughter.

It flitted around me like ghosts. Five? Six? Seven men? No, this wasn't Erik. At least, not directly.

My nostrils flared. I pulled the flap back. "You—"

But I stood on the precipice of a cliff, the star-flecked sea churning beneath me. Waves beat angry against the rocks.

If I took one step forward, I'd teeter over the edge.

More laughter. Laughter all around, howling, skipping, singing like zephyrs. I turned in a circle, trying to pinpoint the source, trying to pinpoint *them*, but they were everywhere—the air, my ears, my teeth.

"Stop this," I said.

"Stop this," they taunted.

I whirled and the tent was gone, the camp was gone, everything was gone, and in its place, a black and gaping nothing, a black and stretching maw.

I groped through the air where I knew the tent should be, but my hands caught nothing. This wasn't real, it *couldn't* be real.

Water dripped down my back. Wind screamed in my ears. I clawed for my tent, I grasped air.

What was happening? Where was the tent?

"Please stop," I snapped.

More snickers. "Please stop, please stop, please stop."

I scrubbed my eyes, but I couldn't turn it off, couldn't lift it. What if it wasn't an illusion? What if this was real, and they'd somehow taken me here to die? Is this what they did to Hans before they slit his throat and dumped his body in the tide pools? Is this *how* they got him to the tides?

Then—

"What are you doing?" A familiar voice, an angry voice. "Stop that right now."

The precipice, the cliff, fell away, revealing three men, one short, one fat, one tall. Each had tattoos knotted across their

127

knuckles, one had tattoos across his cheeks. And behind them—

"Bo."

My hero. My savior.

Bo crossed his arms. "Torturing the guide? Really. That's low, Bengt, even for you."

My heart roared. Gooseflesh pebbled my arms. A few beads of water dripped down my neck.

I glanced at my hand, outstretched and groping.

My fingers hovered inches away from the tent. I must have tangled through the fabric. Why hadn't I felt it?

The short man—Bengt—took a step back and opened his palms in supplication, moonlight playing in the hollows of his cheeks and the space where tongue met teeth. "Come now. Surely our guide doesn't mind a joke."

They'd dumped water in my tent. They'd made me think I was standing on the edge of a cliff. I wouldn't call that a *joke*.

Grass swished around my ankles, a gentle *shh, shh*. A bird arced over the moon.

Bengt took another step back, his hands still raised. "Until next time," he murmured, then turned and left.

"Thank you," I said when they were gone.

Bo shrugged, the gesture quick and boyish. "I know how they can be. With reykr."

"Have they done that to you?"

"Dumped water in my tent? No. Hazed me? Yes. They used to do it all the time until Erik made them stop. He lets them do it to each other, but I'm off limits." A pause. "You could talk to him. Ask him to make you off limits, too."

I squinted at Erik's tent, a wash of orange light against the heathered sky. "He's kind of scary. You know that, right?"

Bo ran a hand through his hair and laughed. "Erik? Oh, he's terrifying. I would *never* want to be on the opposite end of his sword. But," his shoulders softened, "he won't hurt you. Promise. Just go in forceful and be confident. He respects that."

"And you think he'd actually make them stop?"

Another shrug. "I think it's worth a try. Otherwise, you'll have to deal with that sort of behavior the entire trip." Bo must have read the expression on my face because he added, "Yeah. It's terrible. Just remember. Forceful. Confident."

My heart still pounded from the incident with the tent and the cliff. "And you're *sure* he won't hurt me?"

"Isabel, we're going in circles. I'm positive. Now, go on."

Okay. Forceful and confident. I could do that.

I trudged up the hill and stopped outside his tent. The *pound, pound, pound* of my heart grew faster. Bo said he wouldn't hurt me, but did I actually trust that?

"Hello?" I called.

No response.

I tried again. "Hello?" Wind rattled the grasses.

Still nothing, which was strange. I was pretty sure he was in there. I edged the flap open…

Erik sat cross-legged in front of a map, shirt untucked, sleeves rolled, wheat-blond hair ruffled. Two silver beads hung on a cord around his neck. He tugged at them, keeping his attention on the map unfurled in front of him, the corners weighed down with stones picked from the riverbank. Smaller pebbles scattered the coastline—Cobble Cove, North Beach, the farthest point of Saeby.

He gritted his teeth and rearranged the stones, scattering them in different increments down the coast. More in Saeby, less on North Beach. A pause, a frustrated sigh. He snatched up the rocks and—

Forceful and confident. Here we go.

I pulled the flap wide and said, "Hi."

He jumped. "Augh! How long have you been there?"

The map and blankets disappeared, and he stood in front of me, his hair fixed, face stern. Canvas flapped in the wind. Stars, hot and wild, peaked through the cracks.

I blinked hard, blinked again. No, this wasn't real.

"Do you ever knock?" he snapped.

I squared my shoulders. "Your men attacked me. They dumped water on my tent and made me think I was going crazy."

He gave a sardonic twist of the lips. "So?"

"They ruined my things."

"And look at you. You're fine."

"I'm not fine."

"Yes, you are. Come see me if something actually happens."

I was doing exactly what Bo had told me to do, but Erik didn't seem to be listening. If I couldn't convince him, I'd have to deal with those men. Every. Single. Night.

The water, the snickering. *Until next time.*

Tension sparked between my teeth. "Let me be clear. I am a representative for my country. If I don't come back, there will be war."

Liar. The word scraped through my brain. I wasn't worth going to war for. I wasn't worth saving. I was here because I was expendable.

A rush of upward smoke and Erik was ten feet away, pouring a glass of brandy from an amber bottle, his expression carefully neutral. "They're teasing you, Isabel, not trying to kill you. It means they like you."

"They listen to you."

He clucked his tongue and swirled his glass. "I'm their commanding officer, not their mother. If you don't like it, you can always, I don't know, leave?"

"You're brutes."

His eyes dropped from my face, to his cup, then back to my face. The corner of his mouth quirked. "At least we know how to use cups."

Red lined my vision. To hell with him. To hell with all of them. I'd find the weapon, I'd steal it, and then I'd watch Volgaard burn.

The next morning, when a giant spider fell out of my breakfast bowl, I didn't so much as flinch. When a seagull pooped on my head, I waited patiently for it to dissipate. When I found a rat in my pocket, I flung it across the field.

A few of the men snickered, made faces of mock surprise. All the while, I could feel Erik's eyes on me, cool and assessing.

If you can't handle it, you can always leave.

Once, when I was wrestling Buttercup back from a patch of wild garlic, I caught his gaze and tipped my chin in a challenge that said I could handle it. I could handle anything.

Beasts rose from the grasses. Blood rained from the sky. I watched versions of myself die a thousand different ways—fire, beheading, walking straight off a cliff.

"We're falling behind schedule," Erik said when we stopped for lunch. "Kaspar, make sure the horses are watered. Bengt, pack the food."

"Or maybe you shouldn't have taken so many people," I mumbled, reaching for the pot of honey.

A thin line of ants circled the rim. I plastered a smile that showed all my teeth and lifted the honeypot. "Mmm, ants. My favorite."

"Um. Isabel," Bo whispered. "Those are actual ants."

"Shit." I dropped the honey. "Wait. How can you tell?"

"Because I can see them too, and the only person here who can Send is Erik."

"Send?"

He tipped the honeypot right side up, brushing off the ants. "Most of them can only show their illusions to three or four people at once. Kaspar and Bengt can both do sixteen, and that's considered incredibly gifted. Signey can do twenty-eight, which is…almost unheard of. But Erik… He doesn't have a limit. He can just…open his mind and you'll see it, I'll see it. If he makes it big enough, everyone within a hundred miles can see it." Another shrug. "Sending."

I rubbed my forehead. "No one else saw the spider in my breakfast? Or the version of me running around without a head?"

"I saw you staring at the horizon, looking mildly disturbed."

Great. I'd been acting crazy all morning.

"It's because you react," Bo added. "It makes you fun to harass."

At that moment, a naked version of Bengt strolled past. Coarse, black hair speckled his upper chest, a fuzzed trail leading to his—

My cheeks heated. My hand flew to my eyes. "I'm. Not. Reacting."

"Lunch is over," Erik said, standing. "Let's move out." He gave a pointed look at Bengt and his friends. "Don't slow us down."

This was the perfect opportunity to talk to Erik about the

route. If I wanted to get updates from the minister, I'd have to make sure we traveled through Esbern or St. Kilda. I hadn't had much luck with the weapon, but maybe I'd have better luck with that.

"You said you were falling behind," I said, untying Buttercup and scrambling after him. She snorted and tossed her head, trying to lip a cluster of heath orchids sprouting from a rock. "I can help."

A muscle ticked in Erik's jaw. He swung himself into the saddle. "It's not an issue."

"If you were to show me the map maybe—"

"You said yourself, you're just a symbol. A pretty symbol."

And with that, he spurred his horse, leaving me alone with Buttercup and a naked Bengt.

WIND WASHED MY FACE, swept over meadows of copper like a pair of massive hands. Birds colonized the hillocks. A pair of sheep grazed.

I pressed my forehead against Buttercup's neck, her mane snapping against my cheeks. How was I supposed to learn anything when every person here seemed set against me?

Even my horse seemed bent on making things miserable. As if on cue, Buttercup stopped to lip a cluster of yarrow.

"Come on," I said, dismounting and grabbing her reins. Men parted as if we were a stone in a stream. "We're going to be left behind."

Buttercup snorted and skipped over a stem that quivered from the rock face, eating everything but the plant, the petals yellow and variegated, shaped like stars.

I blinked once, blinked again. I swear it hadn't been there a moment ago, but it was like the hand of the earth unfurled and had given me…a gift.

Ragwort.

Suddenly, I had an idea.

Chapter Seventeen

THE ENTIRE CAMP WAS VOMITING. Okay, maybe not the entire camp. Maybe just the ones who'd been harassing me, plus a few casualties.

I shifted, cross-legged, and peered at the line of men waiting outside my tent, their arms around their stomachs, eyes watery, faces various shades of green. Fading sunlight spilled over their leather caps and quilted jackets, the meadow stretching gold behind them.

Okay, maybe it was more than *a few* casualties. I'd had to poison the rabbit stew before Bengt got to it, which meant everyone behind him also got sick. Not my intention, but the pockets of ragwort had been wildly effective. They'd been retching all evening.

I gave the man I was treating a mug of fennel tea. "Remember, second dose tomorrow. Next."

It was one of Bengt's friends, the tall one with thread-thin scars on his knuckles and a crow tattooed on his throat.

"Make it stop." He sank to his knees and clutched his

stomach. Sweat sheened his brow. "Please, make it stop."

I kept my eyes down, shuffled a few of the bottles over the low writing table I'd requisitioned from Bo. After he'd clued me in about how reykr worked, I'd started looking for hints as to who created what illusion—a smirk here, a twitch of the fingers there. I was pretty sure he was the one who made Buttercup sprout fangs.

I pulled a smile across my face and laced my fingers together, elbows on the table. "What are your symptoms? Same as the others? Better? Worse? Do you feel like you're dying?" Men always thought they were dying.

In response, he grabbed my bucket and retched.

"You know, I think this may be an intestinal worm. You can get them from contaminated meat or dirty water. Weren't a few of you drinking straight from the stream?"

The man gripped the bucket, sweaty hair falling over his forehead, his eyes so wide they showed the whites. "Worms?"

It wasn't worms. Just ragwort. But he didn't need to know that.

I touched his elbow and gave him my best concerned face. "Never fear. We *can* get rid of them. My tea works wonders. Kills the worms. Do you have a mug?"

The man began unbuckling a water skin at his belt, frantic and a little feverish. "Help me. Please hel—"

He barely got it off before he grabbed the bucket and retched again. Stomach acid smeared the air, the stench like spoiled cheese. But I'd seen worse. Hell, I'd *smelled* worse.

I lifted the kettle and poured a braid of steaming liquid into the water skin. "Of course I'll help. But first I need *your* help."

"Anything." The word cracked in his throat. Dirty tears streaked his cheeks. "Please, I'll do anything, I'll—"

I tipped the kettle upward, cutting off the braid. The skin warmed my hand, soft and supple, like the fleshy part of a thigh. I wanted to stab it. "Some men have been playing jokes on me," I said, kneading my thumbs into the leather. "Making me see things that aren't really there."

He reached for the waterskin.

I pulled it away.

"It's not me. I swear—"

Liar.

I replastered my smile, so false, so cheery. "*Of course*, it wasn't you. But if you see anyone using reykr, you'll defend me, won't you?"

He ran his tongue over his teeth and nodded.

"And you wouldn't use reykr on me, would you?"

Another nod. His eyes didn't leave the water skin in my hand. I turned it, pretending to study the line of silver fillings studding the strap. "I want to hear you swear it."

"I swear it," he muttered.

"Louder."

"I swear it!"

The other men snapped their heads in our direction.

I tossed him the waterskin. "This is the first of twelve doses. You'll need a dose every morning and evening for the next two days, then we move to evening only."

Why twelve doses? Not sure. Twelve had been the first number that came to mind, and I'd stuck with it. Twelve doses on the regimen I'd suggested would buy me at least a week without reykr, a week where most of the men would have to visit me every day, a week to befriend them and learn about their weapon.

The man stumbled out of my tent and I called for the next to come in.

Tomorrow, I'd ask about their military service. Did they like serving under Erik? What was their role? The next day, I'd ask them about their training. What did it look like? What weapons did they wield? I'd keep asking until I got what I wanted.

I shuffled around a few of the medicine bottles I'd set out as decoration.

I had to pat myself on the back. It wasn't a bad plan. Not a bad plan at all. In fact, this entire journey was looking up.

A shadow passed in front of the tent flap, and Erik settled cross-legged on the other side of the writing table. His eyes burned. "Isabel."

My gut lurched.

It wasn't a bad plan, but it had one very specific rule: avoid being caught. Erik might not be able to send me away, but he could make things worse. So much worse.

"You're fine," I said, nearly knocking over a tincture of comfrey. "Next!"

"You're poisoning my men."

"On the contrary, I'm helping them. You're welcome. Next!"

He caught my wrist and flipped it over. On instinct, my hand curled into a fist.

"I just—" he pried at my fingers. "I don't know how you're doing it." He wedged my thumb open and frowned at my empty palm.

I grinned.

He glared.

"Nothing to see. Buh-bye." I tried to pull my hand away.

He held tight. "I'm not going anywhere until you tell me what's going on."

"Great. You can hold the puke bucket."

His lips pinched. "If you don't tell me what happened, I'll watch you. Put you right next to my tent."

"I accept your offer of protection."

His jaw worked. "We won't wait for you. When Buttercup trots in the wrong direction, we'll keep going."

"Can't." I tugged my hand harder. "You've been ordered not to."

"If you don't tell me, I'll… I'll…" he searched the tent, "I'll tell the camp this whole thing is a farce."

My heart stuttered. "You wouldn't."

He leaned across the table and dropped his voice to a fake whisper. "Oh, yes. I would. So, tell me," his thumb smoothed my knuckles, "what did you do to my men?" Now it was his turn to grin.

His hands really do feel nice.

Stop. Focus.

I could keep lying or I could try a plea for sympathy. My plea for sympathy hadn't worked last night, but something told me that continuing to lie would make things far, far worse.

I stood and shook the flap closed, plunging us both into a ruddy dark. "They kept harassing me."

He snorted. "You're looking for revenge?"

"I'm looking for bargains. Every man I've treated has sworn not to use reykr. Problem solved."

A pause, longer than I was expecting. If I squinted, I could make out the pale outline of his cheek, the slash of his jaw, gray eyes, blond hair, scary mouth.

He stood and stepped around the table, closing the distance between us. "Don't mess with my men."

I tipped my chin to meet him. "Maybe you should have done a better job controlling them."

Woo him. The minister's suggestion. And wasn't I doing a terrible job of that? Maybe I should be nicer.

I pressed a hand to my forehead. "It's fine. I fixed it."

"By telling them they have what? Worms?"

I shot him a glare. "If you're worried about the schedule, don't. They might be a little tired, but the vomiting shouldn't last the night."

"Good. Because I'm holding you responsible for any delays."

An edge crept into my voice. "There won't be delays."

"Fine."

"Fine."

His teeth glinted, white as his irises. Wavy hair fell onto his forehead, curling just above his brow, making him a feral, animal thing. I had the sudden urge to run my fingers through it. My hand started rising of its own accord…

I swiped a strand of hair behind my ear to cover the movement. My cheeks flamed. Shit. And now I was probably as bright as a strawberry. My cheeks flamed hotter. I ducked my chin.

Erik's gaze flicked from my face to my hand, then flicked back to my face. His brow quirked. "Interesting."

He turned to leave, the heat of his presence vanishing, leaving something, something—

"Wait." I hated the note of desperation in my voice.

Erik turned, his hand on the tent flap, edging it open just enough to show the meadow beyond, lined in lemon and spun gold.

"You won't tell them, will you?"

He glanced over his shoulder. "If I told them, they would *actually* kill you."

With that, he left.

I knew I should've called the next man in. After all, I had an entire line of them groaning and retching. Instead, I placed my hands on my knees and took big gulps of air.

What just happened?

It hadn't been anger. Erik's anger was hot and round, a twist of the mouth, a tick of the jaw. This had been lighter, airier, limned like the meadow in shades of gold.

It hadn't been anger.

It had been amusement.

Chapter Eighteen

I WOKE FROM A NIGHTMARE, but it was the pain in my bladder that kept me awake. I threw my arm over my head, rolled to one side, rolled to the other, snuggled my knees to my chest and tried to let the pull of sleep wrap around me, tried to let it drag me down, press like—

The pain persisted, angry and throbbing.

I cracked my eyes open.

Fine.

I slipped outside my tent, runched my nightgown around my hips, squatted like a hen among the grasses, tried to relax.

The sound of the sea echoed off the high ground, the drum of the waves mixing with the low knell of the wind to create a soft *shh, shh*.

The first night, I'd pushed my blankets aside and peed in the corner like a scared dog, but sleeping with it had been even worse. The smell. The shame.

Then the second day, I'd held it. Had crossed my legs and gritted my teeth as if sheer will could drive the urge away, because if Erik's men knew, they would've turned it to cockroaches or coils or flashed the image of me with my skirt hiked up to the entire camp.

Even now, a part of me wondered if they might try something. Was the ragwort enough?

Overhead, the sky swept like a blanket, star-flecked and infinite. Grass bristled my ankles and the backs of my thighs, the cool of it cutting through my stockings and causing a chill to creep over my spine.

Go. Just go. No one else is awake.

A hiss, a patter. A dark puddle formed on the ground between my feet. I balled the wool scrap I'd brought for drying myself and—

A flick of movement, a swish in the field, there then gone.

My heart lurched. I nearly dropped the wool.

The flick again, a blurred shadow.

I yanked my underthings into place and squinted through the knotted dark. Was it actually a shadow or was it reykr?

Boulders rose and fell like the backs of gray whales. A bird flittered up from the darkness.

And there, the flick.

Only it wasn't a flick. It was a person, a silhouette skirting the edges of the camp.

The silhouette disappeared into Erik's tent. Moments later, a light flared, a wash of orange, a beacon, a fire.

I bit my lip and waited for the tent to warp or explode or crumble to dust like moth wings on wind.

But nothing. Only the swish of grasses and a steady orange glow.

Okay. Maybe Erik was awake.

He hadn't slept in Karlsborn Castle, either—his duvet still folded, sheets still tight, no rumple of blankets or muss of pillows. Why was that? What was he doing?

If I was caught spying, I'd have no excuse. My tent was positioned on the opposite side of camp, pitched near a small scoop of rock, more sheltered than the rest. Erik's tent had been placed between the horses and the narrow stream that curved through the meadow like a black-bellied snake. Between us, the men, the bags, everything. The distance had seemed so logical when I'd set up shop to cure the worms, but now I had no reason to be on that side of camp.

A few wild orchids quivered, their lips pale pink against the dusk. Moonlight spilled like a bucket of milk.

If I was caught, I'd have no excuse.

If I was caught…

I sucked in a breath and started toward the brilliant orange glow.

Better not get caught.

I DUCKED FROM TENT TO TENT, sticking to the shadows—not that the shadows helped much, anyway. The moon was full and bright, every leaf and branch rendered in shades of smoke and steel, and all it would take was someone to pull back their door flap and I'd be seen.

Men snored. Horses snorted. An unseemly fart ripped.

I froze.

From inside the tent, the scrape of skin on blankets, a curse, a groan. Another fart.

Bengt.

My heart hammered and I dropped beside a boulder, but I couldn't help it. I smiled.

He'd had at least three helpings of that stew. My fennel tea would have helped *some*, but even I couldn't undo the damage from that much ragwort.

I waited for the groaning and cursing to subside before scooting the rest of the way to Erik's tent. My palms pressed against the freezing soil, my nightgown rucked against my knees.

What was the best way to spy? Could I find a gap in the fabric and peek through? Could he feel me watching him? Would he know I was there? What if he was just fiddling with the map, shuffling around those black and white river stones? What if this entire trip was a waste and—

"You think I encouraged her?" The words a warning. Erik.

"I don't know. Did you?" A second voice. Was that Kaspar?

I pulled myself onto my knees, hovered outside like a ghost, a ghoul, a whisper against the canvas.

"Of course not."

Were they talking about me? About how I'd poisoned the men? If Kaspar suspected… I ran a hand over my face.

Erik might not have plans to tell his men, but Kaspar…?

He'd tell everyone.

I could try to pass the ragwort off as some sort of accident, could say I'd misidentified the plant. Or I could run. Would they let me run? Or would they drag me back and play with me the way a cat plays with a—

"She shouldn't have brought it." Kaspar again.

"No," Erik agreed. "She shouldn't have."

Wait. Erik had complained I'd brought too little, no tent, no horse. But if they weren't talking about me, then who? Signey was the only other woman on the trip.

Wind lifted the door a fraction, revealing Kaspar fingering a silver flask and Erik, sitting on his bedroll, his knees up, head in his hands, his shirt open at the throat.

"You're not going to get rid of it?"

Erik raised his head, his eyes glittering. "I might need it."

I scooted around the side of the tent.

"You can't be serious." Kaspar again.

"We need any advantage we can get."

"Do we? Because this is turning out to be a lot easier than we thought. Or is this still about proving yourself?"

"I don't need to prove anything."

"You sure? Because I think this has something to do with what happened with the ships—"

"Shut up."

"That wasn't your fault. Lothgar was—"

"I said, shut up!"

I dropped to my belly, just as the flap was flung open and Erik stalked out.

He glared at his tent once, his gaze skimming the shadows. Then he threw up his arm and vanished into the hungry night.

"AND SUDDENLY THERE WERE NO ROCKS and I was up to my ass in river water. And guess what happened? Just guess." The man I was treating—Tyr—leaned back against the blankets, beard scruff unshaved, eyes gleaming a bright and mineral blue. Handsome in a roguish sort of way. One of my ragwort casualties.

I pressed the back of my hand to the tea kettle, the iron mostly cool. What happened with the ships? And what did Kaspar mean Signey shouldn't have brought it? Shouldn't have brought what? The weapon?

"I saw a water snake," Tyr supplied. "But was it a real snake or a reykr snake? It's hard to tell. I assumed it was a reykr snake—something about the color seemed off—but then…"

And if the weapon *was* here, did that mean I could steal it and bring it back to Karlsborn Castle? It had to be small if she'd stowed it in her bag.

"… and I thought, surely snakes don't act this way in the wild. Like I said, it had two heads. *Two heads!* I grabbed a stick and—"

"What do you know about Signey?"

Tyr opened his mouth, then closed it, rubbed the scruff of his jaw. "The bitch queen? She was actually pretty cool until Lothgar picked Erik to be his second. Then she went—" He let out a quick whistle. "Yesterday, she nearly had my head off for touching her bag. I was just setting up tents."

I'd noticed the men divided into groups each evening, some on tent crew, some on dinner crew, some on horse crew. Bo claimed it made camp set up and tear down quicker. But Signey came at Tyr for touching her bag? Interesting.

I poured Tyr his cup of tea—ginger because I'd run out of fennel.

"You know, you're easy to talk to," Tyr added.

I wasn't. I knew I wasn't. I was hard like a tortoise, prickly like a sea urchin, all barbs and spikes and iron walls.

Tyr fixed his mineral eyes on me. "I bet you get that a lot."

I stared at my hands, my knuckles reddening, my nails rimmed with dust from the road. "You were setting up tents?"

"Well, yeah. Most people keep extra spikes in their front pockets. Not you, obviously, because Erik gave you the…" He glanced up. "Oh, never mind. Anyway, Signey's tent was missing a spike, so I reached for her bag to see if she had any extras, and she bit my head off."

"Sounds strange."

"Like I said, bitch queen." He nodded at his mug of ginger tea, a smile teasing out the dimple in his cheek. "Anyway, eleven more days, right?"

"Eleven more *doses*." I passed him the mug.

"You wound me. I could do eleven days of worm treatment so long as you're my doctor."

I…wasn't sure what to say to that. Luckily, I didn't have to because he winked and left.

Tyr was my last patient of the morning. The rest of the men were already breaking down the tents and saddling the horses. I gathered up the blanket, the kettle, dumped the rest of the tea into a thatch of carrot blossoms.

Signey, the bitch queen.

Signey and her bags.

It had been more helpful than anything I'd gotten from the other men.

"She's scary," said one.

"Stay away from her," said another.

"Lothgar's lackey. Does his dirty work."

I should stay away from her, I should. Everyone in the camp seemed to give her a wide berth. But if I wanted to know what she'd brought, what she was hiding, then I'd have to get into her bags.

I plucked one of the white flowers, rolled it between my thumb and forefinger.

Ordinarily, I'd have no reason to snoop around Signey's bags, but if I helped with tent duty, then maybe I could rifle through it under the guise of looking for a spike.

My heart hammered. The noose came back around my neck. Because if I could find what she was hiding, then maybe, *maybe*, I could steal it.

Chapter Nineteen

"WHY TENT CREW?" Tyr asked, unraveling a canvas bundle over the sand. "Why not, erm, taking care of the horses? You know, something easier?"

I pushed my sweater up to my elbows and twisted my hair into a high bun. "Just show me how it works."

I'd spent most of the day watching Signey—her strong shoulders, her angry mouth, the way she rode so high and proud.

She had three bags—one big, one small, one nearly empty. Every once in a while, she'd reach back and rub the lacings on the small one, as if she wanted to make sure it was still there…

That's the one I needed to search.

Rolling waves doubled the length of the beach and a colony of puffins surfed the swells, a scattering of gray in orange-ribboned water. Fires smoldered in sandy pits.

"If you let her on tent duty, you'll need to monitor her," Erik said. His deft fingers worked to loosen his saddle bags.

"Why would I need to monitor her?" Tyr asked.

"Any tent she sets up is going to collapse…probably with us

in it." His saddle bags dropped into the sand, one right after the other. *Thump, thump.*

I placed my hands on my hips. "They will not collapse."

The corner of his lip quirked. "Oh? Have you ever set up a tent?"

"I've set up a tent." A lie. But…it was a tent. A few poles, a bunch of fabric. How hard could it be?

Hard, it turned out. The fabric bunched together, didn't like to lie flat. There was only one pole and whenever I got it standing, it would topple over or the pit I'd dug for it would collapse or the wind would snatch away the canvas and drag it halfway down the beach.

I glanced at Signey sitting atop a boulder, a fishing net slack between two fingers. Her oval face tipped toward the waves, shining like a coin. Going straight to her bags would cause too much suspicion, so I'd started with my own, but if I wasn't quick, someone else would set up her tent before I did.

A gust of wind snapped the canvas off the pole and blew it into Erik, who'd donned a lake-blue jacket and crouched over a cook fire.

I dropped the pole and bunched my skirts to tromp after it.

Erik dragged the canvas back to my spot.

"There's a pin here." He flipped over the pole and pointed to a rusted nail driven into the end. "Use it to hook your fabric."

"Right." I dropped to my knees and refolded my canvas. Sand clung to the wax, pilled in my shoes, my socks. I swiped a strand of hair out of my face.

"You have it backward," he said.

I ground my teeth and pulled the canvas around.

"Still backward. You give up?"

"Never."

I tried again, again, again. Collapse. Collapse. Collapse.

The rest of the men moved through the camp with practiced efficiency, tents erected like monuments. The sun disappeared from the horizon, sucking away the yellow hue, replacing it with a fraying black.

"The thing I can't figure out is why you're so set on this," Erik said.

I jumped.

He clasped his hands behind his back and inspected the misshapen tent the way a war general examines his troops. He'd popped his jacket collar against the cold and the wind ruffled his hair. "Frankly, it's weird. Also, the nail goes in the hole. Pointy end, sharp hole."

I stabbed the spike through the fabric. "What do you think I've been doing for the past hour?"

"It's only been an hour?"

I glared.

He held up his hands. "Kidding. Can I help? I don't have an extra, and I don't want you sleeping in mine."

"I'd rather stick a sewing pin in my eye."

Behind me, a gust of wind caught the fabric and the entire thing collapsed.

He shrugged. "Suit yourself. I think I snore. And thrash. And sleep walk. Come find me when you're cold and desperate."

He turned to leave.

I ground my teeth. "Fine."

He paused, the firelight touching his smug little smirk. "Didn't hear you. Can you repeat that?"

"Fine?"

He gestured to his ear.

I resisted the urge to stick a sewing pin in *his* eye. "Fine. Yes. You can help."

He dropped to his knees and began unraveling the mess of fabric and cording. "The thing about these tents—you must get the tension right. If you don't, they'll collapse." He passed me a length of rope. "Hold that."

"Just put it up."

"I'm teaching you. Pins in eyeballs sounds awful. I wouldn't wish that on my worst enemy. Except..." he tapped his chin, "maybe you."

"Stop it."

His eyes glittered with silent laughter, and he leaned forward, the hem of his jacket edging up to reveal a sliver of tattoo cut against a muscled abdomen, a thick black line that curved over his hipbone, disappearing into his—

My cheeks heated.

He shifted and the sheath of a knife gleamed, the stamped pattern barely visible in the fading light. Crows and cornflowers.

But a knife. I pressed the heel of my hand against my eye. *Stop being angry and ask about the weapon.*

"Do they mean anything?"

His eyes flicked to mine. Gray. Guarded.

My heart kicked. "The crows and cornflowers."

He dropped back to the tangle of cording that he was trying to unravel. "The crow is House Rythja's emblem. The cornflower is mine."

"A personal emblem." That was different. "Is that common in Volgaard?"

"Every father in Volgaard chooses an emblem for their child."

"And your father picked…cornflowers?" It seemed strange that, of all the things a father could pick, his had chosen a bright blue weed.

Erik pulled the strings tight. "Lothgar didn't pick cornflowers. I did."

I wanted to ask why he'd chosen his own, but this line of questioning seemed to upset Erik, and I didn't want to make him run off like he had the first day. I settled for something adjacent. "Do you have crows and cornflowers stamped into all your weapons?"

"Just my knife."

"Did you…bring other weapons?"

He gave me a quizzical look. The canvas snapped in the wind. "Did you?"

Again, a catch of the eyes. Again, a kick of the heart.

"A knife," I lied.

"You know how to use it?"

"Yes."

"For cutting herbs?"

"Not just that." Another lie. I wasn't sure why I said it. Maybe because I didn't want to feel weak? Maybe because I didn't want to feel small?

Erik unsheathed the knife. The steel winked.

I held up my hands. "I'm touched. Really. But I already have one."

"Oh-ho, I'm not giving you my knife." The corner of his mouth lifted. "I'm testing a theory."

"A theory?"

His eyes glittered. "I want you to show me how to use it."

Down the beach, fires crackled. Waves crashed. Wind carried

laughter and the muted voices of men. Dusky twilight tangled through his hair, edged his features, stormy and handsome.

My stomach did a little flip. "You know? I would. I really, really would, but I need to help Bo with, uh…" my eyes darted to the men huddled around the fire, "dinner. Yeah. Dinner. Bye!"

He cocked a brow. "Interesting, considering my men are under strict orders not to let you handle food."

"I meant the horses."

"Mmm, sure you did. Here's the knife."

I took a step back. "I don't want to hurt you."

"I doubt you could. Go ahead." He flipped the knife so the blade faced his gut and closed the distance between us. My breath caught in my throat, and now we were so close that I could make out the waves in his hair, the lean slant of his muscles, the faint outline visible through his jacket. His voice dropped to a purr. "Show me, Isabel."

Wind ruffled the seagrass, banded shades of green and blue. The knife's rounded hilt brushed my stomach, the cold metal cutting through my sweater, sending a shiver down my spine.

His eyes swept my face, his gaze deep as the sea. It flashed as if he had me, as if he knew.

Gotcha.

"Remind me not to get on *her* bad side," Kaspar said.

I jumped. "Shit, you came out of nowhere."

"Yeah, well, we have company." He'd tied his shoulder-length hair at the nape of his neck and popped his collar against the wind. Without his grin, he seemed older, tired.

Erik took back his knife. "Where?"

"There. See?" He pointed at a fire that glowed a little way down the beach, dancing like a speck on the wind. "What do you want to do about it?"

Erik drove the last of my tent spikes into the ground. "Nothing. We ignore it."

"What if they're dangerous?"

"They're not."

"You don't know that."

"Are they dangerous?"

It took me a moment to realize the question was directed at me.

"I…" Probably not. Bandits weren't common, but they also weren't unheard of. Three months ago, two shepherds and an entire troupe of actors had been found dead, slaughtered in the hills around St. Kilda. I'd hardly paid attention to it, had chalked it up as one of the many disasters that seemed to plague the Sanokes. But maybe…

"I'll shadow walk," Bo said. He stood a few feet away, his squint fixed on the foreign fire. "Check it out. See if they're friendly."

Erik's eyes flicked to Kaspar. "Not an option. We don't need skygge."

"That's why you brought me. Skygge."

"I changed my mind. It's too dangerous."

Bo's hands balled into fists. "So, I'm supposed to what—sit around, watching puffins?"

Another glance at Kaspar, this one more wary. "If you want to spend your time watching puffins, you're welcome to."

"I'm not useless!" It was almost a shout. Almost. Bo's shoulders rose and fell, rose and fell. Wind ruffled his dark hair, the dim light blurring his delicate features. A few drops of rain fell from the sky. "I'm not useless," he repeated. "Just let me help."

THEY DRAGGED A BEDROLL FROM A TENT, two deer pelts and a blanket with braided tassels. They placed both across the sand.

Bo laid on it, propping his jacket under his head like a pillow. He took a shaky breath and looked up at the gray-streaked sky.

Erik settled cross-legged above his head, his hands hovering around Bo's temples. "You sure?" he asked. "You don't—"

"I'm fine," Bo snapped.

The rest of the men drew their weapons and formed a circle around them. Axes, swords, knives that winked silver in the twilight.

"Why all this?" I asked Tyr, gesturing at the men, their weapons.

"Last time they shadow walked, the connection was…broken."

Bodies don't like to be left empty, Bo had said that first day. *They die pretty quickly.*

He'd been talking about the need for an anchor, but—

Suddenly, it all made sense—why Erik insisted on so many men, why he wouldn't send them home. "You protect them."

Tyr tossed his broadsword from one hand to the other. "Bo nearly died. Kadlin *did* die."

Rain needled my lashes and hair, thin and freezing. I pulled my sweater tighter, the cream wool soaking through.

"Then why not have Erik walk and Bo anchor?"

"Erik…doesn't shadow walk. He's the second, you know? Skygge's dangerous. He almost always acts as anchor."

Of course, *of course.* Let someone less important take the risk, someone who didn't matter.

Someone like Bo.

I glanced at Bo stretched out on the blankets, hands clasped over his chest, gaze fixed to the bleak sky. Rain coated his cheeks, rolled down his face.

"It took him three weeks before he could speak again, another two before he could walk," Tyr added. "After the connection broke, we weren't sure if he'd ever... Well. We're glad he's okay."

"You should know there was literally nothing Erik could have done," Kaspar said, coming to stand beside us. "In Lundar. Bo was just closer to his body."

On the bedroll, Bo's breathing slowed from normal breaths to something rasping and ragged. His skin paled, all color rushing out of his cheeks, almost as if he was sick in bed, as if he were dying.

Then he sat up. Except it wasn't him, not exactly. His body lay outstretched on the ground, empty and still, but Bo—another Bo—perched on top of it, white as shells, white as salt, the edges of him whiskering like water. A spirit. He scanned the men and waved to me—or was it Kaspar?—before peeling off his body. As he did, he became paler, a moonbeam struck by the sun, before disappearing all together into the dusky night.

Erik's chest rose and fell, so slow, so steady. His eyes fluttered beneath his lids. Sweat beaded along his brow.

"Being an anchor isn't easy," Tyr whispered. "None of it is easy."

Signey snorted, and I realized she was here too, a battle ax in one hand, her gaze fixed on that tiny fire.

Would there be another opportunity like this? Would there be something that snagged the entire camp's attention like skygge seemed to? Would Bo and Erik shadow walk again?

My heart thundered. My mouth dried.

Maybe…

But maybe not.

I closed my fist, opened it, wiped my sweaty palm on my skirts.

"How long are they usually gone?" I asked.

"With the mysterious camp being that far away…" Tyr rubbed his jaw. "I'd say five, ten minutes. Why?"

"I'm, erm…wet. From the rain," I backed toward the tents.

"We're all wet from the rain."

"Well, I'm going to change my sweater."

Before he could reply, I hurried down the dark sand and into the line of tents. The crash of the sea thundered in my ears, my heart thundered in my mouth. The patter of rain turned into a full-on pour. I only had a few minutes, but a few minutes was all I needed.

I pulled back the flap to Signey's tent and stepped inside. Rain drummed the canvas, and the tent flap blocked most of the light. Her three packs littered the floor, scattered like boulders— one big, one small, one nearly empty.

I pulled open the small one, golden swede trimmed with bright orange fox fur and a button fashioned from a canine. Inside, a set of playing cards, a pouch of dried fish, a bag of tree sap rolled in powdery flour.

I grabbed the empty one next and turned out the pockets. Nothing. I tossed it on the floor.

My head pounded, my throat thickened, and I couldn't scream, couldn't hear.

This was the woman who killed Hans, who'd dumped his body into the tides. All it would take was her peeling back the flap, striding into the room, and she'd find me. She'd *kill* me. But if I didn't do this, Hans's death would be for nothing, would *mean* nothing.

The entire camp was distracted. This was my best shot.

I grabbed the largest bag and began rifling through it.

A deep red tunic unrolled like a flag, the sleeves and neck trimmed with silver fur. Pants and stockings, a purse filled with foreign coins. I clawed through them.

An empty water skin, a comb, a pouch filled with dark leaves that had the sharp tang of dried peppermint.

My fingers scraped the bottom of the bag and a small chest tumbled out, onyx metal stamped with a lattice of knots and a pattern of falling crows, feathers curled around their bodies, so polished, their wings reflected the blurry outline of my face.

I tried to pry it open, the box and the lid separating a fraction before a latch caught the lock with a hollow *click*.

I tried again, but the lid would not budge.

I ran my fingers around the seam, the place where metal met metal, found a keyhole, round and small, embedded in one of the crow's tumbling feet.

I tried the lid again. Again, the lid and box separated a fraction of an inch. Again, that *click*.

Could I force it open if I had something sharp? A hairpin? A key?

Where would she keep a key?

Commotion from outside the tent. I shoved the tunic and the box back into Signey's bag and ducked outside, hurried down the beach, down the sand, toward the men.

Bo was back, gasping, his hand at his throat. "Bandits," he said after a moment, the words dry and raspy. "They're bandits."

"So, we don't light a fire tonight," Kaspar said. "And we keep quiet."

Erik rested his forehead on his knees. "We can light a fire." His shoulders heaved. "I'll keep us hidden."

Kaspar's head jerked. "What? You'll Send all night?"

Erik gave him a wary glance. Rain soaked his shirt. His hair clung to his forehead and cheeks in wet strands. "I'd rather not deal with bandits."

The men broke up, wandering back to their dinner and their jobs. Bare cliffs rose out of the mist, softened from the deluge of rain. Horses snorted and pawed the earth.

"Hey," Tyr said, coming up beside me. "Weren't you going to change your sweater?"

"I, um…" My eyes met Signey's, cool and searching, as if somehow, impossibly, she knew I'd been in her tent.

Chapter Twenty

I WALKED AROUND THE CAMP TWICE, testing my theory about Signey. Maybe it was my paranoia, but she was definitely following me. I went to pet the horses. She was there. I went to check on Tyr's rash. Watching me. Trying Kaspar's special tea? She wasn't far behind.

I dumped the rest of the tea into a bush. Vold tea had a rancid smokiness. It tasted like I'd eaten a fire pit, and now I needed to find some peppermint to fix my mouth.

I skirted the corner and ran into Erik.

"Sorry." I glanced over my shoulder. "Didn't see you." No Signey. Okay. Maybe I *was* being paranoid. "If you see your sister, tell her I went, um…that way." I pointed my thumb in the opposite direction.

Erik nodded and went to step around me. His shoulders sagged, his hands hung limp. "Yeah, sure."

I studied him—the way his shirt was rumpled, the few strands of hair that clung to his forehead. The color had leached from his cheeks, leaving his skin glassy and pale.

Maybe it was the fact that I knew what it was like to feel exhausted and gutted because my stomach squeezed. "Wait," I called. "You...okay?"

Waves crested. Pearlescent shadows scattered the sand, a lick of froth brushing the shore.

"I'm fine." His voice was a hollow echo.

"You sure?"

"Yeah." He rubbed his eye. "Went through worse in Lundar."

Lundar. "What happened? Kaspar said Bo nearly died." *And Kadlin did die.*

His eyes narrowed. "What's with all the personal questions?"

"I haven't been asking personal questions."

He lifted a hand. "Was your father always the general?" He ticked a finger. "Do crows and cornflowers mean anything?" Another finger. "What happened in Lundar?" A third finger. "Personal questions."

"I'm trying to get to know you," I replied. "Is there something wrong with that?"

Something flickered across his face so fast, I nearly missed it. Confusion? He swallowed and touched the back of his neck. "Okay, um, Vilmar was anchoring Bo, and I was anchoring Bo's sister, Kadlin. Vilmar and Kadlin died, and Bo..." He let out a shaky breath. "I messed Bo up pretty bad."

"Oh."

A weak smile. "Yeah. Nothing like accidentally killing your best friend's sister."

"Kaspar said there was nothing you could have done."

His hand dropped to his side. "I could have Sent."

He stepped around me. The ocean sucked and the sky stretched. Stars freckled the night.

163

I thought of Hans. In the apothecary, on the bluffs. The flush of his curls, the brush of his hand.

You found a poppy.

Erik turned, a flash of cheek, a curve of mouth, and for a moment, he wasn't second-in-command, the general's son, but a boy who'd been lost and hurt and broken. Didn't I know what it felt like to live with ghosts?

"Can I show you something?" I asked, offering my hand.

He glanced at it. "Isabel, I—"

I gave him my warmest smile. "Come on. I won't bite."

He threaded his hand through mine and I felt his heartbeat through his fingertips, quick, a little unsteady.

I pulled him through the tents, past waves that broke along the shore. Mist flecked our faces, our hair, and maybe I should woo him, should lower my eyes and my voice and come at him with swinging hips.

I could get back to that tomorrow.

I pulled him past puffins and up hills. Twin fires glittered, sheltered from the wind—ours, the bandits. They watched like baleful eyes.

"Stand here," I said, leading him to the bluff's edge. Cliffs dropped, sheer and fantastic. "Hold up your arms."

He glanced over his shoulder. Wind tangled his hair, tossed the strands like spun gold. "I'll look crazy."

"You won't." I lifted each of his arms like a bird. "Now scream."

"What?"

The last time I'd done this had been with Katrina and Hans. Tears pricked my eyes, and standing here, at the edge of the blustering world, I wanted to laugh. "Scream!"

"The bandits—"

"The sound goes backward, not out. Watch." I leaned forward and my skirt snapped my legs. "I hate Buttercup! I don't know how to set up a tent!"

Tnet a pu tes, said the echo.

He gave me a quizzical look. "This feels like a bad idea."

"Bad ideas are the best. Here, I'll answer your questions. One, I don't know why it happens. Two, it only works on the bluffs. Three, the sound doesn't carry *that* far behind—we've run tests." I flashed a grin. "Now scream."

His jaw tensed. In his eyes, a war, a wall. They burned with a siege. Then—

"Can you hear me?" The gusts caught the sound and ripped it back.

Em raeh, said the echo.

His hands balled to fists. "The stars are pretty! The camp is small!"

I nudged him with my elbow. "You're supposed to scream secrets."

"Secrets?"

"Yeah, like things you want to get off your chest." I turned back to the sea. It caught the stars. "I peed in the corner of my tent! Erik is a pain in my ass! Your turn."

He squinted over the horizon, fists tightening. "I stole Bo's favorite cup! And, uh… Sometimes my men drive me crazy!"

In truth, I was surprised he screamed an actual secret, the second-in-command, so stormy and austere.

He touched his lips, his eyes widening, almost as if he was surprised, too…

A beat passed, then another. And then we were yipping and shouting. The cacophony ripped away, ripped back.

"I'm feeding your men ginger tea! I don't feel bad about it!"

"Sometimes I pretend I can't hear Kaspar!"

"I still don't know how to ride a horse!"

The corner of his mouth lifted, and I knew, *knew*, what he was feeling.

"Signey deserved to be Second!"

"I wish Stefan would quit!"

"I hate my father!"

I let out a laugh and swiped the tears from my eyes. "I hate my father, too!" I leaned forward and shouted even louder. "And I'm going to prove him wrong!"

His brow arched. "Oh? You're going to prove him wrong?"

"Yeah. I'm going to *BEAT STEFAN!*"

"Well, I want my father to *ACTUALLY CARE!* And I don't want Signey to hate me! And… And… *I WANT TO BE MORE THAN MY MAGIC!*"

Wind howled and tossed, and for a second, it was just the two of us, a boy and a girl standing at the edge of a salt-spewed cliff.

I caught the edge of his cheek, the stormy shape of his mouth. Moonlight ruffled his jacket, dragged fingers through his hair and, for a moment, he looked so…alone.

Our eyes locked.

Wanting to be more.

I knew how that felt, too.

Chapter Twenty-One

MORNING DEW PILLED ALONG the canvas, round dots scattering like confetti.

I raked a hand through my hair, bound it in a fresh braid, and changed into a clean sweater, a mauvey pink with a thin, mock neck and wool flecked through with cream. One of my favorites, warm enough to keep out the nip from spring.

I'd spent most of the night scheming how to open the metal chest. I could always steal it and smash it against a rock, pry the lid the same way a river otter pries open an oyster. Not a bad idea, assuming the weapon was actually *in* the box. If it wasn't, I'd have no way to return it, and it might cause suspicion if the box disappeared or turned up broken.

So I had two options—find a way to open the box without breaking it, *or* confirm the weapon was in the box, then steal and break it. Stealing and breaking it without confirmation of the contents had to be a last resort.

I grabbed my stockings and my pouch of coffee grounds and pulled the tent flap open.

Fog had built along the coast, thick and white, bringing out the crispness in everything—thatches of grass, basalt cliffs. The sea lapped the shore, a dull sapphire, like the inside of a mollusk. No wind. No rain. Just…quiet.

Erik was already up and stoking a fire. His blond hair was mussed, gray eyes fixed on the flames. He wore the same clothes as yesterday—white shirt, blue jacket, fitted pants. At his hip, the same map I'd seen him looking at earlier—a map of the Sanokes with beach stones scattered up the coastline. A pot bubbled water.

"Morning," I said, settling myself next to the map.

"Morning," he replied, his voice thick.

"Sleep well?" I squinted at the map. He'd marked the same locations—Cobble Cove, North Beach, the farthest point of Saeby, but he'd placed two stones along the beach we were staying at, white stones instead of black, each—

The map vanished.

I scowled. "I can help you with that, you know."

He fed another knot of grass to the fire. It feathered and snapped, the grayish smoke mixing with the mist. He probably hadn't slept, had probably been here all night making sure the bandits saw nothing but empty beach.

My hand crept to the linen pouch. "Do you…want coffee?"

"Coffee?"

"Tastes like dirt, but it helps you wake up. Most of the staff drink it. I only started after…" After Hans died? After your people killed him? After the nightmares started, and I found myself at the tide pools again and again? I pressed a hand to my temple. "It doesn't matter. Here, I'll make you a cup."

A dark and roasted aroma filled the air, a grind of rust and umbers flecked the deepest black. The receding tide had left behind a strip of glossy sand, and a few of the men had wandered to the sea or settled by the flames.

I ladled another spoonful of boiling water over the linen. Opening the mysterious box seemed like the better of the two options, but where would Signey keep a key? In the pocket of another bag? I hadn't searched the smaller pockets, but searching smaller pockets meant I needed to sneak into her tent again. I could do that, couldn't I?

"About last night…" Erik said, tugging me from my thoughts.

Coffee grounds swirled, black flecks floating to the surface. Steam fogged my forehead. "You don't have to worry about your secrets. I'm a locked box."

"I was actually going to say thanks."

"Feeling better?"

"Some." He turned his cheek into his shoulder, hiding a smile. "Because of you."

My heart tumbled. Something thick rose up my throat and I remembered last night—the gray of his eyes, the catch of his cheek, the *knowing*.

"What did you mean when you said you could have Sent?" I asked, changing the subject. "In Lundar?"

On the other side of the fire, a few men tossed chickweed fronds into the flames, the green buds crackling and smoking. Another wave rushed the shore.

"In Lundar…" The smile faltered, and he bit the inside of his lip. "We went to spy on House Kynda. House Kynda…they're a lot. Anyway, there were four of us. I could have Sent to hide them, but it was Bo's first time using skygge to walk into Faela Fort, and he was so scared… So Kadlin went too, and I acted as her anchor. We thought we were hidden in the caves. But House Kynda? They found us. Killed Vilmar, who was anchoring Bo. I remember dragging Kadlin's body closer to him, trying to anchor both. And—" His jaw clenched. "I should have Sent."

"You didn't know."

"That's the thing." He grimaced. "I did."

"How?"

"I knew I wasn't a strong anchor. I knew I was better at reykr." He prodded the fire with the stick. "You said you know what it's like…to feel like you could have done more?"

"Every day."

"Does it get better?"

I ladled another scoop of water over the grounds. I could lie, could tell him it did. But—

"I don't know." The truth. "Sometimes I feel like I'll always come up short. Do you ever wonder if some people are made to be…small?"

He thought for a moment. "I think people have different strengths, but I don't think anyone is made to be small."

Fire snapped, the white-hot smoke chugging between us. *I see you, I see you*, it seemed to say.

More men filtered out from their tents, poured cups of tea and warmed slices of bread in the flames until the bottoms became black and charred.

I ladled another scoop of boiling water over the grounds.

"You know," Erik said, "that doesn't smell like dirt." He scooted forward, his thigh brushing mine.

Slowly, carefully, he tugged the cup from my hands. His thumb grazed my index finger and mist clung to him. His shirt hung open at the throat, and I caught his scent—smoke and wool and something else, something wild.

"It doesn't taste the way it smells," I said. The words came out a little breathless.

Above the cup's rim, his eyes flicked to mine, cool, assessing. "Isabel. *A lot* of things don't taste the way they smell."

"Right." Still breathless.

He studied me for one beat. Two. Something dangerous flickered over his expression and his gaze intensified. He set the cup down and, with another slow and careful movement, reached up and traced my cheekbone.

I expected him to brush away whatever dirt was there and drop his hand, but it lingered. His knuckles brushed my temple, his thumb skimming the sensitive spot right below my ear, setting my skin on fire, my body on fire, and all I smelled was him, and it filled my nose, my mouth, and his thigh pressed against mine, the heat of it scalding. His hand moved to tangle gently in my hair, and now he was playing with my hair and—

What was *wrong* with me?

His intense expression fell away. The corner of his mouth quirked. "Testing more theories."

"What theories?" I was almost afraid to ask.

"Secret ones." He dropped his hand and picked up the cup. "Now tell me, why are you trying to befriend my men?"

"I'm not trying to befriend them."

"They say you are. They say you ask all sorts of questions."

"It's called being nice."

"You know, you're not a good liar."

"Why would I lie about that!"

"You tell me. But I've noticed you lie about a lot of things." He used two fingers to trace a lazy circle along the cup's rim. "Having a tent. Riding a horse." A glance at the coffee mug. His eyes flicked up, caught mine.

171

I had the thought the same moment he did.

He tapped the metal hard. "Cups." He took a gulp.

A beat passed, then another.

His hand flew to his throat, and he gave a little cough.

"I forgot to mention, you have to drain the grounds. Whoops." I grabbed the cup and flounced next to Tyr.

"Oh yeah, come hide by me," he said, stirring a pot of porridge. "Just so you know, I'm not protecting you if he seeks revenge."

"I guess you'll have to hang onto those worms forever."

Tyr brandished the spoon. "If you take revenge on her, you'll have to get through me! Raaa!"

Erik flipped him off.

"I mean," Tyr amended, "no sleep and Sending all night? Damn, you look good."

Erik flipped him off again.

I glanced at the mug in my hand. The grounds swirled a rust-flecked umber. "Should I offer coffee again?"

"Nah, he'll be fine. He has amazing stamina. On the way over to the Sanokes, he Sent ships for like, six days straight. Because he could."

That was interesting. Kaspar and Erik had been arguing a-bout the ships.

I settled onto the rock next to Tyr and brought the cup to my nose, letting the sweet steam lick my forehead. Tyr liked to talk. Maybe I could learn more from him. "What do you mean by that? Sent the ships?"

"Sending is—"

"Yeah, I know what Sending is."

Tyr tapped the spoon on the side of the pot. "Oh. Well. He just hid them. With Sending. Conjured a bunch of fog and mist.

At one point we were a black raincloud. I think Lothgar was putting him through a drill. They do that. Lothgar comes up with these crazy challenges—hide a dozen ships for six days—and Erik makes it happen."

"Did he sleep?"

Tyr squinted at Erik. "Honestly? I don't know."

The flap to Signey's tent was thrown open and she stalked out with the lethal grace of a predator finding its prey. Her hair was unbound, some strands braided, others loose, her roots held a greasy sheen. She plopped next to a wiry man, who immediately vacated his spot and scrambled to the other side of the fire. Her eyes flicked to me.

Great.

Erik fed another knot to the fire. "Signey."

"Erik."

Signey snatched a pack off the ground and dug out a clay pot and a few dried fish.

"I trust you slept well?" Erik said.

"I trust you didn't."

"I was Sending." There was an edge to his words. "All night."

"Sending." She snapped a head off a fish and picked the meat with her fingers. "Of course."

The corner of Erik's jaw ticked, and he stood. "Wake the rest of the men," he said to no one specific. "We leave within the hour."

Signey didn't move. She sat on the rock, her hair greasy, shirt rumpled, a dusting of salt coating her fingers.

I needed to find a key to get into the box, which meant I needed to get back into Signey's tent. If I was going to do that, I needed a distraction, something to keep her occupied for at least ten, fifteen minutes. If she was watching me—and I was pretty sure she was—the distraction would have to give me enough time to get in and out, and then escape far enough away that she wouldn't be suspicious.

She cracked the head off another fish, flecks of silver-white meat flaking into her lap.

A distraction.

And I had just the way to do it.

Chapter Twenty-Two

"WE SHOULD TAKE TURNS BATHING," I said, loosening the buckles around Buttercup's saddle and letting my bags drop to the ground with a *thud*. A thin drizzle fell from the sky, giving everything a rusty hue. "This is a good spot for it. The water's deep and the Järne is clean."

The men had already broken into their groups, setting up tents, untying pots, and pulling down sacks of the coarse flour they made into bread.

Streams crisscrossed the grass like troll fingers, jagged and broken, creating squiggles in the dirt.

"Funny thing," I continued. "I actually made a few pouches of lavender bath tea. Does anyone want to try?"

Bath teas were one of my favorite vanity potions, though out here, I'd had to get creative with the ingredients and method. Normally, I would have used orange peels and cotton pouches, but I didn't have any of that, so I'd ended up tearing linen bandages into strips and knotting everything into a pretty package complete with a few sprigs of wispy lavender.

The goal was to give Signey an extra step in her hygiene ritual, buying me a few more minutes to check her tent, but because I couldn't single her out, I'd made bath teas for everyone.

"Great idea," Kaspar said, grabbing a sachet and working the knot.

"You don't want to—" I started.

Salt and lavender spilled out.

"Was this the salt for our food?" he asked.

"Um, maybe."

He grinned. "It smells delightful. Thanks, Isabel."

The men cycled through baths, walking through the camp with shirts slung over their shoulders and furs wrapped around their waists. A few gave me full-toothed grins and flexed their muscles, but none of them used reykr, which I suppose, meant the ragwort had done its job.

I brewed my pot of ginger tea and treated them on a blanket of bear furs under the open stars. If anyone asked, I said the sky was bright and I found the drizzle refreshing, but the real reason I was here was because I wanted to keep an eye on Signey.

She leaned against a boulder, tossing her knife into the grass over and over with a dull *thud, thud, thud*. When she left to take a bath, I'd need to act quickly to search for the key.

"Any changes to your digestion?" I asked, bringing my attention back to the man I was treating. "Bloating? Diarrhea?"

He grunted and handed me his water skin.

Thud, thud, thud went Signey's knife.

I planned to use a bar of soap to make an imprint of the key, then I'd take the soap bar to a blacksmith and have him pour me a new one. Even the smallest towns usually had a smith. We just…had to go through a town. We'd passed several outlying villages, brightly colored houses and crumbling walls, but we'd never gone through. Was Erik avoiding them? If so, why? What did that mean about traveling through St. Kilda or Esbern?

Bo came back from the river, his cheeks a ruddy red, dark hair plastered against his forehead, shirt slung over his scrawny back. "Who's next?"

Signey tossed the knife into the grass with a final *thud*. "Me."

I scrambled after her. "Don't forget your bath tea."

She frowned at the sachet. "Why would I want this?"

The drizzle pattered the bearskin. I took a steadying breath. "The minerals and salt will help with any muscle soreness. It's also good for bug bites, scrapes. You know, that sort of stuff. You just need to find a slower part of the river, tie it to a tree or a rock, and give it at least ten minutes." I wasn't sure how well the bath teas would work in a stream, but she didn't need to know that. I forced a cheery smile. "Fifteen is best."

Fifteen minutes was the longest a person could stay in the freezing stream. Realistically, I had ten. Maybe less.

She snatched the sachet from my hand and stalked toward the river.

I glanced at the man I'd been treating. "I think I forgot something."

The man frowned at his water skin. "It's empty!"

"I know. I'll—stay here. I'll be right back."

I hurried through the camp, past horses and smoke, men playing cards, reading books, making dinner, the air thick with the smoky smell of meats. The cook fire flashed gold among the grasses.

"Isabel," Tyr called, a fan of playing cards in one hand, a pile of coins at his feet.

I tried to dart past, but he dropped the cards and jumped up. "I have this weird red spot on my neck, see?" He tugged the collar of his shirt. "I was wondering if you could give me something to help. Itches like hell."

"Bug bite. I'll bring you chamomile. If you'll excuse me—"

"Wait," a tawny-haired man said. "I have this weird rash right—" He planted his foot and pulled his trouser leg to reveal an ankle crisscrossed with coarse hair. "Here."

I brushed past him. "Allergic reaction. Probably some sort of grass. Wear longer stockings."

Tents billowed, the world flecked, thin and foggy, bringing out the greens and grays. A rainy sort of cold curled up my spine and settled in my bones.

Slip in and out of Signey's tent. Find the key. Get far enough away that I wouldn't draw her suspicion. I could do this. I could—

I rounded the corner—

And ran straight into Erik.

He'd donned his blue jacket, his hair ruffled from the wind. Rainwater clung to his lips, his lashes, making him stormy as ever. His eyes flashed. "Isabel."

Shit.

"What's going on with the baths?" he asked.

"Nothing's going on with the baths." I tried to skirt around him.

He blocked my path. "Something is *definitely* going on with the baths."

"Weird. Well, let me know what you find out." I made another attempt to pass him.

He stuck out a hand. "You orchestrated this. Don't pretend like you didn't."

"Orchestrated what?"

His jaw tensed. "The baths."

"Are you telling me you don't bathe? That's gross, and probably unhealthy. Come see me when you get a rash."

"I'm telling you—" He scraped a hand through his hair. "Why are you making them take baths?"

"I'm not *making* them do anything."

He gave me a doubtful look. "Really? Because I'm pretty sure four people just asked if I was going to try *this*." He whipped one of my sachets from his jacket pocket.

I blinked. "I have no idea what that is."

"Stop lying."

"Fine. It's bath tea."

"It's lavender!"

"And now the camp will smell much, much better. You're welcome." I made a third attempt to skirt around him and got about two steps before he fell into step behind me.

Rainwater pooled around rocks and bushes, glittering like bath bubbles. A petrel swooped.

"Why are you following me?"

He shrugged. "I'm seeing what you do. Where you go."

I skidded around a puddle. "I'm going back to my tent."

"Except you're not."

"How do you know?"

"Your tent's back that way." He thrust a thumb in the opposite direction. "Which begs the question, what's the purpose behind the baths?"

"Guys?" Bo said.

"I told you. There is no purpose."

Erik stepped in front of me and crossed his arms. This close, his height blocked the rest of the camp. His voice fell to a dangerous murmur. "Oh, there is *definitely* a purpose."

My heart hammered. My gaze dropped to his scary mouth, his lips, supple and full and—

"Guys!"

We whirled.

Bo had changed into a clean tunic—deep green—and had combed his still-wet hair to one side so that it showed off his wide forehead and delicate cheekbones. "Bandits. How dangerous are they usually?"

I placed a hand on my chest and tried to still my pounding heart. "I don't know."

Bo's brow furrowed. He squinted at the horizon, and I saw it, too, that butter-yellow speck. "Because I think they're following us."

"Could be someone else," Erik said, stepping back.

Bo shook his head. "They were talking about us when I shadow walked. It's them."

The wind lifted the hairs off the back of my neck. I bundled my sweater tighter.

Bandits. Following us.

Over by the campfire, a few men scrambled away from Signey, who made her way through the camp, wet hair dripping down her back, a fur skin wrapped around her middle. Our eyes locked, then hers slid to the side.

To a tent.

Her tent.

Which I'd stopped right in front of.

"Well, I think dinner's ready," I said, looping my arm through Bo's and pulling him away. "Do you want to check?"

Dinner was indeed ready—roasted rabbit with dark and buttery bread they left on the griddle until the bottoms became black.

As we ate, I expected the Volds' hardness to return, the gruff edges and rugged parts.

It didn't.

Instead, they told stories.

Stories about home and honor, about hearts they won and stole and plundered, about those they left behind on wild shores and in winding mountains. They talked about ships and saddles and reykr, about Lothgar and his two hounds with snapping maws and a hankering for hares, about how they used to dare each other to stick their fingers between the bars of the cage.

Even Signey lost her frown.

Smoke chugged toward the star-streaked sky. Grease winked their fingers gold, and I noticed Erik was missing the tip of his— the skin rounded just above the topmost joint. He rubbed his thumb over it sometimes, a half-hearted habit he did whenever he laughed.

I hadn't noticed that before.

I'd failed to find the key, but I was learning about them. They were opening up around me.

Just listen, Stefan would say.

He was right. This should be good, I should be happy. Just listen, and maybe I'll hear something useful.

But as I sat on the edge of the rock, the stone cool beneath my fingertips, the wind whistling through the grasses, I felt like a wraith hovering at the edges, watching through the glass.

I didn't want to be one of them, was glad I wasn't one of them, but…

I used to laugh like that with Hans and Katrina. We used to stuff our pockets with pastries and run off to my family's apothecary or the bluffs, or we'd take a fishing boat and row and row until our arms gave out or the tide ripped in or until we were sure Katrina's mother would be frantic. But Katrina and I hadn't spoken—*really spoken*—since the funeral, and I wasn't sure we could fall back into those patterns, the grooves of life before—

Hans.

On the beach.

Hans.

On the pyre.

Before I burned the paper.

Before I couldn't say goodbye.

And Hans.

Dark curls, warm smile, who seemed to know exactly what I was thinking, who never laughed at me, but sat with me, and talked with me, and now the dark and gnawing thing clenched at my heart. It smoothed the hair off my forehead and whispered—

You should have been there.

That day in laundry? You pushed him away.

He shouldn't have loved you.

You weren't enough.

You will never be enough.

If I couldn't do this—find the weapon—Hans would be gone and his death wouldn't matter. He would be nothing, nothing, nothing, and we were small and we were sand and we were screaming into the void, and I missed him, and there was a hole in my chest that ate and ate and ate. I swallowed the tears that pricked the back of my throat and glanced at the sky.

Stars.

White and hot and burning and so, so far. Glimmers of light. Thousands of them.

The fire snapped, showering sparks that lifted in the wind.

"Erik," Kaspar snorted. "Oh, oh, oh, do you remember the sheep in Meya's bed?"

A smile tugged at the corner of Erik's mouth as he rubbed his nubbed finger.

I pushed myself up.

"Where are you going?" Bo asked. Firelight glinted off his face.

Anywhere. Away. "A bath."

I didn't think any of them would bother me with reykr, but I still wandered so far from the Volds that their fire vanished behind the rolling hills.

I still needed to figure out how to steer them to Esbern so I could pick up whatever information the minister had sent me about Karlsborn Castle. I needed to find the key, open the box. To befriend them. To be nice.

But I didn't feel nice.

I stripped off my stockings, my shoes, then waded out into the shallow stream. In Karlsborn Castle, we bathed by crouching over three-legged stools with a sponge, a bucket, a bar of lavender-scented soap. Freezing air would pipe our skin and gooseflesh would prickle our arms. Baths were never comfortable, always cold.

But this water wasn't just cold, it was freezing. Made from storms and snow, so clear it glittered like foil over river rocks, the gentle hiss of it, white-tipped, unending, cutting through the valley like the belly of a snake.

It reflected the stars.

I picked my way to the middle, feet sliding over the stones, the wind whistling over my bare arms. It wasn't deep, the ink-pot water swirling around my thighs at the highest point.

Still.

I gathered a breath and let my legs be swept out from under me.

I plunged.

Everything went cold, then warm, then bright, an explosion of white that threw itself, heady, against my skin. Awake. Alive. The exhilarating buzz that tingles through your head and heart until it consumes you.

I came up for a breath and pushed the sopping hair out of my face. It ran in sluices down my spine, cold locks that stuck to my skin the same way skin sticks to ice.

"Enjoying yourself?" The words came out of nowhere.

I jumped.

Signey sat on a boulder, white-blonde hair damp around her shoulders, a knife caught between her fingers. She twisted it, made the beveled edge wink.

And here I was, all of me, naked. Every inch exposed—the scars and ruddy skin. Shame coursed through me, hot and red. I pressed my arms against my chest and crouched.

Signey barred her teeth and tipped her chin toward the sky. "I followed you, you know. As soon as you left. Used reykr. Did you know I can hold for twenty-eight people at once?" Her thumb stroked the blade of the knife the same way one might stroke the cheek of a lover. "It wasn't hard to hold for you."

My heartbeat thudded through my hands. She could kill me, probably *would* kill me. Right here, right now. And I'd end up like Hans, only no one would find me because we were too far away from Karlsborn Castle, so I'd bloat and rot, be picked at by birds.

The wind howled, flattening the grass in giant sweeps. Water continued to drip down my back.

Signey flipped the knife between her fingers and grinned—actually grinned. Moonlight played off her lips, her teeth, made them white against the hollow of her mouth. "You know," she continued, "most men from House Rythja can't even hold for six. But me?"

She disappeared, a wreath of black, a rush of smoke and skin, sleet falling past a window. Then she materialized, another fall, another rush, this one crow feathers that squalled up from the ground like a flurry of bats. Blonde hair. Fur vest. Knife.

"Twenty-eight."

My toes had gone numb, and I pressed my arms tighter against my chest.

I needed to distract her, to get a head start. I'd be running into camp naked, but at least I'd be alive.

I inched my foot through the river thrush, feeling for a loose rock. I'd have to be quick. Pick it up and throw it.

Cold mud. Sand and grit, the flutey reeds of grass stems. A rush of water. And there… A rock. Pocked and heavy. I ran my toes across it, feeling its curves and edges. Big. It needed to be big. I nudged it. It rolled, the weight splashing my ankle.

Overhead, the stars glittered like a carpet, so bright, so hot.

I bit my lip, prepared to squat—

Then she was inches from my face, her lips peeled into a snarl. She shoved me, and I fell into the water with a slosh. My palms scraped the riverbed, my thigh banged a rock.

"I don't know who you are or why you're *watching* me, but if I catch you near my things again, I will carve out your heart and leave your body to rot." She leveled her knife. "Do you understand?"

Ice water poured around me. My heart pounded through my hands. My body screamed, *Run, run, run.*

Moonlight banded her cheeks, her teeth, and that's when I saw the cord nestled between her open tunic, falling between her breasts. The way into the metal box, the thing that I needed to steal.

Everything furled, fell away, and it was only me and Signey and the key.

She was wearing it.

Chapter Twenty-Three

HOT BLOOD TRICKLED DOWN the back of my thigh, pooling at my ankle as I limped back to camp.

Signey kept the key around her neck. *Of course,* she kept the key around her neck.

I should have felt some sort of panic, some sort of worry, should have felt the searing impossibility of the task ahead, but all I felt was numb. Numb head, numb heart.

If I catch you near my things again, I will carve out your heart and leave your body to rot.

She knew, of course she knew. And I *still* had to get the key, the box, the weapon. Or maybe I could just leave, pack my things, and run.

You pushed Hans away when he was alive. Are you turning your back on him in death, too?

Are you going to leave? That's what your father did.

I wanted to laugh. I wanted to cry. I wanted to curl into a ball and never unravel.

Who was I to go up against her? Who was I to go up against

them? Anyone—literally anyone—would have been better at this than me. Stefan. Katrina.

I peeled off my wet and dirty sweater and clawed through my bags, stockings and shirts, dove-gray and fleecy creams.

My knuckles knocked a bottle of lavender oil, blue glass and a stoppered top.

I will carve out your heart.

I hurled the bottle against the ground. It popped like a flower, a spray of glass and herbs and I shouldn't, I shouldn't, but I was already digging through my bag for another, and I was ruining my supplies, ruining my tent, but it felt good to break something and I didn't care.

Another pop, another spray, more glass, more herbs, more breaking. A vial of drawing oil, of rosewater, pieces glittering like diamonds. I wanted to use them, to press the point into my palm until blood welled, but I was over that—*over that*—and maybe if I could break *things,* then maybe I wouldn't break myself.

Chamomile. Comfrey.

Pop, spray.

I scraped through the bottom of the bag and my hand knocked the brown leather box embossed with the letters *HH.*

Hans.

Tears stung my cheeks and that thing, *that thing* tried to claw up my throat. I swallowed.

Two options—find the key or convince someone to tell me what was in the box. Two options, and I couldn't steal the key off Signey's neck.

Two options.

This wasn't about me.

This was about Hans.

I put the letter box back and grabbed my pouch of coffee grounds, took a moment to pull my hair into a high bun, dabbed my wrists in the puddle of lavender oil, tried to make myself *more, more, more.*

If Erik was going to make us invisible again, he'd appreciate the coffee. Maybe we could joke about what happened when he drank the grounds this morning. I'd win his trust, use my womanly wiles to woo him. *Easy.* It should be easy.

The camp had fallen into the swish of sleep, a quiet lull. Grass swayed and the last embers smoldered in the fire. A few moths flittered, wings silver in the starlight. His tent sat at the end of the row. I reached to pull back the flap, but—

"You have to sleep eventually." Kaspar, hard and angry.

I paused, my fingers skimming the waxy fabric.

"Why? I'm fine." Erik.

"You're running yourself ragged."

"So?"

"You can't keep doing it. You'll—"

"I'm fine." The words were harsh, meant to end the conversation.

A scrape, a huff. "What good did Sending do? They still found us."

"I hid us last night and for three-quarters of the day. They shouldn't have been able to follow."

I hadn't realized Erik had been doing that, but he'd ridden behind everyone today, skirting the edges of the group the way a sheep dog skirts the edges of its flock. He'd hardly said two words to anyone.

"Unless," Erik continued, "I'm dropping it again. Like with the ships."

"You can't keep beating yourself up about that. Lothgar shouldn't have pushed you that hard."

"That's no excuse."

"We're not meant to hold illusions for six days." Something scraped. "If you keep this up, you're going to be exhausted when it actually counts."

"I'll be fine."

"Erik, we're launching the attack as soon as we get back."

No, no, no. I pressed a hand to my stomach. Once the Volds attacked Larland, Larland's attention would be pulled away, a snag on a sweater and they'd be too busy defending their own shores. They wouldn't come to help us. There would be no victory, no cannons, no swans, no monuments built in Hans's name. He wouldn't matter.

You'll have failed him.

His death will be for nothing.

Pointless.

You pushed him away.

"We should go on the defensive," Kaspar continued. "Confront them. Kill them before they kill us."

"We stick to the original plan," Erik said.

"I don't like it."

"You don't have to like it."

"And Isabel?" Kaspar asked. "You want an update on her?"

A sigh. "What's she doing now?"

"Nothing bad. She came back from bathing and went straight to her tent. She seemed upset, so we didn't bother her."

"She hasn't left? No...wandering?"

"Not that I'm aware."

"Hmm. Okay." The scrape of blankets, the clink of glass.

"The thing that I can't figure out is why they picked her. If they're still sticking with the 'you need a guide' story, anyone—*literally anyone*—would have been better. She—"

"It's rude to eavesdrop." Signey's voice cut through the night. She reached around me and pulled the flap open.

Erik's head snapped up. Our eyes locked.

"Coffee," I said, thrusting the bag toward him the same moment Signey said, "I want her gone."

I turned and headed back to my tent. Screw them, screw this. Screw all of this because I couldn't, I couldn't, I—

"Isabel," Erik said, chasing after me. "Isa—" He grabbed my arm.

I rounded on him. "What?"

He blinked. Moonlight edged his features, his high cheekbones, his angular jaw, and there was last night on the bluffs and this morning getting coffee. It glinted in his eyes. *I see you, I see you.*

He scraped a hand through his hair. "I'm sorry. I didn't think—"

"You didn't think what? That I knew you didn't want me here? Well, guess what? I don't want to be here, either."

The words cut like a knife, quick and scalding, and I should stop, should go back to my tent, but I was cold and wet and sick of this—sick of them, sick of being that wraith who hovered and hovered and hovered, and they were right: I was a terrible guide, and they were going to attack Larland, and I was running out of time and—

"And you're right," I continued. "They could have sent someone better. But do you know why they sent me?"

No response. Of course not.

"Because they didn't need two apprentice physicians, and *Stefan is better at managing the king.*" I let the words linger along with everything else: *I am expendable, I am small, I am no one.*

Grass shivered, the silhouettes of wildflowers bending and bowing. Clouds hung like razors in the sky.

I stalked into my tent and sank onto my bedroll, my hair wet, my forehead on my knees. Broken glass glittered and shaking. I was shaking.

It didn't matter.

That night, when the nightmares came, I gritted my teeth and lived through them, sand flies and splashing water, the press of his chest beneath my palms.

Pump, pump, wait.

I woke, sweaty and sobbing, and watched the silhouettes of rain drip down the canvas of my tent.

Chapter Twenty-Four

THE NEXT MORNING, I FOUND A MAP.

It sat in the dew-coated grasses outside the door to my tent, a brittle parchment tied with a blue ribbon. I picked it off the ground and unrolled it, the paper thick and soft, the coastline painted with faded greens and muted blues, the sea speckled gray like a fulmar egg with marked points, not stones, but pen and ink—Cobble Cove, North Beach, the farthest point of Saeby…

Erik sat around the campfire, a cup of tea by his hip, his gaze tipped to the pearly sunrise. His fingers tugged at the two beads braided on the cord around his neck almost as if he was nervous.

I dropped the map into his lap.

His eyes flicked up.

"It's a better route," I explained. "One that will help us lose whoever is following us."

And one that would take us through Esbern.

ESBERN WAS A TINY TOWN that teetered on the edge of the metallic sea. Houses lined the streets, steep A-frames and stone siding painted in shades of thistle, beet, and blue. A few seabirds wheeled and chirped, their bodies slicked with sea mist. Whaling ships drove in and out of the harbor, sails snapping.

Erik had sent most his men west, hoping to throw off whoever was following us, and opting to take a tighter group for the rest of the scouting trip. Bengt and his friends were in the decoy group, so was Tyr.

"We'll stay one night in the city," I said, hitching my dress to jump over a puddle. Rainwater pooled between the speckled beach stones and ran, shimmering, through gardens of rhubarb and wild thyme. "Leave in the morning."

After getting the Volds settled, I needed to find the post office and pick up the minister's letter, but I didn't have any information to send to him, and this would be my only chance before we returned to the castle.

So, I had until the end of the day to get the key off Signey's neck and look in the box.

No pressure.

A few whalers sat on a low retaining wall, puffing pipes and feeding cats scraps of salty fish. A woman carried a stack of hatboxes through the street. Laundresses. Fisherman. Merchants. A dozen others dressed in thick wool sweaters and knitted caps.

Erik had only kept five of us—himself, Kaspar, Bo, Signey, and me—but even with the smaller number, we were drawing stares.

"This is fine," I said, grabbing the handle of the inn and pushing myself inside.

A soft bell tinkled.

Paintings decorated the walls—an austere woman, a pair of sheep, a red-gold sunset in a driftwood frame. A book lay overturned on a chair with a curly goatskin throw, and a cup of cold tea sat on a narrow side table, the porcelain stained a dark shade of brown.

The Volds shifted behind me, out of place in their rough canvas and thick cottons.

"Hello?" I called.

A woman brushed around the corner, slight and swanlike, a mountain of linens in her arms. Her blonde hair fell in ringlets down her back. "Sorry about that," she said, easing the linens stack onto the ground behind the desk. "Now what can—" She blinked once, blinked again. A smile cracked across her face. "Isy Moller, is that you?"

Now it was my turn to blink. Delicate, slender, a dapple of freckles across her nose. Her orchid-purple sweater brought out the pink in her cheeks, a color that usually came from standing on windy bluffs and running through grassy meadows, but it sat so naturally on her. It had *always* sat so naturally on her.

Helene.

Helene who'd worked in laundry with Katrina, who'd dangled boys off her arm like bracelets, who'd traded kisses like secrets. Helene who'd quit her job six months ago and went home to care for her sick grandmother.

Home to Esbern. Home to here.

"It's good to see you," she said, pulling me into a hug, the gesture so warm, so alien because we weren't friends. We'd never been friends.

I squirmed away.

"You're here for rooms?"

Erik nodded.

"We're pretty full right now." She squinted at the Volds as if trying to place them. "The Merchant's Market is this weekend. They're setting up on the docks."

"The Merchant's Market?" Erik asked.

"Shopkeepers come from all over the Sanokes to buy inventory for the year." She withdrew a brown notebook and ran a slender finger down the ledger. "We have…two rooms. You can stay here if you're okay sharing."

Sharing. Which meant—

"We're not sharing," Signey hissed. She must have had the same thought. We were the only two girls. If we had to share—

Her thumb circled the hilt of her knife.

I will carve out your heart and leave your body to rot.

"We might check another inn," I said.

Helene closed the ledger book. "Wayfarer's full. Driftwood might have space, but they look over a fish market. It has a smell."

Signey's thumb fell from the knife. "I don't mind a smell. Everything has a bit of a smell."

Erik reached for his coin pouch. "We'll stay here. All of us." The way he said it, maybe he'd decided to stay here *because* Signey didn't want to.

Kaspar grinned. "It's one night, Sig."

She ground her teeth. "Signey."

Our room was narrow and small, containing only a medium-sized bed, a tarnished looking glass and a tufted chair angled toward the window. A yellow stain bloomed over the ceiling.

Signey set her bag on the bed. "I assume you'll be sleeping on the floor?" When I didn't respond, she gave me a hard look. "Let's ignore each other."

"Fine with me."

"But I get the bed."

I slung my pack onto the ground by the armchair and tried not to stare at the little snip of leather cording popping out from under Signey's collar. I could use søven to knock her out, but she'd remember when she woke up. There wasn't really a subtle way to søven someone. So, that plan was out. I could see if she'd take another bath…

Signey's lip curled into a sneer. "What are you looking at?"

My heart leapt into my throat. "Nothing. I'll, um, check if Helene has an extra sleeping mat." I pulled the door open and was grabbed by a flurry of orchid-purple and blonde curls.

"What are you—"

"Shh."

Helene's hand clamped over my mouth. She dragged me down the hall and into a bedroom at the top of the stairs.

The door clicked. Dim sunlight filtered through mauve curtains, illuminating a four-poster bed and rosy pink wallpaper painted with strawberries and duck eggs.

This must be Helene's room.

No. The sweet stink of sickness, the open jars by the bed, the old woman laying in a tangle of blankets, feathered lips ajar, chest rising and falling, rising and falling. Helene's grandmother looked so much like Queen Margarethe with her crop of white hair and the lacy nightgown that went all the way to her neck.

Dying. Helene's grandmother was dying.

"Have you been giving her dandelion root?" I asked. "White willow?"

Helene stepped in front of the woman. Her eyes burned fever bright. "Who are they?"

"The Volds?"

"They're Vo—" She grabbed my arm and glanced at her sleeping grandmother. "They can't be Volds. I mean, I'd heard rumors, but I didn't think—" She scrubbed a hand over her face. "Volgaard has been closed for hundreds of years."

"I know."

"They cut out our ambassador's heart."

"I know."

"Sent it back stuffed in his mouth."

"I know."

She glanced over her shoulder again as if Erik and the others might come through the door. "What are they doing here?"

My heart skipped a beat. Helene and I had never been close, but Hans was dead, and Katrina and I were fighting, and Stefan was Stefan, a brother and a rival. So, I sank onto the corner of her dying grandmother's bed and told her everything. Hans's murder, Larland's letters, the search for the weapon.

I'd meant to keep it short, keep it sweet, to keep it muted like spring's pastel colors, but once I started, the words spilled the same way water rushes from a broken damn.

I reached for the washcloth and the basin, the water frigid against my hands, and damped sweat away from her sleeping grandmother's brow. This felt natural too, the rhythm of it strong and familiar, like a lifeline or a heartbeat.

Helene listened as I told her about the magic, the illusions, and Signey's small, black box.

When I finished, she wiped her palms on her skirts. "So let me get this straight. You took the Volds through Esbern, hoping you'd have some sort of information to send the minister. This is your one shot to send something, but you don't know what's in the mystery box and you don't have any other clues about the weapon. Do you know what they're scouting for?"

"Three locations," I said. "All coastal. But I don't know beyond that."

She took the rag and scrubbed her grandma's skin like a washboard. "So, you need information," she continued. "We should figure out why the Volds are scouting those particular locations. You also need to figure out what's in this box."

"Correct."

"You don't know how you're going to do any of this."

"Also correct."

She straightened, her eyes brightening. "Well, Isy Moller, you're in luck. I have a plan."

Chapter Twenty-Five

I POUNDED ON THE DOOR to the boys' room. Waited. Then pounded again. *Come on. Open up.* Another pound. Another wait. Bits of dust drifted from the rafters, silhouetted like gnats.

No answer.

Their voices carried through the wood, muddled and deep. I pressed my ear against it. A grind. A creak. The bed? Orange light dipped into the hallway in a burnished glow, leaving everything black and fuzzy.

Oh, come on. I knew they were in there.

"I can hear you," I shouted. This was bold. This was reckless, but Helene's plan—our plan—would fall apart if I couldn't get Signey out of her room.

And there was only one way to get Signey out of her room.

"Hello?" I called, pounding again.

A scrape. A click. The lock. The door swung open to reveal Erik. Shirtless. "What?" he snapped.

His hair was wet, curling at his temples. A few stray droplets clung to his lips, his lashes as if he'd just been washing his face. A tattoo spiraled down his chiseled chest, a falling crow and a great black snake that twisted once around his navel and disappeared into the waistband of his—

"Isabel?"

Oh wow.

"*Isabel!*"

"Yeah?"

"My face is up here."

"So it is." The words were a squeak. "But I'm, um…admiring the paint. In the room. It's very white." I couldn't meet his eyes.

He cocked a brow. "Was that the only thing you were admiring?"

My cheeks heated.

Behind him, Bo and Kaspar snickered.

"Pay up," Kaspar said.

Bo rolled his eyes. "This doesn't count."

"It definitely counts."

Erik leaned his arm on the doorframe, blocking them from view. "What do you want?" The tattoo twisted, the snake's body rippling over his lower abdomen, so toned you could probably use it to cut glass.

Don't look at it. Don't look at it. "Helene offered to show us the Merchant's Market."

I snuck a glance.

He smirked and went to shut the door. "No thanks."

I caught it with my foot. "It only happens once a year."

"I think we're fine." He glared at my foot. "Move that."

"Make me."

"Guys?" Bo called.

Erik glanced up, blond hair falling over his forehead, a single

201

lock curling just above his brow. His chest heaved and his eyes went feral. "And how, Isabel Moller, would you suggest I do that?"

From outside, the rattle of wheels over cobblestones, the clop of hooves, singing.

His voice dropped to a husky murmur. "I could make sure you had a good view of my tattoo. I know you like it."

The heat rushed straight to my core and we were so close, and he was staring at me with those scary, feral eyes and—

Bo popped his head above Erik's arm. "So, um…hello. Sorry to interrupt, but I actually want to see the Merchant's Market."

I peered around Erik, who started cackling like an idiot. "Great," I said. "We leave in fifteen minutes."

I tromped back to the room I shared with Signey and attempted to purge the image of a shirtless Erik from my brain. I needed to stick to the plan.

No distractions.

No tattoo.

Okay, it was a very nice tattoo.

Stop. Focus.

Signey was laying belly down on the bed, her arms dangling off the edge, tossing a knife over and over into the wooden floorboards. She'd thrown open the window, letting in the scents of chimney smoke and rain.

I hauled my bag onto the chair and began pulling out clothes—sweaters, skirts, a thin gray cardigan. I shrugged the cardigan on. Gloves. A knitted cap. I pulled those on, too. A fleecy scarf the color of tender lavender.

Waves and rain filled the silence.

I hadn't been around Erik and his group for very long, but hopefully, I'd read the dynamic right. And maybe the cardigan, the scarf, the gloves and the cap were too much, but I needed Signey to notice I was leaving. I needed her to ask—

"Where are you going?"

I flipped open a container of lip tint I'd borrowed from Helene, a rich berry red, and tugged off a glove. "The Merchant's Market."

She pushed herself higher, her expression taut. "By yourself?" The unasked question hovered in her voice.

"Everyone else is coming, too." *Hopefully.* "Helene offered to show us around."

"Oh."

I waited for more, but Signey said nothing.

Maybe I'd misread her; maybe she didn't care about being left behind. After all, she seemed content to sit apart from the men, but I'd seen the furtive glances she gave them, saw the way she hovered at the edges of the group. And if the morning of our departure had been anything to go by…

I patted the creamy tint over my lips and hazarded a glance.

Her hands had stilled. The corners of her mouth quivered and she looked, for a moment, like a child who'd been left hiding.

Before she could give too much away, she schooled her features, the frown replaced with her easy, cat-like confidence. "I guess we're going shopping."

Fifteen minutes later, we met the others at the bottom of the stairs—Erik, Kaspar, Bo, and Helene.

Helene had changed into an oversized cardigan and a cream shift, her loose curls shoved under a knitted cap. "Well," she said, her cheeks rosy. "Shall we go?"

Houses reflected against dark waters and the air hung thick with the scent of sugar cakes and fried fish. Lanterns knocked hollow, their light glinting off merchants' tables. They'd set their wares under a crisscross of tents—oil lamps and clay birds, chippy glassware and adventure novels with thick covers and gold-painted edges. Rain poured.

"You stand out like a gannet in a flock of guillemots," Helene said, threading her arm through mine. Her nose had gone pink from the cold, her eyes bright from the wind. Then lower, she added, "Relax. I'll take care of them."

Kaspar was two tables away, watching a demonstration on throwing knives, but the rest were close, their hands in their pockets, shoulders pulled up against the bump and jostle of the crowd.

The corner of Helene's mouth tugged into a frown. "Not big shoppers, are they?"

"Apparently not."

"Ooh, that's a pretty necklace." She picked up a velvet ribbon with a single black pearl dangling from the end. "Do you think this will work?"

But before I could answer, Helene dropped her grip on my arm. "Hey, Sig." The necklace dangled from her hand. "I think this would look amazing on you."

Erik's eyes flicked up. He'd stopped the next booth over, two fingers resting on the hilt of a ruby-studded knife.

Signey shook her head. "I don't want—"

Helene broke away from the table and looped her arm around Signey's, the gesture all kindness and warmth. She planted Signey in front of the merchant's looking glass and held the necklace against her collarbone. "Humor me," she said.

Signey did.

Maybe I shouldn't be surprised that it worked because this part had been Helene's idea, but Signey pulled back her hair, pressed it into a bun at the nape of her neck, and tilted her head so Helene could clasp the dainty silver necklace.

"This is ruining the effect," Helene said, pulling at the leather cord that held the key. "Take it off. Here. I'll help you."

Helene handed me the cord and I was ready with the bar of unscented soap, had been warming it in my hands until the lye became soft. I pressed the key hard enough to leave an impression and—

A sudden warmth snuffed the wind's chill. "Signey has never been one for trinkets," Erik said.

I jumped, nearly dropping the key.

He shrugged. "She looks good." He shot me a glance as if we were in on some sort of secret, the two of us against the rest of the world.

Helene's hand opened and closed behind her. *The key.*

"Yes," I said, edging away from him, toward Helene. I slipped Helene the cord, who handed it back to Signey.

"I think you should buy the necklace," Helene announced.

"She's not buying the necklace," Erik murmured.

Signey dropped the ribbon back onto the table. The corner of her mouth quirked. "No."

Helene fished in her pack. "Then I'll buy it for you." She pulled out a faded floral purse. "It's criminal to look so good in something and *not* buy it."

As the shopkeeper wrapped Signey's necklace in tissue paper, Helene nudged my ribs. *You got it?* her green eyes seemed to ask.

I dropped my chin into my scarf. A slight nod.

A smile broke out across her face, whole and genuine. Maybe we could have been friends back at Karlsborn Castle.

Helene handed Signey her necklace, and we found the others. "There's dancing and arm wrestling at the end of the pier," she said.

This was the plan. After getting the mold of the key, we'd all go to dancing and drinking. Helene would keep them busy while I'd find her cousin, the blacksmith who was running a tent that sold horseshoes and metal flowers. She thought if I mentioned her name and explained the situation, he'd leave his apprentice in charge of the booth and help me make a key.

Erik fiddled with the sleeve of his jacket. "Hey, Isabel, I wanted to—"

"Come on." Helene hooked her arm through Erik's and pulled him through the jostling crowd. Her cream sweater vanished into the swirl of gray.

I shouldn't, I shouldn't…but I stretched on my tiptoes and there were the tops of their heads, his blond hair, her knitted cap. They bobbed through the sea of brown and black and red.

Helene was helping with the plan. Distracting the Volds was part of the plan. It shouldn't matter how she did it. So…why did I want Erik to pull away?

They stopped beside a vendor selling candied nuts, wax-paper wrapped almonds so roasty and sweet, and he glanced back, his eyes skimming the crowd until they found mine. His gaze went curious.

I see you, I see you. The snap of smoke and feathery grasses, and we were back at the morning after we'd done the screaming thing, just the two of us.

My heart kicked.

"You coming?" Bo asked.

I dropped back to my heels. Erik and Helene disappeared from view. "Yeah. Of course."

The rest of us trudged behind them, the rain giving the world a soft, watercolor-like focus. Bonfires had been lit every few feet, puffing smoke toward the sky, dancing gold along the glass of the shops pushed right against the waterway.

We reached the end of the peer where a troupe of fiddlers played on a pile of overturned crates. Around them, couples danced.

Up ahead, Helene dropped Erik's arm and hurried back to us. She pulled me into the crush of the crowd.

"He said they're scouting for a place to launch ships," she said, a little breathless. Raindrops beaded along the knitting of her hat.

"Interesting." But it made sense considering Erik's map and the handfuls of rocks scattered up the coast. "Erik was practicing hiding ships," I said. "I wonder if those things are connected."

"Ooh! Okay. I'll see what else I can get."

She pulled Erik into the middle of the dance floor, under the paper lanterns, beneath the garlands of marigold and daisies that crisscrossed between rooftops.

She said something and he smiled—a real smile—pulling out a dimple I hadn't even known was there.

She made it look easy, so easy, standing in her loose shift, her curls tumbling out from under her cap. She was wild and giddy, delicate as dandelion fluff, and yet she seemed to have gotten closer to Erik in five minutes than I had in five days, she with her wide-set eyes and graceful bones.

Another twist of my stomach. I leaned my forearms against

the harbor wall, the rock still gritty and damp. The rain had cleared to a drizzle and lantern light shone off the flagstones in halos, glossy puddles that swirled in shades of honey, spun gold, and sand. Beside me, a whaler puffed a pipe, heavy smoke coiling toward the sky.

"You should be out there dancing," he said.

"I don't dance."

"Sure you do."

I didn't. I had two left feet and I always ended up trying to lead.

The fiddlers dropped to a slow song, an old song, a lullaby. The chilly breeze ruffled the flower garlands, knocked them against the hollow lanterns like a pair of hands ruffling the sheets in a notebook. Somewhere to my left, Bo listened rapt to a storyteller. Signey sat in the bar across the street. Rainwater and window glass ribboned her silhouette, drew it out long and soft, but I could see her in there, white-blonde hair falling loose around her shoulders, a pint of something in her hand.

I should find Helene's cousin, should use this opportunity to look in the box.

And yet...

Helene turned back to Erik, a wide grin on her face, her cheeks red and rosy from the rain. She offered him her a hand.

He took it, pulled her onto the dance floor, spun her once, a swish of coral and cream. She beamed up at him, and he down at her. Would she ask him about the weapon? Would he tell?

It shouldn't matter how we got the information, it shouldn't.

And I shouldn't be jealous, I shouldn't.

Erik was an enemy, an invader, and for all I knew, he could have been involved in Hans's death, but the act stirred something within me and I couldn't look away—*didn't want* to look away—from the fairy tale unfolding in front of me.

"Aalto's star is shining bright tonight," the whaler said, exhaling a puff of smoke. "Means Vega hasn't found him yet. It's bad luck."

"I seem to be," I replied.

Helene leaned up and kissed Erik, a soft, swift peck on the lips. He startled, then stilled, his hand sliding up her back, bunching the creamy cotton of her dress.

My throat thickened and I was a gargoyle, a troll, a gnarled, ugly thing, all hands and bones and teeth, and it didn't matter that information came so easily to her, and it didn't matter that he was kissing her, that her laugh eased away the rain. She was searching for things we needed to know, and it didn't matter, didn't matter, didn't—

The fiddlers continued to play, their song streaming out a fresh melody of notes. Amber light danced off the flagstones, the world sheeny and bright.

Helene pulled away, spun Erik so he faced the opposite direction. She raked a hand through the back of his wheat-blond hair and pulled his face into her neck. She scanned the crowd, found me.

"Go," she mouthed.

I shoved my hands into my pockets and slipped away.

Chapter Twenty-Six

I PULLED OPEN THE DOOR to our room at Rose & Thistle Inn, half expecting to find Signey splashing her face in the washbasin or rummaging through her packs or lounging on the bed in the long undershirt and leggings she wore to sleep.

Instead, the room was empty and still. She'd left the windows open, the air turned bitter and cold. A faint smattering of starlight cast everything in shades of white and gray, despite the golden lights that twinkled in the distance. The notes of a fiddle twisted in the wind.

It could have been the song that played earlier when Helene pulled Erik onto the dance floor, when she wrapped her arms around his neck, when she kissed him…

I pressed the heel of my palm against my eye. The kiss didn't matter. Erik could kiss whomever he wanted, and I shouldn't care. I shouldn't care about the way he ran his hand up her back or the way she tangled her fingers through his wheat-blond hair or the way they seemed to fit together so perfectly. None of that mattered. It *didn't*. I should focus on the task at hand—open the box, steal the weapon, then leave.

Open. Steal. Leave.

Helene's cousin had indeed been willing to help, a burly man with heavy arms and a heavy gaze. It had taken him nearly two hours to heat his forge, another half hour to smelt the iron, pour the key, file the flashings so the finished product would fit in the lock.

Two and a half hours filled with the hiss of bellows, the strike of anvil against metal. Two and a half hours of Helene entertaining Signey and the others at the Merchant's Market.

They should have been back by now.

Except they weren't.

Aalto's star is shining bright, the whaler had said. *Means Vega hasn't found him. It's bad luck.*

But maybe luck was on my side after all.

I pulled the laces on Signey's packs one by one, searched through the folds of fur and fabric until I found the box, the black metal stamped with the lattice of knots and falling crows. I smoothed my thumb over the keyhole.

Bad luck.

A sailor's superstition.

I pressed the key into the lock. It fit like a hand sliding into a glove. The lock snicked and I lifted the lid to reveal a smaller box wrapped in a dish cloth.

Interesting. A box in a box.

I let the dish cloth fall away, the smaller box painted linen nailed to wood, whirls of rosettes and heath-spotted orchids rendered in chippy, abstract pinks, and I knew—*knew*—with a sudden sense of immutable certainty that I was holding something old, something ancient. My blood buzzed, a hum that vibrated from the top of my head down to my feet.

Love me, it said. *Use me.*

A call, a pull, and I never wanted to let it go.

I flipped the lid open, the latch a flimsy metal thing and prepared to face whatever was in there, but the box was empty, only padded linen and a tab pull where a board in the lid could detach to reveal a mirror.

I removed the tab, the top sliding away to reveal my reflection—dark hair, high cheekbones, narrow chin.

Love me. The call a scrape on my senses. *Use me.*

I touched my cheek. A jewelry box. An ordinary jewelry box. Why—

Outside, a *thud* and a *thunk*. The door swung open and Signey stumbled in, her hand braced against the doorframe, locks of white-blonde hair falling from her braid.

I stuffed a pillow over both boxes and leaned forward on the bed. *Her* bed. Which meant she could shove me off at any minute, move the pillow, find the boxes. I inched my hand under the pillow, the quilt rough against my palm. Maybe I could slip everything—the metal chest, the jewelry box, the tabbed insert—into my bag…

"*Wait, wait, wait.*" Signey swayed, her nails biting the wood. Dark blood dribbled from her nose, crusting in a blackish ring above her upper lip. Her clothes reeked of salt and stomach acid. "Do you hear it?"

Beneath the pillow, my fingertips skimmed the edge of the tabbed insert, the cold rim of the box. "Hear what?" The bag was too far away.

"Honor beads."

"Honor, what?"

"*Shh.* I have," she frowned at her fingers, "I have… *Waitwait…* I have one."

"Have you been drinking?"

"Drinking." She hiccuped. Her teeth were stained purple, lips swollen. "But I don'tgit drunk."

Okay. New plan. Move everything into my pocket and fix the jewelry box in the hall. Then I'd return the black box and all its contents to Signey's bag when she was asleep.

Good plan.

I eyed her. Kohl smudged her left eye, blood flaked her chin. She'd probably pass out with her boots on. But was she drunk enough to miss the rattle of the lid when I pulled the box out from under the pillow? Or would she hear that? And if she asked, how would I explain what I was doing?

I will carve out your heart. She was drunk, maybe, but she wasn't stupid.

Signey tugged at one of her white-blonde locks falling loose just above her shoulder. "I braid it into my hair… leke dis." Another frown.

I needed to mask the rattle of the lid when I scooted it from under the pillow. And beads. I closed my eyes. "Erik has beads, too. On his necklace."

Scrape, rattle. I scooted the box into the folds of my skirt.

Signey pushed the door closed and stumbled into the room, the stench of her growing stronger. Cold wind pricked the back of my arms, blew in from the open window. "Don't talk about Erik, nnkay? Erik'snot important."

I pushed myself off the bed, the metal chest clanking. A wince, a pause. She apparently hadn't heard it, staring slack-faced at her lock of hair and the single bead braided there.

The metal chest rattled as I moved across the room. My pocket bulged, the fabric pulling open like a maw to reveal the glossy lid. She'd see it right away if she were sober. She might *still* see it if I wasn't fast.

Keep her talking. Deep breaths. Steady hands. Hands. Hans. Hans dead. And now I was stealing from the woman who killed him. Another breath. Just keep her talking. "Erik's not important, hmm?"

I expected her to make some sort of retort, but Signey's expression slacked and she stood there, a lost child, a wayward daughter, her eyes red-rimmed and deep set, hands loose at her sides.

Because no. Erik was the general's son, his second. And Signey...what did that make her?

Are we not enough for you?

"I have to go," I said, grabbing my bag and letting myself out.

MOONLIGHT PUDDLED AT THE END OF THE HALL, bright and silver, glinting off white walls and wood beams. The faint scents of lavender and beeswax filled the air and—

Erik.

He sat on the ground outside his door, chin tipped toward the ceiling, lips parted, chest rising and falling, rising and falling. He'd shucked off his jacket and it lay discarded next to him. A package sat by his hip, a box the length of my forearm, wrapped with brown paper, tied with a ribbon.

I angled my bag away from him and slipped the box inside. "Where's Helene?"

"Gone." The beginnings of a bruise reddened his cheek.

"You drunk, too?"

"Not drunk. Just…tired." The answer was soft, a little husky. "I think Helene's downstairs."

"Thanks." I stepped around his outstretched legs. I'd have to ask Helene what had given Signey a bloody nose and Erik that bruise.

"Wait," Erik said, the word no more than a rasp. The top buttons on his shirt were open, his throat bare against the white fabric. His chest continued to rise and fall. "Is Signey in there?"

"Yes."

"She doing okay?"

"She'll be fine."

He nodded, his eyes fluttering closed.

"Did the two of you…?"

"Someone said he didn't like her hair, and I kept her from ripping out his throat. The present is for you."

My heart kicked. "For me?"

"Try not to sound so excited."

I edged closer to the box, waiting for it to explode or crumple to dust or spring at my face like a snake.

It didn't.

I lifted the lid. A knife sat nestled against a bed of creamy silk, the hilt a polished wood, whorled the deepest red and burnt-honey brown. It reflected the light.

I wanted to reach out to touch it, to trace my thumb along the knots, to feel the smoothness of the handle.

I snapped the lid shut. "I have a knife."

"Stop lying, Isabel. You're not good at it."

"Why'd you buy this?"

He shrugged, one-shouldered, kept his face toward the ceiling.

And maybe that should have been the end. Maybe I should

215

have found Helene and told her about the jewelry box, but there was something else—

"Why did you give me the map?" The question left my lips, whole and formed. I hadn't been planning on asking, but…hadn't I wondered?

Gray noise and light scudded against the window glass.

"You seemed unhappy. I know…what it's like to be unhappy." He was watching me, his head turned just enough that the glint of his eye shone through the darkness.

My mind crawled back to that night, the fear, the anger, the feelings that threatened to eat and eat and eat me whole. "I was fine."

"If you say."

There. Another opportunity to leave. Another opportunity to find Helene and show her the box. But there was another question tugging at the back of my brain, and I wanted to know… "Why'd you become your father's Second?" *Why did he pick you over Signey?*

He knocked his head back and gave a dry laugh. "So many personal questions."

"Most people like to talk about themselves. I'm surprised you don't."

"It's not that. It's just, no one's ever—" He rubbed a thumb over his palm. "Never mind."

"Do you want me to stop?"

A beat, a pause, a wait for a breath.

"No." The word was so soft, I almost missed it, but behind it, an ache, a longing, a wave so strong it nearly swept me under.

You are valuable for one thing.

Oh yeah, keep that up. That's the only thing you're good at.

He's better at reykr than Signey. Better than everyone.

What would it be like to be so good at something that it's all people could see?

I see you, I wanted to say. *I see all of you.*

"Okay." I slid against the wall opposite him. We faced each other. Our legs touched. "What's your favorite color?"

A faint smile pulled at his lip. "Blue."

"Your favorite food?"

"Honey."

"Sweet tooth, huh?"

The smile deepened, bringing out the dimple. "Mmm, maybe."

"If your favorite food is honey—*straight honey*—then you definitely have a sweet tooth. Your favorite season?"

"Summer."

"Why?"

"Why what?"

"Why summer?"

He laughed, light and beautiful, and there was something so shy about it. "Because there's no snow. In Volgaard, every other season has snow."

"What's wrong with snow?"

"What *isn't* wrong with snow?"

"You like warm, sweet things. Remind me to introduce you to cinnamon buns."

"I don't know who cinnamon bun is, but I would love to meet her."

"Who's your hero?"

He thought for a moment. "Baldar Landvik. Ancient explorer. House Skall."

"Your favorite animal?"

"Puffins."

"*Puffins?* I thought you'd say wolves or bears or something scary."

"Puffins do a courtship dance when they reunite with their spouse. It's cute."

"Puffins don't get married."

Erik flashed a grin. "They mate for life, and that's better. It's true they separate for a few months out of the year to fish and feed, but they always find their way back to each other. And then they dance."

"Okay, fine. That is adorable." I adjusted my legs. "What about the silliest thing you can imagine?"

"Hair on a seagull."

"Didn't Kaspar show that to Signey?"

In response, a seagull flitted down from the rafters, a full head of dark brown hair and bangs—

Wait.

That hair.

My hair.

Erik watched me, his eyes bright, shoulders shaking.

"You're ridiculous," I said, kicking him with my boot. "Just as bad as your men."

"I'm worse," he said between laughs. "Way worse."

I kicked him again. "Alright, next question. If you could change anything about yourself?"

The seagull collapsed in a stream of smoke.

Erik rubbed his hand. "You...wanted to know why Lothgar picked me to become his Second?"

"Yeah."

He uncurled his fist. A pony sat in his palm, its body white as the waves, its tail trailing mist. This time there was no revelry in it, no joy.

The pony collapsed into itself, and the mist slipped between his fingers.

Reykr. Of course.

"Why'd you become an apprentice physician?" His gray eyes were watching me now, his cheek angled so that moonlight slatted half his face.

"My father. I…always imagined I'd apprentice under him."

"He missed out. You have a gift."

Something thick rose in the back of my throat and I swallowed. "You don't know what it means. To hear that."

"It means you're going to beat Stefan."

"I forgot I told you about that."

The corner of his lip quirked. "You screamed it. Right after you screamed you'd peed—"

"Ahh, okay." I shoved my hand over his mouth. "We don't repeat secrets outside of the screaming thing."

He smiled against my palm, full and slow.

Again, I realized how close we were, my hand over his mouth, his fingers splayed beside my knee. His nubbed one curled against the fabric of my skirt, almost as if he'd tucked it there to keep it safe.

I pulled my hand away and there was his dimple, his lips…

The smile fell, replaced by a pinch of the brows, a question. His breath hitched.

Below, a bell tinkled, and a man's voice filtered up from the floorboards.

Erik sighed and tipped his head toward the ceiling. "You should get some sleep."

I wouldn't get much sleep. I needed to return the box, then wake up early to mail the letter. But I didn't say that. Instead, I stood and said, "Goodnight, Erik."

A pause so long I wondered if he'd heard it. Then—

"Goodnight, Isabel."

Chapter Twenty-Seven

GRAY-GREEN WATER SLAPPED against the crumbling retaining wall that separated the city from the sea. Seaweed and trash swished in the eddies, and from somewhere, a bell tolled.

I shut the door to the Rose & Thistle Inn with a gentle *thud* and set out into the morning, the letter to the minister already in my pocket.

They're scouting for a place to launch ships. Also, Erik was hiding ships on the journey to the Sanokes. Maybe some sort of naval attack? This means the weapon must either be effective at a distance—cannons, maybe?— or small enough to carry ashore.

It wasn't enough, but it had to be. The Volds were attacking as soon as we came back, and we were running out of time. Maybe the minister could puzzle it together with something else they'd found.

I'd sketched the jewelry box on the other side, the rosettes and heath orchids, the little tabbed insert for the mirror.

I'm not sure what this is, but they have it locked in another box.

A seabird looped overhead. Reflections of shops rippled in the waterway, blackberry, cornflower, lobelia. A dress shop, a flower shop, a church. The post station should be just up ahead past the pub, and there it was, a steep-A frame roof, the word *POST* painted in black letters.

I gathered my skirts, trudged across the street, and tried the handle. Locked.

I cupped my hand to the window and tried to peer through the glass. The room warped and bowed, softened from the rain. A seabird skeleton perched on the counter, rows of parcel shelves lined the wall.

I'd heard somewhere that you could slip a message and a coin under the door and the postmaster would mail it for you but…I wanted to pick up the minister's letter to me.

I rasped on the glass. "Hello?"

No answer, no movement. The inside remained silent and still.

I rasped again. "Hello?"

Nothing.

I took a step into the street and peered at the upper windows, black and dark. Sometimes the shopkeepers lived in little apartments above their stores. It was possible that he was up there.

I picked a pebble and tossed it at the windows. It *plinked* against the glass and fell back into the dirt.

A light flared. Wood scraped against glass.

A man poked his head outside, a beard shadowing his jaw, a nightcap crammed on his head. "What the hell are you doing?"

I held up the letter and forced a smile.

THE POSTMASTER SCRATCHED SOMETHING in his ledger book. "Name?"

"Isabel Moller."

"Parcel or letter?"

"Just the letter."

He jotted the note, his strokes thick and curt. He had the set of a gremlin, thick brows that furrowed over his face and a mouth pinched into a scowl. The lamp reflected the bald spot on his scalp, creating a soft halo on the top of his head.

I glanced at the counter. A single piece of dust quivered.

Would the minister tell me if they'd found anything?

"Where to?"

My head snapped up. "Oh…um. Karlsborn Castle."

"Pigeon or coach?"

"Which is faster?"

He set the pen down. "You know you could slip the letter under the door."

"I wanted to see if you had anything for me."

He shuffled toward the card shelves in the back of the room. "Or at least have the decency to wait until we're open. You said Isabel Moller?"

"Or Isy."

He removed two envelopes and slid them across the counter.

I tore open the first, expecting to find the minister of trade's seal—two scales and a rose compass. Instead, my eyes found Stefan's familiar hand.

Dated three days ago—

I hope you have good news for me, because I don't have any for you. More Vold ships showed up the day after you left, dozens of them. They have an army now.

But that's not the worst of it.

The minister of trade. He's dead.

A lump rose in the back of my throat. I forced myself to keep reading.

They called me to check the body, and there was blood everywhere—the floors, the ceiling. They stuck a letter opener through his eye, cut off his hand and stuffed it in his mouth. It was not a kind death. ~~I wish~~ I'm glad you weren't here to see it.

Stefan.

The minister of trade, dead. For a moment, I could see it. Blood painting the walls, the ceiling, glittering red like cherries, reflecting the room, reflecting his dismembered body. I wrapped my arms around myself and tried to breathe because—

Murder.

He'd been murdered.

We hadn't been close, but the minister had been a good person—one who liked honey wine and raisins and always wore blue. Now he was dead. What did this mean for Stefan? What did this mean for me?

I tore open the second letter.

Dated yesterday—

King Christian and Queen Margarethe have been placed under arrest. Queen Margarethe is in her rooms (they couldn't get her out of bed), and King Christian in the dungeons. The Vold king arrived on yet another fleet of ships and declared the Sanok Isles a territory of Volgaard. He says he owns us now, that he can do with us what he pleases.

And, Isy, I'm worried about our king. He's getting worse. I'm told he spent most of yesterday crouched naked on a bucket. He's afraid, and he doesn't understand what's going on. Queen Margarethe tries to issue edicts from her bed, but the Volds take them before they ever reach the hall.

Some of the staff have talked about rallying the men in the surrounding villages, but if they fight, they'll be slaughtered. They're farmers, not fighters. Some barely know how to hold a sword, and there are too many Volds, not enough of us.

If the Sanok Isles are to remain free, we need Larland's help. Katrina and some others started helping me search for the weapon. That's right. Katrina. I knew you'd like that.

Anyway, I hope you have some good news for me. We've had no luck on our side, and if we can't secure Larland's aid soon, the Sanok Isles will collapse.

Stefan.

I read the last sentence a second time, a third. Things had gotten worse. So much worse.

And Katrina…involved.

Stefan was wrong. I didn't like it. If the Volds killed Hans, if they'd killed the minister, it meant they were willing to kill anyone. Did Katrina realize how much danger she was in?

Blood.

On the rocks.

In the rain.

Her dismembered body mangled and tossed aside, crumbled like a napkin. There would be her bun and there would be her slippers, lilac and felted wool, one kicked off because she fought them—of course she fought them—and they'll be her favorite shoes and now she was going to die, and I was in another town on the other side of the island, making friends with the Volds, and there was nothing I could do to stop it, and I had to remember that they were a job, a job, a job.

Erik was a job, and if he was anything more—a friend, maybe—there would be blood. Stefan's. Katrina's. It would paint the streets and—

Failure.

Bright and burning, staining everything it touched. Wild, uncontrolled, a bonfire in raging reds and scorching oranges and—

Failure.

A sea of it, violent and deep. Choppy waves, a hungry tide. Saltwater flooding my ears, my mouth, and I was drowning, dying, and it was all too big, too vast, and there was nothing I could do, and I was small, and I was sand, and I missed Hans and—

I swallowed it.

Ate the feelings.

Chewed them down.

I couldn't fail.

The postmaster watched me, his hand stretched out, grizzled brows furrowed.

"What?" I asked.

"Your letter. The one you woke me to mail. Two gyllis."

A draft caught the papers, made them flutter. If the Volds were in control of Karlsborn Castle, I couldn't send the letter I'd written. It would implicate them.

But did Katrina realize how much danger she was in?

I shoved the old letter in my pocket and wrote a new one.

Kitty,

Don't work with Stefan. Don't search for the ~~we~~ Don't search. Trust me. Please.

~~I miss you.~~

~~I miss him too.~~

~~I'm sorry.~~

Chapter Twenty-Eight

AFTER ESBERN, TRAVEL BECAME SLOW, the way winding and steep. Fog blew in from the ocean, heavy and thick, causing water droplets to bead along our noses, our lashes, muting the rolling shapes of hills, the jagged cut of the coast.

I destroyed Stefan's letters, had torn them to pieces and fed them to the wick of a whale oil lamp, but his words still danced circles through my head. *Minister of trade is dead. King and queen under arrest. Territory of Volgaard. Fear the Sanok Isles will collapse.*

I just needed to do better.

Erik pulled up on his reins, stopping along the rocky edge of Troll's Finger. The ravine cut through the island of Saeby like a seam, black as soil, black as lead.

I stopped Buttercup beside him, the cold cutting straight to my bones, the fog rolling so shimmery and thick, I could taste it. "The bridge?"

There should be a bridge here. There the fuzzed outlines of two posts, jutting up from the earth like monuments, there was the sign. *Crossing.*

But the bridge…

The bridge…

Signey dismounted and strode to the posts. She fingered the bridge's ends, snapped and fraying, disappearing over the side of the cliff and into the valley below.

"Out," she said.

I steadied Buttercup and blinked through the heavy fog. "The map says there's another. It's not too far."

The next bridge was out too.

Signey didn't even bother to dismount this time. "Out again," she said, her voice flat. Her white-gold braids hung limp around her face. Her lips pulled into a scowl. "So much for getting to the other half of the island."

"It might be a trap," Bo said. "The bandits could try to drive us inland."

Kaspar rubbed the back of his neck "Are we sure the bridges haven't been washed out from the—"

Buttercup wandered off to nibble a cluster of fennel, making me miss the end of his sentence.

"Come on," I said, trying to guide her back to the group. We'd gotten good at this game, which I'd dubbed the eat-pull game. She would eat, I would pull. She'd eat harder, I'd pull harder. Eventually, one of us would give up.

It was usually me.

"This is a bad time to be hungry," I said. "We're missing the plan. Do you want me to abandon you?"

In response, Buttercup snorted and wandered to the ravine's edge, where a cluster of dewy fronds sprouted like whiskers. Mist muted them to a blackish-green, fuzzed their edges like a drop of paint suspended in water.

"Okay. You're right, that was an empty threat. Let's get back."

Another snort, this one coupled with a flick of her yellow tail.

Fine. She'd won. In two minutes, Erik would come get us.

I adjusted my legs so they hugged Buttercup's belly and pressed my palms against the base of her neck. I could return to my original plan: befriending them. But the jewelry box… I'd felt something when I'd held it. Maybe I needed to figure out what it was. The only issue: Signey had never taken it out in front of me. Did I need to—

From the corner of my eye, a flick of moment. There, then gone.

I squinted through the sheet of gray and white, searching for that flick and… There. Something dangled down the far side of the ravine, a little lighter than the rocks.

Something…something…

I squinted harder, mist weaving the thing in and out from view like a pair of hands.

Ba-dum, ba-dum.

A rope.

Not the fraying rope of a cut bridge, but a new one, the palest tan. It hung stiff.

Was someone trying to drive us *into* the ravine?

Buttercup nosed a thistle weed growing over the ledge. The weed bumped out of her reach. She nosed it again. Another bump out of reach.

"Guys," I called. "Come look at this."

Buttercup nickered and edged forward, stretching her neck into the abyss. One clop as she readjusted her footing. Two. She bent her front knees, tilted her whiskered chin…

"Guys?" I said again.

Three things happened at once.

Buttercup screamed. My heart flipped. The rock dropped out from under us.

Everything blurred, a rush of cold. I grabbed the saddle, my bags banging my knee.

Rock and grit poured down the mountainside, engulfing flowers and bushes that grew from splits in the stone. Below, the river rushed, and we were going to—

Hoof met rock as Buttercup found her footing. Her sides heaved.

I glanced around.

The air was colder here, moist like the sea, but with the stagnant stench of limpets and old shells. Fog rolled down the sheer cliffs like clouds, swallowing flowers and grass and bushy-tailed mice that darted in and out of the underbrush. Petrels swooped in and out of high nests.

"Are you okay?" Bo shouted, his voice faint.

"Yes." My heart pounded. I tried to pull Buttercup in the right direction, but she shook her head and pranced in place, yanking the fistfuls of mane from my grasp.

"Come back up," Bo said.

"Working on it."

Buttercup whinnied and pranced again, her hooves ringing over the rocks.

"You on your way?"

I gritted my teeth, tried to swallow the tears. "No. She's— We're stuck."

A pause. "Okay. Erik's coming down."

From above, a horse's nicker and a *clack* as a few loose stones tumbled down the cliff.

A minute later, the blue-black shape of Erik and his horse appeared. He stopped a few feet ahead, mist clinging to his shirt, white and open at the throat. His knees hugged the animal's body.

"You're okay." He scrubbed a hand over his face and glanced toward the sky. "You're okay."

He clucked his tongue and spurred his horse closer, the relief slipping into the hardness of a general addressing his troops. "You can't take your feet out of the saddle. *Ever.* And you have to be more forceful with her. She doesn't make decisions. You do. You have to— Isabel. Isa— Don't— Stay on your horse."

"I'm done," I said, scrambling off. Fog billowed around my ankles. My boots slipped against the gritty cliff face. "Buttercup and I had a good run, but I'll walk." I pulled my bag down and threw it over my shoulder. My hands shook.

"You can't wa— *Isabel!*" He dismounted and caught my wrists. "Will you at least ride Buttercup until we get out?"

A mouse crinkled through the underbrush. A few rocks clacked into the rushing river at the ravine's bottom. I should be brave, shouldn't show that this had gotten to me, but Hans was dead, and the minister was dead, and Katrina was probably going to die, and our home was gone, and all those things were gathered storms and they pressed against my teeth like a kettle screaming.

"No." My voice cracked.

Please don't look at me. Please don't notice how close I am to breaking.
I'm not breaking.
I'm breaking.

The kettle screamed. I pressed a hand to my mouth, splayed my fingers against my lips, tried to hold it all in, but it wasn't enough and it was coming out, water bubbling over.

Erik's eyes flicked between Buttercup and his dappled gray.

"Fine." He dropped my wrists and started adjusting the straps on his saddle.

"What are you doing?"

"Putting you on Helhest. With me."

"I don't want to ride with you." He was my enemy, and I shouldn't, I shouldn't—

"You can't walk."

"You can't stop me."

He grabbed my arm and pulled me to the side. "Hey," he said. Then softer, "Hey." He laced his hands through mine and pinched the soft skin between my thumb and forefinger. "Can you breathe? Good. Take deep breaths."

"That's a pressure point—"

The corner of his lip quirked. "For stress and panic attacks, I know." He adjusted his fingers, drawing me closer. His gray eyes found mine, so steady. His hands were warm, and his body was warm. It shouldn't be calming, but it was, and I wanted to cry. "Keep breathing, Isabel. Good. It's okay. I have you. You're safe with me. Just breathe." He modeled a breath in and out. "Now, I'm going to explain the situation to you like you're one of my men. I'm not trying to talk down to you, it's just how I think about things. Several bridges are out. It means that someone is trying to lead us somewhere. Into the ravine or along it, I don't know. Right now, we need to rejoin the others."

His thumb smoothed my knuckle and his eyes didn't leave my face. "If you don't want to ride Buttercup, that's okay. It really is. You can ride Helhest. But I can't have you walk. If there was a confrontation, it's better if we're not on f—"

At that moment an arrow whizzed through the air and cracked off the rock behind us.

Erik whirled, his eyes wide.

The ravine went quiet. Knife quiet. Cat quiet. No rustle of mice. No call of birds.

He turned back to me. "Isabel. We need to—"

Another crack, another whizz. Erik's body lurched forward, one shoulder twerking over the other. He flung his arms around my neck.

A feathered-tip arrow stuck out of his back, the fletching dark as ink. Something warm and sticky dripped over my hands. Blood? His blood. His weight sagged against me.

The shadows of men stepped from the swirling mist, eight of them with broad shoulders and wide-set eyes.

Whoever had been following us earlier?

They'd found us.

I shoved it all back, the things too big to hold, too large to name. "We have to go," I said, hauling Erik over the rocks, back toward the others.

Erik murmured something, his head lulling. Smoke curled around us, spilling from him the way steam spills from a kettle, and suddenly, we were invisible, my hands, my feet, Erik.

The world spun and I couldn't see him, but I could feel the press of him, the weight of him, the warmth of his body, the warmth of his blood seeping down my hand, sticky like honey. He leaned his face into my neck.

"They're still out there," one of the bandits called. His voice echoed off the high walls of the ravine, everywhere and nowhere.

A volley of arrows clattered against the rocks, some skidding off stone and rolling into the river below.

A second bandit clucked his tongue. "Come out, little mice. Come out and play."

Erik and I scooted over the rocks, invisible boots, scraping over grit. His weight pressed against me, threatening to drag me down. How was he so heavy?

"I know you're there," the second bandit called.

Erik groaned. His arm dug into the back of my neck. I couldn't hold him, couldn't hold him, and—

There was my boot, my hand.

I glanced up.

And Erik. His head lulled, eyelids fluttering, skin cool and ashen. Sweat sheened his brow. Shock. He was going into shock. And—

We were surrounded by trees, then snow, then a thousand horses thundering on a rain-slick plane. A castle. Ghosts. A chest spilling rubies. And there was Kaspar, scrambling down the mountain toward us.

"Do something," I shouted, hoisting Erik higher. "*Do something!*"

Another spray of arrows. Something sharp tore my ear. A pop. A burst. White pain and warmth. Had I been hit?

We were fuzzing in and out of visibility, my feet whiskering like rain, like smoke, like flowers wavering on moonlit bluffs.

Kaspar dismounted his steed. "Help me lift him."

"How many men can you hold an illusion for?" I asked, blinking hard. My ear throbbed. Something hot oozed down my neck.

"Sixteen," Kaspar said. "But I have to see them."

Shit. There were at least one, two… Maybe eleven of them? The fog made it impossible to tell.

Where was Bo? Where was Signey?

A horse's scream, a whinny. The clang of steel up above. We

could run back up to them, but we'd be exposed. Signey could hold for twenty-eight, but Erik—

The illusion wavered, spilling into mountains, markets, wheat fields crushed under a blue-black sky, images so frayed and tattered, the real world and the false one transposed over each other.

My eyes strained against the sheets of white, trying to make out the river rushing below. There was no way we'd be able to lift Erik onto Kaspar's horse under this sort of fire, but if we could make it to the bottom of the ravine, we could shelter behind some of the bigger boulders.

"Erik, stop. *Stop*." I gave him a hard jostle. "You're making it worse."

"There they are," a bandit shouted. "Down there!"

Another volley of arrows clattered off the cliffs.

Erik's body jerked forward. He let out an *oof*, his weight coming down hard against me.

"Down to the river," I told Kaspar. "Let's go."

Kaspar scraped a hand through his hair. "What? Not back to Bo and Signey?"

"You think Signey can see?"

"You think *you* can see?"

I couldn't. But I'd splashed around the Colt enough times to know the biggest boulders were always at the bottom. The Colt wasn't the same as Troll's Finger, but—

"If I find a place for you and Erik to hide, I'll run up and show them the way down," I said. "We go in three, two—"

Another spray of arrows.

We ran. Ran, ran, ran, our boots slipping over the stones, down a path that really wasn't a path, white fog parting around us.

The river rushed, the shapes of boulders sprung up from the earth.

I pulled Erik into the shallows, freezing water splashing up the back of our legs, my skirt swirling. We crouched behind the biggest one.

The river rushed, black water barely visible through the fog.

"I thought you were going to wait until one," Kaspar said. He twisted and glanced at the arrow protruding from his thigh. "Thanks for that."

Blood trickled down my neck. I touched my ear, my fingers coming away bright red. So, I had been hit. How bad was it?

"Next time," Kaspar continued, "if you don't say 'one,' I'm going to—"

"I'm sorry," I hissed. "Would you rather we stick around and get shot?"

"I got shot!"

"Little mice," the bandit's voice echoed, too close. "I know you're down here. There's nowhere for you to go, nowhere for you to hide."

I peeked around the boulder's edge. The world was empty, a sea of white. Up above, more clambering. A shout? Signey?

A shadow seemed to detach from the fog like a fly, unfurled and stretched into the shape of a man, dark hair, dark bones. He smiled, a scar that split his lip. A red armband fluttered around his bicep. His left eye drooped.

"You're wounded." He said the words simply, as if he were talking to a child. "You're hurt. You can't hide forever."

Erik's hand tightened around my shoulder. "An…ight…" he murmured into my hair.

"What?" I asked.

"I can…fight." The words were slurred, heavy like he was drunk. "Help me…stand."

"You can't fight, you're in no position to—"

But Erik was already pushing himself up, the warmth of his presence disappearing. He staggered into the open, the white roar of the water rushing around his legs, his lips blueish, skin so pale.

"Ah," the bandit said. "There you are."

Erik raised a hand, his fingers splayed and the earth rumbled. "I don't know…who you are. Or why…you've been…following us."

The ground split, the space between them opening into a chasm.

Erik's lip twisted into a snarl as his fingers twitched. "But it ends here."

Bugs streamed out of the chasm, beetles and moths, a black and writhing mass that swarmed the bandit, his nostrils, his throat.

"Hey," called one of his comrades. "Are you—"

Erik twerked his hand.

The mass of bugs separated, cleaved in two, and flew at the second bandit, encircling him, *eating* him.

Their screams echoed off the ravine walls, and they clawed their eyes, their chests, their necks. Burning. It looked like they were burning, the bugs pluming off them like smoke.

They were screaming, screaming, screaming, and then, they weren't.

Two bodies hit the ground with a *smack*.

Erik turned to me, his hand still raised, the mass of insects roiling behind him. His eyes burned black as hollows, black as pits.

They found me, and something in his stance softened. "Isabel," he said.

And collapsed face first into the water.

Chapter Twenty-Nine

I GRABBED ERIK'S ARMS and pulled him into the shallows where the cold water could wash away the blood. Sand and sediment swirled in the eddies, sloshing up my ankles and the back of my skirts.

He groaned, his blond hair matting, skin flushed. His eyes fluttered beneath their lids.

Shock. He was going into shock. I needed to stabilize him before I handled the arrows.

I pulled off my sweater and stuffed it under his head. In nothing but my undergarment, cold air needled my skin, causing gooseflesh to pebble my arms. Around me, the water ran red. Red like poppies, red like plums.

Red. The color of the sea the day Hans died.

The day Hans died.

Blood.

Red.

Ocean.

Sea.

And I was back, was pressing on Hans's chest and being hauled away as the sky furled out like a flag, and here is a body, and here is the foam, and here are the flies, their lacy wings quivering. Here are all the big things threatening to spill, and I couldn't—

I couldn't—

I couldn't—

Erik's breathing had gone ragged, wet sucks in and out. Pale hair, pale lashes, lips that were tinged blue. If I didn't act fast, this wound would bleed him out, would kill him.

And there, Erik's friends. Kaspar silent on the strip of pebbled beach, Bo and Signey hurrying down the rocks. Helpless. They were helpless. They didn't know how to save him.

I did.

You could let him die. The thought prickled dangerously soft, desperately gentle, a blush, a kiss, the brush of a feather.

My hands twitched. The water pulled the hem of my skirts, dragged the sleeves of my sweater, a swirl of cream in the eddies. Blood billowed like smoke.

I could let him die the same way Hans died, could let him bleed out here on the beach until he was nothing but a body and bones. He needed the bleeding staunched, his wounds bandaged. Maybe a compress of honey and yarrow. I could see it in my mind's eye, the little rocky outcropping where the white plant grew. It called to me like a tree extending its roots…

This is where it is, it said. *This is how to save him.*

Save him!

I blinked and pushed the thought aside. His friends weren't doctors. They wouldn't know if I did any of that. They wouldn't know if I was helping him or killing him or just letting him die.

My ear throbbed from where it had been nicked. Something wet trickled down the back of my neck. Blood? No. A soft pattering that dappled the water.

Rain.

I should let him die. It was smarter to let him die. Lothgar's second, the general's son, the best person at reykr in Volgaard's army. His loss would be a huge blow, could maybe be leveraged to delay the pending attack, and he was a job—just a job—but…

Why did you give me the map? My question that night at the Salt & Thistle Inn.

The turn of his head. The glint of his eyes, gray, the color of dried heather, of fire ash.

I know what it's like to be unhappy.

Beneath those words, a deeper current, red like life, like heart: *I see you.*

Something in me ached.

Icy water rushed over my hands. Rain pattered his face. Erik groaned, his cheek lulling into the river. It caught his hair, spun it gold in the drifts.

I gritted my teeth and hauled his head higher on my sweater.

Stefan would let him die. Hell, *anyone* would let him die. Anyone who wasn't a Vold.

"Can you save him?" Kaspar called. His voice seemed small, distant, like he was standing at the end of a tunnel and it was just Erik and me.

So many personal questions.

Do you want me to stop?

I clenched my fists, unclenched them. "I need the white willow and two writing quills. Signey, start a fire. Kaspar, find a pot."

His friends hurried along the beach. The clank of pans, the scrape of rocks, the strike of steel on flint-stone.

Erik's eyes fluttered open, a sliver of gray. They met mine and my heart stuttered. Then he let out another groan, and those gray, gray eyes rolled shut.

I UNCORKED THE BRANDY BOTTLE and doused it over Erik's wounds.

He tensed and mumbled something, tried to roll over, smoke pouring off him, his body steaming.

"Shh," I said, smoothing my thumb over his bare skin, the ridge of his spine, the slope of his shoulder, across a rough indent where scar tissue knotted. "Breathe. Just breathe."

Smoke continued to coil, continued to pour, forming shapes. Whalebones and white waves. A cracked door, dark wood ribbed with iron, golden light spilling out onto the pebble riverbank.

I blinked.

Through the door, a woman, her face all angles carved honey in the candlelight. A tiara sat atop her head. "Then send him back," she hissed with a flick of her hand. "I can't have him here."

The door fell apart, a rush of water, and we were on a beach. Hunks of ice. Black sand. Water lapped my legs like puppy dog tongues.

We needed to get him stable. We needed to get the arrows out. "Hold him down," I said to Signey and Bo.

A fold, a fall, and there was that doorway again, a yawn of breath, golden light slatting the beach.

Inside, the same woman, the same honey carved features, a

green dress instead of a blue, her belly round and swollen.

"Hire a tutor and keep him in your rooms," someone just beyond the frame said. "Herleif doesn't visit them, anyway." A pause. "Ginja, he's just a boy."

The woman's voice dropped to a snarl. Red lips, white teeth. "*This* is a boy," she said, pointing to her belly. "*He* is a mistake."

Erik murmured something, his cheek scraping the pebbles.

I ripped my eyes away from the illusion and stretched out my hand. "Quills."

Someone dropped two feather pens into my open palm.

The illusion twisted again, and there was the woman sitting at a table.

"Lothgar's a fool," she said, high and heady, a little drunk. Her waist was slim, her hair braided into a crown that accentuated the real one fixed atop her head. "If he were smart, he'd train him. Send him with the First Born." She swilled her glass and nodded, resolute. "We'd be rid of him before Ylír."

I slid both quills into the wound on Erik's shoulder.

He hissed. Ice shot from his hands, sharp spears, and suddenly, we were on a frozen lake, the stars and moon reflected in whorls. A fox. A man. A herd of reindeer crossing.

I poked around until both quills' hollow shafts hooked over the arrow barbs. There. My eyes locked with Signey's. "You holding him?"

She nodded.

"Good. Whatever he shows you, don't let go."

Then, slowly, carefully, I eased the arrow out.

I BALANCED THE BOWL OF WATER on the pebble-black beach and pulled my hair back. The blood around my ear had crusted a rough black-brown, trickles of it running down my neck, disappearing into the edge of my undershirt.

Impossible to tell how bad it was.

I doused the corner of a rag with brandy and shoved it against my head. The sting of alcohol made me purse my lips. My ear burned.

The river rushed. Bloody brandy dribbled down my arm as illusions spilled from Erik's tent. A pen of lambs. A churning sea. Bones and bells. That woman, over and over and over. And there she was doing needlework, a tapestry in her lap. There she was sleeping, her cheek crushed against a velvet pillow. There she was laughing and singing and talking, playing with a kitten and a leaf on a string.

Beside the tent, Bo drew circles in the pebbles and Kaspar fiddled with the bandage around his thigh.

I tore the rag away from my ear and studied my reflection in the bowl of water. Rain dappled the edges.

It was hard to tell, but it seemed like an arrow had torn the outer shell of my ear, leaving it jagged and ugly. I prodded the flap of skin and blinked away tears from the pain. Luckily, my hearing seemed okay. And I could stitch that. Maybe. Worth a try.

I tied my hair into a bun that kept everything away from my ruined ear, reached for the needle and suture thread, and—

The jewelry box dropped into my lap.

Love me, it said. *Use me.*

"There's a mirror in that," Signey said.

What? There was no way she'd just given this to me. But there was her bag, the bast cording loose, and there was the metal chest sitting open beside it. And here was the jewelry box, rosettes and spotted orchids, the hum of it so strong it vibrated my teeth.

"Don't tell me that bowl of water is working for you," she added, pulling the bodies of the dead bandits along the riverbank. She took off their shirts, their trousers, and laid them prone in the dirt. We'd killed four in total—the two Erik dispatched and two others.

"You're staring," she said.

"Sorry."

I flipped the lid open and pulled down the tabbed board. There was my face in the mirror, the planes of it starker, bruising purple playing beneath my eyes, in the hollows of my cheekbones, my ear torn and ugly. That would take work. But first…

I returned my attention to the painted linen, the rosettes. Could I ask her what it was? Why it hummed? Could it be that easy?

Signey crossed one of the bandit's swollen arms, ran her fingers through his hair. "You know, I used to imagine myself killing him." The words came out of nowhere, and it took me a moment to realize she wasn't talking about the bandit. "It would have been so easy. But tonight, when he almost died, I—"

She glanced over her shoulder and swallowed. Smoke and grizzled shapes poured from Erik's tent, the images sloppy from søven, bears that looked more like demons, a ropy coil of trees, all falling back into that woman with the dark hair, pretty face, crown.

Signey licked her lips. "Thank you."

Stiff wind whistled against the basalt rocks, dark shapes of stone towering around us.

"Tell me what this is," I said, holding up the jewelry box. "It feels—"

Ancient.

Powerful.

Like I never want to let it go.

"Old."

Signey uncorked the bottle of oil and swiped it over the bandit's nose, forehead, lips.

Her own lips pressed into a line. "It's a jewelry box."

Except it wasn't. It couldn't be. I traced one of the pale pink rosettes with my thumb. "It's not Vold."

Signey kept even strokes over the bandit's body. "Sometimes when foreign merchants came, they'd bring gifts, things they hoped would convince us to open our borders to trade." She moved to the next bandit and repeated the same pattern—nose, forehead, lips. Her gaze kept steady on her hands. "This one's from the Sanokes."

I nearly dropped the jewelry box. "What?"

"It came from a merchant who came from the Sanokes."

"I heard that, but…" I stared at it, the creamy white linen, the heath orchids painted delicately along the side, spotted pinks and purples—the same pinks and purples that grew on winding trails and from crags in the cliff. Maybe I should have made the connection, but…there was no way I would have.

"He called it a Lover's Box. You write a message, and the box will send it to a reciprocal box for a toll, something you care about." She plucked the jewelry box—Lover's Box—out of my hand, flipped the latch with her thumb. "It might take your ability to see the color green or smell rain. It took one man's memories of his favorite dog, and Erik can't hear whistling. But they say the lovers who created it would rather live in an empty world than a world without each other."

"You think it's magic?" I asked. It couldn't be magic. The Sanokes didn't have magic.

She shrugged and went back to the dead bandit. "I think it's a mirror."

"You've used it?"

"We try not to."

"Who has the other? Lothgar?"

With an expert crack, she broke the bandit's chest and eased her knife's tip into the cavity. A few quick strokes and she held his heart, raw and fatty, in her hand. "Use the mirror as long as you like. Just don't think too hard about it… It can sense that. And keep your blood off it."

Chapter Thirty

THE LOVER'S BOX CAME FROM the Sanok Isles. The Lover's Box had magic. What did that mean?

The rain slowed, then stopped, leaving the world glassy and clear, slick rocks shining like candles. We lit a fire and I crouched beside it, fed another bloody linen to its maw. It shriveled and sparked, a pair of hands curling in on itself.

Through the heat haze, Signey tucked the Lover's Box away and used her knee to hold the bag as she pulled the strings tight.

The Lover's Box.

Magic.

The Sanokes didn't have magic, we couldn't. We were nobodies, no more important than a grain of sand on a dance floor.

Still, I wanted to hold it, wanted to have it. The way it hummed in my hands, the way it made pieces of me sing… I would trade anything—*anything*—to feel it pressed against my cheek.

The fire dried my lips, made the blood race to my fingers, red and stinging.

I could rush Signey now, could tear her hair and gouge her eyes because I needed it. *Needed, needed, needed—*

I pressed a hand to my temple.

Stop. The Lover's Box was a tool—a useful tool—and maybe I could use it to help find the weapon. That's what I should focus on.

The weapon.

If I stole the box, could I use it to correspond with Lothgar? If I pretended to be Signey, could I get him to tell me what the weapon was?

I hadn't been brave enough to poison the food since Erik discovered the ragwort, but he was still unconscious, fevered illusions spilling from his tent. Valerian should only make them a little drowsier than normal…

That night, I dumped the entire bottle into their skause.

Their snores echoed through the camp.

I changed into a fleeced cardigan and my nightgown, the fabric lighter, smoother than the heavy rustle of my traveling skirts, strapped the knife Erik had given me to my hip and crept outside.

Moonlight dribbled down the walls of the ravine like spilled milk, glinting off limpet shells and bones, the black pebble beach. Horses pawed the ground, tossed their manes. The river rushed.

I eased the flap of Signey's tent and there she was, stretched out over her bedroll, one hand by her face, the other tucked under her pillow, lashes dusting her cheek.

I wanted to hate her, but she didn't look like a villain when she was sleeping like this.

I grabbed her bag and hauled it out into the ravine, the scrape of leather on stone. Without the wind, without the howl, everything seemed so quiet, so still. Stars glittered overhead, bright and burning.

I dug through the bag until I found the metal chest, fit my makeshift key into the lock and—

"Isabel?"

I whirled, my hand going to the knife, and there was Erik, shirtless and bracing himself on the tent pole, his free hand thrown around his bandaged middle.

Shit. I hadn't even noticed the illusions stop.

"Good reflexes," he said, eyeing the knife.

I let my fingers fall from the hilt. "You shouldn't be standing. Do you need something?"

A sheepish smile crossed his face. "I'm actually hungry."

Double shit. I could drug him with søven, but he'd remember when he woke up, and it might be difficult to explain that. New plan. Feed Erik, get him back to bed, then use the Lover's Box.

I glanced at Signey's bag, spilling tunics and blankets, the strings pulled wide. I also needed to keep him away from that.

Far away from that.

I used the side of my foot to nudge it into a shadow. "Craving anything specific? I think I saw some of Signey's dried fish."

"Not her fish. They're—" He grimaced. "To tell you the truth, I've never been able to stomach Signey's fish."

"Then what?"

Another sheepish smile. "Salted porridge with a lump of butter melting in the center?"

"That's...very specific." And would take far too long to cook. "What about cheese? Biscuits?"

He shivered, his eyes red-rimmed. "Do you know where they

put my bag?" A glance at Signey's. "Is that it?"

"Uh. That's not your bag. *Definitely* not your bag. It's fine. I'll make it for you. You shouldn't be standing, anyway. Weird salty porridge it is."

FIRE CRACKLED AND POPPED, embers glinting off sand and bone and empty shells. High above, seabirds soared in and out of nests. An eerie silence stretched through the ravine.

"About what happened," Erik said. I'd brought him a knitted blanket to clutch around his shoulders, but he still sat shivering on a rock.

"I took the arrows out."

He shook his head. "What happened before we were attacked."

Oh. Buttercup. The panic attack. I poked the fire with a stick, sending a fountain of sparks into the sky. "I've been dealing with a lot."

He pulled the blanket tighter. "I probably didn't help by saddling you with Buttercup and letting the men play their pranks. But if you ever want to talk…I'm here."

I bit my lip. Those dark and messy things churned, an angry sea where each wave threatened to capsize me. "I don't think I'm ready to talk. I'm—"

I'm what? Broken? Alone?

Our legs brushed.

"Okay." He glanced at the sky. "Well, then. The other thing I've been dying to know. Did I…Send anything when I was out?"

I shrugged. "A beach. A lake. Some reindeer."

His shoulders relaxed. "Good."

"Why? You worried?"

He scooted forward. "Do you want me to show you how to use that knife?"

I poked his chest. "Ha! You *are* worried!"

He glanced between my finger and my face. That lock of hair fell against his forehead, curling just above his brow. His eyes went feral. "You're deflecting, Isabel."

"I'm not deflecting." I scooted back and stretched my legs. "I want to know what's in your head. What were you so afraid of casting?"

"I'm not afraid of anything. You…"

"Are also not afraid of anything?"

He laughed. "If only. You pretend to be fearless but…" he caught my hand, "I see you."

My breath hitched, and his thumb grazed my knuckle. His gaze didn't leave mine, so fervent, so fierce.

Smoke chugged toward the stars. I licked my lips, smoky and bright like ice. "Sloppy trees."

The corner of his mouth quirked. He let my hand go. "What?"

"Besides the beach, the lake, and the reindeer, you also cast some very sloppy trees."

"What even is a sloppy tree?"

"They had these trunks that twisted like wet hair and branches that bulged like…slugs? I've never seen a real tree, but there's no way they look like—"

He held up his hands. "Okay, okay." Something mischievous flickered in his eyes and suddenly, they surrounded us, a forest of shadowed pine that scraped the stars. Bark curled off their trunks and needles fanned like dainty swords.

I tipped my head back and tried to lean the crown against one of them. "I mean, I've seen *your* trees, and I've seen pictures of them. But they don't grow in the Sanokes."

The tree shivered, then reappeared two inches closer.

"Thanks."

"Of course. But you've never visited Larland? Or Gormark? I thought everyone outside Volgaard traveled."

"Before this? Karlsborn Castle was the farthest I've ever been from home."

From the corner of my eye, I caught him stretch and wince when the stitches pulled. "So where is it?"

"Where is what?"

"Home."

Oh. *Oh.* I blew at a branch of pine needles. They quivered like feather fluff. "It's a tiny town off the coast of…well, you don't know it, but Hjern. It's a tiny town." The dark wood door, the way honey light spilled over the beach. I sat up. "What about yours?"

"Mine," he said with a rough laugh. His expression wavered.

I studied him, the set of his jaw, the way shadows danced along the planes of his face. "You kept casting a woman. She was…pregnant." If Erik had been a tributary, that must be the family he'd been sent to live with.

He ran a hand through his hair. "She's no one. Not important."

I arched a brow. "And you call me a bad liar."

The forest collapsed and we were back in the ravine. The river hissed and Kaspar's snores drifted from his tent. Fire crackled, so bright, so hot.

"Okay. She was my mother."

"But…she called you a mistake?" Why would his mother have called him a mistake?

"Because I am," he said after a moment. "A mistake."

That didn't make sense. He was the general's son. Lothgar's second, better at reykr than—

"I'm a bastard," he added, his expression guarded. "My mother wasn't Lothgar's wife; she is—*was*—from Kaldr-Flodi."

Was. "I'm sorry."

He gave a hard laugh and leaned back. "I'm not. She was a…well, she wasn't the type of person you wanted to know. They say she was different before Herleif married her and made her queen, but I never saw that side of her."

Before Herleif made her queen. "So you're a prince? I mean, if your stepfather is the king of Volgaard, that would make you a prince. Right?"

"A prince? No. Gus and Henny are princes. *I'm—*" He swallowed. "Honestly? I spent a long time wondering if I even mattered."

His mother's words came back to me, the red of her lips, the twist of her mouth.

Then send him back.

We'll be rid of him before Ylír.

This is a boy, he is a mistake.

But—

"You're the best person at reykr. Of course you mattered."

He barred his teeth. "You think my parents cared about *me*? You think they wanted *me*? They passed me back and forth like I was some sort of disease. Children born between houses are almost always dadig, ordinary, and I couldn't do anything with reykr until I was fourteen. So yes, I wondered if I mattered. Not because of magic, but because…because…" He clenched his hands. "You know your stitches hurt like a bitch."

"I have white willow." I pushed myself up and returned with a sliver of bark. "Chew until it becomes soft. Should take the edge off."

But instead of taking it, he fisted it in his hand and kept his gaze on the snap and crackle of the fire. Was he thinking about his mother?

"You okay?" I asked.

"Yes." *No.* He scrubbed a hand over his face. "Just tell me something? About you, the Sanokes. I don't care."

"Why?"

"Because your stitches—"

"Hurt. Yeah, I know." A pause. The char of smoke filled the night. I cocked a brow. "I thought you said I couldn't hurt you."

He grimaced. "I lied. You can *definitely* hurt me."

"Mmm, two lies in one night. I must be rubbing off on you."

"Not rubbing off on me." He shot me a teasing glance. "I'm just better at it."

"Go back to bed."

He scooted toward me. "Tell me a bedtime story."

"No."

He shrugged. "Then I'm not going back to bed. I'm going to sit here all night, Sending trees and keeping guard over that specific bag." He nodded to a pack half open and shoved against a pile of rocks. Firelight gave the leather a reddish hue and glinted off the silver buckles.

"You're pathetic. That's the food bag." I'd been sure to shove Signey's deep, *deep* into the shadows. But— "Speaking of, it's weird you're making me cook for you. I thought I'd been banned."

"You wouldn't poison me. You like my tattoo too much." He winked and leaned onto his palm. "Now about that bedtime story."

Maybe it was the wind or the cold or the fact that it was so late, but I found myself slowing, easing into the moment the same way a dormouse eases into the grooves of a winter-warm house. I knew I needed to send the message, to return Signey's bag, but the porridge was still cooking, and I could wait just a few minutes.

And maybe, just maybe, there was a small part of me that wanted to stay.

A shooting star streaked past, then another.

"Okay. So there's a story," I said, squinting up. "Aalto and Vega. He was from the sea, she from the sky. Some say she was a sorceress, a purveyor of spells and oddities. Others claim she was a spirit, the daughter of ash and air, one of those immortal things that sit on the seams of reality. They met on the horizon, Aalto with his fishing net and Vega with sunlight braided into her hair. They talked, they kissed, they fell in love.

"'Run away with me,' he said one night as the ocean tangled around their legs like a sheet. He smoothed a lock off her forehead. 'Be mine.'

"In some versions, she tells him she needs to wait until after the summer solstice, until those few days when the world grows balmy and sweet, until the nights are short, and her father has his face to the stars. In others, she says she needs to return home to gather holed stones and secret spells. In all versions, she tells him, 'Meet me here in three days. I'll find you.'

"But when Vega's father found out, he stole Aalto away and locked him in a tower that teetered on the edge of infinity. He told her a fisherman wasn't good enough for his daughter. He told her she'd never see him again."

256

"Interesting. And Vega found him?"

"She tore apart the sky. Pulled down the stars and dropped them into the buckets of the sea."

Another shooting star cut through the night—a flash, there then gone. The world had dropped to a chill, the chap cutting against our cheeks, our bones.

I tugged my cardigan around my shoulders, the cream wool soft against my skin, and squinted up. "I remember looking at the stars after my father left, wondering what it would be like to matter so much that someone would tear down the sky." A stick popped. "So yeah…I've wondered that, too."

Erik cocked his head and studied me like I was a puzzle. "Your father left?"

I pressed the tip of my pinky into a pit of a rock. "It's fine. I'm over it."

His eyes darkened. "You're not a good liar, Isabel."

I pulled my hand away from the rock and thumped him on the chest. "I'm a great liar. Fooling you into thinking I'm a bad one is my best lie yet."

"Will you tell me what happened? With your father."

I did my best to imitate his throaty chuckle. "So many personal questions."

"Well…maybe I want to know you, too." The admission, like a blink, a blush, a flower blooming open, the petals furling wide. And there he was—strong jaw, stormy mouth, the lock of hair that was almost a curl. He ran a hand through it, brushing it back from his forehead, and watched with careful eyes.

My heart kicked. "My father. Okay. He—" *Lied? Cheated?* How do you say he ripped apart my world? I finally settled on, "Had another family."

Erik waited for me to elaborate.

"He kept them in a shack on the beach," I said. "Sent them money, stayed the night. They lived right there in Hjern, and no one knew. She was the local witch, and he pretended not to notice, but they had two babies, little boys, ages one and three. When Mama found out, she screamed and screamed and screamed at him to choose: his wife or his whore. He chose them. Said he'd choose them every time."

Those words had burned my ears, scalded my skull, and banged around my brain until I marched to that shack on the beach, thirteen years old, and I pounded on that salt-stained door. Pounded and pounded until Papa pulled it open, shirt untucked, a baby in each arm.

"Are we not enough for you?" I'd cried. "Are Mama and I not enough for you?"

He didn't say anything—*wouldn't* say anything. Instead, he coolly and calmly shut the door. He'd said over and over he didn't want to lie, but he couldn't bring himself to tell the truth—the cruel and ugly truth: we weren't enough.

We would never be enough.

"It hurt," I said. "The babies, the door. But I think the worst part was knowing he was happy. And I realize that makes me a terrible, terrible person, but I had to let go of the life I thought I'd get. Had to watch him give away the love I wish I had because I wasn't enough. People always think you need a body to grieve someone, but you don't. I missed him, and he was standing right in front of me." I opened my hands, closed them, wiped my palms on my skirts. "I'm sorry. I shouldn't have told you that. It's just— I don't know." The fire snapped, sparks scattering like grains on the wind. "They really passed you back and forth?"

258

Erik swallowed. "I mean, they'd try to convince the other parent to keep me. Lothgar once sent me with a dozen racing stallions and three blood rubies. My mother kept the rubies and returned me. No one wants a child who's dadig. And...I think I reminded them of their mistakes."

Shadows raced up the wall, skittering wide like the wings of a sea eagle.

A bastard boy, an unwanted child, the second-in-command, desperate to prove himself, hungry to be seen. But that didn't explain—

"You said you picked your emblem yourself. Why cornflowers, of all things?"

He ran a thumb over his nubbed finger. "No more secrets?"

No more secrets. A dangerous thing to promise when I was here to spy, to steal, to bring his country to its knees.

But—

Maybe I want to know you, too.

"No more secrets."

Erik shivered and pulled the blanket tighter. "Because they're weeds. Beautiful, stubborn weeds." Our eyes caught and this time, he didn't hide it—the hurt, the pain, the longing. "Maybe you're a cornflower, too."

Chapter Thirty-One

THE NIGHT HAD GONE HEATHERY, the sky softening to the blue-gray of predawn. Two bowls sat, rinsed in river water and tipped against the rocks. Embers smoldered in the pit.

I hadn't meant to stay out all night, hadn't meant for us to share stories like we were friends.

We weren't friends. We couldn't be friends. This was supposed to be a job.

And yet…

Images of last night twirled through my mind. The brush of his shoulder, the touch of his hand. His laugh, teasing and rich and *real*.

What's your favorite smell?
What's the biggest lesson you never learned?
Which one of your scars has the best story?

Now, Erik had gone to bed, and the night was too far gone to expect a reply to any letter sent through the Lover's Box. I'd have to send the message and put the box back. One chance, one letter.

I already knew what I'd say.

The river hissed, silk on stone and morning mist knitted like a finely woven shawl. The moisture made my nightgown stick to my stomach and shoulders, and all I wanted to do was fall face-first onto my bedroll. But I could do this.

I yawned and fit my key into Signey's crude metal chest.

If—no, *when*—this worked, we'd have the location of the weapon. All we'd need to do was retrieve it.

The lock snicked, and the Lover's Box tumbled out.

The world tilted. My blood sang.

I pressed the linen against my cheek, felt the buzz, the hum. It vibrated my teeth, and I never wanted to let go, *never, never, never*—

I dropped the box onto the riverbank with a *thud*. The lid splayed open like a clamshell, waiting and patient.

I pressed the heels of my hands to my eyes, scrubbed them through my hair. Wake up. *Wake up*. But the residue of the hum still sang in my skin, my skull.

Hold me, it seemed to say. *Love me. Love me, love me, love me.*

Leave me alone, I wanted to scream, but I saw myself reaching for it, dusting the sand and dirt and my limbs felt so heavy, and why couldn't I just sleep? Maybe I needed the box, maybe if I had the box, I could do anything. Maybe the box completed me, made me whole, and—

I dug my fingers into my scalp.

Stop. *Stop*. The hum, the pull…it wasn't real. It couldn't be real—

If I picked it up, touched it, it could be. How could anything beautiful be so bad?

My fingers slid down my head, my hand bumping my ruined

ear. White-hot pain. The grip of the Lover's Box wavered and pain. Pain had done that.

I gritted my teeth.

Whatever trick this was, I couldn't let myself get caught by Signey and the others. The risk? The stakes?

Cold mud against my feet. Sand and grit, the flutey stems of reed grass brittle in the night. *I will carve out your heart and leave your body to rot.*

I slid my fingers over my ear, my thumb catching the nubby knots of the stitches.

I'd promised myself I wouldn't do this again, promised myself I'd stop.

I had stopped, I had. For two years, I'd stopped, but this would be harder tomorrow, and Erik was observant—*so, so observant*—and I knew pain.

I could handle pain.

I pushed my thumb against the stitches, popped my nail into the wound.

Pain exploded, blinding and hot.

I clenched my fist, pressed a knuckle into my mouth, the prick of pain pushing away the hum of the box, the song until all that was left was the steady thrum of my ear.

I fished the journal from my bag, tore a page from the back.

Our Sanok guide tells us Larland has spies in Karlsborn Castle. She doesn't know who they are, but we know they're there. It would be safer to move ~~the weapons~~ *everything important onto the ships.*

I paused, pen hovering over paper. This was dumb and desperate. The scrawling words looked nothing like Signey's hand, but nothing else had worked, and I was running out of time. The Sanokes were falling apart, and if I couldn't find the weapon before Larland was attacked, Hans wouldn't matter, and this would all be for nothing, and—

Sunlight tipped the ravine, turning everything pink.

I shoved the message into the box, clicked the lid, and waited. My ear throbbed. How was this supposed to work? Was there something to do?

I cracked the lid. The paper was still there, still scrawled in my messy hand, the edges curling like a feather.

Were there magic words? Did it need blood? An offering? Signey said the box took a toll.

"You can have my…ability to taste coffee?" I clicked the latch with my thumb.

A suck, a snick, a tingle in my fingertips that spread to my palms.

My head pounded.

A fire. A flash. Wings. Lots of them.

"No, no, no," I fiddled with the latch, tried to pry the lid open, but it stuck.

Breath. Sky. A whirl of color, of light. Apricots. Stars. A pair of fangs. Waterfalls. Death. A butterfly burst from its cocoon.

The tingle stopped, but the hum remained, brighter, more resonant. I needed to use it again. I should take the box, hide it. What else could I send? A word? A song? A blank sheet of paper?

I patted the ground around me. Where did I put the journal? In the bag? I must have put it in the bag.

Sunlight drenched the cliffs, and now everything was on fire, and I needed lots of paper because I would never give it back, *never, never, never*—

I dropped the box onto the riverbank and stared at my hands.

Shaking. They were shaking, and the meaning of what I'd done hit me. I wasn't sure whether I wanted to laugh or cry.

Assuming Lothgar heeded my warning, he'd move the weapon. Then all I'd need to do was retrieve it.

Love me, the box continued to hum. *Use me, use me. Love me, love me.*

I stripped off my cardigan and used it to push the Lover's Box back into the metal chest. Then slowly, carefully, I eased the lid shut.

FIRE SNAPPED AT KINDLING, sunlight stealing its edges, making it hollow, dry as sand, bleached as bones.

What were the odds Lothgar sent a reply? It had to be low. The box was toxic, the box took a toll. He wouldn't waste energy confirming receipt…would he?

"Isabel?"

But what if he did? What if he had questions? What if he realized it wasn't Signey's handwriting? Had I made a mistake?

And should I continue on with Erik, or should I go back to the castle? If Lothgar moved the weapon to the ships, I didn't need to stay. I could go back, help Stefan and the others. But what if Lothgar didn't move the weapons? What if he sent a reply?

"Isabel?"

If I ran, I'd have to take the Lover's Box with me, cutting off their line of communication. Erik and Kaspar were wounded, and I could probably beat them back. I could send a few messages on the way to confirm the weapon had actually been moved.

But…what if they did more than pass messages? What if they

were the weapon we were looking for? After all, I'd felt something when I used them.

Wings. Fire. Apricots. Stars.

Okay. I'd steal the Lover's Box and run back to Karlsborn Castle. I could fiddle with them on the way back and see what I learned. If the boxes were the weapon, I'd figure out how to wield them. If they weren't, well, I could still use them to make sure the actual weapon had been moved.

Not a bad plan.

The sharp burn of bread bit my nose.

Good plan.

"Isabel!"

I startled. Black smoke chugged from the pan.

"Shit."

I pulled the griddle cake off the skillet and dropped it, smoldering, onto the rocks. It had been Bo's idea to mix the porridge with less water and fry them. He said it would make a lumpy pancake.

"That's the third one this morning," Bo said.

"I know. I'm sorry. I—" I pressed the heels of my hands against my eyes. "I know."

"Do you want coffee?"

Not if the Lover's Box had stolen my ability to taste it. "I'm fine."

Bo cocked his head, his eyes steady. "You…always have coffee in the mornings."

"I do, but—"

But what? I'd bargained away my ability to taste it because I used the Lover's Box to tell Lothgar to move the weapon onto the ships? But I couldn't say that. So fine, I'd drink some. If only to stop myself from raising suspicions.

Water bubbled, beans seeped, dark as fresh-tilled mud. I strained the grounds and braced myself for the taste of nothing.

But…it wasn't nothing. It was dark and loamy sweet, bitter and earthy, with just a hint of smoke. Same thing I drank every morning.

My hands flew to my chin, my throat.

"Everything okay?" Erik asked, settling next to the flames.

"Fine." I prodded the soft skin under my jaw. Shit. "I'm fine. Really. Just…give me a second."

I stumbled to the riverbank and dropped to my knees. The eddies dappled my reflection, ripples catching the tufts of grass and spinning them like watercolors. A fish darted through the shadows.

I cupped my hands and splashed my face, the water minerally and cool. I counted the colors—red, green, blue. Could I hear the birds? Yes. Could I smell wildflowers? I snatched a stem of clover, the petals creamy with notes of honey and grass. Yes.

Because if the Lover's Box hadn't taken my ability to taste coffee, then what *had* it taken?

Chapter Thirty-Two

"SIGNEY SAID YOU CAN'T HEAR WHISTLING?" I said, dropping to a crouch. I pulled a griddle cake off the iron, the underside burned to a crisp. "How did you figure that out?"

Erik cocked a brow. "Signey showed you the Lover's Box?"

"She let me use the mirror to stitch my—" I swallowed. The mangled stitches might raise questions. "It doesn't matter."

"So, you felt the thrall?"

I poked at the griddle cake's blistered bottom. "It's…strong."

Bo placed another on the iron. "You should've seen what it did to King Herleif." Butter browned and foamed at the edges, going warm and nutty. "He became obsessed with the boxes. Stopped bathing, stopped eating. He was passing messages back and forth so often, they said his house was filled with a constant *click, click, click*, like a horse prancing on stone. It's how the boxes ended up with House Rythja."

Kaspar threw open the flap to his tent. "Good morning, friends!" He popped onto the rock beside me and waggled his brows. "Isabel."

"Yes, Kaspar?"

"You can put your hands all over me now." He dropped his voice to a sultry whisper. "I know you've been waiting."

"Shut up," Erik said.

"You know," I said, grabbing my medicine bag, "I actually have."

Water shined on the rock face of the ravine. Mountain avens quivered from where they sprouted in the walls, their white petals coated with dew.

I ripped one of my extra skirts into strips to clean and re-bandage Kaspar's leg. The arrow had struck his upper thigh just below his butt. Riding a horse would hurt and there'd be a scar, but he'd be fine.

"Any idea who was following us?" Erik asked.

"None," Kaspar replied. "We killed four, the rest got away. So did one of our horses."

"Not mine, I hope."

Kaspar shrugged. "Helhest is fine. We actually lost Buttercup."

My hand slipped, knocking the water bowl I'd perched on a rock. "You lost Buttercup?"

"Oh, don't look so sad. At least you have your bag."

It was true. I'd taken off my bag when I'd decided to walk, but that didn't explain—

"My tent!"

Another shrug. "I slept in Bo's and you slept in mine. Not a big deal."

"Wait," Erik said. "You slept in *Bo's* tent?"

"To be fair," Kaspar drawled, "there wasn't a lot of sleeping."

Bo ducked his head, the tips of his ears turning pink.

Oh. *Oh.*

Erik gave Kaspar a fist bump.

A hawk turned through the sky above us. A few fish splashed through the shallows, silver bodies glittering under the sun. Their fins fanned out like lace fans, causing little ripples.

I knotted Kasper's bandages a final time. "You're ready. And you—" I pointed at Erik. "You're up."

He tugged off his shirt and sat before me, his back toned and muscular.

I laid my palm against it.

He tensed against my touch.

Could I beat him back to Karlsborn Castle? Would he chase me when I ran? A thrill ran through me, shivery and wild. I shouldn't *want* him to chase me, but…

I reached for the bowl of water.

"Was there anything on the attackers that could identify them?" Erik asked as I pressed the damp rag against his wounds.

Kaspar shook his head. "No. And that's the strange thing. They had nothing—no packs, no bags. Except…"

"Except?"

"One had this in his pocket." Kaspar extended a strip of red fabric, two fingers wide and as long as my forearm. "It's probably nothing."

Erik grimaced. "How long do I have to sit here?"

"Not as excited as Kaspar to have my hands on you?"

"It's just not how I pictured it."

I…wasn't sure what to say to that.

Erik tipped his head back so his chin angled toward the sky. His voice went husky. "Tell me, Isabel. Did you picture it like this?

Or did you picture us somewhere else? Were we sneaking around my camp? I know you like that." His gaze darkened. "Sneaking."

I coughed.

He cackled.

"Why do you keep doing that?" I asked.

He flipped around so his knees bracketed my body. "Doing what?"

I blinked. I was not expecting to face him when he answered that question. "You...know."

He leaned back on his palm, stretching. No, not stretching. Making sure I had a good view of his tattoo.

Oh lordy.

"Tell me why you think I'm doing it," he purred.

Because you're dreamy, and I sometimes fantasize about your hands all over my body.

Except Bo, Kaspar, and Signey were all in earshot. So nope. "Turn around."

He laughed again but complied.

I uncorked the jar of honey and smoothed it over the wound.

Focus on the wound care. Wounds. Gross wounds. Bloody wounds. Puss-filled wounds. How to treat them. Not his husky voice. Not his tattoo. Definitely not the tattoo. This wound. Right here. Yes. Treat it. How should I treat it? Calendula or yarrow would be best, but I didn't have any left. If I hadn't been planning to leave, I might have climbed back up and went to Esbern. Or maybe...

"I need supplies," I said. "This is the last of the bandages, and I'm running low on everything else. If I could borrow a horse—"

It was the perfect excuse, really. It would buy me a lead, and if I could steal the Lover's Box before I left...

Erik glanced over his shoulder. "Back to Esbern?"

"Yeah."

"For supplies?"

I tried to keep an even expression. "Um, yes? Is that a problem?"

"Take Kaspar."

"Kaspar's injured. He'll slow me down."

"Then Bo."

I glanced at Bo, who was flipping another cake off the griddle. "I don't think—"

Erik lifted his brows in mock surprise. "I was told it would be a diplomatic disaster if something happened to our Sanok guide."

Diplomatic disaster…like he cared about that.

"I'll be fine."

"I'd hate for something to happen to you."

"That is a very different attitude than the one you had at the start of this trip."

His brows furrowed. Mock concern. He flipped around again and placed both hands behind my knees. "I only want to keep you safe."

More like he wanted to keep me watched. Fine. I still had søven. I could drug whoever came with me and escape afterward. Ha. I'd still win.

I gathered up the dirty bandages and tossed them into the fire. They shriveled in on themselves, curling in like—

Something clicked.

Not clicked mentally, but actually clicked. It came from—

I whirled.

Click.

Signey's tent. It sloped and rose, a monument against the morning mist.

My heart hammered. My mouth dried.

What had Bo said about the boxes? King Herleif had been sending messages back and forth so often his house was filled with—

Click.

Had they heard it? Bo smothered butter over his griddle cake. Kaspar tore at a hunk of rye bread. Erik tugged his shirt back over his head. Maybe they hadn't. Maybe it would be—

Click.

"Did you hear that?" Erik asked.

"That's weird," Bo said.

Click.

Kaspar snatched the griddle cake off Bo's plate. "Sig! I think there's someone who wants to talk to you."

"Hey!" Bo said. "That's—"

Signey flipped him off. "Screw you."

Click.

Time sped, time slowed, the seconds falling through my fingers. I had søven, but I couldn't drug all of them. Could I outrun them? Erik and Kaspar were wounded, but they both had reykr. So did Signey.

Bo rolled his eyes. "Fine. You can have that one."

The river hissed. Two sheep wandered down the mountainside, white blots against the gray.

Kaspar opened his mouth to eat the stolen griddle cake, and—

Click.

"*Signey!*" he shouted. "Are you going to get that?"

Signey got up, returned with the black metal box, the one stamped with falling crows. She tugged the key over her head, fit it into the lock. It snicked.

Maybe I could pretend like I hadn't sent the original message. After all, the reply would only be half of the conversation, and Signey kept the key around her neck. There was no way I'd have access to send it.

But no. I'd used the box yesterday when I'd stitched up my ear.

Click.

Signey flicked the lid open. Inside, a single piece of paper quivered.

If I wanted to run, it was now or never.

She scooped the paper up and peeled it open. Her eyes flicked across the page.

My heart thudded. Every muscle in my body screamed *go, go, go*.

"What do they want?" Erik asked.

Signey shoved the paper at him.

Erik skimmed it. Crumpled it in his fist. "Pack the camp."

"What happened?" Kaspar asked.

"Read it yourself."

Kaspar opened the paper. His face pinched, then fell. "Shit. This is—" He scraped a hand through his hair and stalked off. "Shit."

"Wait!" Bo called, rushing after him. "What does it say?"

He thrust it back at Bo, who smoothed it on a rock.

It quivered, blinding and white, a lone leaf left on a bare branch. I pressed two fingers against the page.

The writing was crimped and rushed. Something—A hand? A wrist?—had smeared the ink.

Uprising at Karlsborn Castle. Attempt on Lothgar's life. Poison. Unsure if he'll last the day. Protests. Threats. Fire in the streets. The future is changing. The sooths see a different outcome. Come back.

"WE'LL REPLACE BUTTERCUP IN ESBERN," Erik said, saddling the horses. He glanced at me and grimaced. "I…know she wasn't the easiest animal, but we'll get you something better. Probably a gelding. Not another mare."

I used my knees as a levy to pull the flap on my tent bag closed and scrambled for the buckle. The words of the letter swirled in my head. *Uprising at Karlsborn Castle.* "She hated me."

"Buttercup didn't hate you." The corner of his mouth quirked. "She just liked food better."

Attempt on Lothgar's life. I wasn't sure if that was a good thing or not. Lothgar seemed formidable, so removing him would probably be a good thing for Larland and the Sanokes. But…that was Erik's father. How would he feel about losing him?

Erik extended a hand. "Now come on. I'll help you up."

"Up?"

He cocked a brow. "We're riding Helhest. Don't tell me you planned to walk."

I wouldn't mind walking. I'd be a sore and sweaty mess climbing out of the ravine, though that would be better than another Buttercup situation. But the letter…

We needed to get back.

"Okay," I said. "Put me on your horse."

HELHEST WAS BIGGER THAN BUTTERCUP, all muscle and dominance with thunderous hooves and piercing eyes. His coat gleamed the gray of salt-splattered rocks, and his entire body rumbled when he snorted.

Erik led him to a rock. I grabbed the lip of the saddle and scrambled on. My heart pounded. Above us, birds flew in and out of nests. Storm clouds darkened the skies. Then, a heat behind me. A warmth. Erik's arms reached around and found the reins.

I expected to feel anxious—a normal person would have felt anxious. The last time I'd been on a horse, it had been Buttercup. She'd fallen into the ravine and I'd had a panic attack, and I *should* feel anxious.

Instead, I felt…alive.

The damp air made my skirt stick to my legs and my braid clung to my neck. My ruined ear held a dull ache, and yet, I didn't care about any of that.

Instead, I studied the saddle—the way the leather glistened, the line of brass studs that decorated the seams, each stamped with a little cross, like a bun. And there, padding on the seat. See the way it puckered when it joined the leather, the line of stitches that connected it? I shifted. Shifted again. Shifted a third time. Did Erik have a more comfortable saddle than me? Had he *purposely* given me a bad saddle? Had I been riding on a bad saddle this entire time? I shifted again, shifted—

"Ah, um, Isabel. Stop."

I glanced back. *He* shifted. A bulge jutted from his pants.

Oh, hi. Okay. That was unexpected. Well. Um. What would be worse? Acknowledging it or *not* acknowledging it? But I'd seen, and he'd seen that I'd seen. And now he was waiting for some sort of response and—

"Wow," I blurted. "An actual snake." The words dangled

between us, worse than the cups comment when we first met. Definitely should not have acknowledged it. Nope. Should not acknowledge. But now he was looking at me and his brow was furrowing.

"Like your tattoo," I continued. "A snake to match a snake. Yep, that's a snake."

"Of course you'd make this awkward," he muttered. "How about I teach you how to steer him?"

Blood rushed to my cheeks. "Um."

He scrubbed a hand over his face. "Helhest. I meant Helhest. Just…give me a second to calm down." He took a few breaths, then hooked his boots around my ankles and dragged them back a few inches. "You hold here and here. Don't control him through the reins. We give commands with our feet." He nudged my boots against Helhest's stomach. The horse set off at a slow walk.

My heart thundered. "I didn't— The snake comment—"

"Let's not talk about it. We use the opposite foot for the direction we want to go. If we want Helhest to go left, we nudge with our *right* foot." He eased my right foot into Helhest's belly, and Helhest veered left. "If we want him to go right, we nudge with our *left* foot." Helhest veered right.

We looped around the camp, then returned to the others where they waited, mounted and ready to go.

Erik took the reins back and pushed my feet forward. "No more blabbering about snakes," he said. "And do *not* grind against me in the saddle."

Kaspar took a drink from his waterskin. Signey played with her knife.

Bo fidgeted with the letter, opening and closing it, twisting the corner. "They said the streets were on fire. What do you think we'll find?"

Chapter Thirty-Three

WE SMELLED IT BEFORE WE SAW IT—the acrid bite of smoke, the sear of air.

Ruin.

Broken trunks spilled clothes, all grays and woolly creams. Doors hung off hinges. Inside, dark flashes of movement. The wet gleam of eyes. Sobs. Ash blew through the streets.

I swallowed and pressed my hands to Helhest's neck, felt the steadying heave of each breath.

The letter said there had been protests, chaos, fires, but I hadn't expected…

If you didn't want to be gutted…

I should have expected.

I'd stolen the Lover's Box almost every night on the journey back, sat cross-legged in my tent and fiddled with it until the pull made my eyes blurry and my teeth ache, until my fingers were slicked with the blood from my ear and the skin went numb. No answers, but when I touched the box, the memories seemed to sharpen.

Wings.

Fire.

Apricots.

Stars.

All falling together like…

Drops

Of

Rain.

And I knew—*knew*—there was something bigger, something deeper, a beast lurking beneath the surface, and maybe the clasp wasn't a clasp, but a mouth, and maybe the rosettes weren't rosettes, but eyes, and maybe the box was a living thing that wanted to bite and swallow and chew.

And maybe, just maybe, it wanted to be let out.

Behind me, Erik shifted, the warmth of his body pressing against my back. His arm wrapped tighter around my waist, and we were back in the ruined city, back to the burn of smoke, the bite of char, the clop of Helhest's hooves ringing over stone. Cracked windows. Broken chairs. A scraggly cat slunk through the wreckage.

"It wasn't supposed to be like this," he said. "It was supposed to be peaceful."

We'd never stopped to replace Buttercup, and I'd ridden with him the entire trip back. Awkward beginning aside, I liked the way we sank into each other, liked the way he fiddled with my sweater sleeve, his steadiness, his warmth, and I shouldn't have liked it, I shouldn't have because now a ribbon fluttered, tied to a charred wheel spoke, and now a splintered bell hung off a stoop and—

"Why?" I asked. "Because we're small?"

"I didn't say that."

I bit back a laugh. It might have been a cry. "We may not be big enough to drive you out, but we're not weak."

Behind me, he stiffened. "Without a bigger ally—without *us*—you'll lose the coming war."

"A war Volgaard is starting."

"Larland will demolish you."

"Larland isn't our enemy!"

"We're not your enemy, Isabel." A note of pleading in his voice. "*I'm* not your enemy."

A rag doll lay face-down in the mud.

No, I wanted to scream. *Your people just killed Hans, killed the minister, sacked our city.* "Larland might have owned us," I said, "but they *never* treated us like this." I scooted forward, as far as I could go. A sudden rush of cold washed my back. "I'll ride with Bo."

Erik's knuckles tightened on the reins, but he stopped and let me scramble off.

Bo's body was more slight than Erik's, more willowy. "Don't worry," he said. "You're not my snake's type." He tried to give a teasing smile.

Smoke continued to waft over us.

Bo and I turned down the path that led to Karlsborn Castle. The others broke toward the beach path, Erik spearing the head, jaw set, eyes hard, Kaspar and Signey just behind.

"He's right, you know," Bo continued. "It wasn't supposed to happen like this. We never came to the Sanokes to conquer them."

I tore my gaze away from Erik. "Only if we didn't help you in your war against Larland."

Bo's response was so quiet, I almost missed it. "Only that."

We fell into a guarded silence, the only sound the toll of bells, the shriek of gulls. They might not have intended this to happen, but it had. The Volds were a tempest and there was no stopping them, no way to guard against the damage that would continue to grow and grow.

Unless we secured Larland's help. Unless we found the weapon.

We left Bo's horse at the stables and followed the path of ruin into the castle. Settees had been slashed down the center, bouquets of buttercups sat crushed and browning at the edges.

Bo kept his hands in his pockets and picked his way through the ruin, but I kept my hands out, let my fingers trail across the wisps of curtain lace, the leg of an overturned chair.

The castle wasn't home, not exactly. Still, something curled and knotted in my stomach, and it was a daze, a dream, a delicate, gilded thing.

"It's going to be okay," Bo said. "We're going to fix this. We're going to— Erik will shadow walk. He'll shadow walk and figure out—"

"You can't fix this," I said. "It's done."

Bo turned away, a flash of cheek and jaw.

Down another hallway, light dazzled from broken chandeliers, sparkled from shattered vases, soft as a soap bubble, shiny as a snowflake, and—

Something caught my eye.

A credenza wedged against a door. A chair shoved under a handle. Crates brought up from the kitchen, overturned to form a barricade.

Too small to drive you out, but not weak.

Bo took a shaky breath, ran a hand through his hair. "I should help him. Erik. I should—" A glance over his shoulder. "He'll want to shadow walk. He'll want to know—"

"It's fine." Another credenza. Another door. Another stack of chairs with arms that bowed back on themselves like swans. "Go."

"But he'll want to make sure you made it home."

Broken windows. Smashed locks. We hadn't made it easy for them.

Pillows torn. Scorch marks up the walls.

What happened to everyone? Gone, probably, and I could leave, too, could find work somewhere else. There was no royal physician anymore. There was no royal *anything*.

But Hans…

When history was written, it wouldn't be about his sacrifice. His death would be nothing, would *mean* nothing.

No, I'd stay. I'd figure out what happened here, see what we could salvage from this ruin.

He'll want to make sure you made it home. Bo's statement hung in the air.

I turned to him. "I am home."

THE LATCH TO THE APOTHECARY'S DOOR no longer lined up with the lock. It hit the frame with a soft *tap, tap, tap*. I caught the swing and let my hand rest on the handle. Bo had gone back to shadow walk with Erik, and I'd traveled on alone, past shattered statuettes and torn paintings.

A draft caught my hair, and feathers swept the hall like snow. Maybe sending Bo away was a bad idea, but I couldn't keep him forever, and if I didn't search for survivors, I'd never learn what happened. I'd just put down my bag.

I pushed the apothecary door open…

The long worktable had been overturned. Shattered jars. Broken books. Dried flower buds littered the floor, white and curled, fair like fleece. Rancid smoke gave everything a grayish tinge. I pressed the neck of my sweater to my nose.

No staff.

No Stefan.

But Volds…

Two of them.

They basked in the smoke, their feet kicked on the table, puffing from pipes that dangled between their fingertips. One had his long hair tied back in a ponytail, his cheek crisscrossed with puckers of scar tissue, hands tattooed with so many knots and whirls, they webbed his skin like spiders. The other was missing an eye.

I loosened the grip on my sweater and gave a little sniff. Rancid, yes, but beneath it, the weedy sweet of citrus and mud.

Golden grass, a mild relaxant. Not strong enough to make you high, but it would definitely give you a buzz.

"Oh looksies," said the one-eyed Vold. "A maid."

The other's lips pulled into a sneer, revealing a split tongue and sharp teeth. "One we haven't broken yet."

The tattoos on his hands flared, fire licking up his arms like gloves. Light spilled from his mouth like a lantern and his eyes burned like pits.

I backed toward the door. Oh no. No, no, no. "This isn't… I'm not—"

A fireball blasted the door, spraying wood.

I ran.

Ran, ran, ran. Down one hall, then another. "Bo!" I shouted. "Bo!"

A second fireball scorched the stone right next to my head.

"Come back," one of the Volds shouted. "Let's have some fun."

My foot slipped. My hip banged against a credenza. Pain coursed up my leg, spiraling, spiraling, spiraling—

"*BO!*"

Another fireball splintered stone, and bits of dust caught in my hair, my teeth, and I wouldn't make it, wouldn't—

Bo skidded around the corner, eyes wide, jacket askew.

"Stop. *Stop!*" He held up his hands. "She's under the protection of House Rythja. You can't hurt her."

The Volds came to a swerving halt. Dark hair. Furs. Fire licked the split-tongue's arms in smoky tendrils.

The one-eyed Vold curled his lip. "Says who?"

"Erik, son of Lothgar."

"And you are?"

I rested my hands on my knees. My heart beat through my fingertips. *Ba-dum. Ba-dum.* But safe. I was safe.

"Björn, son of Bror. Erik's Kaldr-Flodi anchor."

"Bror's son," repeated split-tongue. He licked his teeth. The fire coming off him hissed and snapped, yellow tongues inked blue.

Bo's hands balled to fists. "Yes."

"Anchor to Lothgar's bastard."

Bo tipped his chin. A smirk. Maybe there was something feral in Bo, too—kind and sweet Bo—because right now, he had that same wild energy as Erik or any of his men. A flare of nostril. A flash of teeth.

Sweat beaded my brow.

Ba-dum, ba-dum.

With one swift motion, split-tongue grabbed Bo's shirt and whirled him against the wall. Bo's head hit the plaster with a *crack*.

"Bo!" I shouted, and then I was on split-tongue, clawing at his clothes, his eyes, my fingers digging into the fleshy skin of his—

An elbow to my ribs. Another to my stomach.

I stumbled back. My palms slapped the ground.

Blood oozed from Bo's temple.

Ba-dum, ba-dum.

I flexed my hands, wiped them on my skirts.

"You know, I always wondered about Kaldr-Flodi blood," split-tongue continued. "Is it as sweet as everyone says?" He leaned forward and *tasted* it, a slow drag of the mouth against Bo's temple.

"Leave him alone," I said. "You were after me. Come at me! Come on!"

Split-tongue ignored me. His lips came away sheened a bright ruby-red. "Sweeter. Like honey. And warm like milk." His tongue flickered out and caught a stray drop. "We've been looking for you, you know. There's an unskag on your head. A thousand pennigars."

Bo struggled against his grip. "An unskag? For what? I haven't—"

Split tongue pressed a finger to Bo's lips. "Ah-ah-ah."

Bo's eyes found mine. "Find Erik."

Split-tongue shoved a hand over Bo's mouth and pulled him away.

Chapter Thirty-Four

I STUMBLED THROUGH THE HALLS, the events of a few minutes ago playing in my mind. Split-tongue's hand on Bo's shirt. The *crack* of his head. The sheen of blood. Only this time, the blood reflected the room, the domed ceilings and shattered chandeliers. And this time, instead of licking it, he drank and drank.

Metal burned my throat. I needed to find Erik. Tell him what had happened and—

Arms hooked around my waist, pulling me into a storage closet. I stumbled, my feet catching the hem of my dress. Shelves rattled.

I elbowed a hip. A groin. Something—a jar?—fell to the floor with a crash.

Liquid spattered my skirts. Lemon and vinegar.

"Oof!" A familiar voice. "It's me, Isy. *Isabel!* It's me, it's—"

I blinked. Stopped fighting.

The hands on my waist loosened, allowing me to twist.

"Stefan? What…? How…?"

He pushed the door closed, plunging us into darkness.

"Stay quiet. We might've already—"

Footsteps. Voices. Brisk. Gargled, like a mouthful of stones.

Stefan pressed a finger to my lips and cracked the door, letting in a band of light.

Outside, Volds. Not the same Volds who'd taken Bo, but others. Tattoos like gloves. An angry glint in their eyes. Fire licked their arms, coming off them in ropy coils. One flicked out a tongue as if he was tasting the air.

More words. And shouts?

Stefan shut the door and whirled. "When did you get back?"

"Just now. What's going on?"

"When the Volds sacked the castle, most of us fled to nearby cities or retreated to safer parts. We've been hunkering in the kitchens, plotting our next move." A sliver of light slatted his cheek, lit his spray of freckles a pale red-gold, caught the hazel flecks in his irises.

"So those are the Volds who showed up after we left?"

Stefan cracked the door and peeked down the hall. "Yes."

"And they're the ones who sacked the castle?"

"I think it's safe now. We'll have to move fast." He extended a hand. "Come on."

If I left with him, I'd be abandoning Bo.

The corner of his mouth lifted. "Katrina's down there. She's turned into quite the resistance fighter. I think you'd be proud. She misses you. I think she feels bad about the way she treated you. She hasn't said those exact words, but sometimes she—"

"I can't. The Volds—they took Bo. I need to—"

"The dark-haired boy? Yeah, good distraction. Let's go. Stay close."

"I have to help him."

"Ready? One, two—" He grabbed my wrist and dragged me forward.

"Stefan." I dug my heels and tried to wrench my hand free. "You're not listening."

He tugged harder. "Why don't you want to—"

I stumbled back, pulling him with me. My foot knocked an empty mop bucket. "Because I'm busy. Now let me—"

Stefan whirled, the flats of his hands coming to my shoulders and shoving me backward. My back hit the shelves with a rattle. "Dammit, Isy. The Volds? They killed Hans. Not the crazy fire-wielding ones, but the ones you're trying to help. Which side are you on?"

Circles rimmed his eyes. A cut festered above his brow. His expression darkened to something wild.

Pain radiated up my shoulders. The scent of vinegar and washing ash filled my nose, made my head pulse. "How is that even a question?"

He gritted his teeth and pressed me harder against the shelves. The wooden lip cut against my back. "Answer me."

"I'm with the Sanokes, you know that."

"Do I?"

"I am, I'm just—" My body ached, my head throbbed. "Bo's my friend."

Stefan adjusted his grip on my sweater so he held it with both fists. He pulled me higher, my heels inching off the floor. "*We're* your friends, Isy. We are. *Us.* Not them."

We're not your enemy. Erik's words.

I grasped at Stefan's wrists, his shoulder corded with muscle and suffocating. I was suffocating, the cut of my collar pressing against my throat. The mint on his breath burned my lips, my nose. He wove his fingers through the wool. Stars burst behind my eyes. "Stefan. Stef—put me down. You're hurting me."

Stefan clapped a hand over his mouth. "I'm sorry. It's just that—" He dragged a hand through his hair. "You don't know what it's been like."

I slumped against the shelves and heaved in heavy breaths. "I have a pretty good idea."

"Have you watched your friends be burned alive? No, you haven't. We need Larland's help. We need to find the weapon. We're running out of time. Come on. We need to—"

"Who was burned alive?"

"Shit, Isy. What don't you understand? As soon as the Volds move against Larland, they won't be able to send aid. We'll be on our own, even more than we are now. We're running out of time."

"Stefan. *Who?*"

His eyes flicked to me, then away. "Henrik." The word no louder than a whisper.

Henrik, the lamplighter. The last time I'd seen him, we'd been taking bets on whether the Volds used cups. *I'll buy you in.* The flick of a wrist, the flash of a gyllie. His dazzling grin.

Stefan scrubbed a hand over his face. "Look. You were the only person on that scouting mission. We need you. *I* need you."

The way he said it, so fervent and full of determination. But what about Bo? Bo, who had always stood up for me, defended me, even when I had no one. Bo, who taught me how the Volds worked, who let me ride with him when I couldn't—

I swallowed.

If I left with Stefan, would I be abandoning Bo?

"I'll come back," I said, wiggling free. "Tonight. I'll tell you everything. Just…let me do this first."

BIGGER. THE ENTIRE CAMP. At least three times. The other camp had been an outpost, but this? But now? They'd made an army. Smoke billowed a tarry gray.

There were none of the Volds with fire hands, but there were others—spikes embedded into their knuckles, their teeth filed to points. Others with lips tattooed the copper of dried blood, with faces that changed from maiden to crone and back again.

Waves beat like battle drums and flags snapped, green and gray, a troupe of them in blazing cerulean. I pulled my sweater tighter and kept my head down.

Find Erik. Tell him about Bo.

"Watch it," hissed a man leading a goat. Between one blink and the next, the goat grew fangs and snapped its jaws.

"Get outta here," said another.

"Wait," I called, chasing after him. Sand nipped my ankles, speared my skirts. "Do you know Erik?"

The man snorted and kept walking.

"Erik?" My voice cracked.

I side-stepped a flea-bitten dog, a crate of overturned apples with dewdrops scarring the skin. I grabbed a woman's arm. "Erik?"

She barred her teeth and pointed a wraith-like finger toward the beach.

And there he was, standing, smiling, handsome in a dark green jacket, the crest of a falling crow embroidered on his breast. He'd combed his hair to the side, tucked one hand into his pocket, the other resting on the hilt of a sword. "Erik," I called, stumbling toward him.

A blink and he was gone, a furl of smoke and shadow, and there was the beach and sun-tipped waves, the rhythmic *pound, pound, pound* against the shore. Seagulls screeched. Puffins squabbled. A clutch of them bobbed in the shimmering blue water.

I pressed the heels of my hands against my eyes. *Shit.*

And—

Behind me, Erik leading his dappled gray. He grinned and caught fire like a candle. And Erik talking to a dark-haired man. He melted into a snake, a sea. And Erik, Erik, Erik.

The camp spun, a whirl of color and faces. Some leered, some laughed. Chickens clucked, coins clinked, spindles whirred, and—

"Isabel?" A familiar voice, a familiar accent. I whirled and found myself face to face with Tyr. He'd changed from the travel leathers he wore on the road, and his beard had grown out, no longer trimmed so close to his jaw. His eyes still shone that mineral shade of blue.

We stared at each other, and maybe he would change into a goat or a ghost or some black-headed beast with cracked horns and missing teeth, but a smile split his face and I was swept into a giant hug. I didn't think Tyr and I had ever been *this* close, but in that moment, I'd hug a ferret if it was real.

He pulled away, swept his hands down my arms.

"I heard you were back. Wanted to find you, but I wasn't sure… You'll be happy to hear we cleared up the worms. That bit of tea? Did the trick. After you left, Bengt was… Well, you know how Bengt is… He—"

"It's Bo," I said, clawing at his arm. "They took him. I need to—Erik. Where's Erik?"

Tyr blinked once. Blinked again. He ran a thumb over his jaw. "Ah. Um. I think he's with Signey. Maybe I can help. Who took Bo?"

"The snake people."

Tyr looked at me like *I* was the crazy one. "The…snake people?"

"Yes."

"Okay. Snake people. Like…people snakes? Or actual snakes?"

I clenched my teeth. "You know, snake people!"

"I'm just trying to understand. Tell me more about these alleged 'snake people.'"

Fine. "They have tongues cut down the center, and their hands burn like… Is Erik one of them? I mean, he has that tattoo—"

Tyr grabbed my arm. "Okay. Yep. This is an Erik thing. Come on." He glanced around and dropped his voice to a whisper. "And stop calling them snake people. They won't like that."

We reached a tent, twice as big as the others, a green flag out front, a falling crow emblazoned over the canvas.

Signey's voice leaked through the fabric. "How can you be so *dense*?"

"You went along with it." Erik. "In fact, you were the one who brought it with—"

A scrape. "I *went along with it*? I only took it so they wouldn't be—"

"Don't pin this on me. It was your idea to—"

"If I'm stripped of my honor bead, I swear, I'll—"

Tyr pulled the flap back.

Inside, Signey and Erik were locked in battle stance, chins tipped, fists balled, teeth barred. A smoky mass roiled off Erik's back and shoulders, spinning into storms, into seas, into snow. A shark swam through the sky above us, and dozens of white-furred wolves growled and snapped. They all turned toward me like puppets in a play. Blood dripped from their maws.

"Delivery," Tyr said.

Erik's jaw hardened. "Now isn't a good time for—" He glanced up. "Oh. Isabel. Hi. You're back? I mean—" The wolves fell away. "You're back."

Signey snatched her bag off the ground. "It's fine. I'll check on Dad. Come see me when you have a solution."

"You probably couldn't see Signey's illusions," Erik said, "but, uh...she was also casting some wild stuff. Powerful emotions. It's hard to control it. Anyway." He shot me a cagey glance and skirted to fix some blankets.

Tyr inched toward the door. "And this is where I depart. Good luck with the snake people."

Erik paused, a quilt dangling from his arm. "Snake people? Is that another euphemism for...?"

I shook my head. "They took Bo. Chased him down and drank his blood."

"Snake people?"

"Yes. Aren't you listening? Their hands turn to fire, and they have split tongues, and they took him and—"

Erik's hands erupted into flames.

I jumped back. "Holy shit! You're one of them!"

The fire stopped. "Sorry," he said. "Couldn't help it."

I grabbed his pack and prepared to swing. "Stay away."

"Isabel. Isa—" He dropped the blanket and grabbed my wrists. "That was a bad joke. A really bad joke. Snakes are Kaldr-

Flodi—my mother's house. They shed their skins. Their symbol is a snake. You're talking about *helvedeshunds*. Hellhounds. House Kynda. Not— They're not snakes."

"They took Bo. We have to get him back. The heaven hounds—"

His thumb smoothed the back of my hand. His gaze found mine. "Helvedeshunds."

"Them. They said something about an unskag?"

He was…weirdly calm about this. "Breathe," he said.

"What's an unskag!"

He dropped my wrists and folded the blanket. "It's an arrest warrant, issued by the king. Pretty formal. High bounty. Not something you want your name on."

"I just told you your friend was arrested, and you're going to…clean?"

The room wasn't messy. A canopied bed had been dragged down from the castle and made up with thick pillows. His packs sat at the foot of it, tugged open, then shoved off to the side. A sheep hide hung over a chair back, curly and gray, and copper tub sat in the corner, stolen from one of the Karlsborn Castle's noblemen. The scent of salt and impending storm drifted through the door.

"How's your dad?"

He hauled his pack onto the bed and unpacked a bundle of clothes. "Dying."

"How are you feeling about that?" I knew Erik didn't like his father, but…

Erik let out a heavy sigh. "Can we focus on one problem at a time? I knew Bo was arrested. They arrested Kaspar, too."

If he didn't want to talk about his dad, that was fine. I wasn't sure how I'd feel about my dad dying, either. "Why'd they arrest Kaspar?"

"Stealing." He tossed me a jacket. "Put that on."

"What did they steal? Also, I'm not wearing that." I tossed the jacket back.

"You can't run around the camp in your sweater. It makes you a target. And with all the syn rót floating around, I can't hide you from everyone." He tossed the jacket again.

"Syn rót?"

"It's a root that lets you see through illusions. Put the jacket on."

Fine. I threaded my arms through the sleeves. The quilted fabric smelled like him—the crackle of kindling, of campfires, of warmth and wool. I pressed the sleeve to my nose, breathing in the familiarity. The frantic patter of my heart eased.

"Maybe if we returned what Bo and Kaspar stole, we could fix this." I released the sleeve and tugged my braid out from beneath the shoulders. "What did they steal?"

The first beads of rain flecked the canvas.

Erik fiddled with the pack's buckle, a silver medallion etched with House Rythja's falling crow.

"What did they steal?" I asked again.

More rain drummed like fingers. From outside, the squeal of pigs, the shuffle as pelts and cooking pots were pulled under awnings. Shouts.

"Erik?"

"Bo and Kaspar didn't steal anything," he said after a moment. Candlelight carved angles in his stormy cheeks, shaded the set of his jaw. He glanced up, eyes burning. "I did."

Chapter Thirty-Five

MY JAW DROPPED. "*You* stole something? Alright. This is an easy fix. We just need to tuck our tails between our legs and give it back. What did you steal?"

Erik's mouth set into a line. He grabbed an armful of shirts and dumped them into a leather-bound trunk at the foot of his bed. "It's not that simple."

"Why?"

"I stole from the king."

"My king or—"

"Volgaard."

Well, that complicated things. "So, we tuck our tails *extra tight* and give it ba—"

He shut the trunk with a *thud*. "He already took them back."

"Then what's the problem? The thing's been returned. The king's been made whole. What did you steal?"

"The Lover's Boxes."

Well, shit. If that was the weapon, and if the King of Volgaard had taken them back, I now had a problem. A major problem. "Why did you steal the Lover's Boxes?"

"Here. Untangle this." He handed me a ball of fishing twine and moved to refold a stack of blankets. "You've felt the thrall…how strong it can be. Different people seem to have different tolerances. Signey says she hardly feels it, but King Herleif is susceptible. He became obsessed. Stopped eating, bathing—"

"Bo mentioned that. Are you okay? I feel like this is stress cleaning."

Erik shot me a glare and slunk to put the blankets on the bed.

Not okay, then. I picked my fingers through the knots, bristly fibers catching under my nails. "Why did you steal the Lover's Boxes?"

"King Herleif was running Volgaard into the ground—same thing he's doing to the Sanokes, only worse. We stole the boxes and things got better until—"

"You can't let your friends take the fall for this."

He snatched up a few empty bags. "You think I *want* Bo and Kaspar to take the fall? I'd rather be the one rotting in prison."

"Let's not be dramatic. Maybe if you talked to him—told him it was you—you could—"

That lock of hair fell over his forehead, and he pulled himself higher, feral eyes, white teeth. "Oh-ho, he knows it was me."

"Okay, now you're being *really* dramatic."

Erik shot me a sulky look and hung the bags by the door.

"Then why arrest Bo and Kaspar?" I continued.

"Because I'm Rythja's general while my father is dying. Arresting one of his generals would look bad. It's a power play. One that House Kynda is more than happy to—"

House Kynda. "The heaven hounds?"

"*Helvedeshunds.*"

I wedged a loop free. "Helv-dah-sounds."

He threw his hands in the air and stalked toward the bed. "You know what? Just call them snake people. Or hellhounds. Anyway, I'm convinced the Lover's Boxes have something to do with what happened to the Sanokes. That city? That wasn't supposed to happen." He found a coil of rope. Where did he find a coil of rope? "Now, look. I know you're a spy—"

My hands slipped, a piece of flax splintering my thumb. "I'm...not a spy."

He pursed his lips and wagged a finger. "You're not a *very good* spy. There's a difference. But go ahead." A little flourish of the hand. "'I'm not a very good spy.' Say it."

The splinter throbbed, pulsing and warm.

Was this another one of his games? Was he trying to trap me? And if I admitted I was a spy, then what? Would he drag me out of his tent? Kill me? If I died, no one would know about the Lover's Box, about Hans. If I made a run for it, how far could I get? I was in the middle of the Vold camp. Probably not far. But if I stayed...

If I stayed...

Outside, waves cracked. Rain pattered hard against the tent, dappling shadows.

I lunged for the door.

Erik caught my waist, spinning me back.

I elbowed him in the ribs. "If you think I'm going to go quietly—"

"Relax, Isabel. I just—*oof!*—want to hear you—"

My knee hit the bedpost, rattling the lamp and the inkwell on the side table. My shoulder collided with his jaw.

I reached back, tangling my fingers through his shirt. My knuckles grazed something cool.

I snatched the knife and flipped it on him. My hands trembled. "Don't come any closer."

His eyes flicked between me and the knife. He smirked and leaned into the blade. The tip pressed against the hollow of his throat. "Or what?"

With one strong motion, he grabbed my wrist and spun the knife out of my grip, and then I was on my back. He tucked the knife back into his belt and straddled me, sitting on my hips.

"'I'm not a very good spy.' Say it."

I dug my fingers into the weave of his rug. "I'm not a spy."

He puffed his chest and tipped his chin, a champion, a god. "Close, but not quite. Let's try again. 'I'm not a *very good* spy.'"

"I'm not a spy!"

"Shall I list how I know?" He held up a hand and ticked his fingers. "The worms. The baths. That time I caught you snooping outside my tent."

"Because I was bringing you coffee! I was trying to be nice."

He crossed his arms. "I should clarify. I caught you outside my tent *on more than one occasion*."

"I like to take walks."

He gave a skeptical look.

"Outside your tent." I shoved at his chest. "Now get off."

He leaned forward, placing both arms around my head, and now his body was a cage, and I was caught beneath it. "'I'm not a very good spy.' Your turn."

This close, I could see the curl of his lashes, the faintest fracture of blue in his eyes, almost the catch of light on quartz. This close, I could smell his smoke and wool scent, the way it clung to his hair, his clothes, the way his shirt hung open, exposing the barest sliver of chiseled chest.

I could kiss him if I tried.

I wanted to try.

I tipped my head back, caught the upside-down slant of the world, the honey-wood legs of his chair, his bed, the little slit in the tent flap where rain darkened the rug to cobalt. "You're not a good spy?" It was childish, it was, but I didn't have anything left.

He caught my chin, pulled it back. "On the contrary," he said, "I'm an excellent spy. You're not. Go ahead. Say it." His thumb lingered on my jaw.

My heart hammered.

Now his mouth was so close to mine, the softness of his lower lip, the dip of his cupid's bow. If I tipped my chin a little higher…

He slid his hand down my neck, stopping to play with the collar of my shirt. "I could always…" his voice went husky, "make you say it." He rolled the fabric between his thumb and forefinger, a fleecy, blue-flecked gray. His knuckles grazed my chest. "You wanted me to make you do things at the Rose & Thistle Inn. Do you remember?" He traced the arc of my collarbone, his touch feather-light.

Chills swept through my body.

"I wonder what other naughty things you might enjoy." The back of his nail dipped just inside my sweater. "I've noticed you like using your talents to do naughty things. I can always…use mine." He leaned forward, took the shell of my unharmed ear between his teeth, and gave a little nip. "Tell me you're not a good spy."

I gritted my teeth. "I'm…not a very good spy." The words came out breathless.

"Say it again," he murmured, nipping my jaw.

"I'm not a good spy."

"Say it," his voice dropped to a growl, "louder." His hips rolled against mine and his nip turned into a suck, drawing a bruise to the skin's surface.

"I'm not a good spy." Another breathless gasp. "Are you giving me a love mark?"

"Was that louder, Isabel?" He grabbed my hands and pulled them above my head, stretching me long.

"I can't. The walls… Someone will hear."

"No one will hear." Another murmur. He adjusted his grip, lacing our fingers together. His palms were rough and warm, and his eyes locked with mine, intense and unwavering. "Say it again, Isabel. Say it loudly. Scream it."

"I'm not a good spy! I'm a terrible spy! The absolute worst. What else do you want?"

His gaze dropped to my lips. It followed the curve of my mouth, the line of my jaw, before landing on what must be that love mark. Light lit him from behind, tangling its fingers through the waves of his hair.

His eyes flickered with something unreadable. "Isabel?"

"Yeah?"

From outside, a drunken laugh.

Erik blinked once, blinked again. He sat back on his heels. "See? Was that so hard?"

"What were you going to say?"

"That you're not a good spy. *Clearly*. And you crack easily under pressure." He slid off and skirted to the desk. "Now, look, here's my theory. Lothgar's Lover's Box swept up King Herleif in its thrall. Lothgar's box made Herleif seek out our box. Now he's letting House Kynda run wild, which is causing problems for everyone. It's exactly what happened in Volgaard. If we remove the boxes, we remove the thrall. Herleif will reassert dominance over Kynda and, *hopefully*, release Bo and Kaspar."

"And the Sanokes?" I touched the place he'd sucked, the skin still warm and throbbing. Was that all the love mark had been? Pressure so I'd crack?

He pulled out a map, smoothed it on the ground, and dropped a handful of black and white stones across the coast. "This was the original plan. To use the Sanokes as a foothold into Larland. It's what we were scouting for—places to launch ships. There's a corruption growing in Larland, a darkness, and it's going to spread until it devours *everything*. The sooths saw a better chance at victory if we moved first. It's a preemptive strike."

Erik moved the stones into a circle surrounding the Sanokes, clustering the white stones at the tip of our island, Saeby. "This is Herleif's plan now. I'd be willing to bet the change has something to do with the boxes."

"Do they mean anything?" I asked. "The colors?"

"White stones for House Rythja. Black for all other houses."

"Because of reykr?"

He shrugged. "Because of me. I can hide any ship I can see. So those are white. Stealth ships. An important part of the plan…or, the original plan."

I moved to touch the ear he'd nipped, and something stung my finger. The splinter. Right. I dropped my hand to my mouth and fished it out with my teeth. "Why are you telling me this? You know I'm a spy."

"Because I trust you. Mostly. I think."

My heart ticked.

"And stop doing that," he added.

"Doing what?"

"Eating your thumb. It's weird."

"Can't. Have a piece of rope stuck. Must remove."

I expected some quip, but instead, he settled cross-legged in front of me and flipped his palms up. His knees brushed mine. "Can I look?"

I gnawed my thumb. "Why?"

"Maybe I can help?"

"I can do it."

"You probably can."

"Better than you."

"Stop being weird."

I peeked over my knuckles. "Fine."

He took my hand and twisted it until he spotted the splinter, thin as a bristle on a boar-hair brush. Then he poured a knuckle's worth of water into a copper mug. "Put your hand in that."

"Why?"

"Because we're going to soften the skin."

"I've never soaked a splinter. I just use drawing salve."

"I used to get them from training swords, and I didn't have your fancy salves."

A few shadows passed over the canvas. Waves lapped the shore and this close, I could make out the rise and fall of his chest, the way the lamplight highlighted his nose, his mouth.

Was he going to kiss me earlier? Would he kiss me now? Or did a love mark count as a kiss? And if I leaned forward and pressed a quick peck against his lips, would he kiss me back the same way he kissed Helene?

A part of me still wanted to try.

He flipped my palm and smoothed my fingers flat. "That's fate," he said, skimming the line down the center. "Life." An arc around my thumb. "Heart." A sweep over the topmost line. He lingered, his thumb doubling back and tracing it again.

Heart.

"Now, I'm not a sooth," he continued, "so don't ask me to read your life line or your fate, but I do know something about your heart."

"Is it something terrible? Let me guess. I'm going to end up alone with a thousand chickens." Instead of kissing him, I tipped my head against the bedpost, the wood lemon-scented and smooth.

He laughed, light and sweet. "Not chickens. The line fractures here." He stopped in the middle. "That means that Skýja, weaver of bonds between souls, will conspire to keep you from the people you love. But it reunites here—" Right below my pinky. "Meaning you'll always find a way back to them."

"Like a puffin?"

"A what?"

I pulled my head up. "You said they mate for life."

Another laugh. "Oh. I guess like a puffin. The sooth said defying the gods, and I thought that sounded exciting. But puffin works, too."

I cocked a brow. "The sooth was telling you about my palm? When was this?"

"Not yours." He held up his palm. "I have the same."

I see you, I see you.

Slowly, carefully, he lowered my hand into the mug. "Now we wait."

"Can I count this as evidence of cup misuse?"

A smile plucked at his mouth. Lashes shaded his cheek. "Stop."

"You like it."

The water was cool, the bottom pitted and grooved, the copper seams soldered to metal.

Erik leaned back on his hand. "Herleif isn't a bad king. We just need to get the Lover's Boxes away from him."

If there had ever been a time to dig deeper about the boxes, now was it. "Do they do anything...other than pass messages?"

Erik gave me a quizzical look. "Not that I'm aware of. Is that what the Sanok rebels sent you to find?"

"No."

He quirked a brow.

"Yes. Sort of."

"Did they ask you to do anything else?"

Woo him. The minister's words. But would telling Erik fracture the fragile bond of trust growing between us? Plus, the minister was dead...

"They just wanted information," I said. Not a lie. Not exactly.

"Would you pass information back? If you found something?" He lifted my hand out of the water and squinted at my finger.

"No."

"Isabel."

"Maybe," I amended. "Are you going to kill me? If so, I will fight you. With the knife you gave me."

He grabbed the knife from his pack and scraped the blade over the pad of my thumb, roughing the skin and loosening the splinter. "Don't pass information back. I'm trusting you. I...hope you'll trust me, too."

My heart kicked. "What do you plan to do with the Lover's Boxes after you steal them?"

"Truthfully?" His jaw set in concentration. "I don't know."

"Can I…have them?"

He glanced up. "Why would you want the Lover's Boxes? They're toxic."

"When I…handled them, I felt something. Wings. Fire. Death. I think there's something inside."

The corner of his mouth tugged into a frown. "You want to let it out?"

"No."

"I wouldn't blame you. After what we did to the Sanokes, I'd want to use them against us, too." He set the knife behind him and rubbed my thumb. "Is it out? I think it's out."

I twisted my hand, hunting for evidence of the splinter. "Yeah. It's out."

"Look," he continued. "I'll make you a deal. If stealing the boxes from King Herleif doesn't fix the problems in the Sanokes, then I'll help you unleash whatever is lurking inside of them myself."

"You would defect to the Sanokes?"

"I'm not defecting to the Sanokes. I'd defect because House Kynda will ruin everything if they're not controlled. The only person who can control them is King Herleif, and the only reason he can do *that* is because he's bound their general with some sort of freaky ancient fealty magic. So, yeah." A shrug. "If stealing the boxes doesn't work, I'll help you unleash whatever's lurking in them, and we can use it to control Kynda together. And you know what?" He stood, rerolled the map and dropped the black and white stones into a leather pouch. "That's actually not a bad idea."

"What's not?"

Another shrug. "You."

"Me?"

"I can't steal the boxes because I'm being watched. So is Signey. Bo and Kaspar could, but they're in prison. But King Herleif doesn't know about you…"

"What are you saying?"

The corner of his mouth quirked. "I'm *saying* I'm going to make you into an actual spy."

STEALING THE LOVER'S BOXES.

I hooked my stockinged feet and fiddled with Hans's box of letters, the freckle of leather, the creamy soft of it, the embossed *HH*.

The candle snapped and sparked, chewing the wick like a hungry dog and casting ribbons of orange over the coarse rugs and canopied bed. Outside, laughter and stories, snatches of songs.

"*…hips full and round…*"

"*…bigger than a ship…*"

Erik had gone to a war council with King Herleif's other generals and left me here, alone in his tent.

I flicked the latch, then closed it. Inside, paper and powder, seals of wax, and scraps of ribbon.

Stealing the Lover's Boxes.

Then what? Did I trust Larland? Did I trust myself?

And Hans…

What would that make him?

Click, latch.

"You've been playing with that for hours."

I glanced over my shoulder. "How long you been standing there?"

Erik shouldered the tent pole. He'd pushed his shirt sleeves to his elbows and crossed his arms. Rain flecked his hair. "Long enough. You okay?"

I don't know if I can do this.

I miss him.

I want to be enough, but I don't know if I am.

I let out a shaky breath. "I don't know why I'm still here. I should get back to Karlsborn Castle."

His brows furrowed. "You don't have to leave, Isabel. You can stay with me." He studied me and added, "It's probably safer until we get things with Kynda figured out, anyway. And...I'd feel better knowing you were safe."

I bit the inside of my cheek and nodded. "Okay."

"I brought you something." He set a wax-paper-wrapped package on the floor in front of me, still warm. The air filled with the heady scent of butter and caramelized sugar.

Cinnamon buns.

I pushed myself onto my elbows. "You brought *you* something. How did you—"

"Tyr found a cookbook and was determined to make you a treat. A thank you for curing his worms."

"I didn't know Tyr bakes." I pulled off the wax paper, the cinnamon bun inside lumpy and misshapen, half-scorched on one side, raw on the other.

"He doesn't."

Looks aside, it couldn't be that bad. It was butter, flour,

sugar, almost impossible to screw up. I broke off a piece, took a bite and—

Salt scorched my tastebuds. "Okay, this is—"

"Awful?" Erik wrinkled his nose. "Yeah. Don't tell him. He was so proud."

"You're terrible, you know that?"

He grinned, bringing out his dimple. The candle crackled and sputtered, casting shadows up the wall.

"Tell me about your council meeting," I said.

He laid on the wool rug beside me, propped one hand under his head, ruffling his hair. "Oh, you know. Herleif's still hellbent on keeping the Sanokes. They're still looking for the rebels who poisoned my father. Kaldr-Flodi wants extra patrols tonight. Kynda doesn't because that means more work for them. That sort of stuff. Mostly boring."

"How is your father?"

"One day at a time." He reached for the letter box, ran his thumb over the embossed *HH*. "This…means something to you."

My throat thickened.

Erik must have read my expression because he added, "You don't have to tell me. I was just—"

"It belonged to my friend Hans." The words came out thick like cotton. "He was the apprentice postmaster, but this was his letterbox from before…"

Erik kept his face neutral. "I see." He toyed with the latch. "And, ah, are the two of you…?"

"He's dead."

I'd screamed, I'd sobbed. I'd been angry. So, so angry.

I hadn't let it out.

"You asked if it ever gets better," I continued. "I want to believe it does, but I'm afraid if I let go—"

A beat, a breath. He paused, his hand outstretched, almost as if he couldn't decide whether to touch me.

Touch me.

He tugged me to his chest, a wave crashing, smoke and softness, my cheek on his shoulder, and I was safe and warm and *here.* "You don't have to." He smoothed a few wisps of hair away from my forehead. "You don't have to let it go."

The world stretched and looped, doubled back on itself, the seconds tumbling together, a kaleidoscope of greens and grays, of summer and storms, of *him.*

Our legs tangled together.

And it shouldn't matter, it shouldn't, but the patter of my heart eased.

You're betraying everyone.

You're betraying Hans.

"He died right after you came," I said. "At the tide pools. I was… I found him. The body, I mean."

I waited for Erik's shame, the telltale sign of stillness that said he'd been involved.

His fingers continued to comb my hair. He hooked a strand behind my ear, let his knuckles linger against my jaw as if I was something precious.

I curled my chin to my chest. My nails pricked my palms. I should just come out and ask. It would be so easy to ask, to shatter this fragile thing. I cared about Hans, I did. I wanted him to be remembered, I did. And this wasn't about me; it was about Hans and his legacy, and I needed to know, needed, needed, needed—

"Tell me anything," I said.

Coward.

Hans deserved more.

Deserved better.

This isn't about you.

The thing inside me smoothed my hair and whispered, *This is only about you.*

Erik's fingers stilled, then started. "There's this story about a sorceress and a fisherman—"

The fist in my heart released. I lifted my head off his chest. "Hey. That's mine."

He laughed and squeezed my shoulder. "Okay. Calm down. What I meant to say… There's this story about a prince and a weaver. The prince was cursed as a baby, and anyone who saw him turned to stone…"

As Erik told the story, the world went hazy and golden at the edges, his voice hollow and far, and it was an anchor, a lifeline, all rich reds and starling blues, and we were infinity, and we were heartbeats, and we were *gravity*, hurling through the black expanse.

It

fell

apart.

"Isabel?" His fingertips smoothed a stray lock from my cheek. Or maybe it was a kiss. "I see you."

Then the swell of sleep swept me under.

Chapter Thirty-Six

I WOKE WITH A KINK IN MY NECK and pain in my bladder. The candle had burned out, washing the world in sweeps of shadow and gray. Moonlight shone off the walls of the tent, illuminating the fuzzed outline of a bed, a chair and—

Erik.

He'd grabbed a pillow and a blanket and hauled them onto the ground beside me. His breath came out deep and even. Lashes shaded his cheek.

The memory of last night swam through my mind, the tangle of his hand in my hair, the brush of his knuckles against my jaw…

The pain pressed harder.

There was a chamber pot on the nightstand near the bed, but there was no way I was going to pee in Erik's tent, especially with Erik sleeping right there.

I pulled on his soft blue jacket and piled my hair into a high ponytail. I caught my reflection in the mirror—gaunt cheeks, bloodshot eyes. I hadn't slept long enough.

Still, from a distance I might pass as Vold, especially if I kept my head down…and there had to be rocks farther down the beach.

I'd just pee and come right back. It would be quick. Erik wouldn't even know I was gone.

I fumbled through the dark, searching for my shoes. Not there. Not anywhere.

Fine. I'd go barefoot.

THE WORLD WAS SHARPER OUTSIDE, starker. White sea. Black sky. Silver moonlight spindled shadows into hands, into puppets, into a play. Foam tumbled like threads of cotton.

My bare feet left a string of footprints in the sand, and there was careful silence, a sucking silence, a dreamy silence filled with the lap of water and the *tink* of shells on the tide, and I was a seed, a spark, a small thing set against the sky.

I went a little ways around the side of the cliff, found a secluded spot between two rocks, and maybe I shouldn't have gone so far, but I couldn't shake the sense of being watched. It needled the base of my neck.

Wind and foam, the ink-black bodies of birds and the mouth of dreams yawned wide.

A flash of color, of warmth.

"Isy!"

I jumped. "What the hell?"

Katrina threw her arms around me, and then it was all wax and wool, the rosemary scent of her soap. "You're back!"

The last time I'd seen her, she'd been hitting me. Now she was hugging me, and I didn't even care because this was Katrina and she was okay. *Okay*. But now I really couldn't ignore the pain in my bladder. "I was going to the bathroom."

She squeezed harder. "I missed you. You—"

"You said you'd come back," Stefan supplied. Fog matted his hair, darkened it to a ruddy red and caused water to pill along the strands. He'd shoved his hands into his pockets, popped his jacket collar against the cold.

I wiggled out of Katrina's grip. "You should have waited for me to come to you. It's not..." I glanced over my shoulder. "It's not safe."

Stefan gave me a hard look. "*Were* you going to come to us? Or were you going to—"

"Oh save it," Katrina said. "We were trying to figure out whether or not to kidnap you out of that tent. I said yes, Stefan said no. But you're here now, so that doesn't matter. Do you want to see what we've been up to?" She shrugged off her shoulder bag and flipped the flap to reveal bottles—rows of them, all filled with the same cloudy liquid.

She plucked one out and held it up to the moonlight. Not cloudy. Amber. The color of fresh-strained honey. The sharp tang of lamp oil cut through the air.

"What...?" I asked.

She grinned, pulling out something devious. "They're incinerates. For the Vold ships. We're going to torch the fleet."

I plucked the bottle from her hand, a perfume vial with a curving neck and glass butterflies that scalloped the edges. Pink. The color of starfish or slippers. The butterfly wings caught the light, casting rainbows across the sand. "You're going to... Why?"

"Think about it, Isy. When do you use a weapon? If you're attacking or if you're *under attac*—"

Down the beach, a dog barked. Shouts.

Stefan grabbed Katrina's waist and hauled her into the shadow of a rock. I snatched the bag and ducked after them.

"That's not—" Off the shore, hundreds of boats floated. It wasn't a bad idea, but it wasn't a good one, either. "If you torch the fleet, you'll be trapping them. You'll be making things worse. Erik said there was a corruption growing in Larland, a darkness. He said it's going to devour everything. Maybe if we—"

"Why are you defending them?" Stefan shot back. He pressed himself under a rocky outcropping. "They literally conquered us. What don't you understand?"

"We could steal the weapon for ourselves. Instead of turning it over to Larland, maybe we use it to—"

Something blinked above the cliff side, a glint of light, a speck of silver, there then gone.

Stefan dug a mirror out of his pocket. "He's lying. I've been to Larland. I have *family* in Larland. I visit them every summer. There's nothing there." He tipped the mirror, sending back a flash of light. "Our best chance—our *only* chance—is maintaining our alliance with Larland. That's it. And torching the fleet is the best plan we have. So unless you have a better idea—"

"That was the signal," Katrina said.

My stomach lurched. "Wait. You're going tonight?"

"Yeah, silly. You coming?" Katrina offered her hand. There was an eagerness in the gesture, a giddiness that reminded me of sneaking out.

But this wouldn't solve the problem. I'd spent more time around the Volds than anyone. We'd be trapping them. No trees meant they wouldn't be able to rebuild the fleet. They'd be stuck and the hellhounds would burrow like ticks into the island. If Erik

314

was telling the truth—and I believed he was—torching the ships would cause more destruction, not less.

I needed to talk Stefan and Katrina out of it.

"What if we wait a little while?" I asked. "Watch the patrols? Maybe I could get the information from Erik—"

Stefan snorted. "We poisoned Lothgar and stole a crate of syn rót. We've snuck in and out of the Vold camp dozens of times. We'll be fine. Let's go."

"*You* poisoned Lothgar?"

"Yeah. Pipe root."

"But there isn't an antidote for pipe root…" Once it was in the system, it would be a slow death like a caterpillar eating a leaf, consuming the muscles until the lungs gave out and the heart could no longer squeeze.

Stefan gave me a sharp look. "Why would I give him something with an antidote? Come on. We're out of time."

Another flash of light above the ridgeline.

He grabbed my wrist and—

I had to stop them. Stefan and Katrina were like caged cats, desperate animals, and they were about to make things worse, so much worse.

"I think I know what the weapon is," I blurted.

Stefan paused, his fingers still on my arm. Fog rolled around us like water, like dreams.

"They're called the Lover's Boxes," I continued. "You can pass messages for a toll, like the ability to see the color green or smell rain. Erik can't hear whistling." My heart pounded, *ba-dum, ba-dum*. Erik had told me not to pass information, but I had to get Stefan and Katrina to back down.

"That doesn't sound like a weapon," Stefan said. "You didn't find anything else? What were they looking for?"

"A place to launch ships."

"They told you this?"

"I saw the map. White stones and black. Rythja and the other houses. Erik was going to make them invisible, but that doesn't matter. When I used the boxes, I felt something. Wings. Fire. Death. I'm going to help him steal them from the Vold king." *Ba-dum, ba-dum.* I was floating, falling, outside my body looking in. "They're from the Sanokes. I-I think they have some sort of magic."

The sea tossed, a roll of foam, a sweep of hands. A pair of petrels skirted the sky.

Stefan's brow furrowed. "The Sanokes don't have magic."

Katrina shrugged. "I mean, there's the screaming thing."

Another blink of light on the ridgeline, this one more frantic. *Blink, blink.* Pause. *Blink, blink.*

"We have to go," Katrina said. "They're moving."

"Time," I continued. "That's all I'm asking for. Give me time to steal the boxes. I think that will fix things. If it doesn't, maybe we can use the boxes to drive the Volds out ourselves." *What about Hans? His memory? His legacy?* "Just…" I pressed a hand to my forehead, "trust me."

"How much time do you need?" Stefan asked.

"Ten days?"

He glanced between me and the ships, his jaw set, hands curled. He was going to torch the fleet, anyway. He was going to—

He pulled out the mirror and gave three sharp twists of the wrist. "You can have seven. Come on, Katrina."

Katrina hesitated, her mouth drawn. "I thought you died," she said after a moment. "I thought you went off and got yourself killed. I thought…" She pinched the bridge of her nose. "It doesn't matter."

I bit my lip. "I get it. I was pretty sure you were going to die, too."

"You *don't* get it. I *grieved* you. You made me grieve you. *You* did, Isy. And I was still grieving Hans and it was—" She pressed a palm to her temple and shook her head. "I don't want to fight you. I'm sick of fighting you."

I tucked my hands under my arms. "I'm sorry you grieved me. What did you write?"

Something in her expression softened. She laughed and swiped a tear. "I said you were an idiot, but you were *my* idiot, and that I hate you, but I also love you."

"Sounds about right."

She slipped a silver ring off her pinky, one of the bands the carrier pigeons wore. "It reminds me of him." She gave my hand a squeeze. "Maybe it'll remind you, too."

SEVEN DAYS TO STEAL THE BOXES.

It wasn't enough.

It had to be enough.

Alone in Erik's tent, I balanced the pigeon ring on the lid of the letter box. Made it stand. Made it spin. Each rotation caught my face, caught the light. *Face. Light. Face. Light. Face—*

"We'll work on your lying first," Erik said, grabbing two blunted knives and heading toward the beach. "Repeat after me. Erik isn't attractive."

The sea spit like a cauldron of foam, all smoke and sleepy

white. The morning held a clean sort of cold.

"Erik isn't—wait!" I fell into step beside him. "Why do I need to be a better liar?"

He smirked. "I am not sometimes flustered by Erik's incredibly impressive abdominals."

I swiped my nose. "You realize I'm stealing boxes, right? No lying involved. Also, I wanted to talk about the timing of this heist. How does next week sound? Maybe before Thursday?"

He kept an even stride. "We need to figure out where Herleif's keeping the boxes. The best way to do that is to shadow walk, and the only person I trust to shadow walk is in prison. So first step: break into the prisons and shadow walk with Bo. And yes, you will need to lie for that. So, 'I'm not sometimes flustered by Erik's impressive abdominals.' Say it."

"Erik is a grump."

He cocked a brow.

"Fine. Erik isn't attractive."

He waited.

"I'm not saying the thing about the abdominals."

Back in the tent, the ring scraped against the cracked leather, spinning and spinning. *Face. Light. Face. Light. Face—*

"We need more information," Stefan said. It was two days later and we were in the cellar, shadows spilling over sacks of potatoes and radishes with pink-colored tops. "Where are they keeping the weapon?"

"I don't know," I replied.

"What can we use against them?"

"I'm working on it."

He pounded the table. "Dammit, Isy."

Time blurred, slowed, slipped between my fingers, an hourglass with the sands running backward, running up.

318

Face. Light. Face. Light. Face—

Erik took my hands in his, flipped my wrists over. "The key to lying is to maintain your baseline. You get nervous. It's a tell. Take a deep breath." His eyes found mine, so steady, so sure. "Good. Now," he traced the heart line on my palm, "tell me you don't think I'm attractive."

We're running out of time. Stefan.

"Take your time." Erik.

Always keep your eye on the enemy. Stefan.

"Always keep your eye on the *environment*." Erik. His leg swept out, knocking me to the ground.

The knife skittered out of my hand.

"Rude," I said, shaking the sand from my skirts. "And against the rules."

Rain pattered and a thin fog rose from the sands. Streams squiggled toward the beach.

"Stop trying to act like a Vold warrior. You're not a Vold warrior, and you probably won't ever be one. That's okay. You have different skills. Use them." He picked up the knife and placed it in my hand, correcting my grip. Thumb on top, fingers underneath. He smoothed my knuckles. "Again."

To be clear, Stefan said. *You don't know where they're keeping the Lover's Boxes. You don't know what the Lover's Boxes do. What are you doing?*

"Erik isn't attractive," I said, braiding my hair.

"Erik isn't attractive." Spooning bites of porridge into my mouth.

"They took another city," Stefan said.

"The hellhounds are getting worse." Erik.

The ring wobbled. *Face. Light. Face. Light.*

"Come at me," Erik said.

Rain came down in sheets, hard and heavy, blurring the world into a river. That clean sense of cold curled up my back.

I lunged for his bicep, scraped the blade across it, and dove for his thigh.

He whirled and struck my heart. "I win."

"Wrong." A fluttery feeling swept through my hands. "Your bicep controls arm extension, your inner thigh, your ability to run. You'd be disarmed and on the ground."

Rain matted his shirt, his hair, darkened the strands to a straw-spun blonde. He flashed a smile. "I knew you'd figure it out."

You're supposed to be stealing the boxes, Stefan said. *What are you doing instead?*

"Erik isn't attractive." Brushing my teeth.

"Erik isn't attractive." Washing my face.

"Erik isn't attractive." Hunting for a place to pee.

"Erik isn't—"

I pulled back the flap of Erik's tent. "You are the ugliest person I have ever seen. You are a gargoyle, a troll, and your abdominals look like a wheel of cheese. They offend my eyes. Sometimes I lie awake and think about how terrible and ugly they are. I hate them, I hate them, I hate—"

The ring clattered to the lid of the letter box.

Erik glanced up from the stack of papers on his desk. The corner of his mouth quirked. "I think you're ready."

"I'm ready?"

He stood and stepped around the furniture, leaving his palm against the wood. "Provided you promise me one thing."

I cocked a brow. "Depends on the thing."

"If it comes to a physical fight, I want you to use your skills to disarm them. Then I want you to run. Run as fast as you can."

My heart sunk. "So you don't have faith in me."

He laughed and stepped closer. "Isabel. You were *so* fast when you tried to bolt out of my tent."

"You still caught me."

He captured my hand and pulled me closer still. "I'm exceptionally quick. And I was motivated."

"To use your…talents?"

His eyes flashed. "To keep you with me." He swept his thumb over my palm. "After all, you are a dangerous spy."

I caught his scent. My knees wobbled. "I'm…dangerous?"

"Oh, the most." His thumb continued to circle. He took a step forward, then another, walking me against the desk. "Poisoning my men. Befriending everyone. I'm fairly certain you stole the Lover's Boxes a few times on the trip back."

"I…" My chest buzzed.

He dropped his voice to a purr. "Were you a naughty little spy? Are you going to confess?"

"No."

"Liar." He tangled his hand through my hair and tipped my chin back, exposing the column of my throat. He pressed his lips there, gave a little nip, a little suck, drawing another bruise to the surface. "Come now. Confess to me." Another nip, another suck. His mouth moved lower. Nip, suck.

My palms went sweaty. I wanted to faint. "Are you trying to get me to crack again?"

"Oh, I'm not just *trying*." He turned me to face the desk, positioned my hands on the wood, and knocked my stance wider. "Did you steal the Lover's Boxes, Isabel?" He wrapped one arm around my waist and brushed his mouth against the back of my shoulder. Nip, suck.

"I...did." The words came out breathless.

Nip, suck. "I thought so."

"Every night."

Nip, suck. He moved my braid aside. "I'm not surprised." His hand fell to the front of my skirt, untucking my sweater. Without the bulk, the waistband slipped lower, and he toyed with one of the buttons, his knuckles skimming the bare skin of my stomach.

Chills swept through my body. "Sometimes I stole them multiple times a night."

He sucked harder, rocking slightly, and his hand doubled back as if he might slip his fingers beneath the fabric and touch me lower.

My heart thundered, and something inside me said *yes, yes, yes* and *please, please, please.*

"Like, a lot of times. More times than you think. Are you going to make me scream it?"

The heat of him disappeared. "Withstanding interrogation is like withstanding any other type of torture. It's all mental."

I turned, and he stood by the door, tugging on his jacket.

He grinned. "We'll practice it again sometime. Later. Right now, we have work to do."

Chapter Thirty-Seven

THE SCREECH OF THE PORTCULLIS tore through the prison, the ring of metal on metal. Water dripped off the spiked ends, swirling rainbow from grease.

Erik gave my hand a squeeze.

Breathe. Just breathe.

My job was simple. I wasn't even the one taking the biggest risk. I could do this. I could—

The portcullis disappeared into the abyss above.

Behind it, a galley for the guards. Behind *that*, the cells. The order of it—portcullis, guards, prisoners—prevented escapes. The portcullis only stayed open if a guard was holding the crank, and the theory was that no guard would ever willingly let a prisoner get away.

But the entire system meant that the galley guards were stuck behind the gate until someone came to take their place. Since no one liked to be stuck, they were usually a little sour.

My job was to distract the guards.

But these weren't any guards.

The portcullis stopped with a *crack*. Beyond it, a beckoning gloom, a brittle gloom. A breeze blew over the floor, licking my ankles and whistling over lime-hardened walls. My eyes ached.

Erik shoved his hands into his pockets and glanced up. "Interesting how the guards are locked in here with the prisoners."

"The prisoners have their own cells." I grabbed his arm and pulled him into the galley.

The portcullis rattled shut.

And now we were at the mercy of the guards.

One lounged on the stone-slick bench, dark eyes, straight nose. The other shouldered the crank, wide hands and muscled arms shoved under a cotton shirt. Tattoos peeked through the stubble on his head.

"General," he said, smiling, revealing a split tongue and sharp teeth. "Come to see your friends?"

"She's here to treat the Sanok king," Erik replied. It was the cover we'd decided on. He and Bo would shadow walk to search for the boxes, and I'd treat King Christian to buy them time. Erik had escorted me to the castle to treat the queen's bedsores this morning, so it was good cover. If he couldn't find the boxes, I'd "treat the king" again in a few days.

But I didn't have a few days.

I was running out of time.

Dust drifted through eddies in the air. From the hallway of cells, a scrape. A cough.

"Erik?" Bo's voice. "Is that you?"

Bo.

My stomach squeezed, and I peeked around Erik and down the hall of cells.

We're here, I wanted to say. *We're going to fix this.*

The hellhound clucked his tongue. "Shame." He lifted one of his fingers. It sparked to life, a flame gnawing at his skin. "They could be out tomorrow. Tonight even."

I turned to Erik. "What?"

Erik gave a slash of his hand. A warning. *Stay quiet.* "Not true," he said to the hellhound.

The hellhound laughed. "Sure it is. You know the price. You just don't want to pay it. What kind of friend does that make you? Not one I'd want." He twisted the burning finger, leaving a trail of smoke. "And fealty. Such a simple thing…"

Erik's jaw ticked, his nostrils flared. He stepped forward, boxing the hellhound in. The hellhound was bigger, bulkier, but Erik barred his teeth. The whites of his eyes gleamed, and he was wild, feral, poised and ready to strike. Lamplight seeped through his hands, his hair. His voice dropped dangerously low. "Take her to the Sanok king."

We passed through the dim-lit entrance and to a hallway lined with cells. Salt bloomed like spindly flowers, crept up the walls like ivy, streaks of white watching, waiting.

The first hellhound—the one who'd been sitting on the bench—fumbled with the keys. He hadn't said anything and kept glancing at Erik from the corner of his eye.

Erik kept a stony mask. "I'll wait up front."

The cue.

Fifteen minutes.

I needed to keep both guards distracted so Erik could shadow walk with Bo.

Fifteen minutes.

I could do this.

If Erik was caught, the connection could be broken and he would die.

Or I could be trapped. The double-gated prison meant that the guards had to let us out, and King Herleif had made clear he would use the people in Erik's life as leverage. We'd decided the best way to protect us both was if the guards didn't know we were working together. As such, I'd made complexion cream to hide all the love marks and resolved to treat him like a stranger, at least while we were down here.

But now Erik laced his fingers through mine, squeezed.

The first hellhound's gaze dropped to our hands. It lingered.

The door to King Christian's prison cell swung open.

The warmth of Erik's hand disappeared, replaced with a rush of cold.

Fifteen minutes.

Time to put on a show.

A kneeling cry tore through the stone. "You're here!" King Christian said. "The dark devil!"

He scrambled to the back of the cell. Dirt dabbed his cheeks, darkened his hair to a yellow-gray. A tattered cape fluttered around his waist, blue silk studded with emeralds and onyx crystals shaped like pears. No shoes, no shirt. The sores around his mouth had worsened and angry red blisters freckled the side of his cheek, crusting over his ear. His skin flushed fever-red.

"Your Majesty," I said, dropping to a crouch beside him. I pulled out a mug and a bottle and set them on the ground. Dessert wine. "I brought you something. You love cherries. Remember?"

The king pressed himself into a corner, wrapped his arms around his knees. "I will not drink. Not from your cup of suns."

I glanced at the mug, the same one I'd soaked my finger in. No suns. Although, maybe to an addled man, the dapples gleamed?

326

The king puckered his lips and tears rolled down his cheeks. "He makes me drink from the cup of suns, but I do not want to drink."

I'd thought that by offering him wine, I could get him to spout something interesting to hold the guard's attention. But now, looking at the way the king's body trembled, the way he hugged himself…

It wasn't funny.

It was sad.

I corked the bottle and slid the mug back into my bag. "That's fine. You don't have to. Can I look at your face?"

King Christian uncurled from his ball and peeked over his knees, his eyes bright as blackberries. "Will it…protect me? The drink?"

"It might." I set the søven bottle by my hip. Not vinegar. I wouldn't make that mistake again. "Do you want some?"

The king's eyes flicked to the søven, then to me. Søven. Me. Søven…

Me.

Søven…

Oh no.

"You're working with him!" the king screeched. "The dark devil! You're his helper. You want me to drink."

He tried to shove past me, but I grabbed him around the waist, hauling him back.

"The bottle," I said, pushing the king against the wall. "Right—"

"This?" The first hellhound plucked the søven off the ground.

Beneath my palms, the king thrashed and writhed.

327

My grip loosened.

I couldn't let him leave his cell. If he got away, there was no telling which direction he'd run. Toward the galley, yes, but maybe toward Bo and Kaspar.

And Erik.

I struggled with the king. "If you could—*oof*—uncork… Thank you."

I snatched the bottle from the hellhound's hand and dumped the contents on my sleeve. The cloying scent of strawberries filled the air. My eyes watered.

I shoved the sweater sleeve against his face. He let out another piercing shriek, this one burbled by the søven.

His nails raked my arms, my neck. They caught the tail of my braid, his fingers twisting through my hair and—

Breathe. He just needed to breathe. I pressed my sweater sleeve harder.

Something warm flooded around my knees.

I glanced down.

A dark puddle.

Great. He'd peed himself.

The clawing stilled, his eyes fluttering…fluttering… King Christian's head lulled to the side. He let out a snore.

I pushed myself off.

Pee drenched my skirt, søven slicked my sleeve, but all things considered, that could have been worse.

Much worse.

"I guess you're done?" the hellhound asked. "I mean, the king's done. We'll escort you out?"

Shit.

I licked my lips, salty from the beach. "I, um…still need to clean his sores. The ones around his mouth. They'll fester."

The hellhound thrust a thumb toward the door. "Great. Well, it doesn't seem like you need us anymore. We'll be up front."

Double shit.

If they went back to the galley, they'd realize Erik wasn't there. If they realized Erik wasn't there, they might go looking for him and find him shadow walking with Bo. Even if the connection *wasn't* broken, there was no way they would've been able to find the boxes that fast.

I needed to buy more time.

"Help me out?" I asked. "We should make him comfortable."

A second snore tore through the prisons.

The muscled hellhound rubbed his chin. "There aren't a lot of places to do that."

I glanced around.

He was right. Stone floor. Straw. A little brass water bucket knocked to one side, a three-pronged dinner fork, and—

"The pallet," I said. "Help me move him to the pallet. We'll want to go slowly. Really slowly. He's, erm…delicate."

I grabbed the king's arms while the first hellhound grabbed the king's legs. We dragged the king across the floor, his cheek lulling, white hair sweeping straw like a broom. Drool trailed behind him.

"Can you go any faster?" the hellhound grunted.

"Actually," I said, "it would be better if we slowed down. The king…he's heavy and—"

"It's just—" The hellhound gritted his teeth. His left leg dragged behind him, the side of his boot hitting the floor with a steady *thunk, thunk, thunk.* "It's hard for me to—"

Oh. I stepped over the bucket. "Ouch. I didn't notice. Is it your foot?"

He let the king's legs drop. "I've heard some men from Ryth-ja talk about you. You cured them from a…" his voice dropped to a whisper, "bowel illness."

"Worms," supplied the other hellhound. "Just say it. She cured their worms."

The king smacked his lips and tossed his head from side to side, still asleep.

I dragged him toward the pallet. "I, um…did. Yes. Their worms. Why?" Almost there. How slow could we go without looking suspicious?

The king grunted.

"Would you look?" the hellhound asked. "At…me?"

"If you don't have bowel issues, then you don't have the worms."

The hellhound glanced away, color rising in his cheeks and staining the tips of his ears a rosy pink. "At my foot. I meant my foot. But you definitely don't have to. I shouldn't have asked. Anyway, yeah, let me help you move the king." He grabbed hold of the king's ankles, grimaced as his foot took the weight. "You said the pallet?"

He hobbled a few steps.

There was something about the way he dragged his foot behind him, about the way it faltered on the uneven ground. His boot scraped stone and his pant leg inched up to reveal the ribbed hem of a stocking, the cream wool flecked dark blue. There was a fray at the edges, a pucker pulling the seams. Loose threads looped like teeth. And over it, a heart stitched in red, the shape of it crude, as if someone had decided mid-mend to make it special.

I could almost imagine his partner, a handsome husband or a wild-haired wife. Maybe fire crackled up the wall and maybe there was snow—Erik said there was always snow in Volgaard—and I should be afraid of this man, this hellhound with a straight nose and hawkish eyes. After all, hellhounds had destroyed the castle, had taken Bo.

I *should* be afraid.

He maneuvered his foot around the bucket, wincing, and something in me softened.

Didn't I know about taking care of feet?

I set the king's arms on the floor, dragged the pallet across the room, and pulled the king on top. "There. Now let me see your foot."

The hellhound settled on top of the bucket, eased off his shoe, then his sock. A deformity. Not the foot itself, but the angle. It bowed like the body of a harp, the sole turning toward the opposite ankle.

Clubbed foot.

There'd been an entire treatise about the condition in *Harrison's Ailments of the Feet*, which I'd become familiar with after I'd started caring for Queen Margarethe.

"I've heard of special types of shoes that are made to guide the foot into the correct place," I said, touching the skin. "Sometimes they'll use stiffened leather or plaster. And there are some stretches that may help. Do you...want me to show you?"

The hellhound nodded.

I cradled his heel in my palm and stretched the foot until the muscles would go no farther. This was stalling, only stalling.

But...maybe it was more than that.

Something about this moment reminded me of Queen Margarethe—the pale pink of her room, the rosewater scent of her sheets, the way sunlight skirted through open windows, the rain that flecked the sill.

It was a funny thing to think about, the queen's feet.

How many hours had I spent studying discourses and diagrams? Remedies for wound care? I probably knew more about that than Stefan, even Jens-Kjeld.

"You want to hold it for five to seven seconds," I said. "Don't force it, but don't keep it comfortable, either." I eased my hand up the arch, taking care not to tickle his toes. "The goal is to go a little farther every day. It won't be healed tomorrow, or even in a week, but maybe over time…"

It took me a moment to realize that Erik had reappeared in the cell door. He shouldered the frame, the top buttons of his shirt undone, his head resting against the metal.

Here I was, covered in pee, cradling a hellhound's foot.

Yet there was a softness in Erik's shoulders, in the ruffle of his hair.

And pride.

It lit his face like a candle.

Our eyes locked.

Sorry, I mouthed.

He gave a little shrug, a smile pulling at his lips. *Take your time*, he mouthed back. Then he waved his arm and disappeared into the dark.

"How do you do that?" Erik asked as the screech of the gate echoed through the prisons.

"Do what?"

"Make friends with literally everyone."

I hauled the medicine bag higher on my shoulder. "I don't make friends with *everyone*."

He cocked a brow. "Half of my men are begging to be smuggled into my tent so they can see you, Kaspar just told me he wished I *was* you, and, weirdest of all, Tyr is baking."

"Because I told him he had worms."

"Exactly."

"That's not a great foundation for friendship. Speaking of Bo and Kaspar, how are they?"

"They're…okay. Mostly. They were wondering when I was going to get them out. Which, fair. I'd be wondering that, too." He started up the narrow staircase.

I bunched my skirts and tromped after him, our footsteps ringing over the stone. "Bo's head? Did you pass along the tea?"

"He said it tasted like a bog."

"You warned him, right?"

Erik grimaced. "So, I might have forgotten…?"

"Erik."

"Sore. His head is sore."

"But the Lover's Boxes? You found them?"

He made another face.

Shit. I jogged to catch up. "Please don't say we have to come back. I mean, as much as I like palling around with King Christian and the hellhounds—"

"It's not that."

"Then what?"

Erik threw open the prison door.

Rain came down in sheets, heavy, blurring the world into a river.

"They're going to be almost impossible to steal."

Chapter Thirty-Eight

"WHAT DO YOU MEAN, they're going to be almost impossible to steal?" I shouted over the pound of rain. It rinsed the world, flecked the granite in the doorway.

"Herleif has them well guarded," Erik shouted back.

"Okay. I'll be extra careful. Problem solved."

He shook his head. "You don't understand. If you're caught, I won't be able to help you."

Okay. I could do this. I *had* to do this. If I didn't, Stefan and Katrina would torch the ships, the hellhounds would be stuck to ravage the island, and Hans's memory would be forgotten, his death unanswered and meaningless.

I still had three days to steal the boxes. Three days. It had to be enough time to make and execute a plan. "What if we got Bo and Kaspar out?"

The rain pounded harder.

Erik furrowed his brow. "What?"

"Bo and Kaspar. The hellhounds said you could free them."

The corner of his mouth ticked. "Herleif offered, but I'd have to *bind* myself to him."

"What does that mean?"

He smoothed a thumb over his nubbed finger.

"What does it mean?" I shouted again.

"It means I'd be his. Forever. Like Kynda's general. And I can't—" The expression faltered. He turned away and I caught the edge of his cheek. A lock of blond hair curled just over his ear.

I took his hand. His fingers were rough and warm. They trembled.

"Do you want to walk over to the beach and talk about it?"

He shook his head. "I have to check on my dad. He's… It's worse."

Water ribboned the world, poured off the eves of the castle in torrents, brought out the colors, the greens and grays and white. The flagstones glittered.

"Come with me to change?" I asked. "We'll go together?"

"You don't understand. He's *dying*."

I glanced at my skirt, the pee spots darkening to a muddy brown. I didn't want to leave him like this, but I couldn't stay in these clothes.

"Okay," I said, stepping into the pouring rain. "Your dad. I'll meet you there."

IN ERIK'S TENT, I STRIPPED OFF MY SKIRT, hauled a bucket of wash water to the copper tub and scrubbed the pee off my knees. I scrubbed and scrubbed, and the bubbles were black, dark as pine. They reflected the room.

I needed to be there for Erik, needed to get back. I knew he was a Vold, knew we weren't on the same side, but the curve of his cheek, the flash of his hurt, the way his fingers trembled.

He didn't feel like my enemy anymore.

Rain battered the canvas, lashed the walls.

I splashed everything away, the bubbles, the pee, and pulled on a clean skirt, a cozy olive twill.

Strands of hair curled at the corner of my vision. I pressed my palm against them. My braid had been torn from the frantic struggle with the king, but it didn't matter. I could fix it there.

I grabbed my brush and the bag of medicines, and—

Stefan.

He stood in the tent's doorway, water running in sluices down his face.

"You can't be here," I said.

He stepped inside, letting the flap fall closed. "Were you going to tell us you went to the prison?"

I swiped away the strand of hair. "We were looking for the boxes. Erik shadow walked. It didn't seem important. You can't be here."

"And where are the boxes?"

"I forgot to ask."

Another step, light like a tabby. Lamplight glittered in his hair, his teeth. His face went grim. "You forgot to ask? Or are you lying?"

"I'm covered in the king's pee, and I haven't slept all week. Erik's dad is dying, and he just shadow walked. So, yeah, I forgot." I tried to step around Stefan.

He blocked my path. "We're running out of time."

"I'm doing my best."

"I need better."

A thousand thoughts welled in my mind, a ship, a storm, they hammered and hammered and—

Tell him it's not enough.

Are we not enough for you?

Stefan. He's better.

He grabbed my wrist.

I yanked it free. "Then torch the fleet," I hissed. "See where that gets you."

Lightning streaked, casting everything in sharp relief—fingers of black. White. Black. White. Stefan. His hands clasped behind his back, his mouth pressed in a line.

Thunder boomed.

Stefan's jaw ticked. "Three days."

"Or what?"

No response.

I laughed and stepped forward, and now I was the predator and he was the prey. "You need me. I'm the closest thing you have to the Volds."

No response. Of course not.

"From now on," I continued, "you'll do things on *my* time. You won't come to the camp again. You won't seek me out again. If I have something to report, I'll go to you."

Stefan circled the tent. He let his fingers trace the curving back of the chair, the sheepskin throw, the rows of medicine bottles I'd lined up on the desk.

Tick, tick, tick.

He stopped. Pressed two fingers against the map. Stones for ships—black and white. He picked one up, rolled it between his thumb and forefinger. "You were right, you know. About torching the fleet. I came to tell you we have a new plan." His thumb circled the stone. "Poison the officers. The captains. The seconds… The generals."

I'm Rythja's general while my father is dying. Erik's words.

My heart thudded. "Why?"

"It'll scare them. If the Lover's Boxes are really the weapon, we'll flush them out amid the chaos. If the weapon is something else, then we'll find that, too." Stefan twisted the stone, ran his thumb down the fissured groove. "You might not be keeping us involved in your plans, but I'm keeping you involved in ours. You can thank Katrina for that." He pocketed the stone. "Fix this. You have three days."

Chapter Thirty-Nine

I'VE DEBATED WHETHER TO WRITE what happens next. I know it isn't something you'd want to hear, and I keep trying to find a way to skip it. I've wasted two pages of starts and stops, but beginning again is like trying to pick up a thread when you've dropped it.

So, I'm going to be honest, I am.

I'm going to tell the truth, I am.

Even if it hurts.

I'm sorry if this hurts.

I write this for you, mostly, but I also write it for myself. I suppose it's my way of processing everything, of chewing my story until it softens enough to suck meaning off the skeleton.

I want this sacrifice to be worthwhile. I guess in the end, we all do.

I'm sorry.

I never had the chance to tell you that.

Chapter Forty

TORCH THE SHIPS.

Poison the generals.

These plans were getting worse and worse. I should tell Erik. But…

Katrina. Did I want to implicate her?

And despite everything, Stefan was my friend, too—more like a brother than my real ones. We'd fought, we had, but I didn't want him dead or imprisoned or worse.

I couldn't tell Erik.

I *had* to tell Erik.

The rain slowed to a drizzle, sheening off the cliff faces and the birds nested there. Pocks dappled the sand and droplets gleamed, clung to cook spoons and cast irons, the silver-orange coats of cats. In the dim and dizzying dark, their eyes flashed.

A hiss, a yowl, the cluck of chickens and shapes of the Sanokes rose wild. And there were the cliffs, the sea, everything hard and heavy, hewn from mountain stone. And me, a whisper, a ghost, there then gone.

If we stole the boxes, it wouldn't matter. There would be no need to murder the generals. Either the Volds would leave to attack Larland, or Erik and I would release whatever was in there and drive them out.

If we stole the boxes, everything would be okay.

If we stole the boxes.

And if we failed?

Icy winds threaded through my hair. Black waves tumbled down the beach.

If we failed?

We couldn't fail.

I had three days.

The vents in Lothgar's tent had been peeled back, letting in the ocean, the scents of salt and lightning, fresh and clean, but beneath them hid the ripeness of unwashed skin and the sour stench of death.

Lothgar was laid out on a mass of bedrolls, the great general tucked between layers of pelts and silver furs. His beard had been shaved and his hair combed out of his face, making him seem younger.

Signey sat at one side, her fingers laced through his, squeezing tight. Erik sat at the other, a bowl of water at his hip.

His gaze flicked to mine.

My heart stuttered.

I won't let them do this to you.

I won't let you die.

Three days.

"How's he doing?" I asked, settling beside Erik.

The heat of his leg brushed mine and he shrugged. "He's…how I expected."

"And you?"

Another shrug.

I laced my fingers through his, felt the thrum of his heart. It was easy, so easy to sink into this, into the rhythm of the past few days.

Pearls of water pilled on the canvas, a scattering of stars.

"We've been telling stories," he said after a moment. "Signey just told how she got her honor bead."

"Tormod's Keep," she added, pressing Lothgar's hand to her cheek. "And you got yours from catching a horse."

"A very big horse."

"Tell me about it," I said. "The horse."

Erik stiffened. "Catching Heggi? Alright." He released my hand and pulled the leather cord from under his shirt, showing me the two silver beads I'd seen him fiddling with. "Heggi is Volgaard's heart."

"Volgaard's heart is a horse?"

He traced his thumb along the lattice of the beads. "All places have hearts, Isabel. Don't you know that?"

I shook my head.

"Heggi came by our house every morning, trailing smoke and stars. I watched Dad watch him, and I knew he wanted him. Wanted Heggi. So I decided to catch him."

Signey wet a rag and wiped it over Lothgar's forehead. "This is when you find out Erik is really stupid."

Erik shot her a glare. "I was fourteen."

I placed my hand between the furs, the silken strands slipping through my fingers. "So let me get this straight. You caught the heart of Volgaard when you were fourteen?" Somehow, I wasn't surprised.

He tucked the beads back into his shirt. "That's the first time I ever Sent. In my panic, I made a second version of Heggi. The real Heggi stopped to look at the mirror one, and I put the halter on. Dad was so proud, he gave me two honor beads. One for Heggi, one for Sending. But I didn't care about the beads. I cared about Dad. I wanted him to…" He scrubbed a hand over his face. "Well. It doesn't matter. But that's how I caught Heggi."

The distant roar of waves filled the silence.

"Hey, Erik?"

His gaze cut to mine. "Yeah?"

"It matters."

He let out a shaky breath. "Thanks."

"So, what happened?" I asked. "Where is Heggi now?"

Signey shrugged. "Dad rode him once and decided he liked not having a broken neck. Plus, I don't think things like that are meant to be owned. So we let him—"

Lothgar's breathing fell out of rhythm. Dry sucks became rasping exhales. One hand went limp, the other spasmed, his knuckles flushing red. It opened and closed.

"Something's obstructing his air," I said. "I need a knife. Some alcohol and…and poppy."

For a moment, the tent dropped away, and I saw it growing along the base of the cliffs, ruffly petals corrugated with wrinkles, delicate veins that seemed to connect everything and there, the heartbeat, the pulse, and I was reaching for it, grasping, crawling on my knees, and the world seemed to be a hand, gentle and smooth, fingers outstretched, a mother reaching through the darkness.

Reaching back.

The breathing stopped. Lothgar's hand stilled and fell, lifeless, between the furs.

The thoughts of the poppy, of the reaching mother dropped from my mind, fish wriggling free from a net. I leaned forward and placed my fingers at the base of Lothgar's throat. There was no thrum of a heartbeat, no throb of a pulse, only the cooling touch of a body just dead. I went to find Erik's eyes, but instead, I met the fragile gray of Signey's.

I half expected her to cry. After all, that would be the normal response. Instead, she nodded once and left the tent, coming back a few minutes later with a knife and a fresh water bowl. Together she and Erik stripped the blankets and Lothgar's yellowed clothes. Signey sponged down his arms, his legs, cleaned the grime from his nails. She eased the knife into his chest cavity, then used the flat of her hand to crack the ribs.

She peeled them open and pulled out his heart.

And the way she cradled it, it felt too bizarre, too intimate. I pushed myself out of the tent and let the cold air wash over me.

Waves beat against the rocks and sand. I should have gone back to Erik's tent, but I needed to crawl out from the clog of sickness. I needed to breathe.

I stripped off my shoes and stockings and walked barefoot up the moon-beamed beach, leaving behind a string of footprints that were pearled away every time the waves rushed the shore.

She'd carved out his heart.

She'd *cradled* his heart.

I wasn't sure what that meant.

Wet sand glittered like glass as foam blew across my feet. The sky stretched black and endless.

No stars tonight.

When I came back down, a lone figure sat in a scoop in the rocks, his face toward the horizon. I climbed next to him, blew on my freezing fingers, and stared out at the wild sea.

"You okay?" I asked.

"Yes." *No.* Erik squinted at the sky.

I wished I knew what to say, but I wasn't good with words, didn't have Hans's easy heart. I couldn't make him laugh or smile or smooth away the pain.

I could just…be.

Here.

With him.

And maybe that was enough.

"He was the first person who believed in me," Erik said after a while. "As soon as he realized I could Send, he took me in and made me—" He clenched his fist. "I should be grateful. Instead, all I want is to make him hurt."

"You're not—" I followed his squint to the sky. "That doesn't make you a terrible person."

He glanced at me, wary. "He wanted me. You're telling me I'm not terrible for hating that?"

"I'm telling you, you're human. At least, I'm pretty sure—" I reached up to pinch his cheek, but he caught my hand.

I waited for him to release it.

He didn't let me go.

I laced my fingers through his and pinched the soft webbing with my thumb and forefinger.

He sighed. "That's for panic attacks."

"I know. Tell me something. About you."

"So many personal questions."

"You like them."

His eyes flashed, greedy, a little raw. "After Lothgar learned I could Send, he would…train me. Days without food, pushed to the brink of exhaustion." Erik slid his hand away. "Reykr is like a muscle, it has to be worked. It's why the men... Well, it's why they cast stupid things for each other. It's why I had the forest in the bedroom."

"And the ships?"

"Which I dropped." Erik shook his head. "Yeah, he wasn't too happy about that."

"Weren't you Sending for six days? Did you even sleep?"

"Sleeping, eating, Sending. That was about it. Lothgar...he didn't just make me work my reykr, he—" His fists tightened. "He said he was making me strong."

"I don't blame you for hating him."

"I was being honed into, I don't know. *Something*." Erik laughed, short and bitter. "He treated his dogs better."

"Is that how you lost the tip of your finger?"

The corner of his mouth lifted. "Oh. *That*. Trying to impress Signey. You know, little brother stuff."

Ocean spray dappled our clothes, our hair.

"We were close once," he continued. "If you would believe it. She helped me sneak out of Lothgar's house on more than one occasion. She'd stand guard while I went swimming."

"Swimming?"

He shrugged, one-shouldered. "It was the only place I felt like myself. Lothgar was making me into...whatever he was making me into, and I liked the feeling of water—of not being able to tell where I started and the lake began. I guess that's a funny way to feel like yourself. But yeah. Swimming."

Swimming. I hadn't been since...well, a long time. Maybe before I left Hjern. But I knew what that was like, not being able to unravel into your own skin.

And swimming.

The only place he felt like himself.

Waves broke, dark and wild, a little unsteady. A clutch of puffins floated offshore.

Reckless and suddenly brave, I ducked out from the scoop of the rock and tugged my sweater up and over my head, tossing it on the sand beside us.

His brows pinched, a question, and I knew what he saw— the knots of scar tissue beginning beneath my chest and disappearing into the folds of my skirt, the discolored skin so ugly, so raw.

"How did you…?"

They're terrible. I know. "Don't worry about it."

He blinked, shook his head. "*What* are you—"

"Swimming."

"You can't go swimming. You're in the middle of my camp."

"You're right. Which is why—" I loosened the buttons of my skirt. *One, two, three.* I shimmied out of it, tossed it away, and I was standing in front of him in nothing but my underthings.

Cool air whisked my legs, made gooseflesh pebble. Another wave licked the shore, a spray of mist settling over us like a shawl.

"You should come with me."

His eyes raked over my body, his gaze molten, and now he wasn't looking at the scars… He was looking at *me*.

"You can Send and—"

With one decisive motion, he waved his hand and the camp pearled away like dust. He stripped off his shirt, pulled off his boots, and dropped them into the sand with a *thud*. It was just the two of us, alone on a sweeping beach. Grass thatched. Moonlight spilled.

I see you, I see you, said the wind.

"Isabel."

"Yes?"

His mouth tipped up, whatever spell between us broken. He grabbed my hand and pulled me toward the waterline.

A white-tipped wave swirled around our ankles. Followed by another so frigid it made my entire body constrict, but he pulled me deeper into the belly of the ocean, through the bend and break of waves, and into dark waters. When our feet no longer scraped the sands, he let me go.

"There's Fiski," he said, paddling into the freezing black. "Can you see it?"

The ocean curled around my body, stung my eyes.

I squinted to where he was pointing, but all I saw was the moon, waxy and full, the night sharp as steel. No stars. There hadn't been since—

It hit me. I laughed. That's what the Lover's Box took.

I couldn't see the stars.

Waves slapped around my shoulders, the water salty and cold. I paddled toward him. "Can't see it."

"It's right there," he said, gesturing at the empty sky. "There's his boat, his pole."

I stopped a few feet away to tread water. "Mmm, still can't." Not that I'd ever tell him why. "Why don't you—"

He hooked his arm around my waist and spun me to face him, and suddenly, my hands were pressed against his chest, the heat of him cutting through the chill of the waves.

"I can show you," he said. The words were hot, a little breathless. Spray dappled his cheeks, freckled his lips. Dark water lapped around us. "With reykr. I can make them brighter, connect the lines. Fiski...it's so beautiful."

He wasn't looking at Fiski. His eyes dropped to my mouth. His breath hitched and he reached up, smoothed a strand of hair behind my ear. His thumb lingered on my jaw.

I leaned forward and kissed him, a quick peck. There, then gone.

He startled, his eyes going wide.

Shit. That hadn't been what he wanted. I'd thought—*shit*. I tore out of his grip and paddled toward the beach. "It would be great if you could show me Fiski. I—"

He caught my wrist, pulled me back. "Isabel Moller," he growled. "You are *not* allowed to kiss me, then awkwardly swim away."

His mouth found mine and suddenly, I could taste it—the hurt, the pain, the longing—everything he kept locked up, and I could see him, all of him, and I kissed him back, clutching his chest, his skin taking and taking, and—

His teeth scraped my lip and he nipped. I nipped back. He groaned, his knee coming between my thighs, one hand cupping my hip. The other pressed against the small of my back, guiding me closer. He pulled away, lips swollen, before dipping his head and trailing kisses down my neck, stopping at my collarbone and sucking lightly.

"You like that, don't you?" he asked, dragging his tongue over the spot and sucking again. "You like when I mark you."

Yes, I liked it. A lot. Too shy to say, I tilted my head back, exposing more of my throat to him.

He trailed kisses along it, stopping sometimes to nip and suck, and I was *absolutely* going to need a lot of complexion cream after this. *A lot*, a lot.

"Your body is so responsive," he murmured. "Which I love."

He anchored me to his leg and hoisted me higher, cold night air washing my shoulders and chest. He nuzzled down my breast band and trailed kisses toward my—

Wow.

Yes.

Okay.

He could suck there.

A soft whimper escaped my lips.

His eyes flicked up, his mouth still on my skin, and he sucked harder, his lashes dark, making me gasp and shiver while he *watched*. Some primal part of me wanted to rub myself against his leg, but he held my hips, keeping me in place as his thumbs traced little circles over the bones there.

I wanted to melt.

He lowered me into the water and caught my unharmed ear between his teeth. "So fucking responsive. But as much as I like making you make those cute sounds, I think I'd rather…"

"Rather…?"

"Get back to this." He traced his fingers down my cheek, tilting my face toward his, and capturing my mouth in another searing kiss.

I tangled my fingers through his hair and kissed him back, pressed my body against his chest to steal some of his warmth. He moaned, and something in me surged because his body was *so fucking responsive* too. I deepened the kiss, letting my tongue dart out to meet his.

He must have read it as a request to set the rhythm, because he slowed and let me take the lead, but my technique was clumsy, my inexperience showing. A familiar thing clawed at my chest. Was I doing this right? I'd had pecks on the lips, brief and chaste.

He'd kissed Helene in the Merchant's Market, and who knows how many girls before that. Suddenly, I couldn't breathe and maybe—

He pulled away, eyes dark, a little hazy. "Are you okay?"

Was I okay? I searched for that doubt, for the things that whispered *you're not enough*, and they were there, were lurking, were shadows sitting beneath the surface, but Erik was looking at me now like I was an angel, a dream, the answer to every prayer he'd ever whispered. And with that look?

He

chased

the

doubt

away.

"I am." The words came out a little breathless. "Okay. More than okay."

Water splashed around his shoulders. He loosened his grip, letting me slide off his leg. "You sure? We can stop."

I crawled back onto him. "I don't want to stop."

Then I gathered the pieces of my heart, scarred and broken.

And I gave myself to him.

Chapter Forty-One

DID YOU KNOW puffins mate for life?

Chapter Forty-Two

WE WERE LAYING IN HIS BED, my body curled against his, warm and muscular, a little flushed. Our clothes lay discarded on the floor, worn in, then stripped off, a flurry of hands and fever and teeth. Now, his thumb traced lazy circles over my ribs. Our legs tangled through the sheets.

"Tell me something," I said.

"You are amazing, and I would absolutely do it again," he murmured, half-asleep. Smoky tendrils came off him, threading through my hair.

"Not about that. Why do you cut out hearts?"

"Why do we cut out hearts…" His knuckles grazed my breast. The scent of him, smoke and wool, threatened to sweep me under. "Burial rites. It's a way of showing the deceased you respect them."

"All Volds do that?"

His hand curled around my hip, and he pulled me closer, burying his face in my hair. The tendrils came in tight. "Why are we talking about this *now*?"

I twisted to face him. "All Volds?"

He was more awake than I'd thought, content as a cat warmed by the fire. He shrugged. "The decent ones."

"Always?"

"I don't know, Isabel. Do your people always write goodbyes and burn them on the pyre?"

I rolled onto my back and stared at the ceiling.

That was the thing. It didn't make sense.

Overhead, stars twinkled. Not real ones, but stars made from reykr, whorls of light that blew out the ceiling, brilliant and bottomless, a timber of porcelain and pearl and the palest blue. The constellation of the fishermen shone the brightest. Erik had been calling it Fiski, but I'd recognized it as something else.

Aalto's star.

"Now it's your turn to tell me something," he said.

"It is?"

His thumb skimmed the arch of my waist, and he drew a star around the knot of scar tissue at my hip. "Will you tell me who hurt you?"

"I…" How did I tell Erik about the hurt, the pain?

If he knows, he won't want you.

You're broken.

Ruined.

No one wants a damaged thing.

I pushed myself to sit. "I wanted to make him come back."

He pushed himself up, too, the sheet slipping off his bare torso. The smoky tendrils fell away. "Who?"

"My father. He was gone and he wasn't coming back, and I thought maybe—"

Thirteen years old and I wanted to make him hurt the way I

355

hurt. The door in my face, the babies on his hip. I wanted to see him vomit and cry and howl.

So, I heated the tallow wax, tipped the pot over my stomach, and listened as it sizzled and scalded, the skin going up in a braid of steam.

Then I waited. Waited by the window, blisters bubbling.

I wanted him to scold me, to hold me, to scream. I wanted him back, and why, *why* wouldn't he come back? Couldn't he see what he'd done to us, to me?

The groan of wind. The clot of blood. A piece of goose down dragged across the floor.

A day passed, then another, waiting and waiting, until they all swept together, a handful of cards.

"He never came," I told Erik.

Then I wanted the sores gone, wanted to scrub them off, scrape them clean. I wanted to peel them away like an onion and to step back into the world, shiny and perfect and new.

An embarrassment, said the tailor's wife.

Attention seeking, said the salt maker.

My father knew. Everyone knew. The whole damn town knew. Still, I waited and waited and waited.

The sores darkened, then scabbed, a smattering of deep and copper brown that splotched my skin like mud.

Should know better, they said.

Delusional.

Thirteen years old, and applying marigold and black tea, a paste of egg yolks to make it go away. Thirteen years old, and everything so thick, the scabs shimmered. Bandages boiled, the corners pressed. Salves lined up on the shelves, calendula and chamomile, yarrow and yellow dock.

See? I healed myself. See? I don't need you after all. See? I'm better off alone. Go back to your babies and your beach. Go back to taking care of everyone but me. Go back, go back, *come back*.

I gritted my teeth and twisted so Erik could see my left side, my right arm. The scars and everything else. Every hurt, every heartache written on my body.

You're ruining this, said the sharp-set thing inside me.

You ruin everything, said the barbs.

Just like you ruined yourself.

"It wasn't just that one time with the tallow wax," I continued. "I also did it with hot coals and hot soup, a slice of firewood." I touched a mark so big and jagged.

My mother had sat by the hearth, a shell of herself, while I scabbed and scarred. Fourteen, now fifteen, and I wasn't doing it for my father—I was doing it for myself, doing it because I liked pain, because I *deserved* pain.

Hans had asked about them once, had brushed his thumb over the blister fluid bleeding through the arm of my sweater. "You're not still—"

"Of course not," I'd said and laughed it off as a smudge of plant sap because Hans was good—*too good*—for my hide of scars. He shouldn't have to know.

He found out, anyway.

When he did, he came to my house every day and held me as I cried and scratched and tried to stop because by then, I *wanted* to stop. I did, but I couldn't, and I was a mess and maybe showing Erik had been a mistake because he wasn't saying anything, just sitting there, watching, listening, and the way he was looking at me right now...

My face burned. "I'm sorry," I said, yanking the blanket

against my chest and reaching for my sweater. "They're horrible, I know."

"They're not," he replied, and the declaration was so fervent, I stilled.

He cupped my cheek and brought my eyes to meet his. "All I see, Isabel, is you."

He pressed his mouth to mine, hot and hungry. The sweater slipped from my fingers.

We took each other again.

I WOKE TANGLED IN HIM—his smell on my skin, his taste on my lips, all smoke and honey and something else, something wild. There was a sweetness in the way his hand rested on my waist, in the way his foot tucked around my ankle, and I wanted to stay like that forever, cheek on chest, listening to the rise and fall of his breath, to the steady thrum of his heart.

It had taken some time to ease myself away.

He'd stirred once. Only once.

And maybe I should have stayed tucked next to him until he woke, but the words from our conversation last night swirled round and round my head and something…something didn't seem right.

I'd watched Signey cut out the bandits' hearts, and then she and Erik had done it again right after Lothgar died. Volgaard had a history of cutting out the hearts of merchants and sending them back to us. So that made sense.

But Hans didn't have his heart cut out, and neither did the minister. *They stuck a letter opener in his eye,* Stefan had written. *Cut off a hand and shoved it in his mouth.* The murder was so similar to the ambassador killed by Volgaard.

But the minister had lost a hand.

A hand, not a heart.

All Volds do that?

The way Erik watched me, careful in the steely dark. *The decent ones.*

Now, in the dim light of his tent, I flipped open Hans's letter box, searched through correspondence, through scraps of paper left behind.

I'd assumed the Volds killed Hans because he'd been the messenger between the Sanokes and Larland, but...maybe that wasn't right. If the Volds cut out hearts—if they *always* cut out hearts—then they hadn't killed him. And if they hadn't killed him, who had?

The fact of the matter was, Hans *had* tried to show me something before he died. He'd stood in the apothecary doorway and fingered that paper with so much reserve. Maybe it hadn't been the letters from Larland, but then what was it? *Where* was it?

So back to the box of letters, the one marked with HH. I skimmed through the contents, pages torn from notebooks, card stock with dried rose petals, bookmarks with ribbons sewn through the top, and letters, so many letters, from Hjern, from home.

I picked up the journal, leather worn and supple, flipped it open, skimmed the contents, a catalogue of his days. Nothing important, nothing needed.

I went to shut it when a paper tumbled out. It sat there, bright like a lily and brittle with water. It smelled like him—not pigeon, exactly, but cotton and charcoal and something clean and crisp like rain.

Had this been what he'd been trying to tell me?

I peeled it open, the corners clinging to each other like an embrace.

Isy,
~~What I meant to say~~
~~I want~~

A confession. The whole damn thing.

Suddenly, we were back in the apothecary, just the two of us, Hans leaning against the door, his faded sea foam jacket rolled to his elbows, dark curls matted from the rain.

You're not with your pigeons, I'd said. A stupid thing to say.

~~What I meant to say~~
~~I want~~

Tears burned my vision. Hans hadn't been holding some great secret. He'd been trying to tell me this.

This was no secret, either, no surprise. I'd known he loved me the day he chased after the coach barefoot.

Still, I should have felt relief.

Instead, I felt a prickling sadness, the type that cracks you open and eats you raw.

~~What I meant to say~~
~~I want~~

I shoved the letter into my skirt pocket and hauled a bucket of water to the copper tub, stripped naked and scrubbed.

360

Scrubbed away the salt, the memories, scrubbed and scrubbed and *scrubbed* until my fingers were red and raw, so shiny with soap, they hurt.

Hans hadn't come to warn me about Larland's letters. He hadn't come to tell me about the weapon. His death wasn't my fault, and there was nothing—*nothing*—I could have done.

I should have been happy. *Be happy. Be happy.*

I placed my face on my knees. Cold air caught my arms and my hair hung wet down my back. In the bed, Erik slept, a hand tucked under his cheek, and I wouldn't cry.

Don't cry.

Don't—

I remembered the soft skim of Erik's fingertips, the steady thrum of his heart. Could Hans and I have had something like that if I hadn't pushed him away?

Everyone wants something. And there was Hans in the doorway, every hope and dream and want laid bare.

What do you want?

Chapter Forty-Three

I DECIDED TO TELL Stefan what I'd learned.

About Hans.

About hearts.

This was my first mistake.

Chapter Forty-Four

I KNOCKED ON THE DOOR to the kitchens. Paused. Knocked again.

"Come on," I said. "Open up."

Once Stefan realized the Volds hadn't killed Hans, he'd listen. I'd stop him from torching the ships, from killing the generals. We'd put together another plan, a better plan.

Wind pearled through the gardens, rattling the rose bushes, rustling the hedges, the smell of it full and floral with a hint of herbs, lemon balm, rosemary, and thyme. Night rendered each leaf in sharp black.

I pounded harder. "Guys. Come on. It's me."

A shuffle, a scrape. The door swung open to reveal Pehr, blond hair, bright eyes. Without the steward's uniform, he seemed younger. For whatever reason, he wore his cream sweater backward.

"Isyyyyy," he said, resting his arm above the frame. "Finally joined the party?"

I ducked around him. "Where's Stefan?"

The long table had been shoved off to the side, covered in maps, and not one, not two, but eight clay pipes and bowls filled with green powder. The other steward, Loren, plucked one up and took a drag.

Great. They were getting high.

"What is this?" I said, wrinkling my nose and waving away the smoke. "Hemp?"

Pehr tweaked my cheek. "Why so grumpy? You knock, we answer. You come, we play." A shrug, as if this should all be obvious.

"Stefan," I snapped. "I need Stefan."

"Katrina and Gretchen are around back. Carl is…" Pehr scratched his chin and nodded.

"Stefan."

"Ooh, someone's grumpy. You wanna know what else we got?"

"No."

Pehr fumbled with the pouch and shoved a handful of withered roots in my hand, white like tube worms and coarse with dirt. "We stole it. From the scary man with the forky tongue. Try it." He shoved the roots harder. "Try it, try it, try it."

I batted his hands away. "I don't want to try the root. Where's Stefan?"

"Mmm…dunno."

"You do. Tell me."

He shrugged. "Downstairs?"

The hemp smoke made my eyes water, clung to my clothes. "We're in the kitchen. There is no *downstairs*."

Pehr giggled and reached for a bowl of cookies.

"The cellar," Loren supplied.

Oh. Right. The cellar.

The cellar was outside, around the corner and down a flight of narrow steps built from splintered wood and swept with leaves. Spiders crept through shadows, their forelegs gleaming. Each razor hair stood straight.

I reached the door at the bottom and tried to push it open. It stuck. I threw my shoulder against it once, twice.

It scraped.

In the room at the bottom, baskets of blood-oranges, barrels of beer. And crates, dozens of them, all packed with lamp-oil incinerates. They'd dragged a table down here, cluttered it with empty bottles and yellow rags. A knife sat beside a half-cored apple, the blade sticky with juice. A single candle burned.

"Hello?" I called.

Cobwebs crusted corners. The candle guttered.

"Stefan?"

Wherever he went, he hadn't been gone long.

A few bottles had been corralled off to the side of the table. I picked up the first and sniffed. Søven. No surprise they'd kept it out. I'd brought my bottle on the scouting trip with the Volds. There was another bottle with a peeling label and the cherry-citrus scent of white wine. A jar of vinegar, good for scrapes, and—

A flash, a glint, a silver flask, two suns embossed on the front, dark red liquid crusted along the rim, but—

Suns. I traced one with my thumb, the metal textured and cool.

He makes me drink from his cup of suns.

It wasn't…? Could it…?

I unscrewed it, sniffed. I'd teased Stefan about drinking in the morning. But this? It wasn't wine. It didn't even smell alcoholic, the liquid subtly acrid, syrupy sweet, all the smoke and velvet, dark like cassis berries soaked in sugar, so strong it made my eyes hurt.

It smelled like plums.

It smelled like honey.

It smelled like…like fly agaric.

The speckled mushroom grew in the forests of Larland, shaded by trees and temperate things. In small doses, it could treat muscular pain.

But in large doses…?

I poured some on the back of my hand, my face reflected in the blood-red drop.

I do not want to drink, I do not.

In large doses, it would cause hallucinations, fevers.

Madness.

Why would Stefan be feeding this to the king?

A door creaked.

"Isy." Stefan stood in the doorway, his jacket shucked over a shoulder, hair curling over his ears. Circles rimmed his eyes and his cravat hung open at his throat. Red. The color of—

He licks me with his frog tongue, ties it round my neck.

Had Stefan been poisoning the king to win the royal physician position? Or was there a more sinister plot? What would he do now that I'd discovered him?

I liked Stefan, I did, but suddenly, we were back in the apothecary scrambling over Hans's journals, his fingers digging into my hip a little too hard, and we were back in the closet, his hand tangled through my sweater, the scent of him, mint and musk, and he was pushing me against the shelves harder, harder, and I couldn't breathe and his eyes blazed, dark and murderous, and didn't he always have that violent edge?

367

I had to keep him distracted so I could get out.

"You're here." I shoved the flask against the other bottles. It rattled. "I came looking for you."

"You have the boxes?"

"I'm working on it. I have…news."

Every muscle in my body screamed to run, run, run. Pretend I don't know, didn't see.

You get nervous when you lie. It's a tell.

Candlelight shaded Stefan's lashes, his teeth. He shut the door and lowered his eyes, demure. "You do?"

Lie!

I slid my fingers along the rim of the table, edging for the door. "Yes." The word was no louder than a breath.

"What's this news?"

A hiss, a crackle. Beads of wax pattered down the shaft.

"I wanted to tell you…about the plan to steal the Lover's Boxes." The lip of the table ran out. My hands met air.

Stefan cocked a brow. "The plan to steal the Lover's Boxes?"

"Yes." Another breath.

He took a step forward.

I took a step back.

"What is this plan?"

If it comes to a physical fight, I want you to run. "We're going to do it. Tomorrow. We have a plan. It's a good plan. It's—"

His gaze flicked to the open flask. His lips curled into a predatory smile. "Oh, Isabel. You've been poking around where you don't belong."

I snatched the knife from the table. "Don't come any closer."

He lunged.

I ducked, slashing his inner thigh.

Blood spurted, hot and metallic. It coated my hands, my lips, made everything slick.

He screamed. Something—his elbow?—knocked against my ruined ear.

Pain erupted across the side of my head. The world rippled, pulsed.

I dropped the knife with a clatter and hobbled to the door.

It stuck. I jiggled the handle, my hands squelching over the metal, the blood like fat, like oil. It caught between my fingers.

No, no, no.

Behind me, a sweep, a scrape.

"Help," I called, pounding on the wood. "*Help!*"

No answer.

My ear pulsed, my head throbbed. The wood seemed to buckle, seemed to bow, a swirl of chestnut and honey.

Behind me, the drag of a foot across dirt. Jars rattled.

"*HELP!*"

I got a grip on the handle and wrenched the door open. Stony cold air washed my face. In the stairwell, a lantern burned. Up ahead, the vague outline of a door and—

Stefan grabbed my leg, pulling me to the ground.

His fingers tangled through my hair. My knee on his chest. A hand clawing at my ears, my throat. "You know, you were always—"

At the door, a flash of a figure, slim frame, short hair. Gray sweater.

Katrina.

"The bottle," I said. "The clear one. It's søven. I need—"

The shift of shadow. A *tink* of glass.

I tilted my head.

Katrina picked up the søven bottle and fingered it. Her eyes flicked between Stefan and me. Candlelight flickered off her irises, her cheeks. She swallowed.

I had my knee on Stefan's stomach, my fingers tangled through his hair. My vision prickled and air, he was cutting off my air, and I was suffocating, but all we needed to do was drug him. Katrina would drug him and—

Something warm and wet shoved against my mouth, the scent of it cloying and sweet, like sugar and strawberries.

"I'm sorry," Katrina sobbed. "I'm sorry, but the Volds corrupted you. And Hans—"

"They didn't kill him!" I screamed, but the søven slurred the words, and they came out wrong, all garbled, and they made me inhale. The rag pressed harder, linen fibers sticking to my tongue, my teeth, and suddenly I was drowning, floating, dying, a burst of light, a flash of silver, and my eyes became heavy, so, so heavy.

I reached up, the back of my fingers catching her cheek. Her eye. I needed to find her eye, but the smell of søven, of sweet strawberries, was dragging me down, down, do—

Chapter Forty-Five

VOICES DRIFTED THROUGH MY DREAMS like leaves caught on a current—whirling through the ebbs and eddies and spinning through the sediments.

"*… move her here…*"

"*… will have to wait…*"

"*… letter sent…*"

Though the words carried only a vague thrum of meaning, I let myself bob between the bumblings and babblings like a boat, falling between the slips and swells of—

"The ship arrives tomorrow." The words cut sharp against my brain.

"About time." A second speaker. Something creaked. "It would have been easier to use a merchant's ship."

I knew I should listen, knew this conversation was important, but the scent of sugar and strawberries burned hot against my throat and threatened to drag me down, down, down—

"Too risky," the first speaker said.

I kicked toward the voices.

"We could have kept him quiet." The second.

"Hmm maybe." A scrape. A shuffle. "But King Wilhelm will be disappointed if something happens to his new weapon. Better to be safe. Are we sure he'll show?"

"For her?" A warm hand brushed my cheek and looped a strand of hair behind my ear. "He'll show."

I tried to open my eyes, but it was like someone had glued my lashes shut.

"She's waking."

"We're not ready. Dose her again. Stefan? Stefan!"

Another scrape. Another shuffle. And boots, heavy and measured across the floor.

Hands on my shoulder. Breath on my cheek. "Shh, Isy. It will be easier if you don't fight."

The *glug* of a bottle. My head lifted.

No, no, no. I tried to fight it, tried to wiggle free. Stefan.

Stefan!

The wet rag was shoved under my nose. Again, the scent of strawberries and sugar.

Darkness came quickly this time.

WATER DRIPPED, SLOW AND RHYTHMIC, pattered like paint on a page. My cheek pressed against something gritty and hard, my limbs heavy as if someone had pumped them full of salt.

Drip…drip…drip…

I went to pull my knees to my chest and stopped. If I moved, would they dose me with søven again? Maybe. Probably. I needed to stay as still as possible until the full effect of the drug wore off, then I could try to escape.

I let my head fall to the ground.

There was something…something… What was it? Something about a weapon, a rendezvous and—

"I know you're awake." The voice came from in front of me. "It's fine. You can open your eyes. We're not drugging you again."

I cracked them, just enough to make out the rolling shape of the world, the barbed spike of rock, a roof of solid stone, and Stefan, crouched next to me, his face grim, cravat tied around his upper arm.

Not a cravat.

An armband.

A red armband.

Just like the one the bandits wore.

He offered a bowl of yogurt marbled with a deep purple jam. "Eat. And when you're up for it, there's a basin for washing. No baths, but we sponged you off. I had Katrina bring a change of clothes."

Moonlight filtered in through the cave's jagged entrance, leaching the color from the meadow and setting it in shades of silver. Cold air pushed through the opening, damp with dirt. A few men stood watch, their backs to us.

"Why are you doing this?" I said, letting my cheek fall against the grit. My mouth throbbed like someone had shoved cotton against my teeth.

"You're still my friend," Stefan said. "You're just confused."

"I stabbed you."

"Eat."

"Is it poison?"

"If I wanted you dead, you'd be dead. You've been asleep for almost three days."

You've been asleep. The way he said it—so calm, so casual—like he hadn't been the one to drug and kidnap me.

But he was talking, and maybe I could get answers.

I pushed myself up and swirled the spoon through the yogurt curdles. Grit stuck to my palms. My ear ached. "I know what you were doing," I said. "To the king. Were you trying to kill him or just drive him mad?"

Stefan's brow rose. "Christian made a good soldier but a bad king. We were doing you a favor."

"That didn't answer my question."

"The goal was to kill him. Eventually. The Hyllestad Treaty prohibits us from interfering with the Sanokes' independence, so an outright murder would look suspicious. Better to let Christian devolve into madness and wait for the ensuing succession crisis." He must have read my expression because he added, "The Sanokes aren't really equipped to govern themselves. Better to let us do it for you."

"Us?"

"Larland."

"So Larland was trying to retake the Sanokes?"

I took his silence as a yes.

"Why?" My lips stuck to my teeth.

He shrugged. "I don't know, Isy. Why do kings like pretty things?" He got up and came back with his own bowl of yogurt, sat across from me, and swirled the spoon through the berry jam. "To tell you the truth, I don't understand the fixation. But I can tell you that everyone wants these islands—Gormark, Nysk-lland...even little Forelsket, though I don't know how they'd manage."

Everyone wanted us? But why? We were—

I let my head tip back and stared at the ceiling, glittering mica, and suppressed a laugh.

Of course.

It's what drew in the whalers and the wanderers, the same thing that caused us to be conquered and owned, passed like rubies in dowries. It's why the sound looped backward when we screamed off the bluffs.

The islands had a pulse, a pull, a thrall of their own. Just like the Lover's Boxes.

I set the yogurt aside—too thick and sour—and went to the washbasin, a ceramic bowl perched on a rock. A folded pair of clothes sat beside it, one of Katrina's skirts and a pale pink sweater with a mock neck and sleeves that ballooned at the wrists like teardrops.

I let my fingers trace along the knitting of the sleeve. I'd always teased her about stealing this one because it had been my favorite. It was her favorite, too, and I wanted to hate her, *should* hate her. After all, she'd drugged me, betrayed me.

But…

Katrina.

Katrina, who snuck out, stole candies, who screamed off the bluffs. Katrina, who was all smiles and secrets and summer. And she'd brought me her favorite sweater.

A part of me—and not a small part—wanted to know where she'd gone after drugging me, but if I took the conversation in that direction, I might never get answers about the Sanokes.

I pulled my hair back, brushed my bangs aside, and dipped my fingers into the cold water.

"The string of disasters—the sick guards, the torched grain ships. That was your doing?"

Stefan's lips pulled into a line. "Not *mine*, exactly."

"But Larland's?"

Another pause. Another yes.

"Because you wanted to rule us?"

More silence. He wasn't going to feed me answers, but fine. He had a habit of correcting me when I was wrong, so I'd keep forging ahead until he stopped me.

"When Erik and I were traveling around the island," I continued. "We were attacked by people wearing armbands like yours. Also Larland?"

Stefan sighed and set the bowl down with a *clank*. "When Volgaard showed up, we knew nothing about them except for their stated intent to wage war. We needed to learn who—*what*—they were, how they reacted under pressure. *They* were planning to attack *us*. We're the victims."

"Was Larland ever planning to send aid? Or were the letters just a farce?"

More silence. A farce, then.

"Are you going to explain that?"

He held up his hands. "What is there to explain? We needed help, and the letters were a way to get that."

"You planted them?"

His lips pulled back from his teeth. "I...placed them where I thought you might find them."

"With Hans's things?"

No response. Of course.

My hands rippled beneath the water's surface, sharp and clear. I took a breath. "Hans?"

"What about him?"

Wind whistled. A leaf floated across the water.

376

Drip…drip…drip…

The cave walls caught the light, fragmented it like veins or tangled roots, and I was rising, floating and I didn't want to know.

I needed to know.

"You killed him."

The fall of a knife.

I'd meant the 'you' generally. You, as in Larland, the others with the red armbands, not Stefan, but a slow smile spread across his face and I knew—*knew*—by the curve of his mouth, by the gleam in his eye, that it hadn't been Larland in the vague sense of the term.

It had been him.

"You know," he said, reclining. "You're smarter than I thought. You'd make a good asset."

That was it? That was all he was going to say? Skim past it like he had with the rest of the questions, act like he hadn't shattered my world, torn my sky, like he hadn't *tried to comfort me.*

"Tell me about Hans," I said, the words were a clog, a choke.

The leaf spun, the edges curling in on itself, the center dissolving into a lattice of spider webs, dark as veins. Water continued to *drip…drip…drip…*

"It was his own fault," Stefan said. "You know that, right?"

I pressed a palm to my forehead. "It can't be."

"Oh, Isabel, it could. And it very much was." He got up. Crossed the room. Placed a hand on my elbow. His brows pinched. Mock pity, mock concern. "It didn't have to end that way."

I kept my hands plunged in the water, the freezing cold pricking my palms, reddening my knuckles, and maybe if I focused on the cold—

"Explain."

"He liked to open letters. Bad habit. We tried to avoid sending messages through the regular post because of it. When the Volds showed up, the next information drop wasn't scheduled for over a week. So, I sent a letter. Hans found it, confronted me, and… It was his own fault. If he hadn't opened the letter, if he hadn't *threatened* me, I wouldn't have had to—"

My vision flashed and suddenly, I was on top of Stefan, clawing at his eyes, his throat.

His knee came up between us, trying to wedge me up and away.

"Isy," he grunted. "I didn't— It's not—"

Tears blurred my vision. Metal tanged my mouth, and it didn't matter because I'd kill him, *I'd kill him.*

Guards rushed inside. Hands on my waist and I was lifted away, shoved against the ground. A hand pinned my face. Fingers tangled my hair. Skin scraped stone. A bottle *glugged.*

"Leave her," Stefan barked. He towered over me, an angel, a god. His shirt hung open, torn at the neck, exposing the column of his throat. His shoulders heaved. "We need her awake."

Blood trickled from his nose. He swiped it with the back of his hand. "You should know he died like a coward. *Begging* for his life."

Chapter Forty-Six

AFTER THAT, THEY MOVED ME closer to the cave mouth. Crisp air shuttered the grasses, whisked in through the opening, lifted the hair off the back of my neck. I fought against the bindings, bit against the gag. If I could get my hands free, I could work on the leather straps they'd wrapped around my ankles.

Or maybe I should work on my feet.

That actually wasn't a bad idea. If I got my boots off, I could run. If I made it past the cave entrance, I could hide in the tall grasses until they gave up and stopped looking.

New plan. Better plan.

My fingers tingled from the loss of blood. My jaw ached.

I maneuvered myself so my knuckles grazed the soft leather of my boot, the hard edge of the buckle. I flexed my wrists and pushed, tried to ease my heel out and—

Nothing.

I tried again. The thin rail of metal caught the pad of my thumb. I wiggled my foot up and out, up and—

My heel caught on the spot where the rope had been wrapped.

A few feet away, guards puffed pipes of rosemary and mullein.

"Can't do Tuesday," one of them was saying. "Maybe Wednesday?"

"Wednesday's goat racing," said the other. "You coming?"

"Of course, I'm coming," said the first. "When have I ever missed goat racing?"

Smoke tickled my nose, bright and herbal, caught the back of my throat. It mixed with the cold air and made my eyes water, but I could do this. Breathe. Focus. I just needed to wiggle one foot out. One foot.

One.

Foot.

I pressed my thumb against the shoe buckle, holding it in place. I tried to slide my foot out of the boot, my heel raising a fraction of an inch and—

Erik strode in. He had a sword buckled at his hip, and his mouth was hard, eyes smoldering. A cloak billowed behind him, black as shadow, black as smoke, a falling crow emblazoned down the center.

Pieces of conversation filtered back, hazy and round.

For her? He'll come.

The ship arrives tomorrow.

We could have kept him quiet.

I should have seen it, should have known, but I'd been half drugged and unconscious. Me as bait, and Erik…

And Erik…

I had to get the gag off.

Erik glanced at me, bound and feral, then to Stefan, dried blood crusting under his nose. The corner of his mouth quirked.

I rolled the fabric with my shoulder. *Stop being smug*, I wanted to say. *It's a trap.*

Stefan made a broad sweep of his hands. "Sit. We have drinks. Food."

Erik slung a bag off his shoulder. It skidded over the ground. "As agreed."

Stefan waited, his arms outstretched, palm facing up, as if he were a vicar greeting friends.

Erik didn't move.

"Alright, then." Stefan scooped the bag up and flicked it open.

A wave of sickness and desire hit me. I needed to scoot forward, to have it, to hold it. But how? Erik had said the boxes would be nearly impossible to steal.

No. Stay focused.

Remove the gag. Warn Erik.

Stefan lifted the Lover's Boxes out, two of them, cream as paper, cream as bone, identical down to the pink whorls and painted rosettes.

I tucked my arms to my chest to keep myself from moving. My body strained. My muscles ached, and I wanted—

I wanted—

I wanted—

Erik gave a feral grit of the teeth. "Go ahead. Try them out. See how they work."

"Let's talk."

"You have what you asked for."

Stefan tucked both Lover's Boxes back into the bag and tossed it to one of the guards. "Does Herleif know you're here?"

I tried to roll the gag down with my shoulder again. The fabric caught on my tongue, thready and dry.

"That's none of your business."

Stefan's eyes flicked to me. "I heard you bound yourself to him. And to a king like Herleif. *Tsk, tsk.*"

A pause. The only sound the whoosh of wind beyond the entrance.

I stopped fighting and tried to meet Erik's gaze.

Look at me. Please tell me you didn't do that. Please tell me that isn't true. Please—

Erik's hand went to the pommel of his sword. He flashed his teeth. "That's not your concern."

"It is when you're readying yourself to attack."

"Oh. You don't know." Erik gave a sharp laugh. "Your king's been corrupted. You were going to attack us in three years' time. The sooths saw it." He glanced at me. The mask slipped and there, on his face, the fear, the desperation, and I knew, *knew* that he'd done it. Bound himself.

For me.

He slammed the walls back up and turned to Stefan. "Give me what you promised."

"Here's my problem." Stefan stepped forward and pinched my cheek as if I was a dog. "I'm looking for Volgaard's greatest weapon. And those…" A gesture at the bag with the Lover's Boxes. "They aren't it."

"You're out of luck, then. Volgaard doesn't have any special weapons."

"Oh, I think they do." Stefan circled like a wolf drawing in for the kill. "She's been helping me look, you know. She told us so many interesting things about Volgaard. About you. But the most interesting thing was about the ships."

Erik's eyes cut to me, confused. "We don't keep weapons on the ships."

"No," Stefan agreed, "you don't." He stopped behind me. Placed a hand on my shoulder. Squeezed. "What did you tell me about the map? White stones for Rythja, black stones for the other houses?" He released me. "Sit. We have yogurt. Plum wine. Apricots from last fall's harvest. A few of Larland's delicacies."

Erik didn't move.

"If you intend to conquer us, you might as well see who we are."

Stefan turned away, and I went back to trying to shrug the gag down. My cheeks throbbed.

Wouldn't poison be Stefan's weapon of choice?

He pulled out a glass bottle and two tumblers.

"I'll admit," he said, "at first, I was disappointed. Volgaard didn't seem to have any advantage we could steal. It would come down to a contest of wills, of brute strength. As the defending army, we have the upper hand. But who knew how many ships you were bringing? With your magic, one of your men might equal five of ours. It wasn't until Isabel told me about the map that it hit me. Volgaard's greatest strength, their greatest *weapon*. The people." He handed Erik the glass. "You can thank her for that."

Erik raised the glass to his lips, the contents deep purple, reflecting the light, the world, ribboning the facets.

My fingertips needled, and I needed to warn him.

Stefan leaned his elbow against the cave wall and smirked.

It's poison, I wanted to shout.

Lashes shaded Erik's cheek. He took a deep breath and—

With a flick of the wrist, Erik dumped the contents into the dirt. "You think I'd drink anything you handed me?" His eyes gleamed. "I won. I will win every time. Remember that."

Stefan stared at the wine, a swirl of black and grit. His face faltered, then collapsed into something savage. He fisted my hair and dragged me across the cave. Spots flared at the edges of my vision.

"You still want her? The Lover's Boxes for your lover? That was the deal, wasn't it? I have to admit, she did her job well."

Erik laughed. "I knew Isabel was a spy the moment she waltzed down that beach."

"Not that job." Stefan pulled my head back, tipped my chin toward the ceiling.

No. Not the ceiling.

Toward Erik.

"What else did the minister tell you to do?"

The earth seemed to tip, seemed to sway.

That wasn't supposed to come out like this. That wasn't supposed to come out *at all*. I tried to tuck my chin to my chest, tried to squeeze my eyes shut.

Stefan jostled my head. "Look at him, Isabel. I want you to see the moment you break his heart."

Erik swallowed.

The gag tightened, then loosed, a rush of air.

"You have to understand—" I started. "It wasn't—"

"He's waiting," Stefan interrupted.

"They told me to...but I didn't. It's not... Stefan." I licked my lips. "Please don't make me do this." The words were no more than a whisper.

Erik's brow furrowed. "Make you do what?"

A release of hair. I fell forward, my bound wrists scraping the ground.

Stefan's voice pitched higher. Mock surprise. "Oh? You didn't know? She was supposed to seduce you. Get you to fall in love with her. Convince you to tell her secrets using her pretty mouth."

Erik didn't respond.

"And she wrapped you so tight around her finger—"

"Shut up," Erik said.

"You ran as soon as we—"

"I said, shut up!"

The words echoed off the ceiling. Erik's chest heaved. Sweat gleamed on his brow.

Stefan smirked. "Take her. That is…if you still want her."

And then he was gone.

I doubled forward, rested my forehead on the cool cave floor.

"Help me with my—"

But there was no movement, no rush to aid. Instead, Erik watched me like I was a swindler, a snake. "You were…using me?" The words were slow, almost as if he didn't believe them.

"It's not like that."

"Oh-ho." His teeth flashed. "Then tell me, Isabel. What was it?"

I twisted against the bindings. "It's— I can explain."

"So, you're telling me you weren't explicitly tasked to get to know me? You're telling me you weren't explicitly tasked to get me in your bed? You're saying you weren't—" His voice broke. Black tendrils spilled off him, snatching at empty air. Snow fell, glittering. It wove into windows, into wolves.

He drew back. "You know, the one thing I could never figure out was why they picked you. But it makes sense. It makes so much fucking sense, and I was so stupid for not seeing it. Somewhere deep down, I knew you were using me, but I wanted—I needed—" He gritted his teeth. "I was so fucking *desperate* for someone to care, I played right into your trap. I—"

He swallowed and scrubbed a hand over his face. "I never want to see you again."

"Erik…it's not—" My voice cracked. "Let me explain."

"There is nothing to explain!" Thunder cracked, and it all exploded—the storm, the snow, the wolves. "You could have told me. You had *so many* opportunities to tell me. Instead, you used me. You fucking *used* me. Just like everyone else. Did I ever matter, or was I just another job?"

Tears pricked at my eyes. "Why did you bind yourself to him?"

"Because you *left*. You fucking left, Isabel, and I didn't have a choice!"

He stalked forward and dropped into a crouch. The smooth press of fingers beneath my jaw. He lifted my chin. Our eyes met and his were a fortress, the bridge drawn up. His next words were dangerously quiet. "You could say a million words and I would *never* trust you again."

A whistle cut through the air.

"Goodbye, Isabel."

"Erik, look—"

Someone grabbed Erik around the waist and dragged him back. One of the guards.

Erik twisted, barreling into the man.

Then suddenly, the guard was on the floor, pinned beneath Erik's legs as Erik punched him over and over again.

The man let out a cry. Blood streamed from his nose and mouth, and shit. Erik was going to kill this man, was going to kill him right here with his bare hands.

The second guard peeled from the entrance, this one larger, a bald head and thewed shoulders, black coat.

I fought against the rope. "Erik, behind—"

The second man grabbed Erik's forehead, shoved a rag into his face.

Erik thrashed, elbowing the man in the groin. The man let out an *oof*. The rag parted from Erik's face and—

The man pressed it harder.

Erik stilled, then slumped.

Stefan stepped out of the shadows. He clapped once, twice. "Well done." He spared a single glance at Erik, unconscious on the floor. "Tell me, what should we do with Larland's new weapon? Should we break him like a stallion? Breed him like a dog? I hear reykr is hereditary. Perhaps he'd pass on his ability to Send." He smoothed a strand of hair behind my ear. "King Wilhelm was *very* interested in Volgaard's magic."

I tried to bite his fingers.

He pulled them out of reach.

"Ship's here," someone called.

"Take him down," Stefan replied. "Make sure you keep him drugged."

"And the girl?"

Stefan stepped back, his lips grim. "I'll take care of her."

They hauled Erik out of the cave, and it was just me and Stefan. He pulled my knife from his belt, let it dangle between his fingertips. The hilt gleamed the deepest red and burnt-honey brown.

I struggled against the bindings, pulling frantic. "Stefan," I said. "Please. We're friends. It doesn't have to—"

The knife clattered to the floor.

Stefan's chest heaved. Sweat glistened on his brow and matted his hair.

"If you know what's good for you, you'll go back to your quiet life," he said. "Become the physician of some tiny town. Forget about him."

"Stefan!" someone called. "The ship is leaving."

His lip tugged into a snarl. He stood. "If I see you again, I'll kill you."

Then he was gone.

Chapter Forty-Seven

IF I SEE YOU AGAIN, I'LL KILL YOU.

I gritted my teeth and scooted toward the knife, holding back tears that were threatening to spill.

They'd captured Erik.

They were going to use him, to *breed* him.

Their prize.

Their weapon.

The hurt in his eyes, the way they burned.

You could say a million words and I would never *trust you again.*

Wind drove in through the mouth of the cave, cold and biting.

My hands tingled. I twisted so the knife was behind me, wedged the rope against the blade.

I hadn't meant for this to happen. And yet…

The knife slipped, falling with a clatter.

I repositioned it, cord on steel, and bit the inside of my cheek to keep from crying.

And Erik?

For a moment, we were tangled in his sheets and on the beach, in the ravine, and the memories were traitors, so strong my teeth hurt. We were drinking coffee, on his horse, swimming, and he was pulling me into the ocean, that dark belly of the sea. Water lapped at my ankles, a sting of salt and foam, and I wanted to scrub them out, out, out.

Because I wanted that, wanted him.

I pressed the bindings harder against the blade, and we were back at the Rose & Thistle Inn, he on the hallway floor, head knocked back, mouth ajar, chest rising and falling, rising and falling.

I know what it's like to be unhappy.

Who was I to go against Larland? I wasn't smart or strong. I couldn't command ships, hold armies. I was Isabel Moller, apprentice physician from Hjern. A nobody.

The bindings broke and the knife slipped. Something stung my palm and heat welled between my fingers.

I wiggled my hands out and studied the damage.

Blood. A sheen of it.

I yanked the rest of the ropes with my teeth and crawled to the washbasin and dunked my hand into the icy cold, hissing at the ache.

Through the ripples, I studied the wound. A nick large as my knuckle, thin as a thread. It skimmed the center of my palm.

Blood bloomed.

Outside, the meadow lightened, the pale blush of morning. Grasses swayed, and the silence threatened to swallow me.

Drip, drip, drip came the sound of water from somewhere. Drip, drip, drip, and it matched the hollow knock of my heart.

If you know what's good for you, you'll go back to your quiet life.

I could go back, could slip into that life. Maybe I could apprentice to the royal physician for Gormark or Nysklland.

I smoothed my thumb over my bloody palm.

Wasn't that what I wanted? Wasn't that *everything* I wanted?

But no. *If you'd been good enough for Jens-Kjeld, he wouldn't have hired Stefan.*

That thought, a mirror of another.

If you'd been good enough for your father, he wouldn't have shut the door.

The shack. The beach. The seagull's cry.

My reflection rippled, and I caught my eyes, wide and brown.

My father's eyes.

My brothers'.

Staring back at me.

I hurled the basin to the ground. It shattered, a shower of water and glass. The bowl of yogurt, the spoon. I threw them.

Crack. Spray.

Tears pricked. My throat tightened, and I was scrambling for something, anything, to hold, to ruin.

Drip, drip, drip.

I snatched the change of clothes Katrina had brought and a paper tumbled out.

It quivered, the edges crisp and white, crinkled from rain. It had been in my pocket, but Katrina must have taken it out when she cleaned me up.

Blood oozed from my palm, soaking into the twilling of my skirt.

My fingers twitched.

I didn't move.

The paper waited, careful, patient.

You know you want to read me, it seemed to say. *You know you want to pick me up.*

I'd already read the beginning, had branded the words into my brain, but Hans had written more than that.

I crept forward, scooped it off the ground and cradled it like it was a secret, a snake. The paper crackled. I unfolded it.

Isy,
~~*What I meant to say*~~
~~*I want*~~

I pressed my lips together, stared at the ceiling. Why was I doing this? To hurt myself? I thought I'd moved past that.

I glanced at the page again, the way his writing ran together, the familiar scrawl of it, loose like water.

I took a deep breath.

And read the rest of the letter.

I botched it yesterday. I don't want a fishing boat. I want you. I chased you to Karlsborn Castle because you were worth chasing. You will always be worth chasing. ~~I love you.~~ ~~I love you?~~ I love you.
~~*I don't think*~~
You say this job is what you want. If that's true, I'll stay for you. I'll stay as long as you ~~want~~ let me. But I know you better than ~~anyone~~ that.

You think some people are better than others, that being the royal physician is the "biggest" thing you can do. But you're not that small. You have <u>never</u> been small.

Your father was an idiot for shutting the door. You are ~~beautiful~~ ~~capable~~ enough.

I read the words a second time, a third, traced each line with my thumb, the curve of the 'a', the arch of the 'h.'

He hadn't signed it, but I could almost picture it, his name scrawled across the bottom, bold as his declaration.

Hans, who'd held me crying behind the chicken coop, who'd helped me overcome self-harm, who'd been there again and again.

You think some people are better than others, that being the royal physician is the "biggest" thing you can do.

Through the tears, I laughed.

He was right. My entire life, I'd felt small, insignificant, no bigger than a grain of sand on the dance floor. I thought I'd come from a tiny town on a tiny island and that meant I was destined for tiny things. Abandoned by my father, sent away by my mother, I thought some people were born less than and lacking, that my deficiencies stitched like scars.

I thought I was a nobody.

But…what if I wasn't?

I bound a shred of skirt around my palm and ran out of the cave, past the sheep and gardens of rosemary and wild thyme, up, up the path that led not to the beach, but to the bluffs.

You are ~~beautiful~~ ~~capable~~

Wind tangled my hair, flattened the grasses, howled along the sheer cliffs that dropped into the sparkling sea.

This was the edge of the world, a stop off for whalers and wanderers, a waypoint. This was a place with a pulse, a pull, a heartbeat that thrummed through every leaf and blade and fiber.

I stood at the lip of it, unbound.

I, Isabel Annis Moller, apprentice physician from Hjern. I was a friend and lover. A daughter. Radiant. Not small like sand, but a fulmar unfurling her wings.

And I was going to save Erik.

Chapter Forty-Eight

MIST GATHERED ALONG MY LASHES, pilled inside my nose, giving the air an almost wet and sheeny shimmer. Waves lapped at scattered shells, the gentle rush of blue-gray water that made them tinkle. The sea seemed to hang off the sky.

I was used to the cabal and chaos of the camp, to illusions that gnarled and twisted, but the emptiness, the stillness, was new.

My hand curled around the strap of my medicine bag. I skirted around a pile of trash.

I was fairly confident this plan would work. If Stefan and the other spies had slipped seamlessly into the Sanokes, shouldn't I be able to slip into Larland?

After all, they'd owned us, had hammered and smoothed our edges until we were a gold and gilded thing. Their prize, their pet, something to be paraded, soft and feathery, put on pillows and made to smile.

They wanted to build us in their image.

They showed us how to make them bleed.

Twenty years of independence was not so long to drift apart.

And didn't I know better than anyone how royal households were run? Hadn't Karlsborn Castle been patterned after the more opulent Salborg one? And wouldn't they want to show King Wilhelm his new weapon.

So, Erik would be at Salborg Castle, at least for a little while.

But I couldn't save him alone.

Rock faces glittered from the ocean spray. Gulls darted in and out of pockets on the cliff. The world held a sleepy haze.

A handful of Volds sat by a dying fire, hair long and wrists tattooed, their shirts a rumpled cotton, soiled from sand and sweat. They prodded the fire with a stick.

"Do any of you know where Signey is?" I asked.

All eyes flicked to me, beady and hungry, a little wary. One man glugged from a bottle. Another spooned porridge out of a wooden bowl. A third held a half-skinned fish, its body limp and silver. Blood slicked the man's fingers, red as poppies. It pattered the sand with a slow *drip, drip, drip.*

Maybe I should be afraid, but I knew how House Rythja worked. I'd stared down their monsters, and I'd won.

I held the man's eyes.

"You again," he said, shifting forward. His mouth curved into a smile that showed every one of his teeth. "Decide to have a drink with us after all?"

I blinked.

You again? After all?

I'd never seen this man before. He wasn't one Erik brought on the scouting expedition, nor was he one I'd encountered in the camp. He—

Oh. Wait.

Rat face, dark lips.

395

The man who'd made the better me the first time I'd come into the camp.

A whisk of wind and there she was, sitting on his lap, her hair a glossy shade of brown, her eyes dark with desire. Her dress clung to her hips, her breasts, nothing more than a nightgown. She shimmied her shoulders and grinned.

"I don't want a drink," I said, ignoring her.

The better me fell away, a wisp of smoke. The man wedged his knife under the fish's remaining scales and peeled them off. "Then why are you here?"

"Signey. You know where she is?"

He laughed. "You think I follow the bitch queen?"

"I think you know which tent is hers." A statement, not a question. And it was early enough in the morning, hopefully she would still be there.

One of the other men scratched his neck. "Signey? She's gone. Left this morning."

My gaze snapped to him. "You know where?"

He huffed a laugh. "Why would I know?"

The third Vold took another glug of his bottle. "Heard it was another scouting mission. Erik sent her off to...Shoe Cove?"

"Cobble Cove," said a fourth.

The third Vold licked his teeth. "Down by the horses if they're still there."

I sprinted down the beach, sand nipping my ankles, wind spiking my hair. Seabirds wheeled overhead. The sky stretched blue and long. *Please don't be gone, please don't be gone. I don't know who else I'd take.*

The fact of the matter was this plan hinged on finding support. I couldn't trust anyone at the castle, not after Stefan. But

Signey cared about her little brother. Hadn't I seen that? If anyone would help, it was her.

I found her with two dozen men. She'd braided her honor bead behind her ear and changed from her typical fur vest into a dark green jacket with House Rythja's crow emblazoned across the front.

"Isabel," she said. "Glad you're back." She ducked around a man carrying a bundle, stepped over a crate of foodstuff. "If you see Erik, tell him he owes me a horse. And some dried fish. His men dumped mine into the ocean."

Bengt loaded saddle bags onto a stallion. Tyr brushed down a mare.

"Also," Signey continued, hauling a bag off the ground. "If you see Erik, tell him he's late."

She turned and prepared to leave.

I sucked in a breath. "Erik's gone."

Horses whinnied. Waves crashed. Spray from the ocean tarted my lips, dampened my sweater.

Signey paused, her back to me.

"I'm sorry," I continued. "I tried. I—"

She stalked across the sand, grabbing my wrist and pulling me a little way down the beach, away from the earshot of the others. "What do you mean, he's gone?" The words were a growl, a warning.

I took a deep breath and fought the urge to run, to hide. All the times Signey had scared me, threatened me, they were scars, and right now, under the press of her fingers, the heat of her gaze, my body was tensing, a pipit setting flight against a falcon, but I couldn't do this alone, and she cared about Erik, she did, and maybe she wasn't my friend, but she wasn't my enemy, either. We could be allies. At least in this.

I shook my hand loose.

"It was a trap," I said.

Her brow rose. "They let you go?"

I thought back to the heave of Stefan's chest, the blood crusted along his nose, the glint in his eye. *If I see you again, I'll kill you.*

"I don't think they saw me as a threat."

Signey's hands balled to fists, and she stalked off toward the horses.

"Where are you going?" I hurried after her.

She kept her eyes steely and ahead. "To save my brother."

"By yourself?"

She glanced over her shoulder, the corner of her mouth quirked. "I assume you're coming, too? You're trotting after me like a puppy."

"I'm not a puppy."

"What's in the bag?"

I wrapped my hand around the leather strap and jogged to match her stride. "Um. It can't just be us. We need a few more people. A group."

"Wouldn't it be better to keep the mission small?"

"Agreed. But you won't get Erik out by storming in there all by yourself."

"I have you."

"We need more than that. At least four."

"Fine. I'll gather men."

"I had a few in mind. Did Bo and Kaspar get out of prison?" Erik had said Herleif would release them if he bound himself to him. Not that far-fetched of a thought.

She rolled her eyes. "*Anyone* but them."

398

I scrambled to keep her pace. "Kaspar can hold for sixteen people, *and* he's the best swordsman in Volgaard. We might need that."

"Have you seen Kaspar use a sword?"

"No."

"Do you know how many swordsmen there are in Volgaard?"

"No, but—"

"Exactly. He's *not* the best swordsman. Erik just says that."

"He's Erik's best friend."

She eyed me, dubious. Fog dampened her hair, her jacket.

"You know it's true."

She opened her mouth, then closed it. "Erik has bad taste in friends."

"But why *don't* we want someone like Kaspar? He's loyal, willing to stick his neck out for Erik."

She reached a rowboat with a curving hull. The wood warped like a sheep's horn, speckled with gray-green lichen. She toed it with her boot. "Any of Erik's men would stick their neck out for Erik. We'll take Bengt."

My gut lurched. I rushed to the boat's other side. "Bengt?"

"Yeah. Bengt."

"We can't take Bengt."

"Why?"

The thought of being stuck on a boat with Bengt made me nauseous. "Anyone but him."

"He can hold for sixteen people too. That's just as many as Kaspar."

"A talent he used on me."

"So?"

"He *tortured* me."

Signey shrugged and tossed me an oar. "I'll order him not to."

I tossed the oar back. "He smells."

"We'll make him take a bath before we leave."

"We don't have time for a bath."

"Bengt isn't so bad once you get to know him. Plus, he's better with a sword than Kaspar."

"So Erik *did* get Kaspar get out."

At that moment, Kaspar rounded the corner of the bluffs. He must have spotted us because he dropped his packs by the horses and sprinted across the beach.

"Hey, Sig," he said. "Have you seen Erik? I thought he was coming to see us off."

Signey's jaw feathered. "*Signey*," she said. "My name is Signey."

"You've seen him?" he asked again.

"No," Signey replied.

"You know where he is?"

"No."

Kaspar's gaze swung to me. "You've seen him?"

Signey stare went murderous. *Do not say anything*, it warned.

"I have...not," I said.

Kaspar cocked his head. "Really? Because he got us out, we stole the Lover's Boxes, and then I thought he said he was going to rescue you."

"He...did? Then he left?"

There. I'd lied.

Signey was still pinning me with a stare that said if I told Kaspar, she'd eat me alive. But this plan needed at least four people, and I wanted Kaspar to come. Even if Bengt promised he'd never use reykr on me again, I wasn't ready to forgive him.

Kaspar crossed his arms. "You *really* don't know where Erik went?"

Signey kept her gaze on mine. She gave a slight shake of the head. Another warning.

A wave thundered up the beach, white foam and bubbles nearly catching our ankles, licking at the boat's hull.

Kaspar didn't believe me, which was fine for Signey. She would run him off with her grumpy attitude and we'd be halfway to Larland before he circled back to get me alone. We'd end up taking Bengt, which was exactly what she wanted. Or...

"Okay fine," I said. "Erik was captured by Larland. They're taking him to be their new weapon. Signey and I are going to save him."

Signey smacked her forehead. "Isabel!"

I threw my hands in the air. "What? I'm a terrible liar! You guys have been telling me this for weeks."

"Captured?" Kaspar echoed.

"Yes."

He looked at Signey. "When do we leave?"

She stiffened. "*We're* not going anywhere."

"Sure we are. I'll get Bo." Kaspar disappeared down the beach.

"Two minutes," Signey said, rubbing her temples. "You couldn't keep your mouth shut for *two minutes*."

I shrugged and turned my cheek to hide my smile. "Now we have our team."

She eyed the horizon. Wind ruffled her hair, washed her face in a soft flutter. The water had gone a dull sapphire blue, the color of a clamshell or a summer sky. "Do you know where they took him?"

"Salborg Castle. Lillefjord."

"That's a four-day journey."

"If we leave now, we won't be too far behind."

She nodded, kept her eyes ahead. "Do you know how I got my honor bead?"

The question startled me, pulled me back. "Tormod's Keep?"

"But do you know the story?"

"No."

Her hand went to her scalp, the silver ball braided there, and she twisted it. "House Kynda was out of control again, pushing into other people's lands. They'd taken the keep from Rythja a couple months earlier, and we wanted it back. And by 'we,' I mean mostly Lothgar. He had me sneak inside because I was small. Only seven, I think, maybe eight. It wasn't hard. All I had to do was lower the bridge and run like hell. But after the battle, he acted like I was the hero. He cut the bead right out of his hair." Her fingers stilled and her eyes slid to me, the same smoky gray as Erik's. "They don't mean you're important. Well, they do, but that's not all. They mean—*eljun*. That's our word for it. It means you have heart. And you, Isabel Moller, have heart."

I opened my mouth, closed it. "That's...maybe the nicest thing I've heard you say. Ever."

She stiffened. "I'm not nice. Now, let's go save my idiot brother."

Chapter Forty-Nine

WE DRAGGED THE ROWBOAT ASHORE, water sucking at our ankles like a hungry mouth, our faces slick with spray and rain.

My legs wobbled from four days on a ship—three sailing along the coast of Larland and one sailing upriver. Before this, the longest I'd ever been on a boat had been the few hours sailing with Hans and Katrina.

I twisted my hair out of my face and pressed my forehead against the pebble beach. It was cool and grainy, the sweet musk of salt and leaves. I'd stood on riverbanks thousands of times. How had I never noticed that smell?

But that wasn't the strangest thing.

My body felt wrong, felt empty, like someone had torn a hole from the center of my chest and left me bare. In its place, a throb in the direction of the Sanokes, a vein leading to a heart.

Ba-dum, ba-dum.

Come home, come home.

A pair of boots entered my vision. "When I said I'd make you want to kiss land again, I didn't mean you actually had to kiss it," Kaspar said.

I groaned. "You couldn't pay me to get on another boat." Except I *did* want to get on another boat, because I wanted to get back. It wasn't the frantic want of the Lover's Box, but a warm want, a gilded want, all gold and satin, like the gentle hand of a mother.

"I have bad news for you about the trip home…" There was a note of humor in his voice. "Here. Let me help you up."

He pulled me to standing.

The rolling shapes of trees cut through the landscape. Hundreds of them, rough and spiked, barbed like brushes. Pine, maybe? I'd never been so close to them. In the distance, a city twinkled, the lights ribboning the river, set off against the steady browns and hardened grays.

Lillefjord.

The capital of Larland.

Come home, come home, come—

Salborg Castle sat a little higher than the city, bright white and glimmering, a monument. Turrets turned on high spindles, balconies and balustrades swooped over the city, and a domed atrium occupied an entire level. It glowed.

I'd always known Karlsborn Castle had been based on the Salborg one, that the architects had drawn inspiration from its white stone and clock towers. Hans had once said the gold-leaf gilding in the dining hall was a direct replica. But seeing it here, seeing it now, it was like trying to compare a candle to the sun.

Signey lifted my bag out of the boat and tossed it to me. "You said you'd tell us your plan when we got here. Spill."

Home, home.

I pushed the thought away.

Signey wouldn't like my plan, so I'd delayed telling her as long as I could. Now, I reached into my bag and pulled out the two laundry smocks—each a pale pink and white poplin that could be cinched at the knees. I tossed one to Signey. "Put this on."

She stared at the smock, her mouth falling slack. "I'm not putting that on. I'll look like…like one of you!"

"That's the point."

"It's a dress."

"So?"

"A *short* dress."

"Yes."

"I don't see you handing dresses to Bo and Kaspar." A muscle in her jaw ticked. Her eyes went hard as chips. "I'll look ridiculous."

"You know what's more ridiculous? Heading into Salborg Castle dressed like *that*." I gestured at her cotton pants and tunic. "And relax. You won't be wearing it long, anyway."

A pale brow rose. "Oh?"

"We need guard uniforms, but Karlsborn's are blue and Salborg's are different. Probably red. The only way I could think to get guard uniforms is to steal them. Pretending to be with laundry makes the perfect cover for that."

Hopefully that was enough reason to convince her to cooperate. The alternative was to leave Signey with the men and get the guard uniforms myself, but it would be safer to bring someone who could fight.

Signey stared at the smock. Her brow furrowed. Maybe she wouldn't do it? Then—

"Alright," she said.

She stepped behind the boulder and began tugging off her pants and tunic. "What are we going to do with guard uniforms?"

I ducked behind the same boulder and tugged off my sweater. The cool air nipped my skin, made gooseflesh pebble. "Like Sanok, Larland's prisons are designed to be inescapable. They can only be opened from the inside, and someone has to hold the crank for the portcullis to stay open. We'll pose as replacement guards, smuggle Erik out, then two of us will stay behind and wait for the next set of guards, who will let *us* out."

"You're going to have Larland's guards hold the door for their inescapable prison. Clever, Isabel. But you forgot something."

"What?"

She tossed the soft pink fabric back at me, naked from the waist up. "We don't need uniforms. I can hold for twenty-eight men."

I tossed the shift back. "They have syn rót. We can't rely on reykr."

She frowned and tugged the shift over her head. "Then what are we supposed to rely on? Kaspar's swordsmanship?"

Kaspar popped his head over the rock. "I am an excellent swordsman."

Signey whirled. "It's a good thing I'm dressed."

Kaspar grinned. "It's a good thing I'm in a relationship."

Bo popped his head over the rock, too. "Really? With who?"

"With you, idiot."

Signey ground her teeth. "Go away."

"Can I fix your hair?" I asked, reaching for Signey.

She glared.

"It's the style," I continued. "It's not popular in Larland. You wouldn't see that on a laundry girl."

She didn't move.

"Or a guard."

"Fine." She sighed and leaned forward, offering me her head.

I loosened the row of tight braids, let them fall in soft locks across her shoulders, and wiped the kohl from her lids with the back of my sleeve.

When I was finished, I took a step back. She no longer looked like a Vold, hard-edged and stiff. She looked like Katrina, Sofia, or any of the other girls from laundry, younger than her age of twenty-one, blonde hair framing her face, her pale pink smock hitting a few inches above her knee. Her legs glinted in the moonlight.

Her question from earlier still hung in the air: *Then what are we supposed to rely on?*

I probably looked the same as she did—kind and quiet, a little young. But for a moment, I felt bigger, taller, powerful as one of the pines that stood by the river's shore.

What are we supposed to rely on?

I straightened.

"Me."

SALBORG CASTLE WAS A MAZE OF COURTYARDS and clock towers. Gardens spilled roses and peonies, hyacinths as big as my hand. Doors opened to rooms filled with canopied beds and domed ceilings. Chandeliers dazzled and candles burned, perfuming the halls with the faint scents of beeswax, lemon, and thyme.

It took a half hour of creeping around before we found the guardhouse.

There were a couple of places uniforms could be kept, laundry being one. But if laundry girls in Salborg were half as close as laundry girls at Karlsborn, we'd be outed as impostors immediately. The guard house was the other place that might have a surplus of uniforms.

"Signey and I will poke around until we find them," I told Bo and Kaspar before heading up the moon-beamed steps.

The snores of men echoed down the hallway, plaster walls set with dark wood trim. Wrought-iron sconces threw light over doors.

"Follow my lead and don't say anything," I said, skirting around the corner.

"Why can't I say anything?"

"It's your accent. It gives you away."

Signey snorted. "My accent's fine."

I pulled open the first door. Guards. Snoring. I shut it. "I didn't say it wasn't. It's just… It's not Larland."

"And you can do an accent from Larland?"

I pulled open a second door, this one a closet filled with brooms and buckets and cobweb-encrusted feather dusters. A few daddy long legs scurried away. "Larland's accent is my accent. It's the same."

A third door. A uniform closet. "Help me grab what we need."

I began shoving the items into my bag: red jackets, white gloves, belts filigreed with Larland's flayed rose. Footsteps clicked down the hall.

Signey froze.

"Relax," I said, reaching for another jacket. "We're dressed like laundry. Laundry would be in here all the time. They shouldn't question it."

"You sure?"

"Yeah, it's fine."

A voice rose through the footsteps, low and male and—

Familiar.

"Never mind," I said, dropping the guard uniform. "We have to get out of here, we have to—"

It was too late to run. The hall was too long, and he'd see us when he rounded the corner. Instead, I grabbed Signey's arm and pulled her into the closet.

The latch clicked and the light disappeared, plunging us into the dark. The round lip of a shelf dug into my back.

"What the—"

I clamped a hand over her mouth. "Shh."

"You said no one would know."

"*That* someone would know." My words were only a whisper.

Because that voice? Those footsteps.

They belonged to Stefan.

Chapter Fifty

SIGNEY AND I HURRIED DOWN THE STEPS of the guardhouse, night sweeping over the courtyard, skipping over the fountains and benches, those bruising purple hyacinths.

Two figures stepped from the shadows.

"Quick, huh?" Kaspar said. "You were in there a half hour."

"We got stuck. A few guards stopped outside the supply closet, but it's fine." I opened the laundry bag and dumped a bundle of clothes on the grass. "Signey, will you stand watch while we put these on?"

Kaspar reached for a pair of pants, the tension falling from his shoulders. "Oh. Learn anything that might help?"

"They're—" Signey started.

"The prison guards rotate at midnight." My fingers worked the toggles on the coat.

Signey glanced at me, a slender brow arching in a question. *Are you going to tell them?*

I ignored it, and she didn't say anything else.

Good.

They didn't need to know.

"Midnight," Kaspar repeated, tipping his chin toward the clock tower. "That's in fifteen minutes."

I grabbed a pair of satin gloves. "Then we'd better go."

THE CLOCK TOWER LOOMED as we made our way across the courtyard, white as lilies, white as bone. Wind snarled through my hair, raked its fingers against the empty fountains and rosebushes, the statues of bronze horses.

Fifteen minutes.

That would be enough time. It *had* to be enough time.

I stopped outside the iron door leading down to the prison and turned to face them.

Signey had pulled her shoulders up, her eyes bright and glassy. The tips of Bo's cheeks blistered red from the cold. Kaspar blew on his hands and bounced from foot to foot.

Me. They were waiting for me because I knew Larland, because I knew how to get Erik out.

And I *would* get Erik out.

I straightened and tipped my chin toward the door. "Kaspar and I will pretend to be the replacements." The clock tower shone bright. *Fifteen minutes.* "Don't follow until you see the old guards leave."

"What if the old guards don't leave?" Bo asked.

"They will." They had to.

I pulled the door open and headed into the dark.

The tang of sulfur hit my nose. Lanterns lit a narrow staircase. Water wept down the walls. A pair of mice scooted over the stair's rounded lip.

411

"We'll need to convince them to leave their shift early," I whispered, running the tip of my glove against the rain-slick stone.

"Shouldn't be too hard," Kaspar replied.

"And we'll need to get the keys to the cells."

Fifteen minutes.

"How do we get the keys?"

"We'll figure something out."

He opened his mouth, but before he could reply, we reached the bottom of the steps and the prison opened up like the inside of a ballroom, fit with towering walls and ornate pillars carved with hollow-eyed faces, strong chins and straight noses, mouths twisting in agony.

Two guards lounged on the galley benches behind the portcullis, one muscled, the other old. His pillowing of white hair stood out from his head like goose down.

Step one: meet the guards.

"You're early," the old one said, checking his watch with a flick of the wrist.

"Not by much." *Fifteen minutes.* I gave him what I hoped was a bright smile. "It's my first day. I asked Klaus," a nudge toward Kaspar, "if we could get a head start. Mind letting us in?"

The guard muttered something about newbies, but the iron grate groaned, rusty water dripping off the finial spikes.

"Any issues?" I asked, ducking inside. "Anything we should know about?"

The muscled one wrinkled his nose and swatted the air. "Nah. It's been pretty quiet. Night shift usually is."

Step two: get the keys.

Kaspar noticed them at the same time I did, a brassy ring sitting by the guard's knee.

A hint of a smile played at his lips, and he nodded as if to say he had this. The keys flickered, melting into the gray-flecked stone the way butter melts into a piece of warm bread.

Then, as if he remembered we couldn't rely on reykr, he sat on them.

My heart kicked. I wanted to laugh. This was too easy.

The muscled guard had apparently said something and was waiting for a response.

"What?"

"It's why they give it to newbies," he said. "The night shift?"

I dragged my attention away from Kaspar and the keys. "Right. Of course. Night shift. The easiest. So, um, this is where we let you out, right?"

Step three: replace the guards.

The old guard raised a hand. "Aren't you going to do the check?"

The...check?

The guard waited, his face patient, one weathered hand folded over the other.

I released a breath. "Oh. Right. The check." *Fifteen minutes.* I peeked down the cell-lined hallway. Lanterns hissed, their light reflecting like pools of oil on the smooth black floor.

I tugged at the hem of my sleeve. "All good."

"Come on." The old guard started down the hallway. "I won't tell the captain you nearly missed it. We all need a little slack the first day."

I shot one glance at Kaspar, who nodded, but stayed at the front. He couldn't come. He couldn't leave the keys.

"You coming?" the old guard asked.

I hurried to follow, the reek of sulfur growing stronger. Bodies hunched behind bars, ragged clothes, ashen faces.

The guard let the hilt of his dagger clink against the bars as we walked. "We have fifty-five prisoners in here right now. You should have gotten that number from the captain before you started the shift." He paused. The blade of his dagger flashed. "You got that number, right?"

"Of course."

Fifteen minutes.

"We load them front to back, two to a cell, so first twenty-eight should be full. They're numbered." He tapped a rusted nameplate. "Do you want to check the rest?"

"Where's the Vold general?" It was dangerous to ask, but—

"You've heard of him?"

"A little," I said, unsure how much information had been shared. "I was…curious."

The guard leaned close and tapped two fingers at the knot of scar tissue beneath his left eye. "Best to stay away from him. You took syn rót?" A nod. "Good girl. Do you want to check the rest of the cells?" He drew back and dug his watch out of his pocket. "Nine minutes until midnight. We have time."

Nine minutes.

I hurried down the hallway, the heels of my boot ringing against the black stone steps.

Backs and blankets, a man with a scruffy face, each cell illuminated by the lamp affixed to the pillar by the door. Shivers and snores. A woman scraped food from a bowl with her hand and—

There. Erik. Cell twenty-eight. His cheek was pressed against the floor, his eyes shut. Dirt smudged his brow, matted his hair. Something dark red crusted around his nose, his ears. Blood? Every muscle in my body screamed at me to find a way in, to haul his head into my lap, to pick the dust from his hair, to hold him.

"All accounted for," I said, returning. "Now we hold the door for you?"

Step three: replace the guards.

The guard's gaze flicked to my hands. "You bring a book? Cards? Something to do?"

"I'll be fine."

Nine minutes. Less now.

The guard sighed and pulled a book out of his jacket.

I glanced at the cover, pale blue leather embossed with a boy and a girl. The boy sat in the window of a tower, a hand on his cheek, his gaze toward the sky. Below him, the girl stretched on her tiptoes, a silver star caught in the press of her palm, a dozen at her feet. Her hair fell in a single braid down her back and the way she perched...

Aalto and Vega.

"A love story," I said. An interesting choice for a guard.

"Not a love story," he replied. "A *war* story. Or did you forget the hell Vega's father raised after she freed Aalto?"

"Didn't he sink a city?"

The guard rasped the cover. "A little more than that."

Kaspar must have smuggled the keys into his pocket, because as soon as we reached the front galley, he began cranking the shaft to the portcullis. The wood spokes ticked with each rotation. Metal screeched.

"I bunk in Harbell House," the old guard said. "For when you return it. You'll probably finish it before the end of your shift. It's a tiny thing, but don't let that fool you. Sometimes the small things are the strongest."

The guards ducked under the portcullis and headed toward the winding stairs.

"Wait," I called. My voice rung out over the stone, and I flinched. "Can you tell me the time?"

The older guard flicked open his watch.

Tick, tick, tick.

His brow scrunched. He tipped the clock face, trying to find a beam of light. "Five minutes to midnight." With that, they disappeared up the stairs.

Five minutes.

It wasn't enough.

It had to be enough.

"You think we can…?" Kaspar asked.

"Hold the gate," I said, keeping my face toward the dark.

A door creaked open, closed, then open again. The drum of footsteps, smooth like a mooring, steady like a heart. My hands tingled.

This was it.

Signey and Bo rounded the corner in their uniforms, breathless.

"We don't have much time," Signey said. "Only—"

"Five minutes."

"Four."

And then we were sprinting down the hallway, past the backs and blankets, the lines of cells.

"He's in twenty-eight."

"He's—"

"I didn't get a good look at him."

Kaspar threw the keys at Bo and tore off his guard jacket. "They check the cells. We'll pad the blanket with the extra clothes. Make it look like he's sleeping."

The cell door swung open, and I was on my knees.

"Erik? Erik?"

I pressed two fingers against his neck. Hot. His skin was hot and—

Shit. How much søven had they given him?

"We have to move," Signey said, glancing behind her.

Erik groaned, his lids fluttering. "Isabel…" A rasp, a scrape. "Wow. I must…really be…hallucinating…" His head lulled.

I fumbled with my bag, pulling out a flask of coffee, just as Kaspar stole the entire sack and shoved it at the head of his makeshift Erik.

"Sorry about this," I said, tipping the entire flask into Erik's mouth. "Swallow. Good." Not pleasant, but the caffeine would act as a stimulant and hopefully counteract some of the søven.

"Help him up?" Signey asked.

"One second," I replied.

I hooked my fingers beneath his chin and brought his face to meet mine, handsome and stormy, all angles.

"Listen," I said. "I want you to know something, and you might not remember when you wake up, but I'm going to say it anyway. You matter. Not because of your magic or whatever you are in Volgaard's army, but because of who you are. That's why I'm doing this. *You*. Because I see you. I see *all* of you, and it is beautiful and wonderful, and *you* are beautiful and wonderful. And I… I wish we'd had more time." The confession was rushed and awkward, chaste as a closed-mouth kiss. I could feel the tips of my ears turning pink. I laughed and swiped tears from my eyes. "The minister told me to woo you, but that's not why I did it. I understand if you never trust me again but…yeah. I just, I hope you heard that."

With the amount of søven in his system, I doubted it. He'd

probably wake hating me, would probably hate me for the rest of his life. Still, it felt nice to say the words out loud.

I see you. You matter.

I glanced at Signey, jitters flitting through my palms. "Help him up?"

She was already at his elbow.

Then we were barreling back down the hall of cells, Erik suspended between Signey and Kaspar.

The other prisoners were on their feet, clapping, cheering. Their cries filled the halls.

The clock tower rang. Shit. It would be worse if we weren't able to get everyone out. If we were all trapped here when—

I reached the crank wheel, the spokes cool and slick under my palm.

With a heavy twist, I threw my weight against it. I did it again. The portcullis began easing, metal spikes lifting from stone.

Twist, crank.

My arms ached. My muscles burned.

Twist, crank.

Twist, crank.

The prisoners' cheers echoed into the galley. The clock tower's tune finished, and the deaf knell vibrated through the walls. *One... two... three...*

I blocked it out and focused on the crank. My hands shook.

Twist, crank.

Twist, crank.

Stefan's words from the guardhouse looped in my mind like the strain on a sonnet.

The transport will be ready in fifteen minutes. They scheduled it with the change of the guard. And—

I don't know where the Vold general's going. Somewhere he'll never be seen again. And—

Thirty men, most from Wilhelm's personal guard. Probably overkill, but the Red King isn't taking any chances.

Signey had looked at me like she knew what that meant. Because if the transport was showing up with the change of guard, it would be impossible to make them believe Erik was in his cell.

"We can't take thirty men," she'd said, her voice low. "Not if they have syn rót."

Another swirl of memory. The strike of flint against stone. A leaf on a tongue. Tendrils of tar black smoke snake from a lamp. The sooth's white irises, her pupils nothing but pricks.

I see... A threshold... she said. *A mighty threshold.*

"Go," I screamed. Chains rattled. Metal bit into my skin. The shouts of prisoners grew louder.

Kaspar stopped in the doorway. "The change of guard—"

It will be...difficult...to pass...

Tears pricked the corners of my eyes. *"GO!"*

They were pulling Erik under the metal spikes. His feet scraped the slick stone floor. His head lulled.

And you...you will hold the door.

The knell of the clock tower stopped, its hollowness filling the prison like a vacuum, a void.

Signey ducked back into the galley. With the slash of a knife, she cut a lock of hair and pressed something small and cool into my palm. Her eyes found mine. "Thank you."

I clasped my fingers around it. "They'll come after you."

"I know."

"You know where to take him?"

"I do."

"Be careful."

"I will."

Then they were hauling Erik back up the stairs, disappearing around the corner, out of sight.

I glanced at what she'd given me, at the silver bead sitting round and perfect in my palm, stamped with a lattice of knots and whorls.

This doesn't change anything, I'd said. We were back in the guard closet. The smell of leather and cotton filtered around us. I had my knees pulled to my chest, eyes fixed on the slat of light that banded under the door. Signey crouched beside me, death-still. "We stick to the original plan."

"But the transport—"

"Trust me."

A pause. Footsteps faded down the hall.

"I won't let you stay behind." Her words came out as a choke.

"They're after magic. *Vold* magic. You, Bo, Kaspar. You all have it. You're the strongest Volgaard has to offer. Someone's going to have to stay behind." My chest ached, my heart split. "And I'm the only one who can."

With a crack, the spoke pulled out of my hand and the portcullis thundered shut, the metallic clang filling the walls of the prison.

And I was alone.

Chapter Fifty-One

TIME MOVES DIFFERENTLY IN PRISON. It pools, then flows, rushes, then ebbs. It's too slow and too fast.

When Stefan and the new guard came, I opened the portcullis for them, let them rush in and take me.

I suppose I could have sat in the galley, could have stayed safe behind the bars, could have taunted them until dehydration made me delirious, until I became dead-eyed and dead-faced.

Maybe I would have if it'd been just my life.

But it wasn't.

Fifty-four prisoners in twenty-seven cells. Fifty-four prisoners with lives and families, who cheered for us as we raced down the hall. Fifty-four prisoners with hopes and dreams, and maybe some deserved to die, but maybe some didn't.

I'm a physician, not a judge. A healer, not an executioner.

So, I opened the portcullis and Larland took me, pinned me against the wall. They stripped the knife from my stocking and searched my body with roving hands, the scent of their leather filling my nose, my mouth. I kept Signey's bead pressed under my tongue, and I couldn't breathe.

I wanted to scream.

I wanted to cry.

I wish I was brave.

I'm not brave.

They sent out a search party for the Volds, the thirty men meant to escort Erik. They tore Salborg Castle apart, then tore me apart, tried to make me turn, to tell. Where'd they go? How'd they leave? Maybe it would have been better to die in the galley, to die before I opened that door.

But fifty-four prisoners...

The sores are healing—cattail strips up and down my back, red and angry welts that blister and sting against the cotton shift I wear now.

Where the Volds went, I will not say.

But you should know they never found them.

Chapter Fifty-Two

KING WILHELM VISITED ME about two weeks later.

He ducked under the lintel of my cell, a painting, a fairytale, a storybook character with his gold diadem and fur-trimmed cape, red and clasped at each shoulder with a swan.

An entourage gathered in the hallway outside, dukes and earls, mistresses and foreign princes, a swish of cotton and silk, damask and rose, a strong perfume that made my eyes water.

He stopped in front of me, pressed two stiff fingers under my chin and tilted it to meet his face. "I hear you've been difficult."

My heart knocked against my ribs. *Run*, something in me said. But I wouldn't make it past the portcullis.

Instead, I bit my lip to keep from crying.

"My spies tell me the Vold general has yet to return to Karlsborn Castle," he continued. "They tell me he sends orders to his men from a secret location. They tell me the Volds are gathering along the coast like a storm. They tell me war is coming. Is that true?"

I took a steadying breath. "I don't know what the Volds are planning, and I don't know where the general is." I'd repeated the words so many times they might have been true.

Might have been.

I braced for the jerk of my neck, a slap on the cheek. Instead, the king's eyes brightened. He pinched my chin. "You're a terrible liar, but I admire your persistence. Do you know why they call me the Red King?"

I shifted. "I don't."

"Ambition. The Grain Wars left us stripped and weak, a shadow of our former self. But I plan to rebuild our empire and bring the other nations under our wing. They will fly our banners—red—and I'll make a better life for them. For us all. So won't you tell me where they went?"

I forced myself to meet his eyes, the pale blue of his irises threaded with something wiggling and dark. "Never."

The brightness collapsed into a frenzied hate. The king grabbed the front of my dress and pushed me back, back, back. My shoulders hit the wall.

"Set an execution," he said. "Tomorrow. Dawn."

A strangled cry escaped my lips.

He pressed me harder. "I want her body hanging from the gallows. I want carrion to feast on her eyes. I want—"

Wisps of black smoke escaped from beneath the king's fingers, curling up my chest, my neck, searing, blistering. They slithered down my arms, leaving trails of burning flesh, and I could taste it—ash, soot, and bitter tar. It scraped against my tongue, my brain, two claws prying at my mouth saying, *Let me in*, and *Oh? You are hers*, and *I want you, I want you, I want you.* I pressed my lips together, but the thing was *inside* of me, flooding me, and

424

it was like standing under a waterfall, trying to drink, and it was saying *You are mine,* and *I am going to take you away from her,* and—

"Come on, Wil," one of the lordlings said.

The smoke disappeared. The king still held me against the wall, his fingers tangled through the front of my shift, his knuckles gone white.

I glanced at the lordling who'd spoken. He leaned against the cell bars, and dark hair framed an arrogant face—strong cheekbones, chiseled jaw. Had he seen the smoke? Had anyone else?

The lordling's mouth tipped into a wicked grin. "I don't know if she deserves to *die.* Give her one last chance. A confession. It'll show the people you're generous. I mean, look at her. She's just a nobody." He gave me a quizzical expression.

The king's grip on the front of my dress loosened, then released. He turned and gestured toward a red-faced seneschal. "Paper."

The seneschal dug in a satchel.

King Wilhem snapped his fingers. "*Paper!*"

The seneschal pulled out several crumpled pages.

King Wilhem tossed them on the floor. "Write." Then he stormed out.

The act of throwing the papers was probably meant to degrade me further, to make me crawl on my hands and knees in this filthy cell while everyone watched. Except I wouldn't do it. I wouldn't kneel.

Something shifted in the periphery of my vision.

I looked down.

The lordling had crouched beside me, scooping them up. He stood. "He's been irritable lately. I don't think you've helped." He held out the pages.

I didn't take them.

The lordling rolled his eyes. "Don't go all noble. This is your last chance. Tell us where they went. Write a confession. Don't squander it."

I flashed my teeth. "You shouldn't trust anything I write."

"Then write telling me to go south, and I'll be sure to send my army north. Write a ballad. A song. Something. But if you help us capture the Vold general, we'll let you go free. You have my word. Around these parts, that's pretty strong."

I studied his face. I'd guessed lordling from his jacket—dark green studded with pearl buttons and roses embroidered around the cuffs. Expensive. But the way he spoke…

I bit the inside of my cheek. "Who…are you?"

The lordling cocked a brow. "I'm Alexander. *Prince* Alexander."

He set the papers on the floor and turned toward the lintel.

The women and courtiers had begun filtering out—powdered faces and fluffy dresses, their chatter idle like birds. *"…just a nobody from the Sanokes…"* they tittered. *"A nobody, a nobody."*

I stared at my hands, streaked with grit, ringed with grime. I'd spent weeks in prison, starved and tortured. Kept in conditions worse than a dog. And yet—

"I'm not a nobody." The words were only a rasp.

Alexander paused near the bars. "What was that?"

I lifted my head, my hair falling loose around my face. The moment wasn't grand. There were no statues, no cannons, no poems, or ballads. Swans didn't fly, and it wouldn't go down in history. Still, something flared, a seed, a spark, a kindling that lit a fire and saved…me.

"I'm not a nobody," I repeated.

Alexander waited, his back to me. Torchlight gilded his

shoulder, played off his iron-dark hair. For a moment, I didn't think he was going to respond at all, but the corner of his mouth lifted and I caught his eye. "Okay. Somebody."

Chapter Fifty-Three

MY PEN NIB STALLS ON THE PAPER. My teeth grit. I've been writing all night, and I don't know how to end this. The feelings are still too big, too raw, like teetering on the edge of a precipice, like diving into the sea.

The lantern they brought me burns low and the faint tang of sulfur fills my cell. I've been keeping an eye on it, watching the wick shorten, the pool of amber shrink, careful not to let it snuff out.

One of the guards whistles, a dull sound that bounces off the ceiling. "You done already? Or did you run out of ink?"

I drop the pages onto my lap and lick my lips. "Paper." Nearly. "I thinned the ink with broth."

"Blow out the lantern and get some sleep. I'll send someone to pick up the pages in the morning." He drops his attention back to his book.

I stare at the words, at the spindly handwriting crammed into margins and the ink that smudges the page. The bottom sheets have been rinsed from rainwater and marks have blotted to the top, feathering like flowers. They are illegible, nearly. I flip back through them, the story unfolding in reverse and then I'm at the beginning.

At my memory.

It's that morning on the bluffs. I'm dashing away to take care of the queen's feet, and I'm worried about being late. The Volds will eventually show up, the king will strip, and I'll be forced to be their guide. But I don't know any of that. I stop and look over my shoulder and see Hans and Katrina silhouetted in shades of green and gray…

A message.

You were right. You've always been right.

But how do you put pain on a page? How do you say goodbye?

I think for a moment before gathering the pages, my words, my heart, the whole damn letter.

This.

This is how you put pain on a page. This is how you say goodbye. It is flawed and ineloquent, but it is me and it is enough.

From the other side of the prison, there is a shout and a shuffle, something about the stars.

The lantern sputters and cracks, sucking up the rest of the oil. Sparks snap around the flame.

I unlatch the glass door. My hands shake.

If they catch me, they will try to stop me.

If they catch me, they will take the papers away.

I glance at the guard. They moved me to the front cell to monitor me while I had the pen and lantern, but he's busy reading his book, one boot crossed over the other, reclined in the chair. He has the face of a father, and I've heard him talk about his two little girls. They are his light, his world.

I hope he doesn't get in trouble because of me.

I roll the papers like a spyglass, then edge one corner into the flames.

The pages burn orange, then black, then a sooty and smoky gray. They curl into themselves like hands.

Suddenly, the prisoners are roaring, shouting, banging on the bars. My neighbor peers at the sky.

The guard is making a pointed effort not to look in our direction. It isn't the first time something like this has happened. There are only so many things to do, and seeing how far they can push the guards is one of the prisoners' favorite pastimes.

It's a good thing the guard isn't looking, or he'd be rushing at me, screaming to put the fire out. But he doesn't see, and the scent of sulfur covers up the char of paper as long as I need it to.

I stretch to my tiptoes and push the burning papers through the window grate and into the courtyard outside, empty, save for a flea-bitten dog curled around a trash heap, and a few puddles that glitter like glass.

"That you find your way home," I say.

"I miss you," I say.

In Volgaard, they cut out hearts, but in the Sanokes, we build bridges—bridges of paper and pyre smoke.

It might be too late now, whatever bridge Hans crossed may be gone, but I want to send the slivers of this story out into the universe with the hope they find him, wherever he is.

He would have loved it.

The letter burns and the smoke is a braid, thick and white. It coils toward the night sky.

A sky that is too bright, too clear for a night right after rain. A sky that is bruising black, a little wild. The sky—

And the thousand stars shooting through it.

Erik

SHADOWS OF PINE PEPPER THE COASTLINE. Waves lap the shore. In the distance, Salborg glitters. Someday soon, I'll come back and take it. I'll lead a fleet of ships and claim the city, kill the Red King.

But tonight I'm here for another reason.

Isabel.

I think back to the last time I saw her—the hook of her fingers beneath my jaw, her confession.

I see you.

You matter.

Afterward, in my drug-induced haze, I'd imagined her hands on my body, twisting through my hair. In my dreams, she'd straddled me and smiled, her locks lighting a honey-soft brown, and she was beautiful, impossible.

She was home.

I woke in the hull of a ship sailing back to the Sanokes with sheets that stuck to my body and air so thick, I could barely breathe.

"Isabel?" I'd said, stumbling onto the deck. The ocean glittered, blue and bright. "Isabel? Isa—"

Signey and Kaspar chased after me, grabbed me around the waist and dragged me back, held me as the residue of whatever Larland had been giving me worked its way through my system.

Last time I'd been like this—dazed and delirious—I Sent my mother.

This time, I Sent Isabel.

Over and over again, the memories knitting together, then falling apart. There she was standing on the beach, in my tent, the hallway at the Rose & Thistle Inn. And I was sweating and shivering, clutching the front of Signey's shirt.

"She's gone," Signey had said, pulling me closer, running her fingers through my hair. "She's gone. She's— I'm sorry. There was nothing... We couldn't—"

Behind me, a twig *snaps*. I turn to see a figure make its way toward me, its silhouette matching that of Larland's guards.

"Any news?" I ask, standing.

"Today," Signey says.

"I'm surprised they aren't using her as bait."

"They still might be."

"The syn rót?"

"Swapped. Easy. You'd think they'd have it guarded better."

"You are a guard."

Signey glances down at her outfit, a coy smile pulling at her lips. "Mmm, true." She reaches into a bag and offers me a matching coat, dark ruby red with a high collar. "For you."

Blood trickles from my nose, my ears. My hands burn. I open them, close them, wipe them on my pants. I'm disobeying an order. Not a direct one, but the magic knows I'm testing the limits, pushing the bounds.

It will only get worse.

It's why I sent Signey into the city initially, why I stayed by the river.

The coat dangles from her fingertips. "You coming, Vega?"

I take one last look at the sky.

I'm not Vega. I'm something bigger, something worse.

Now, I let my reykr stretch, let it unfold to its bounds. I've always pictured it to be a great white bird, but tonight I picture it as fire. The world tips on its axis.

Every star in the sky streaks.

I am a blacksmith at his billows, a smithy at his forge, and with every strike of the hammer, I Send the illusion, send her shooting stars.

It is a prayer, a promise.

I'm coming for you.

And I'm ready to tear down the world.

Want to see how Erik found out Isy had been kidnapped?
(Basically, do you want to see Erik panic?)

Help me out with one thing and receive an exclusive bonus chapter.

SarahPageStories.com/Erik

Dear Reader,

LET ME TELL YOU ONE MORE STORY.

This one is mine.

I survived three grueling years of law school, graduated in the top 20% of my class, and landed a job at a fancy law firm. I was just finishing my first year as a "baby attorney" when the partner in charge of hiring took me to lunch.

"Look," he said, waving his fancy croissant sandwich. "I wanted to tell you the truth because I don't think you're hearing it from anyone else. You know Cornelius[1] and Victoria? The interns? They're better than you and they're still in law school. The firm is offering them full-time positions and when they start, they'll push you out. Everyone wants to work with the best and you? Well, to tell you the truth, you're not good at writing, and you're not good at research. You're only good at filling out forms."

After the lunch, I called my husband and sobbed. "I think I need to find a new job," I said.

"Get through the rest of the day and we'll start to look when you get home."

So, I started to look.

And I started to write.

I wrote a story about a nobody who became a somebody because *I* felt like a nobody and desperately wanted to become a somebody.

---

[1] With the exception of Sarah Eliason, all names have been changed.

Then, I started querying.

If you had talked to me a year and a half ago, I'd tell you for sure I'd have an agent.

My first ever full request turned into a revise and resubmit, and I had a lot of other agents who wanted to see the manuscript. Fifteen total. Which is...amazing considering some people only have one or two.

And then the rejections started pouring in.

One agent said she liked the voice but just didn't get into the story. Another said she didn't like how everything was resolved at the end. No fewer than *six* agents said, "Love this, but I didn't love it *enough*. Send me your next project!"

One night, I sobbed to my husband about how my book about being good enough just didn't seem to be...well, good enough.

And then I met Madison who was being housed by my friend Sarah Eliason as a part of an addiction recovery program for troubled teens. When Madison said she wanted to be a librarian, Sarah Eliason waggled her eyebrows in my direction and said, "I know someone who writes."

"It hasn't been picked up by anyone yet," I said. "At this point, I'm starting to wonder if it's any good."

Guys, this girl was so sure *Illusion of Stars* would be swooped up and was shocked it hadn't been yet.

So, I printed a single copy and I sent it to her. I wasn't there when she received it, but I saw the video.

The book is wrapped in brown paper with white polka dots. Madison opens it slowly. You can tell she's not used to receiving gifts. When she sees the title, she puts the book on top of her head and sobs.

She spent the next day reading it.

That's why I wrote *Illusion of Stars*. It's not for the accolades or the awards, though I've had both. Instead, I wrote *Illusion* because I'm not the only person who's felt like they're not good enough or pretty enough or smart enough. I'm not the only person who's felt like everyone is miles ahead of you, and there's no way you'll ever catch up.

I'm not the only one who's ever felt like an imposter in her own skin.

If you've ever felt that way too, I hope you'll stick around.

Maybe we can help each other.

So, thank you for reading *Illusion of Stars* and for spending time in my world. I am deeply honored that you trusted me to tell this story.

In gratitude,

P.S. Want to know what happened to those interns? Gone. I outlasted them both.

P.P.S. If you made it this far, would you consider leaving a review? Reviews help new readers discover this story, and that's something that is so, so important.

Acknowledgements

SO, I'M THAT CRAZY PERSON who flips straight to the back of the book the acknowledgments first. If that's you: Hi! Welcome! You can sit with me. That said, **there are spoilers in these**.

You've been warned.

But here's the thing. A book is really only as good as the people you surround yourself with. If it wasn't for my amazing team, I would have made some very…weird choices.

Here we go.

To my developmental editor, book coach, and best friend, Sarah Eliason, thank you for looking at the blurry sketch of a girl barging in on a boy in a forest and saying, "He seems like he's in the military." The seeds of *Illusion of Stars* were born with you. Thank you for your million rereads, late night phone calls, for forcing me to develop things like politics (*ugh*) and romance (*yay*) and for letting me swim around in your head. You have an amazing eye for story.

To my critique partner Caitlin Foley, thank you for not letting me make dumb plot decisions like having Isy waltz straight into a camp of very tropey bandits (*bad*) or setting the kissing scene over Erik's dying dad (*even worse*). Everyone needs a wing woman like you.

Speaking of romance, thank you to Kelsi Lane, thank you for helping me fix my romance scenes. All of them. Your knowledge of tropes is unparalleled. Also, thank you for making me remove all references to "sheep-rutted trails." You're right. I didn't understand what that meant.

To Christina Ferko, thank you for sending me treats and wish candles, for screaming with me when things worked out and crying with me when things didn't. There have been days your support has literally brought me to tears. I'm so grateful I found you. You deserve everything good that's coming.

To Alexandra Kennington, thank you for helping me smooth over the few remaining issues with pacing and for being my go-to girlie for all things marketing. I feel like we could take over the world together. (Also unrelated, thank you for putting up with my trolling on social media. You know I love you.)

To Arianna Padbury, thank you for sending me pictures of your pets. They do make everything better.

To my line and copy editor, Silvia Curry, thank you for helping my words shine.

To my proofreaders, Crab and Kristie Wagner, thank you for helping me ferret out all those pesky remaining typos. And to Rae Harding, thank you for being my final typo boss.

To Jourdan Gandy of @old.enough.for.fairytales, thank you for the bazillion voice memos and helping me get ready to launch this thing into the universe. Even though you refused to admit Midnights is the better Taylor Swift album, your insight into the indie publishing market is invaluable, and I truly believe that every author should hit you up for coaching. (Authors, seriously. Hit her up for coaching. She's fabulous.)

To Christina Marshall of @bookedtildawn, thank you for your tough love feedback on my reels and for your cheerleading of this book. You have an amazing eye for hooks and are an absolute gem in the indie marketing world. Your 1:1 coaching on how to position Illusion was vital in making this a successful launch. (If you're an author or bookstagrammer, check out Christina's Bookstagram 101 course. It is worth its weight in gold.)

To Jessica of @jessabibliophile, thank you for loving this book and helping me hype it. You are a joy to work with and you do the most gorgeous annotations. They are #goals.

To Megan McDonald of @ireadromantasy, I swear you are the one who started the wildfire and are living proof that you don't need to have a massive following to make a big difference. Thank you for including Illusion in Enchanted Pages PR and for helping me champion it. You are such a gift to the indie author community.

To my beautiful ARC readers who took this book under their wing and decided to champion it, you made me cry about a billion times during the six-week launch with your love and support, but I guess you'd say that's payback for the emotional roller-coaster I put you through with the book. Thank you for taking a chance on me. I would list you all by name, but I am *terrified* of forgetting somebody. Please remember that I know you. I love you. I see you.

To everyone else who offered feedback on this story at one point or another: you shaped it into what it is.

To my husband, Brandon. Thank you for supporting my dreams.

And finally, to my cat. You are beautiful and fluffy and—

JK. The final thank you goes to myself. You turned your pain into something beautiful and wrote the damn book.

SARAH MARIE PAGE spends her days engaging in intense battles of wits, fueled by copious amounts of tea and the occasional dramatic slamming of a briefcase. AKA: She's a lawyer. When she's not doing lawyer things, she can be found sneaking off to make-believe worlds filled with romance, betrayal, and steamy enemies-to-lovers tension. If she got a pity laugh out of you while reading this book, she thinks you might like her newsletter where she will make you pity laugh some more. You can find that on her website: sarahpagestories.com. She's also a frequent flier on Instagram: @sarahpagestories.

Sexual Content

THIS STORY IS FADE TO BLACK, meaning there is no on-page sex. There is, however, foreplay, which includes:

CHAPTER 35: A very brief mention of grinding while both characters are fully clothed. The male main character nips the female main character's ear and gives her a hickey on her neck.

CHAPTER 36: The male main character gives the female main character several more hickeys on her neck and shoulders. The male main character untucks the female main character's shirt and plays with the waistband of her skirt. The female main character wonders, briefly, if the male main character may touch her lower. She wants him to do this. He does not touch her lower.

CHAPTER 40: Heated kissing and biting on the neck, shoulders, and mouth. The male main character says the female main character's body is very responsive to him, and he places a hickey on or near the female main character's breast. The exact location is not described. The act of placing the hickey (e.g. sucking on skin) is described. The female main character thinks that she would like to grind on the male main character, but is unable to do so. The chapter ends with the implication sex occurred. The characters are in underwear for most of the scene and are never fully naked, although there is a reference to the female main character's breasts being exposed.

CHAPTER 42: The couple is shown naked in bed and cuddling. The male main character traces lazy circles on the female main character's ribs. They kiss and there is the implication sex occurred again.

Want Spice?

An open-door spicy bonus chapter is available through the Prosecco and Pages book club, of which Illusion of Stars was the August 2024 pick. https://proseccoandpages.mn.co/

TRIGGERS

ILLUSION OF STARS includes content that may be upsetting to some readers. This includes discussion of **parental infidelity**, discussion of **parental abandonment**, crass jokes, **hazing**, catcalling, on-page **death of a parent**, on-page **death of a friend**, a very brief mention of sibling death, a very brief suggestion that a man might be raped (no rape occurs), **self-harm ideation** (non-suicidal), **on-page self-harm** (non-suicidal), brief mentions of torture, **strong language** (including the use of f*ck), poisoning, stereotypical depictions of a mad king, and themes of **grief**.

The bolded triggers are the most prevalent in the book.

If you have questions about how something is handled or would like the corresponding page numbers for a particular trigger, please reach out:

sarah@sarahpagestories.com

The most important thing is to make sure you're taking care of yourself.

www.ingramcontent.com/pod-product-compliance
Ingram Content Group UK Ltd.
Pitfield, Milton Keynes, MK11 3LW, UK
UKHW040659110225
4543UKWH00024B/176

9 798989 983117